LONG MAY SHE
REIGN

Also by
RHIANNON THOMAS

A Wicked Thing
Kingdom of Ashes

LONG MAY SHE REIGN

RHIANNON THOMAS

HARPER TEEN
An Imprint of HarperCollinsPublishers

Library of Congress Control Number: 2016952956
ISBN 978-0-06-241868-5

Typography by Torborg Davern
17 18 19 20 21   PC/LSCH   10 9 8 7 6 5 4 3 2 1

First Edition

For Rachel,
who made the science work

ONE

A HUNDRED DOVES BURST OUT OF THE PIE.

I don't know why I was surprised. Of course there were a hundred doves in the pie. The king wouldn't open his birthday celebration by actually feeding his guests. Not when he could amaze us all with his extravagance instead.

I just wished someone had considered what would happen to the doves *after* they were released. The king had skewered a couple in his enthusiasm to cut open the pastry, and the survivors were determined to get as far away from that knife-wielding maniac as possible. Many of them settled in the rafters of the banquet hall, forty feet above us. More crashed against the huge arched windows, their claws and beaks scraping the glass. One settled in the bell of a trumpet and refused to move, no matter how violently the player waved his hands.

I sank into my chair and kept watch on the doves overhead. I wasn't afraid of them, not exactly, but I already felt on edge, with the entire court around me, with their judging eyes and vicious whispers, surrounded by gold and laughter and fountains of wine, and the doves were moving so erratically. Flapping and skittering. I knew they wouldn't touch me, but I jumped every time they swooped either way.

If only the king would serve the first course. Then I'd be one step closer to leaving. My father usually allowed me to skip the king's festivities—as the king's fourth cousin once removed, I was hardly considered *important*—but this time my father had insisted I attend. To represent the family. To show we were people who mattered.

He couldn't really have believed that would work. No one had spoken to me since I'd arrived. Even my father had abandoned me for "necessary business conversations" on the other side of the hall. So I sat at my table near the door, empty seats on either side of me, half wanting to join in the conversation of the people opposite, too scared to appear to be eavesdropping on them to try.

King Jorgen, for his part, looked completely relaxed, and completely unconcerned about his potentially starving guests. He lounged on his throne, legs thrown over one arm, his golden goblet full of wine, his golden plate free of food, while the golden paneling glittered on the wall behind him. He was talking to a girl about my age, whose smile was so wide that the corners might have been pinned to her cheeks.

The king raised his goblet to her lips. When she shook her head, still smiling that strained smile, he tossed the goblet over his shoulder, wine and all. "This drink does not please my lady!" he shouted. "Bring us something better."

Queen Martha sat on his right. I'd always thought she looked like a praying mantis—tall, thin, and bug-eyed, with a ruthless personality to match. Her dress was the biggest in the room, with silk ribbon at the end of every layer like icing on a cake. Her hair reached up toward the ceiling, studded with berries. She held a peacock-feather fan in front of her mouth to hide her yawn, and pointedly avoided looking at her husband.

A dove landed next to my still-empty plate and fluffed its wings. It looked at the foodless platter, and then looked at me, as though blaming me for the lack of treats.

"I know." I ran my fingers along the feathers at its neck. They were softer than I'd expected, and pristine white. Only the best could be baked in the king's pies, I supposed. "I'm hungry, too."

"Freya, what are you doing?" Sophia, the woman sitting opposite me, waved a ring-covered hand in my direction. She was in her forties, her hair a rich henna red. A black-silk moon and two stars had been stuck to her forehead, either as an affectation or to conceal any scars. "Don't encourage it. It's filthy."

"Pigeons all over the tables," Sophia's neighbor, Claire, said. She was in her forties, too, and rather portly, with a silk heart placed to the right of her pink lips. "I suppose the pie was entertaining, but—"

"Doves," I said, without thinking.

Claire raised a single, perfectly arched eyebrow. "What was that?"

"Doves," I repeated, a little louder, forcing the word out. "They're not pigeons, they're doves."

Claire laughed. "Oh, Freya, you are strange." She waved carelessly at the bird. "Pigeon, dove, whatever it is. We really don't want it on the table."

I pulled my hand back and stared at my plate as she shooed the bird away.

People had been calling me "strange" since I learned how to talk, although usually they only said it when they thought I couldn't hear. When I was younger, I had chattered constantly, stumbling over the words in my eagerness to express them, asking question after question until I was at least five explanations deep. People commented on my strangeness to my mother, as though she had somehow missed it and would surely take action now it was revealed to her, but she would just laugh and say, "Isn't it wonderful?" like my strangeness was my greatest strength.

Even then I'd known what it meant. That something was wrong with me. That I didn't belong.

Then my mother had died, and my strangeness had become

far more concerning. An insult to her memory. An accusation: "Why can't you be more like your mother, and less like *you?*"

It was fine, I told myself. Claire should have been the one embarrassed, for making such a stupid mistake about the birds. It was fine.

But whenever I tried to convince myself my worries were all imaginary, that no one judged me, I remembered every scrap of evidence I'd ever gathered to the contrary. Every time someone had sniggered after I spoke. Every sideways glance shared by friends when I approached. The moment I had walked away from Rosaline Hayes and her friends and heard them repeating my words in high-pitched, laughing voices.

I'd been reluctant to say anything to anyone after that.

At first, my father had comforted me—"Court is an odd place, but you'll get used to it, you'll make friends, you'll figure it out"—but I continued to stumble, and "You'll make friends" became "You'll survive" became "Freya, could you at least try, for my sake?"

Five years later, I still had no place here. Or, I did, but it was sitting by the wall, practically invisible, the butt of jokes if I was mentioned at all. Awkward Freya, strange Freya, silent stuttering Freya who said rude things by accident and was so very, very plain. Did you hear she does experiments in her cellar? Did you hear she nearly burned her house to the ground? What was she even doing in court, behaving like that?

Or that's what I assumed. No one gossiped about me in front

of my face. No one said much to or about me at all.

I'd decided long ago that I didn't care. I was going to escape this court as soon as I could. My father insisted I had to *try* and find a good match, to get married and play a role in court life, but no one had ever shown any interest in me. I'd never found anyone who interested *me,* either. As soon as my father accepted that, I'd be gone. I'd travel to the continent, perhaps, where research was taken far more seriously, and conduct my experiments there. One day soon.

Because, it turned out, I did care. I cared what people thought of me. I cared what they were saying. And I needed to get out, before their judgment changed me.

"Hi, Freya."

I turned toward the voice, smiling. I'd only ever had one good friend, but Naomi was so wonderful that I couldn't imagine needing anyone else. She'd been drawn to me, somehow, when she first moved to the capital with her brother, Jacob, joining me in the corner of awkwardness and pulling me into quiet conversation. We had little in common as far as interests went—she loved novels, stories, romance, and adventure, while I was much happier with equations and research—but our souls clicked.

She looked pretty tonight. She always looked pretty—not the court's version of beauty, but something softer and sweeter. She had large brown eyes, a tiny pug nose, and ever-present dimples. Her black hair was piled in a dome on top of her head, every twist studded with a gem, and her dark skin shimmered with whichever crushed-jewel powder was currently in fashion.

"Hi," I said. She slipped onto the chair beside me, wobbling slightly as she maneuvered her massive skirts into place.

"Should you be sitting here, Naomi?" Sophia said. "Not that we aren't delighted to have your company, but His Majesty worked so *hard* on the seating arrangements . . ."

"His Majesty won't mind if I sit here for two minutes, I don't think," Naomi said, although she looked down as she said it, her expression unsure. She ducked closer to me. "The people at my table are horrid," she murmured.

"And you're surprised?"

"I guess not. But then my brother abandoned me, so it was just me thrown to the wolves. How are you coping?"

"I'm alive. That's something, isn't it?"

"Here? Definitely."

"What are you girls whispering about?" Claire said. "It's awfully rude to have secrets, you know. We'll be thinking you're talking about us next."

"We'd never gossip about you," Naomi said. She glanced at the table again, then quickly back at Claire, correcting her gaze. "What would we even say?"

Lots of things, I thought. But Naomi probably meant it. She made fun of the court, but she was always eager to forgive the courtiers themselves for their cruelty and vanity. Every insult became a harmless misunderstanding or good people having a bad day if you allowed Naomi to sit with the story long enough.

"Well, I hope I'm not *that* boring," Claire said.

"Tell us," Sophia said, leaning forward slightly. "How is your brother, Jacob?"

"He's—well. Thank you."

"What a handsome young man. I suppose he'll be finding a girl soon? Or is he enjoying life too much to settle down?"

"I don't know," Naomi said. "You'd have to ask him."

"But surely, as his sister, you must have some inkling. Women's intuition, no? Young men so rarely know what they want, but you must have a *feeling*—"

"What about Madeleine Wolff?" Claire said. "She's not connected to anyone, is she? They would be a wonderful couple. Think how beautiful their children would be!"

"Yes!" Sophia said. "Is your brother close to her, Naomi? We should arrange an introduction, when she returns from her estate. Something so adorable they can't help but fall in love."

Naomi was saved from answering by a hush that descended on the room. The king had stood, arms swept out toward the crowd. "Before we enjoy our next course," he said, "I've arranged a little entertainment."

Other rulers probably had entertainments arranged *for* them on their birthday. But the king would never leave anything to chance. He had to show how extravagant and benevolent he was, and that meant planning every detail himself.

A troupe of performers ran into the hall through its rear

doors. One woman backflipped her way along the hall, passing just behind my and Naomi's chairs. She shot us a sideways grin as she went. She was followed by more acrobats, people cartwheeling, a man walking on his hands, and jugglers, too, rings flying through the air. Their outfits sparkled, catching the light as they danced, so it almost hurt to look at them.

When they reached the front of the room, they bowed to the king before continuing their performance. One of the jugglers clapped, the sound chasing through the room like thunder, and their rings seemed to transform into knives.

I looked past them to the high table. The king's best friend, Torsten Wolff, sat two seats to the king's left. He looked distinctly unamused. But Torsten Wolff always looked distinctly unamused. If he ever smiled, his face would probably shatter. He was much younger than the king, probably in his early twenties, but they were inseparable. It often seemed as though the king gave Sten all of his worries to carry, leaving himself as the carefree side of the pair.

For once, I felt a connection with Sten. He looked as uncomfortable as I felt.

One of the performers clapped her hands, and the juggling knives burst into flame. The court gasped and applauded as the group continued to juggle, continued to dance and contort, the flames flying through the air so fast they became a blur. More performers ran in from the sides, holding torches aloft. They threw them into the paths of the burning knives, so they caught fire, too, and then the performers bent back, faces to the ceiling, mouths open wide, as they seemed to swallow the fire.

Then they started to *breathe* fire, shooting streams into the air. It caught on ribbon hung across the ceiling, too thin to be visible before, and raced along it, spelling out the king's name.

The crowd applauded again, and the king grinned. "Ah, now, our performers need a volunteer." He glanced up and down the high table in faux contemplation. Torsten Wolff looked like he had swallowed a lemon, and I thought the king would choose him, a punishment for his lack of enthusiasm. But then: "Fitzroy! Why don't you come up here?"

Fitzroy. Even I heard the danger in that word. William Fitzroy was the king's bastard son, and although most people referred to him by his surname, the king's name for him changed with his mood. He was "my son" when Fitzroy was in favor, or "William" if a name was really needed. *Fitzroy* was a hint of dismissal, a reminder of his place in court. A surname they invented for the bastard son, the boy who wasn't supposed to exist.

But Fitzroy sauntered forward without hesitation. His blond hair fell across his eyes, giving him an air of casual confidence, and he was smiling, like he couldn't wait to suffer what his father had planned.

"Whatever my adoring fans demand," he said. People laughed, and danger flashed in the king's eyes. The performers positioned Fitzroy in the middle of their group, and then began their show again, tossing flaming rings to one another over

Fitzroy's head, sending knives spinning inches from his arms, breathing fire so close that his hair must have been singed.

Fitzroy did not flinch. He mugged for the audience as the flames flew past, like nothing was more fun than nearly dying for everyone's entertainment.

Fitzroy, I decided, was an idiot.

The performance ended, Fitzroy bowed, and his father flicked a hand to send him back to his seat without a word.

The performers departed the way they'd come, tumbling and dancing. The backflipper passed behind us again, and as she did, her foot caught on my shoulder. She didn't pause to apologize—she probably hadn't even noticed, so focused on her performance—but I jerked, shoved forward by her momentum, and my heart sputtered into triple time.

The conversation in the hall started again, and Sophia and Claire leaped straight back into interrogating Naomi about her brother. I couldn't concentrate on the words. They were at once too loud and too far away to understand. My hands began to shake.

The kick had triggered something in me, the awareness that people were too close. There were too many of them, and I couldn't leave, couldn't escape, couldn't do *anything*.

No, I thought. Not here. I was safe. I was fine.

It was too late. There were too many bodies, too much breath and too many eyes. It was so loud, so crowded, and I couldn't leave.

No, I told myself again. I would be calm. I tugged at the pins in my hair, and looked around the room again, searching for something to ground me. The fountains of wine, the cascading flowers, the doves that still seemed confused about their inability to fly through the windows. Everything was safe. I'd be all right.

I tugged at another hairpin, my hand shaking, and it slipped free, sending a section of hair tumbling to my shoulder. I grabbed it and tried to shove it back in place.

"Freya?"

I pressed my palms against my knees, willing my hands to still. I tried to force air to the bottom of my lungs.

"Freya?" Naomi said again. "Are you all right?"

I nodded, up and down and up. The world had turned fuzzy, and all the sounds were too loud, and people were so *close,* even those far away seemed to loom and press toward me, and I couldn't breathe, and—

"Come on," Naomi said. "Let's get some air."

I couldn't leave the table, it wasn't allowed, but Naomi was already standing, not touching me, just standing and waiting, and I felt myself standing, too.

Naomi led the way to the doors at the back of the hall. They hadn't seemed far away before, twenty feet at most, but the distance stretched out now. Everyone was watching us leave, I knew, thinking about how *odd* we were behaving, and my father would be watching, too, glowering . . .

The doors stood slightly open, and we stepped out into the gardens beyond. An October chill was in the air, and I gulped it in, stumbling farther from the palace. Calm. I was calm.

The world slowly came back into focus. The vast lawn had been decorated with floating lanterns and glistening ice statues, and couples walked between them, hands entwined, faces close.

The river meandered through the garden at the bottom of a slight incline, reflecting the lanterns and the stars. I staggered toward it, listening to the gurgle, looking at the lights. I was calm. I was calm.

Naomi hovered about a foot away, watching me closely. "Are you all right?"

I nodded. "Yes. Yes, I'm fine." If I said it enough, it had to be true.

"You don't have to be fine, you know. If you're not."

Naomi said that every time this happened, and I always nodded, like I actually believed her. It was one thing to be uncomfortable in court, to hate all the pretenses and be desperate to leave. It was quite another to panic, to become so frightened of the people around me that I forgot how to breathe.

But she understood. She said her father reacted the same way to court, or to anything too crowded. That was why her parents lived out in the country, while she and her brother represented the family in the capital. Whenever I panicked, she would appear beside me, ready to talk me back to reality.

She swept her thirty-six layers of skirts forward and sank

onto the grass. It must have been cold, but she simply looked up at me with a smile until I settled beside her.

At least I could breathe again. The chatter and music floated through the hall's open door, but it felt safer now, farther away.

"Want me to take your hair down?" Naomi asked.

I nodded. Naomi moved behind me and began pulling the pins loose with quick fingers. With every tug, my lungs relaxed, just a little.

"How's the experiment going?" she said. "Any luck?"

I shook my head. I'd been working on a way to create portable heat for weeks, something that could keep your hands warm and perhaps even banish the cold from my laboratory without fire. So far, all I had for my efforts were a whole lot of notes, and a whole lot of burns.

I plucked one of the loose hairpins from the grass and began to twist it between my fingers. The diamonds gleamed. "I've been experimenting with different metals," I said. "But nothing yet. I'll figure it out." Naomi tugged the last of my hair free, and I leaned back, falling onto the grass beside her.

"When you figure it out, you'll be famous." She wrapped a loose strand of my hair around her fingers, moving it gently back and forth. Prickles ran across my scalp, and I closed my eyes.

"Of course."

"Cold hands are the worst, Freya. People'll pay you a lot of money if you figure it out. You could do anything you wanted after that."

I shook my head. But secretly, I agreed. Not that I'd be famous, perhaps, but that this would work, that *this* was my solution. If I could solve this, and sell it, I'd have my own money. I could travel wherever I pleased. Travel to the continent, convince a scientist to teach me there. Stop living on the edge of other people's lives and start living my own.

I couldn't admit it, though. Not even to Naomi. The thought was too thrilling and terrifying to share. If I said it out loud, even nodded at Naomi's suggestion, I felt, madly, irrationally, that it would be snatched away from me, just to punish me for believing.

Naomi tucked her legs underneath her. "Well, you can be boring and unromantic if you like. *I* believe it'll happen. I'll miss you, though. When you're gone."

"I won't leave you." It was the one downside to the plan, the one detail that made me hesitate. I wouldn't know what to do without Naomi beside me. "You'll come with me."

I knew she wouldn't, she *couldn't*, not with her parents' approval, at least. But I wanted to pretend.

"I suppose I would like to see the continent. But what would Jacob do without me? He gets into too much trouble as it is."

"He'll have to come and help you on your adventures," I said. "Rescue you when that dashing rogue you meet turns out to like girl-bone soup."

"Because of course that'll happen to me."

"It happens to all the best heroines. And if your brother doesn't have to rush to your aid, how will he employ that handsome stranger to assist him who falls madly in love at the sight of you?"

She laughed. "Well, when you put it like that." She glanced toward the palace. "Should we go back inside soon? They'll be missing us."

"They won't miss us." Everyone had already seen us go, and my father was going to be furious about that, whatever I did. At this point, I might as well leave entirely.

I tapped my fingernail on the hairpin. Brand-new, special for the banquet. Made from aluminum, which was the stupidest thing I'd ever heard. Someone on the continent had discovered a new metal, and what did everyone here do? Rush to make it into jewelry, without a thought to what better uses it might have.

I'd be there soon. On the continent, with real intellectuals, with people who actually cared, rather than the vapid, fashion-hungry mob here. I just had to solve this one problem.

Another tap of the hairpin. Metal hadn't worked. Not even close.

But I hadn't tried aluminum.

I sat up.

"What is it?" Naomi said.

"Aluminum. I haven't tried it yet. For my experiment." My

thoughts were racing. "What if—what if I combined it with something? Maybe iodine?" Yes. *Yes.* That would produce heat. Wouldn't it?

There were carriages around the front of the palace, waiting until they were needed. Surely one of them could take me home. My father must have noticed me leaving the hall, but he hadn't come looking for me. I could slip out for an hour or two, then come back, and say I'd been in the gardens all along. He'd be angry, but he wouldn't be able to disprove it. The gardens were huge. He couldn't search them while I was gone, not without leaving the ball for longer than he'd deem acceptable himself.

I could go back to the laboratory, try out my thoughts, and be back before the end of the feast.

And if this worked—if it worked, I'd never have to go to a banquet like this again.

Naomi grinned back at me. "All right," she said. "Let's go make your fortune."

TWO

IT WAS EASY ENOUGH TO FIND A CARRIAGE. NO ONE wanted to leave the social event of the year and miss whatever drunken gossip would fuel the next two months of court conversations, but the coachmen had to wait outside the gates with their horses, just in case.

The streets were jammed with people. The king would never pay for commoners to celebrate with him—that would be a waste of good gold, in his eyes—but if the taverns could use the king's birthday as a way to make a profit, and the people could use it as a way to have fun, then little things like invitations weren't going to deter them. It seemed I was the only one who wanted to hide at home tonight.

It made me nervous. All those people, filling the road, blocking our escape. They were just people, nothing more than that, people who didn't even care who we were in the slightest, but *knowing* they were out there, all around us, that they had beating hearts and judging minds, that they might do anything and I couldn't predict it, that I couldn't run past them all . . .

I twitched the curtains closed, but the shouts and laughter cut through the window, so I gripped my hands together in my lap, trying to remember to breathe.

It must have taken half an hour or more to fight through the crowds, but finally, the carriage turned onto my street. Only nobles lived here, in black-beamed buildings from hundreds of years ago. Normally, that meant that anyone stepping out of the front door risked being accosted by nosy matriarchs and young social climbers, but the road was quieter now, and no lights flickered in the windows. Who would be here when they could be at the palace instead? Perhaps a few dedicated servants, an elderly relative telling the younger ones to have fun. And now us.

As soon as the carriage stopped, I shoved the door open, stumbling slightly as my heels hit the pavement. Naomi handed the driver a couple of coins, and I hurried to find the spare key tucked under the windowsill. The servants had been given the night off. Adviser to the king he might be, but my father remembered what working life was like before he married a noble, and he always thought about what the servants might want. He'd never admit to such improper behavior to any of his new peers, of course, but that didn't make his concern any less genuine.

If only that concern stretched to his daughter. *My* happiness could never come before the expectations of the court. I had far too many supposed duties to fulfill.

He wouldn't take it well when I finally left. He wouldn't hate me for it, exactly, but he wouldn't understand. So I couldn't tell him about my plans. I couldn't ask for any assistance. One day, I'd inform him that I was leaving, and then I'd be gone.

I wished things could be different. I wasn't close to my father, but I didn't want to hurt him. I wished he could *understand*, that he didn't wish for any daughter other than me, but wishes didn't mean anything in the end. This was how things had to be.

The front hall was dark, the chandelier looming above us. I strode underneath it, to a narrow staircase at the far side of the room. Anyone visiting the house would probably dismiss it as a servants' passage, and one step into the run-down corridor at the bottom of the stairs would seem to confirm it. I didn't want anyone interrupting my experiments, and my father didn't want anyone to stumble across them.

My laboratory wasn't perfect. The cellar room was cramped, for a start. A scarred wooden table took up most of the space, and I had personally fastened several sturdy but slightly lopsided cupboards to the walls. The only windows were high up, long rectangular panes of glass that looked straight on to the grass of our garden. They could be opened to let out smoke, but they were far less effective at letting in light. Books spilled off the shelves, and every spot of counter space was covered in bottles and vials and notes.

But the busyness was comforting to me. Everything had a system, even if it was one I couldn't express in words. I knew where everything was. When I stepped into that room, all the doubt that defined my life in court melted away. I knew what I needed to do. I knew who I needed to be.

I'd been interested in science for as long as I could remember, for longer than I'd had a word for it. I'd driven my mother and father insane with endless questions—why is the sky blue? Why is fire hot? Why does food change when it's cooked? Why do people in different kingdoms speak different languages from us? Why, why, why, why, about anything and everything. My mother always indulged me with some ridiculous answer. Food cooked because it had big dreams, and it wanted to be the best it could be. The sky was blue because we were being watched by a giant and she had the bluest eyes anyone had ever seen. When it rained, she was crying. And at night, it got dark because she was asleep.

My father took the questions more seriously. He saw my curiosity as a good thing, then, and as a merchant who traveled far, he had some answers, if not all of them.

Of course, both approaches led to more questions, about the giant or the languages spoken across the sea. But the first time I'd learned about *science*, the first time I'd realized that we didn't have all the answers and that some people worked to find them, was when I was about eight. My father mentioned his enthusiastic daughter to a scientist he'd met abroad, and the man gave my father a book called *The Scientific Method*, designed for students just beginning their studies. He'd said it was probably too dry for a child, but I became obsessed with it.

The accompanying letter said I sounded like a very intelligent young lady, and he hoped I would keep asking questions. So I did.

After my mother died, my father stopped traveling, but he also stopped caring about the court, for a while. He just wanted me to be happy. So he let me build my lab. But as I got older and my mother's death faded from trauma into fact, my father became more concerned with her legacy. He needed a proper daughter with a future at court, not a stuttering scientist who planned to run as soon as she could.

I'd left the laboratory door ajar. I stepped inside and began to light the lamps.

Dagny was curled up on the center table, a perfect circle of fluff. She was precisely the wrong breed and color for a laboratory cat—all the dust and dirt stuck in her long gray fur, making her look like she'd been crawling up a chimney—but that didn't matter. She was my partner in science, even if her contributions were restricted to meows that Naomi called "assertive" and I called "needy." She watched me as I talked through my ideas, like she was listening, like she already had the answer in mind and was just waiting for me to catch up, and her intelligent eyes always coaxed the greatest breakthroughs from my brain.

Now I picked her up and move her aside. She mewed with annoyance. "Well, what do you expect, sleeping there?" I said. "I've got work to do." I deposited her on a stool, and Naomi offered her a comforting rub under the chin. Dagny shut her eyes and tilted her head back, a ripple arching along her spine.

Naomi was the world's best tamer of cats. Or maybe cats were excellent tamers of Naomi. She had no pets of her own, so she fussed over Dagny whenever she saw her. I'm not sure which one of them enjoyed it more.

I squeezed past them, toward one of the cupboards on the far wall. "Can you grab that flask from the countertop? The round one, wide at the base, narrow at the top?" Dagny trilled as Naomi moved away.

I opened the cupboard door to reveal rows and rows of jars, each with a different substance stored inside. The iodine was near the back. The silvery flakes were volatile, to say the least, so it was best to keep them tucked away, safe from mishap. I pulled out the jar and carried it back to the center table. Then I took the hairpin from my pocket and held it up to the light to consider it again.

A butterfly clung to one end, its wings studded with diamonds. I snapped it off and placed it to one side. I couldn't allow it to adulterate the aluminum.

Naomi, meanwhile, picked up the jar of iodine and considered the metal inside. "How much do you think you should use?"

"Three pinches, I think." That would probably be safe. Less wouldn't tell me anything, and more might work a little *too* well, if things didn't go as I expected.

Dagny was too busy rubbing her head against Naomi's arm to give her opinion.

With my thick leather gloves firmly in place and my goggles tight over my eyes, I twisted open the jar and used tongs to move three pinches of iodine into the flask. Then I carefully added the hairpin. Nothing happened. "It needs something," I said. "Something to encourage it to react."

I glanced at Dagny to make sure she was still a safe distance away, and then grabbed a pipette and went to fill it up with water. "Maybe you should stand back for this," I said to Naomi. "Just in case."

"But it's okay if it explodes in *your* face?"

"It won't explode in my face." I wasn't going to be wrong. I could feel it. "But—just in case."

Naomi made a face at me. But she did step away.

I squeezed a couple of drops of water into the flask. For one second, and then two, nothing happened. Then bright purple smoke began to billow from the hairpin.

Not what I had been expecting.

The aluminum sparked. I jumped back just before it burst into flames.

The smoke billowed from the flask, getting thicker and more

purple. My lungs tightened as the smoke swelled toward me, and I coughed. Dagny hissed in protest and dove under the chair.

The smoke grew and grew, the fire casting purple light across the room. I held my breath and counted to three, giving myself time to note the exact shade of purple, the intensity of the reaction, the speed with which it seemed to burn. Then I ran to the window and heaved it open, letting fresh air rush in.

Naomi clambered onto the counter to haul open the second window, her toes balanced between more flasks.

Dagny meowed again. She wasn't pleased.

"I know, I know," I said, as I fanned the smoke toward the open window. "But breakthroughs don't come from being cautious. And nothing bad happened. Iodine is only a *bit* poisonous."

"Only a *bit* poisonous?" Naomi said. "Freya—"

"Only if you eat it! Or touch it. Or inhale its fumes." But we hadn't breathed in much. "We'll be fine."

Naomi glared at me, eyebrows raised. Which . . . yes, all right, perhaps she had a point. It hadn't been entirely safe. But science wasn't safe. You had to take risks. And I was wearing goggles, and gloves, and I'd made sure she stepped back! Plus we'd learned something new. Wasn't that the most important thing?

"That was amazing," I said, as I moved back toward the flask. "Did you see that smoke?"

"That purple was pretty impressive. Not quite a hand warmer, though."

A distorted white lump remained stuck to the bottom of the flask, and it split when I tried to remove it. Even I wasn't eager enough to add more water to it without further research, so I put the pieces in a jar of their own and labeled it "aluminum iodine." Maybe I'd have a use for it once I learned more.

I grabbed my journal from its spot on the far end of the desk, while Naomi sank onto the stool beside me. *Aluminum,* I scrawled, the ink smudging slightly. *Did not react as expected.*

I frowned as I wrote, making sure to describe the exact color of the product, the scent and thickness of the smoke.

That attempt had failed, but there had to be something useful in it. If you mixed metal with iodine, and added water, it burned. This one had been too hot, obviously, and reacted too fast, but maybe if I tried something else, something that changed gradually but still produced heat . . .

I glanced at the clock on the wall. Ten p.m. One more attempt, and then I'd return to the ball.

Three attempts later, Naomi settled on the chair in the corner and pulled a book from between the cushions. She always had at least one novel stashed somewhere in the lab, so she could sit with Dagny purring on her lap, half listening to my rambling as she read and I worked.

My whole body buzzed. I was on the right path, I knew it. Every metal that burned too hot or barely reacted at all brought me closer to finding the one that was *right*, closer to finally starting the life that *I* wanted. How perfect would it be, if I solved all my problems on the night of the king's birthday, if I sealed my escape from the court on the one night a year when I *had* to be there? I'd never have to step inside that ballroom again.

After the seventh attempt, I checked the clock again. Two a.m. That didn't seem right. It had only been an hour, I was sure. But the king's parties always went on forever. I had plenty of time to return.

I glanced at Naomi again. Her eyes were closed now, and she was breathing gently. Dagny had curled up with her paws, chin, and tail on top of the book, to make sure that Naomi couldn't ignore her. But Naomi was clearly asleep, and Dagny was, too, their chests rising and falling in sync.

The sun was peeking in through the windows when I became aware of time again. I was pouring spirit of niter into a flask, holding my breath, willing my hand to remain steady, when heavy footsteps crossed the floor above.

I jumped. Spirit of niter flew across the table, and I swore, earning a startled look from Dagny. The party must have ended. My father was going to *murder* me. I grabbed a cloth and quickly mopped up the liquid. If anyone touched this with their bare hands . . .

Naomi sat up. "What's going on?" Her hair had half collapsed, revealing the wire structure underneath. She shoved the dome back onto her head.

"I heard something upstairs. Probably my father." Maybe the feast wasn't over. Maybe he had noticed my absence and finally come looking for me. I wasn't sure if that would be better or worse. When I had left the new year celebrations early to study, he'd locked me out of my laboratory for a month. No experiments, no research, not even access to my books, even though I'd attended the ball for at least an hour. That should have been punishment enough for any later transgressions.

More footfalls, pounding down the stairs. They were too heavy to be maids, but too many to be just my father. Had he brought the whole court to berate me?

It had to be somebody else. Thieves, perhaps. Opportunistic criminals who expected the manor to be empty during the ball. I'd assume that intruders would at least try to be stealthy, but if they thought the entire place abandoned . . . I grabbed a pair of iron tongs and held them in front of me, staring at the laboratory door.

"Freya?" Naomi swiped the small shovel from the fireplace. "Who do you think it is?"

I didn't reply. It couldn't be anyone good. But if we kept quiet, they probably wouldn't look here. It was a run-down old laboratory underneath the house. Not a likely hiding place for jewels.

"Freya! Freya, are you down here?"

It was my father, but he didn't sound angry. His voice was too loud, almost desperate, fearful. Something was wrong.

Before I could even lower my weapon, the door crashed open, and my father barreled into the room.

Titus Nystrom was usually a calm and collected man, with a smile for everyone and a quick wit to match. He had to be, to convince the court that a merchant, of all people, could be allowed to walk among them.

He did not look calm now. His hair was rumpled, his skin blanched and clammy. He wasn't wearing his jacket, and he had lost his cravat somewhere on the way. My father never looked anything less than polished. Dread settled in my stomach.

"Freya!" He ran over to me and pulled me into a hug, squeezing so tightly that the breath rushed out of my lungs. "You're alive."

"Alive?" I scrambled to make sense of the word. "Why wouldn't I be alive?"

"There was an attack." He seized me by the shoulders and inspected my face. "I thought—but you're here. You're here. You're safe."

Four palace guards crowded into the laboratory behind him. They wore dark-blue coats, embroidered with the king's three gold stars. A sword and dagger hung from each of their left hips. I stared at them, the way they clutched the hilts of their weapons. I'd never seen the guards *do* anything before, except stand silently behind the king, but they were alert now, ready to act.

I had to ask my father what had happened. I had to force the words out, had to know, but they got stuck somewhere in the knot that had formed at the top of my chest, and I just stared.

"Sir?" Naomi said. "What's happened?"

My father let go of me and stared at her, like he hadn't even realized she was there. "Naomi," he said. "Is there anyone else here? Anyone with you?"

"No," I said. "No, no one but us. Father, what's going on?"

"Poison," he said. "At the banquet. Everyone is dead, Freya. Everyone."

The words didn't make sense. I stepped away, the small of my back thudding against the table. Dagny butted her head against my side, and I dug my fingers into the fur around her neck. I could feel the rise and fall of her breath.

"What do you mean, everyone is dead?"

"Everyone is *dead*. Something was poisoned, the food or the wine . . . and it killed them. The king, the queen, the king's brother, his nephew . . . they're all dead."

Cyanide could asphyxiate its victims in under ten seconds. The thought floated across my empty skull, so clinical, unwanted. *Everyone was dead.* Dead.

Naomi grabbed my arm to steady herself. "My brother was at the ball," she said to my father. "Did you see him? Is he all right?"

"I don't know," my father said. "Several hundred are dead. Too many to know exactly who—when I couldn't find you, Freya, I thought . . ."

I stared at him, running over the words, checking and then checking again that I'd heard correctly. It didn't make sense. It couldn't make sense. "But you're alive."

"I was lucky. I was distracted, I wasn't eating at the feast . . ."

"So other people survived?" Naomi said. Her grip on my arm was painfully tight. "Other people are still alive?"

"Some," my father said. "Not many. I haven't seen your brother."

"I have to go." She let go of my arm. "I have to look for him."

"I'll go with you." That thought, at least, made sense to me. Naomi needed help. I could help her. I clung to the idea, the clarity of it. But my father grabbed me, holding me in place.

"No. It isn't safe, Freya. You can't go back."

"You said they were poisoned. So it won't be dangerous to go back now."

"Some are still—not everyone is dead yet, Freya. And I can't risk you. *We* can't risk you. Not now."

"You can't risk me? There's no risk." No one would ever want to attack me. "We'll bring gloves. We won't touch anything. It'll be safe."

"No, Freya!" He grabbed both of my shoulders again. "Listen. Hundreds of people died, and more are close to it. The whole line to the throne is *dead*."

"So we should help those who are left!"

"Listen to me, Freya. Everyone is dead. Everyone before *you*. That makes you queen. You can't go back there."

I laughed. It wasn't funny, not any of it, but the sound ripped out of me, the only way I could react to the ridiculousness of it.

I'd seen them, alive, only a few hours before. "I can't be queen."

"This is not a joke, Freya." He spoke sharply now, almost aggressively. "The first one in the line of succession to survive is *you*."

"No. I'm twenty-third in line." I was as likely to rule as Dagny was. That was why I was allowed to skip balls, why I was permitted to spend my time in the laboratory, why no one would even have noticed that I left the grounds tonight. I didn't matter. I was nobody to them.

"Freya, listen to what I am saying. Someone wanted to destroy the court tonight. They wanted to kill the entire line to the throne, and they almost succeeded. You are the first one left."

I couldn't be queen. I *couldn't*. So many people would have to die for me to inherit the throne, and they couldn't be gone. I'd seen them, a few hours ago. All alive, completely themselves. I'd never liked most of them, but I hadn't wanted them to *die*.

Dagny butted against my hand, and I swept her up into my arms, hugging her so tightly she mewed in protest.

"But my brother," Naomi said. "He's ahead of me in line to the throne. Ahead of me, but after Freya. What happened to him?"

"I don't know!" My father was almost shouting now. "I didn't see him. He may have left, himself."

Naomi stumbled toward the door. Her legs didn't seem able

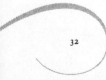

to hold her weight. "I have to get back to the palace. I have to know. I have to look—"

But the guards blocked the doorway, and they did not step aside.

"We cannot let you go, my lady," one said.

"I have to see my brother!"

"No," my father said. "No, they're right. You're in line to the throne, too. Thirty-sixth before tonight? You have to be protected, as well."

Naomi shook her head, over and over, but the guards still didn't move.

"We must act quickly," my father said. "I'm sure our enemies are already planning to take advantage of the situation. We have to move now, before they have time to act against you."

"We don't have enemies," I said. "How could we have enemies?"

"You're queen, Freya. And we must ensure you remain that way. We need to leave—now. We will have the servants fetch whatever you need later."

He gestured for me to place Dagny back on the table. I tightened my grip. I was not leaving Dagny behind. Not now. Contrary to what many people seemed to think, I wasn't a fool. I read my history books. I knew how these things ended. The fights over who was the rightful heir, the fate of hapless girls shoved at the throne because of tenuous family connections, the overbold young men with dreams of glory. If I claimed my supposed throne, I'd be sticking out my neck for anyone to take a swing. And if I failed to hold the crown . . .

But if I didn't claim the throne, I'd still be in danger. Who would leave the rightful heir alive, if they wanted to control the throne themselves?

I wasn't going to leave Dagny behind tonight. Dagny helped me think. Dagny helped me *breathe*. I was going to need both of those things if I was going to survive this.

"I'll go," I said. "But someone needs to look for Naomi's brother. They have to help her." I looked at the guards, waiting for them to move. Instead, they looked to my father.

"Very well," my father said. "Someone will look for him. But Naomi must come with us." He gestured at the door, but didn't move. I didn't move, either.

He was waiting for *me* to walk through first. Because I held precedence now. Because I was the queen.

I couldn't be the queen.

I grabbed Naomi's hand and squeezed it before stepping forward. My legs shook.

Queen. I was *queen*.

THREE

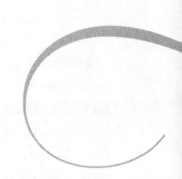

NEWS OF THE ATTACKS HAD CLEARLY ALREADY SPREAD. Even more people crowded the streets now than they had last night, and the air seemed to have changed, heavy with fear. People shouted at our carriage as we squeezed past—is it true? Is the king hurt? Is the king *dead*?

Crowds bumped against the carriage, and the horses danced out of the way. Our curtains were clipped shut, barely letting any light through, preventing anyone from seeing me and my guards. But what would they think, even if they could see me? I was just a girl clutching a cat. Not exactly someone who looked like they had information.

"There should be guards on the streets," my father murmured. "This could turn into a riot."

I clutched my hands in my lap, squeezing my knuckles until they turned white. A riot. I could picture it like it was already happening, the people screaming, running, our carriage knocked over in the panic . . . but it wasn't happening now. It wouldn't happen. It was fine. It was fine.

"We are trying, my lord," one of the guards said. "We were all taken by surprise."

I looked across at Naomi. Her fear was a physical presence in the carriage, but I couldn't think what to say. Anything reassuring felt like a lie. I was terrible with words, and now that they really did matter, I didn't have a clue how to help her.

As the carriage jerked around a corner, Naomi began to shake, and Dagny struggled out of my arms and crossed the seat. She butted against Naomi's side and licked her hand, purring. Naomi stroked her, but she did not turn to look.

I squeezed my eyes closed. Calm. I had to remain calm. But all my fears jumbled together, each one passing too quickly to process. Everyone was dead. I was queen. Someone had tried to kill us all. I was queen. How could I be queen? Each idea felt disconnected from the others, and I couldn't focus on any of them. I couldn't breathe.

No. I could handle this. I just needed to focus on the problem. I couldn't solve the deaths, and the thought of being queen was still too big, too impossible. So I would focus on the murders, the abstract concept of them, the logic behind it.

Someone had tried to wipe out the entire court last night. But who? Why? I hadn't heard so much as a whisper of discontent, and the king's spies couldn't have, either, or this would never have happened. There had to be some motive, something that made sense . . . someone at the feast, probably, with some connections to the kitchen, in order to kill everyone so quietly and effectively.

And who had they intended to survive? Intended to rule? My life was an accident, that much I was sure of. No one would plot to place me on the throne. So had the murderer intended to wipe out everybody, every single noble in court? Or had they had another ruler in mind, another survivor further down the line?

Our carriage moved against the flow of the crowd, away from the palace. Once the sounds of the crowds faded, I unclipped the curtains and peered out.

"Freya!" my father hissed. I ignored him.

The same. Everything looked the same. The world had not shifted. It looked like the start of another normal day.

A stern stone castle loomed on a hill ahead of us. I didn't know its official name, but everyone here called it the Fort. The name did little to capture its true terror. It was a single, square tower, built of black stone, surrounded by a dark moat. Once, it had been the home of the king, when warring nobles were a constant threat. Then it had become a prison, for the kingdom's most dangerous enemies, but even that was rarely needed any longer. The Fort was more of a warning than a weapon these days, but it was kept in readiness, in case the king needed protection.

"We're going to the Fort?" I said.

My father nodded. "It's the only place that's safe."

The drawbridge across the moat hadn't been raised for at least two hundred years. I'd thought the chains and pulleys must have rusted closed from disuse, but the bridge had been lifted now, preventing anyone from approaching.

Another two guards blocked the road at the edge of the moat. "Halt!" one shouted, as the carriage drew near. "Who goes there?"

"It is your queen," my father said. "Let us through."

The guards did not lower their swords. "Step out of the carriage."

I pinched the skin between my thumb and my forefinger, swallowing my fear. If these guards didn't want me as queen, they could easily kill me. In all the chaos, no one would ever notice. My guards stepped out of the carriage, their own swords raised, and my father nodded for me to follow. I grabbed Dagny before I moved. Her wriggling warmth kept my hands steady.

The men on the road frowned as I emerged, like they were trying to figure out who I was. They relaxed slightly when they saw my father.

"Titus," one said. "You survived."

"I did. As did my daughter. Please, let us through. Who knows what may happen if we linger here."

"Of course." The guard bowed to me. If he thought bowing to a soot-covered teenager clutching a large cat was strange, he didn't show it. "Please, follow me."

He led us partway around the moat, to a point where the bank was slightly less steep. A man sat in a boat halfway across, and when he saw the guard, he rowed for the shore. Rubbish floated on the water, detritus from the river that had been swept here and become stuck. Something to do with tides, I thought vaguely. The sea was miles and miles away, but I was certain I'd heard that. The Fort's moat always stank because of something to do with tides.

The boat bumped against the shore, and a guard grabbed it before nodding for me to step inside. It bobbed as I shifted my weight onto the deck, and I squeezed Dagny tight, suddenly certain I was going to go flying into the water.

"Keep good hold of that cat, young miss," the boatman said. "Don't want it to take a sudden swim."

"Young miss?" my father said. "This is your new queen."

The man stared at him. "I apologize," he said. The words were almost a question. "Let us cross then, quickly."

I perched on the bench, and two guards climbed in the boat behind me, taking up all the remaining space.

"Wait," I said, as the boatman pushed off. I looked to Naomi and my father, still waiting on the shore.

"The boat will come back for us, Freya," my father said. "You must go ahead."

They couldn't make me go ahead alone. "The guards can wait," I said. "We can cross together."

"The guards cannot wait, Freya. Did you forget what has happened tonight?"

Of course I hadn't forgotten. But the guards were as likely as anyone to hurt me now. We had no idea who had attacked the king. I'd be safer with people I knew. And as useless as I was, I didn't want to leave Naomi alone. But the boatman had already rowed several lengths away, and I knew he wouldn't turn back.

I pressed my chin against Dagny's fur. The Fort loomed ahead, a dark shadow against the sky.

The boatman deposited me on the bank on the other side, and my remaining guards hurried me up the steep, pathless hill. My shoes slipped on the mud. I glanced back at the opposite shore. I should wait for my father and Naomi—but my guards were relentless.

Finally, we reached the Fort's official road, and climbed it to the entrance of the castle itself. Its large iron doors stood open, but the portcullis blocked the way. My guards shouted for it to be raised, and someone inside must have heard, because it shuddered up, the chains shrieking.

I looked down at the city. The winding streets, the jagged roofs, the old Minster tower reaching past them all. The palace was a sea of green in the chaos. I could still see the lantern lights in the garden, shining with determination even in the dawn. The palace itself was all tall windows and stone columns, unchanged by the horrors it had seen.

"Come, Your Majesty," one of the guards said. He had a gentler face than the others, with a tightly cropped gray beard and concerned black eyes. "We should not linger here."

I glanced again at my father and Naomi. Their boat was already halfway across the river. They were as safe as they could be. I would see them again inside.

I'd never been inside the Fort before, and from the smell of it, no one else alive had, either. It stank of must and neglect, a chill hanging in the air. The walls pressed in on either side, free of adornment, supporting the ceiling fifteen feet up.

My guards led me down the corridor. We passed almost nobody. Some maids were hurrying from room to room, but few even glanced at us. None of them paused to bow or curtsy.

They led me to a tightly spiraling staircase in the far corner of the Fort. There were no lamps, and no windows, so one of the guards seized a lantern to light the way. We climbed, to the second floor, and the third.

A door opened on the fourth floor, and someone barreled out, slamming into me.

They were tall, even taller than me, well built. My nose slammed against their collarbone, and they flinched back, feet stumbling on the steps they had just descended. I yelped, more in surprise than pain, and Dagny leaped out of my arms.

It was William Fitzroy. I swayed from the impact, staring at his face. His blue eyes were bloodshot, and his golden-blond hair was spattered with a dark substance that might have been blood. But he was alive. Another survivor. I hadn't even thought of Fitzroy since I left the palace, hadn't even considered the possibility of his death, but relief rushed through me when I looked at him now. He was kind of an idiot, but he didn't deserve to die. He, at least, was here. Solid and breathing and blinking at me in confusion.

"I am sorry," he said, with a distracted shake of his head. His grief was like a physical presence in the air, painful to breathe in. "Excuse me." He stepped around us and hurried on. I stared after him, unwilling to look away until he was out of sight.

He had survived. Someone, at least, was left.

I scooped Dagny up again and nodded for my escort to continue.

The guards led me to the top floor of the Fort, where the royal apartments were kept ready for times of crisis. No one was watching the entrance when we arrived, but one of the guards peeled off to stand there, while the other led me inside and through to a large room clearly intended for the queen's use. Embroidered red cushions had been piled on the four-poster bed, and a thick rug covered the otherwise bare floor. A harp stood against one wall—the queen had loved music—and I could see many unworn dresses through the open door of the wardrobe, each worth more than a year's income to most people in the kingdom. Pots of color had been lined up on her dresser, along with a brush and jewels. Even in an emergency, the queen would look her best.

"Do you have everything you need, Your Majesty?" The guard hovered by the door. He looked rather eager to leave. Of course. He couldn't leave my presence without permission.

"Naomi," I said quickly. "Will she be coming here, too?"

He opened his mouth, then closed it again. He looked nervous. "These are the royal apartments, Your Majesty. Everyone who comes to the Fort will be given accommodation, but only you can stay here. For your own safety. Is there anything else you need?"

"No." My voice cracked on the word. "No, thank you."

"Then I will leave you to rest, if that pleases Your Majesty. It has been a long night."

I nodded, and, with a bow, he stepped out of the room and closed the door.

But I was in the wrong place, I realized, as the lock clicked. The monarch should have been in the king's room, not the queen's.

So much for asserting my place. I was as out of the way here as I would have been in my lab. But perhaps that was the point.

It suggested respect, without putting me in the most obvious place for another attack.

I dropped Dagny onto the bed. She kneaded the sheets, her claws snagging on the silk.

A diadem rested on the dresser. Diamonds glinted in the dim light. I picked it up, careful to avoid touching the jewels, and slid it onto my head. It perched there, looking gaudy in the reflection against my black hair.

Queen. I was queen.

My reflection didn't seem to believe me. Who would? I didn't look like a queen. Ruling in Epria meant being as glamorous and luxurious and beautiful as possible. If you dripped with gold, if you were spoiled and selfish, if you looked like a fitting idol at the center of the court's intricate dances . . . then, you could be queen. I just looked like a gangly child, dressed up in my mother's jewels. I looked ridiculous.

And not the good kind of ridiculous, the one that everyone in court adored. Weak. Laughable. But what did it matter, I thought, as I tossed the diadem back on the dresser. Everyone was *dead*, weren't they? What court did I have left to lead?

I hoped Naomi was all right.

Queens probably had servants to help them undress, but no one would be coming now. I stretched my arms around my back, reaching for the laces, but I couldn't grasp them, so I kicked off my shoes, washed my face in the basin by the window, and sank onto the sheets. My arms fell around Dagny, and she snuggled close.

I buried my face in her fur and let her rhythmic purring soothe me to sleep.

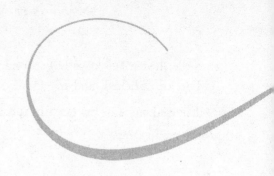

FOUR

I AWOKE TO SHARP KNOCKING ON THE DOOR. I SAT UP, shoving my tangled hair away from my face. My eyes felt sticky, and a dull ache pounded at the back of my head. I hadn't slept nearly enough.

"Freya?" It was my father. "Are you all right?"

I tried to step out of bed, and stumbled. I was still wearing that ridiculous dress from the banquet, with its thirty-six layers of skirt and sleeves up to my ears. It had become twisted while I slept, and I fell as I tried to right it, my elbow slamming against the floor. I bit back a cry, tears stinging my eyes.

"Freya?"

"Yes," I gasped. "I'm all right. What's happened?"

The lock clicked, and my father stepped inside. "Did you sleep well?"

He could not honestly be asking me that. I had *slept*, but it had been a strange sort of half sleep, always on the verge of waking.

"What's happened?" I said again instead, standing up as my father closed the door with the guards on the other side. "Have you found who was responsible?"

"Not yet. But we will."

"Do you know how many . . ." I couldn't finish the question. It was too awful, and it wasn't even what I really wanted to ask. I wanted to know if another heir had been found. Someone to rule before me.

"We don't have a count. Over four hundred, at least. It will take days before we know for certain. But that can't be our priority now. We must act quickly."

"To catch the killers?"

"To have you crowned. We cannot allow the kingdom to remain without a monarch any longer than absolutely necessary. It makes it too easy for someone to challenge you."

"But what about the funerals?" There would need to be so many. "And the investigation?"

"Not as pressing as your coronation. The dead will remain dead, no matter if we delay. We cannot say the same for your throne. If you take some of the old queen's things, we can have you crowned tomorrow."

"But—" It would be an insult to dress up in finery now, while everyone else was dead. "It's too soon."

"It isn't soon enough. You are vulnerable, Freya, as long as you are not the anointed queen. Once we have you crowned, in front of everybody, people will hesitate before they hurt you. Until then . . . we cannot risk it, Freya."

I raked my hands through my tangled hair. "What happened last night? What—what did you see?"

"It was very sudden." He looked away, eyes focused on the embroidery of my bed hangings, as though they might provide the answer. "After the last course of the feast. People—some people began to complain of stomach pains. Then—" He swallowed and dragged his gaze back to me. "I will spare you the details of what proceeded."

"Don't spare me the details. I want to know." I needed to know, needed to *understand*. People were *dead*, and if I could understand that, if I could really *know* . . .

"You do not want to know. They will remain dead either way. You have one concern now, Freya. Be queen. You will have a whole council of people to investigate these murders. You need to focus on your own safety now."

But a council of people weren't *me*. Someone had killed many of the most influential and well-protected people in the kingdom. They'd succeeded, even though simply mentioning the idea would have led to their arrest. They were dangerous people, dangerous and clever. I needed to know who they were. I needed to know how they had done it, *why* they had done it. And I couldn't trust anyone else to find out the truth on my behalf.

"What about Naomi's brother?" I said. "Did you find him?"

He sighed. "I don't know what happened to him. If he was at the banquet, then—it is unlikely he survived."

"But it's possible."

"Yes, Freya, it is possible. For now, Naomi has been given accommodation in the Fort, and our protection, as well. But I have been working all day to take care of the details for *you*. Other people's brothers . . . right now, they cannot be my concern."

"But it's *my* concern. Naomi is my best friend."

"I know you want it to be," he said sadly. "But you can only deal with so many things, Freya. You have to focus on staying alive and holding on to the throne. Her brother is either dead or alive. We can't change that." He shook his head, and then straightened, as though shedding his grief. "We need to get started. We'll have to fit you for a coronation gown, and I will go over the protocol with you."

The rest of the evening passed in a blur. My father returned with four seamstresses in tow. They carried Queen Martha's coronation dress between them, but one glance told me that it would never, never fit.

It took longer to convince them. They squeezed me into it,

urging me to breathe in more, as though that might make my shoulders less broad. When they'd finally forced the dress into place, unfastened but on, they fussed with the buttons and the hem, politely avoiding saying what was obvious to everyone. The dress was several inches too short. It strained around the waist and across the shoulders, while the chest gaped. Short of adding a patchwork of new cloth, even the Forgotten themselves wouldn't be able to make it fit.

"The problem," one of the seamstresses said, as she stepped back to survey the damage, "is that the dress is rather old-fashioned. It is twenty years old, after all, and it was never intended to crown a *monarch*. It might be best if we salvage from Queen Martha's dresses and make something new for our new queen."

My father frowned, but his impatience couldn't change the fact that the dress wasn't going to fit. "Could you have it complete by tomorrow?"

"We must, mustn't we?" the seamstress said. "We will work through the night."

"Then see it is done."

They freed me from the dress, and then they measured me, talking a mile a minute as they went, about regal colors that would suit me, about how many jewels were suitable for such a somber yet important coronation. When their talked lulled, my father threw etiquette at me—as an unwelcome newcomer in court, he had made sure to learn every rule for every situation, and it was coming in handy now. I repeated the instructions in my head, but they jumbled together, nothing quite making sense.

Tomorrow, I would be on display for all the grieving kingdom to see.

The seamstresses left to begin their work, but my father remained, running over the coronation rules again and again, making me walk around the room with a regal air, correcting my posture, correcting my gaze, correcting everything about me.

Was he remembering, as I was, all the times I'd skipped my etiquette lessons, how I'd sulked and shouted and fought until he gave up on courtly elocution and dancing classes? Maybe if I'd gone to those lessons, actually *tried*, instead of assuming it was all useless to me, when I planned to go as far away from this court as I could . . . maybe then, this would have been different.

The seamstresses returned in the middle of the night for a fitting. The new dress didn't exactly calm my nerves. Jewels weighed it down, although only half of them had been added, and the mass of them made it even harder to breathe.

By the time morning came, I was dizzy with tiredness and fear. But the preparations weren't over. It took two hours for the four seamstresses to dress me, even helped by an apparent army of maids. They sewed me into the dress as they went. Jewels were stitched into the cloth, hung around my neck, studded on my shoes, and draped around my waist.

And still my father reminded me of all the things I must not do. The most important one, the one he repeated over and over, was that I must not speak. Not one single word, beyond the ritual itself.

I had to wonder: Was that tradition, or was that rule only for me?

The Minster reached taller than a castle, its bell tower hidden by the clouds. Every inch of its stone exterior was covered by intricate carvings and gargoyles, and when its bells rang, the sound echoed through the entire city like singing. It was a building crafted by the divine Forgotten, before they left this kingdom behind.

Rickben, the peacemaker. Elandra, the fierce. Garret, the trickster. Valanthe, the just. They had ruled Epria when it used to be *better*, but abandoned it in disgust at the kingdom's growing corruption. Now only a few relics remained, miracles of architecture and engineering, a reminder of how great the kingdom had once been and could be again.

It always sounded like nonsense to me. We had no records, no real *proof* of their existence, just a bunch of old buildings and a collection of legends. Everyone knew the names of at least twenty of the Forgotten, but even these were just tradition. As far as I was concerned, the Forgotten were just an excuse. People saw things they couldn't even dream of creating, and decided that they must be divine.

I kept my eyes on the Minster now, staring at one of the

grimacing male faces above the doorway. Crowds had gathered on either side of the path, but I couldn't let myself look at them, couldn't let the fear take hold. All I had to do was walk.

My legs shook underneath my skirts, but I did not fall.

The inside of the Minster had always amazed me. We were rarely allowed inside—once a year for the midwinter celebration, once a generation for a coronation—and every time we were, I spent more time staring at the ceiling than I did listening to the words of the priest. I glanced up again now, taking in the carvings and paintings sixty feet above me. *How?* I wondered, every time I saw them. How had anyone climbed so high to paint?

The people inside rose. I fixed my eyes on the altar at the far end of the Minster—miles away, surely, from where I now stood. The rear pews were crammed with the commoners invited to see my coronation—the merchants, the bankers, the lawyers, the doctors. All here for a glimpse of this unknown queen.

They had already judged me, I was sure. The moment I stepped through the door, they had decided what sort of queen I would be.

The front half of the Minster was almost empty. I should have expected it, should have *known*, but my stomach still dropped when I saw empty pew after empty pew. These boxes were designed to fit at least five hundred nobles. Less than twenty stood there now—the remnants of the court, or at least those willing to see me crowned. It was possible, *possible*, that some of them had decided not to attend. Possible, but unlikely. None of them would want to miss this.

I glanced at the back of their heads—who were they? I didn't know most of them well enough to tell from a quick look at their hair, but I recognized Naomi. Her black hair was in a simple bun at the back of her head, strands falling loose. Her brother was not beside her.

My stomach dropped, and I dragged my gaze away. I had to concentrate. I couldn't think about . . . I couldn't get distracted. I focused on the steps ahead of me, the platform, the gold throne, and the chanting priest.

Somehow, I reached the dais, and the hours of practice clicked. My knees hit stone as I knelt for the priest's blessing. I bowed my head as he dabbed oil on my forehead. I sat on the throne as someone handed me the ceremonial scepter and orb, as a red sable cloak was placed over my shoulders, as the priest stepped behind me and balanced a crown on my head. The ritual flowed past, like someone else was moving my body, and I was just watching, too.

"All kneel before Queen Freya, first of her name, ruler of Epria. Long may she reign!"

The priest stepped back, and the crowd fell to their knees.

"Long may she reign!"

I let myself glance at the nobles before me. My eyes went straight to Naomi, and she gave me a gentle smile. But she was alone.

Maybe Jacob was ill. Maybe he was shunning me. *Something*. It didn't mean he was—her brother wasn't dead.

My father knelt with a group of men and women I vaguely recognized—some of the king's old advisers, I thought. Torsten Wolff knelt by another pew, and Fitzroy. A smattering of people.

This couldn't be everyone who had survived. It couldn't be. The others must have simply stayed away, unwilling to see me crowned queen. That was all.

Don't lie to yourself, I thought, anger rising out of nowhere. No one else was left.

The priest quietly cleared his throat. It was nearly over. All I had to do was leave, and lead the court out of the Minster. Just one more thing. I stood, and the priest lifted my cloak so it did not snag on the throne before spreading it out behind me.

I wasn't allowed to touch the cloak. My father had told me over and over last night, and this morning as well. I couldn't touch the cloak. I couldn't lift the cloak. But I definitely, definitely should not *stand* on the cloak.

But I had no idea how I was actually supposed to do that. Even at five foot ten, I was too small for this thing. It must have weighed more than I did, and the train that spread out in all directions. I took a small step forward and teetered on my jeweled heels.

Another step, and another, and I had reached the edge of the dais. Five stairs between me and the courtiers, and then a straight walk to the door. Easy. I stretched my right foot out, feeling for the steady reassurance of the step below. Once I found it, I shifted my weight and brought my left foot to meet it. Four steps to go. Three steps.

My heel caught on the hem. The cloak yanked down, jerking me backward. I wobbled, fighting for balance, but the crown was too heavy, throwing me off, and I stumbled, falling to the left. I spiraled my arms, fighting to stay upright. My knee slammed onto the step.

The crown tumbled. It landed on the step with a clang that shook my teeth. Priceless jewels scraped against the floor.

I couldn't react. I watched as it rolled, bouncing down one step, then the next, each time landing with a sound like a gong. Nobody spoke. Nobody moved. The entire room stared at the crown.

It stopped just below the bottom stair. Undamaged, I thought, but still *on the floor*, not on my head, and I didn't know what to do. My face felt like it was on fire, and my cloak was still tangled around my shoe. Should I retrieve the crown myself? It might be bad luck for me to touch it, like it was bad luck for me to touch the cloak. Would it be unqueenly to hurry after my own jewels? Even more unqueenly than falling and tossing them to the floor to begin with?

I closed my eyes and took a deep breath. I was a queen. Officially now. I could deal with this. It was the first test, and I would handle it. I had to handle it.

I reached down and untucked the cloak from the jeweled heel of my shoe. I spread it carefully out behind me, away from anywhere I might step. And then I stood.

At least nobody was laughing. Everyone was staring, but no one made a sound.

The priest hurried forward and picked up the crown. "Rulership does not sit comfortably on any worthy head," he said, in the same ringing, serious voice he had spoken in before, as though this were all part of the ceremony. "Our sovereigns may be guided by the Forgotten, may they one day return, but their power should be a weight, a burden, and not something they grasp with both hands. But Queen Freya, we beg of you to take on this duty." And he placed the crown on my head again.

I could have hugged him.

This time, I made it out of the Minster without mishap. An open carriage waited by the steps, ready for the procession through the city, and I climbed inside in silence.

The journey back to the Fort was a somber affair. My father had tried to make it grand, he really had, with fanfare ahead of me, and guards pounding drums, and me perched in an open-topped carriage that seemed to overflow with gold. But people did not want to celebrate. Everyone in the city seemed to have come out to watch, but they did not cheer as the carriage passed. Most just stared at me, or murmured to their neighbors, wondering why this plain teenager girl was dripping with jewels in the royal carriage, instead of the gregarious king they all knew.

Asking why I, of all people, could claim to rule them.

My father had forbidden me to smile, or to wave. I needed a show of power now, he said, and openness was weakness. It wasn't hard to look serious, with so many people glaring at me. But I knew they weren't impressed. The queen was supposed to be *more,* somehow—more than a person, more than human, demanding the attention of everyone around her. I just looked like I'd stumbled into the carriage by accident.

Which I guess was true.

I looked forward, focusing on the horses pulling my carriage along. The music drowned out any sound from the crowd.

If I wanted to survive, I needed to think small. Focus on my council, and the nobles at court. They would deal with the wider world. That was how it had always been, the responsibility cascading down, the ruler only ever needing to look at the next tier. So I would have to impress the court, and everything else would fall into place from there.

Because if I thought not just about the surviving nobles, but about *everyone* in the kingdom, the hundreds and hundreds of thousands of people, each with their own wants, their own opinions, each ready to be disappointed by me, each wishing their ruler was anyone other than me . . . stars flared in my vision, and I shoved the thought away.

Even the famously irreverent court couldn't possibly stomach festivities when hundreds of people lay dead, but a halfhearted feast had been laid out in the old throne room at the Fort. There were no pies filled with doves, no elaborate desserts, no decorations on the walls. Someone had set out long tables, as though they needed seats for hundreds of courtiers. The spaces seemed to mock us all. There were more empty chairs than there were living guests, and the survivors were scattered in small groups around the hall.

I sat at the high table, positioned above them all. Normally, the monarch's family and favored guests would join the table, but so few people remained that my father insisted I sit alone. Twenty people could have been seated here, but instead the space stretched out on either side of me, a queen with no allies at all.

Naomi was seated halfway down another table, similarly alone. Her black hair was piled into another elaborate style, but it was drooping to one side. She didn't seem to have noticed. I needed to talk to her. I needed to find out how she was, what had happened to her, but I didn't dare move. I had a few more hours to endure.

There was food, at least, pheasant and raspberries and wild boar, but how could anyone eat it with the memory of the last feast so fresh? Servants brought out dish after dish for my approval, but I selected them at random, and barely ate a bite.

The room was almost silent. I could hear every groan of a chair, every splash of wine in a cup, every brave scrape of a knife against a plate. Everyone was trapped here until the end of this charade.

Nothing was going to happen, I told myself, as I forced myself to chew a piece of boar. But beneath my stage fright, beneath the awareness of everyone's eyes on me, genuine fear lingered. I was a target. We had no idea what had happened at the last banquet, so it could easily happen again. Someone could try and complete the job, catch the heir they had missed.

And I was making it easy for them. Sitting here, eating this food, acting like I thought I was invincible, when I knew I wasn't. They could hurt me as easily as they'd hurt everyone else, and I was just *sitting* here. Making it easy for them.

I stood. My chair scraped against the floor. Everyone stared at me. But I couldn't bear it, not for another moment. I had forgotten how to breathe.

This wasn't a real coronation. King Jorgen would never have been isolated like this. He would have had music, dancing, wine, a table so crammed with people that everyone's elbows bashed together.

But I couldn't be like that. Everyone had died, and I was supposed to rule, but I didn't know how, and no one would be convinced by this, no one.

The room blurred at the edges. I needed to *breathe*.

I swept out of the room, forcing myself not to run. My guards marched behind me. I needed air. I just—I needed some *air*.

The corridor beyond was quieter, at least, the cold air refreshing. I fell back against the wall. I closed my eyes, shutting everything out, and focused on my breath. Breathe in, breathe out. I could do this. I could.

"What do you want?"

I opened my eyes. William Fitzroy stood farther down the corridor. His eyes were slightly red.

"I didn't know you were here." What else could I say? My voice was too breathy, but at least I managed to speak.

"Quitting already?" He laughed, and the sound rattled through me. Fitzroy usually sounded so light, mocking at his worst. Now he sounded cruel. "They never should have had you crowned. You don't belong here."

I looked at him, his messy hair, his bloodshot eyes. I couldn't deny it. I didn't have the strength to build any lies. "You're right. I don't." Any fool could see that. "But I'm here anyway."

He blinked, and his eyes widened. Had he just realized what he'd said? He opened his mouth to speak again, and then stopped. *What,* I wanted to say. *Tell me.* All the silence, all the pretense of the day had eaten into me. Everything was fake, grief and weakness buried deep, but not him, not then. I wanted his words, his honesty, whatever cruelty ripped out of him. But he just shook his head and stepped back. "Excuse me."

He walked away. My hands shook.

"Your Majesty?" My guard stepped closer. "Are you all right?"

No. No, I wasn't all right. I wanted to scream at them to

go away, that I needed to be *alone*, to breathe, to think, but that wasn't fair. This wasn't the guards' fault.

Fitzroy was right. I didn't belong here. But if I showed weakness, if I ran and hid, my head would be on the chopping block before I could blink. If someone took the throne from me, even if I stepped aside . . . I was queen now, for as long as I breathed. And I did not want to die.

"Yes," I said to the guards. My voice shook, but I said it, at least. "I should go back inside."

I stumbled back into the hall.

FIVE

A COUPLE OF HOURS LATER, I STOOD OUTSIDE NAOMI'S door, trying to work up the courage to knock. One of the guards had shown me the way to this fourth-floor corridor that housed some of the surviving nobility. It looked like it hadn't been touched in the hundreds of years since the court had lived here. It stank of mildew, and the few lamps were sparse, making it feel more like a dungeon than a home.

I needed to see Naomi, to speak to her, but now that I was here, I had no idea what I could possibly say. Her potential grief terrified me. I hated myself for the thought, but the fear screamed inside me, that I did not know what to say, that I would say the wrong thing. That I'd make things worse some-how. I wanted to be able to stride in there and see her and make all of her sadness vanish. I wanted to give her a plan, at least, a way things could be improved. But if her brother was dead, *if* he was dead, I couldn't change that, and that helplessness froze me in place. What good was a friend who couldn't help?

But I couldn't let myself avoid her. What sort of friend would I be, if I abandoned her because I didn't know what to say? I wouldn't let her think she was alone.

I rapped three times on the door.

A long minute passed before it opened, and Naomi peeked through the gap.

She looked like a fraction of herself. She'd released the complicated hairstyle from the coronation banquet, leaving half-braided ropes hanging over her shoulders. Dark circles like bruises ringed her eyes.

She stared at me for a moment, and then threw herself for-ward, her arms flying around me. "Freya!" We collided, and she burrowed into me, her head pressing into the space under my chin. She murmured something into my shoulder, and I couldn't understand the words, so I squeezed back, pulling her closer still.

She was crying, I realized. "I'm sorry," I said, the words rushing out of me. "I'm sorry I abandoned you outside the Fort, I'm sorry I haven't seen you before this. I wanted to, I kept ask-ing, but everything was so chaotic, and my father—"

She shook her head. "I know you couldn't see me. I just—I

missed you. It's been . . . I missed you." She squeezed me again, and then shifted back. "Do you want to come in?"

"Yes," I said. "I mean, if that's all right. I wanted to—we should talk." I glanced over my shoulder at my guard, who hovered a few feet away. "Do you mind waiting out here?"

"If that's what Your Majesty wishes."

I nodded, and Naomi pulled the door closed behind us.

Her room was barely salvaged from decay. Storage crates were still piled against the right wall, and Naomi's clothes hung over boxes. Her bed was hidden under a pile of blankets, and the few lamps were still dusty, the light distorted by grime.

"Naomi, this is awful. Why did they put you here?"

"They haven't had a chance to clean all the rooms yet. And I haven't—I didn't ask anyone. At least I have somewhere to stay."

"You can't stay here. Move up to the top floor, with me."

Naomi shook her head. "I can't. Those rooms are for *you*."

"And I can do whatever I like with them, can't I? I want you to stay. Please."

I should have come sooner. Why had I left it so long? I should have fought harder. "Jacob," I said, my voice raspy. "Did he—"

I already knew the answer, even if I couldn't admit it, but when Naomi shook her head, I still felt like someone had punched me in the chest, knocking all the air from my lungs. "He didn't make it."

I hadn't known Naomi's brother well, but I had known him. He'd always winked at me, every time he saw me, and from him, it always felt like affection, never a joke at my expense. He called me Frey, too, "Hey, little Frey," with that wink, whenever I went to find Naomi and he was nearby. For him to be *gone* . . .

"I'm sorry." Such useless, meaningless words. I wanted to wash her grief out of her, to swallow it up so she wouldn't have to feel it. I wanted to drag her brother back from death, so she'd feel whole again. I wanted to do *something*.

"Thank you." Naomi glanced over at the arrow-slit window. "I still can't believe it. How can they all be gone? It feels like this is just—I don't know." Her voice shook, and she swallowed, squeezing her eyes closed. "I'm just glad to see you." She opened her eyes again, her voice turning determined. "How are *you*? How are you coping?"

"With what? Being queen?"

She nodded.

"It doesn't matter."

"Yes," she said fiercely. "It does. Sit down, and tell me."

I perched on the edge of the bed, and Naomi sank down beside me. "I'm all right. I mean, I'm not all right, not really. I have no idea what I'm doing. But I'll learn."

"You'll do it. I know you will." Naomi pulled her bare feet onto the bed and rested her chin on her knees. "And you don't have to be all right, you know. If you're not."

The familiar words made me smile, just slightly. "I'm still alive. I still have you. That's more than most people can say now."

Naomi wrapped an arm around me again, pulling me closer. A knot in my chest loosened as her head fell onto my shoulder, honesty swelling inside me. "I'm scared," I said quietly.

"Because you have to be queen?"

"No. Well, yes, but—I only survived by accident, Naomi. I wasn't meant to be here." The words felt too dangerous to speak aloud, as though speaking them made them true. "What if the murderer decides to finish the job?"

"Then I'll kill them first," Naomi said fiercely. "Nobody hurts my Freya."

"You are terrifying when you're angry."

Naomi nodded decisively.

"I can't trust anybody," I said. "Not until I know. I'm supposed to have a council meeting tomorrow, and I just keep thinking—what if one of them was responsible? How can I possibly protect myself from that? But I don't know how to be queen, and if I *don't* trust them—"

"You have me," Naomi said. "I'll help you."

I nodded. I knew that. Just her presence gave me strength, reminded me of all the things I could be. I sat up straighter. "I have to find out who the murderer was," I said. "I have to solve this myself. It's the only way I can keep myself safe."

"Do you think you can?"

"I have to." I'd figure out who was threatening me, I'd learn how to be queen. It was a vague, almost laughable plan, but it was a plan nonetheless, and that was what I needed. A goal to frame things with, a way to approach all of this confusion.

"I'm sorry," Naomi said quietly. "I know you wanted to leave."

I'd never do my research on the continent now, I realized. I'd be tied to this court for as long as I remained alive. The knowledge was a crushing weight, lurking in the back of my mind, demanding to be mourned. But I couldn't admit it, not when Naomi had actually lost a brother, not when everyone had lost so much. "I'll figure things out here," I said. "I could never have left you, anyway."

Naomi's shoulders shook. I turned to look at her to see tears rolling down her cheeks, her lips pressed tightly together.

"I'm sorry!" I said quickly. Why did I always say the wrong thing?

"No, no," she said, through her tears. "It's just—it's stupid, Freya."

"It's not stupid."

"I thought—I thought we wouldn't be friends anymore. Now that you're queen. And I thought—well, I've lost my brother and my best friend, all at once. I didn't—I'm just so glad you're here, Freya."

I hugged her again. She pressed her face into my shoulder. "I'm not going anywhere. Come on, Naomi. Come and stay with me in my rooms. I don't want to leave you here."

"I don't know if it's allowed."

"I make the rules now, don't I? And that'll be my first decree."

"It's not much of a decree."

"Well, everyone has to start somewhere." She laughed softly, and I smiled. "Please, Naomi. I can't do this without you."

"I guess that's good, then," she said. "Because I can't do this without you."

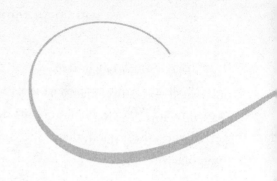

$\text{S}_{\text{I}}\text{X}$

"PERHAPS WE SHOULD BEGIN. IF IT PLEASE YOUR
Majesty."

Rasmus Holt was a rather stern-looking man in his sixties,
with a white beard that grew into a point, and a sharp nose to
match. He had been in King Jorgen's council for the past twenty
years, or so my father told me, and was now the leader of my own
council.

I'd hoped to arrive early to the meeting, to settle in and
greet my councillors one by one, but when I entered the new
council room, everyone had already been waiting inside.
Holt and my father were there, along with a narrow-faced

woman called Sofia Thorn—the master of intelligence, I was informed—and a woman with a severe braid down her neck, called Joanna Norling, who was the master of justice. Torsten Wolff completed the group. He was so tense that the muscles in his neck looked close to snapping. He sat at the other end of the table from me; the perfect place to glower at me without turning his head.

He, Holt had told me, would be responsible for issues of security.

"Security?" I said. "As in the army?" Epria was a peaceful island kingdom. Guards protected the cities, of course, and the countryside had peacekeepers who answered to local nobles, but we hadn't had anything resembling an army for over a hundred years.

"No, no," Holt said. "Nothing as dire as that. But Sten is an expert in military history, and he served on the last king's council, as a general adviser. He's the best mind we have in case of any . . . disturbance."

Disturbance. The word made me shiver. Was he really expecting something that dramatic? Not just poison at dinner, but soldiers, military strategy?

"Not that we need to worry about such things," Holt said, as though he had read my thoughts. "But the past few days have shown us it is prudent to be prepared."

I was pretty sure that the old council had included more than five people. But I supposed this small group was all that was left now. All survivors of the banquet, all suspects, all people I needed to rely on.

Now we were seated around the lone table in the room, trying to ignore the many empty chairs. The entire remaining court could have fit around it easily. Someone must have cleaned the room overnight, but the memory of dust lingered in the air, scratching my throat. The stone walls were bare, with arrow-slit windows protecting us from sunlight as well as invasion. Oil lamps hung around the room, but they only seemed to emphasize the darkness.

Holt watched me, waiting for my permission to continue. I nodded. "Very good, very good," he said. "Well, then. I know that tragedy has brought us here today, but we must look forward. This is the first council meeting of Queen Freya the First, long may she reign."

"Long may she reign," my councillors murmured. I stayed quiet. It seemed too strange to say that about myself.

"Thorn," Holt said. "What do you have to report about the attack?"

"Not enough," Thorn said. She had a rasping voice, like the words were passing over sandpaper. "It seems the poison was hidden in the cake served as the final course. None of those who survived seem to have eaten any. One girl had a few bites and was unwell, but she recovered. Everyone else—well, we cannot interview the dead, but it seems likely that they all had a piece."

"And the poison?" Holt said.

"The symptoms suggest arsenic. Nausea, stomach pains, racing heart, and enough of a delay that the tasters did not fall ill until after it was served. We have no way to prove that, of course, unless someone confesses, but the evidence is fairly clear."

That made sense to me, as well. I wasn't an expert on poisons, but the description matched what I knew. A little more research would be necessary, to ensure the symptoms didn't fit a rarer, stranger poison, but the explanation worked for now.

But the important question wasn't what, but *why?* "But who would want to poison so many people?" I said. My voice sounded a little too loud, and I swallowed, fighting the urge to soften it with rambling.

"We do not know," Thorn said. "We have yet to find any clues in the cake. The king ordered it himself. We will track down the ingredients and see who might have had contact with it, of course, but it is all just speculation as of yet."

"One possibility," Norling said, "is that the Gustavites were involved. Are you familiar with them, Your Majesty?"

"I've heard of them." I'd heard of the book, anyway. *Gustav's Treatise.* He'd been something of a radical, a hundred years ago. Claiming the nobility were corrupt, that we were all a gold-devouring plague on the land. The corruption part was definitely true. He'd wanted all the crown's wealth to be spread equally across the kingdom, and he wasn't quiet about his views. He'd been exiled, along with his words, but he'd never stopped talking, and people had been far more interested in his book once it was forbidden.

"A small group of them have been meeting in the capital, and they'd have the motivation. They are dangerous people."

But it felt a little too convenient. They'd never acted against the court before. I hadn't heard a single rumor about them. Wouldn't *something* have happened, before they resorted to mass murder? "Do you have any proof?"

"It is only a theory as yet," Thorn said. "But if they were responsible, we will prove it."

"How many of them are there? Do we know who's involved in them?"

"They are being very secretive, Your Majesty. Another reason to suspect them. But we will learn all we can."

It made sense that a group like that would be secretive, whether they were planning murders or just meeting for weekly book discussions. My councillors had no evidence that they had any connection to the poisoning.

"Regardless, we must be wary of them," Holt said. "They may use this as an opportunity to increase their influence."

Of course. I was so far down the list of inheritance that calling me queen was almost laughable. All order had already vanished. They'd only have to push slightly for me to fall, as well.

"So what should we do?" I said.

"Show your strength," my father said. "Continue as before, unfazed by any of this. If you are convincing as queen, it will be much harder for them to fight against you."

All I had to do was be convincing. That was all. I tried to fight back a laugh, but it escaped anyway, ringing off the walls. Everyone stared at me, and my face burned. "I—yes," I said. "I just have to be convincing."

"We will guide you, Your Majesty," Holt said. "You are new to this, we know, but we can help you. You can trust us here."

But I couldn't trust them. I couldn't trust anyone, except my father and Naomi. Everyone here had survived the banquet. Any of them could have been involved in the murder. And none of them had any reason to be loyal to me. There was nothing to stop them from finding a better candidate to rule.

I looked at the table, gathering my courage again. "Were you all at the banquet?" I asked. "When it—when it happened?"

Thorn shook her head. "My husband was taken ill, so I could not attend."

"Is he all right?" I asked.

"He is well now, Your Majesty, if weak. He may not appear in court for some time."

That was convenient. But I nodded at her.

"The rest of us were all there, I believe," Norling said. "I remember speaking to Rasmus, at least, and your father. I was lucky that I was no longer hungry, and didn't eat any cake."

And Sten had been sitting at the high table. I'd seen him clearly. I looked at him now, and he frowned. "The cake did not appeal to me," he said. "I am not the sort to eat gold."

"Torsten, your cousin," Holt said, cutting the tension left by Sten's last words. "Have you heard from her since this happened?"

"She sent a letter ahead," he said. "I told her to stay at home, but she's returning to the capital, as quickly as she can."

"Madeleine is your heir, now," Holt added to me. "Perhaps you are friends already? Such a delightful girl."

No, Madeleine Wolff and I were not friends. I'd seen her many times—every time I came to court, she was at the center of it, smiling at everyone, twittering with her bell-like laugh, flirting with Fitzroy when he was in favor, ignoring him when not. Everyone *adored* her, but she had always seemed rather empty-headed to me. Too beautiful for her own good.

Not that I'd ever actually spoken to her, beyond the odd "excuse me." She was too refined to ever stoop low enough to talk to me.

If I hadn't left the banquet, she would have become queen. Everyone would have been far happier with that. Including, perhaps, Madeleine, judging from her flirtations in the court.

"I told her she wasn't well enough to travel," Sten said. "The doctor told her to stay away until the new year—but when has she ever listened to what the doctor says?"

"She isn't well?" I asked.

"She hasn't been for some time, Your Majesty," Holt said. "It is always such a loss to the court when she retires to her estate.

She is most dedicated to her charity work, and a lovely girl besides. But the country air is said to do her good."

"How long was she gone? This time?"

"A couple of months, I believe. Is that correct, Torsten?"

"Yes," Sten said. "That's right." He was watching me carefully. "Did Her Majesty not realize my cousin was away?"

"I've never spoken to her," I said. "I didn't know she was gone."

"Do not worry, Your Majesty," Holt said. "I am certain you will like her. She is a kind girl."

A kind girl who just happened to be away from the capital during a mass murder. A kind girl now one step away from the throne.

"Speaking of journeys—I know this is a delicate subject," Holt continued, "but we must discuss the funeral arrangements for King Jorgen. He must have a fitting ceremony. The funeral will of course involve the traditional rites, and the queen will travel alongside him. But it has been suggested that the other victims should be included in the service, too, in one show of respect for them all."

"It has been suggested by *you*, Holt," Norling said. She had a sharp, decisive voice. "And it is completely unsuitable. To let people share the funeral arrangements of a *king*—"

"It would make the queen seem gentle hearted," Holt said firmly, "and it would be fitting, considering how they all died together. It creates a sense of unity in mourning—"

"It creates the sense everyone is equal," Norling said. "Which is *not* what a new queen wants."

I picked at the loose splinters underneath the table as they continued to argue. It wasn't what was *usually done*, but that didn't mean we shouldn't do it. Everyone had died with the king. They'd probably died *because* of the king. And people like Naomi's brother deserved just as much respect as he did, in the end. "I think it's a good idea."

"Then we shall proceed."

"Your Majesty," Norling said. "It is a good idea in theory, but you cannot understand Holt's true meaning. He does not just mean the king and his relatives. He means all of them. The servants. Everyone who died."

"They died the same as anyone else," Holt said. "They deserve respect."

"They deserve respect, yes," my father said. "But at another time."

I didn't know what the wisest choice might be. But I felt like I knew the *right* choice, the thing that should be done, and that was all I had to go on. "We will do what Holt suggests. Everyone will be included."

"Your Majesty—!"

"Her Majesty has spoken," Holt said, "and we do not have time to delay. We still have to discuss the arrangements for our guests. Nobles from all over the kingdom will be traveling to the capital. I propose we offer them rooms in the Fort, to guarantee their safety—"

"And *I* say that is ridiculous," Norling said. "They will not consider it suitable accommodation, and we don't have time to improve things here. We will look poor. *Weak*."

"We will look safe and secure," Holt said. "Behind solid walls. We cannot expect our guests to live out in the city, considering what has happened."

"We can make the Fort more inhabitable," my father said, "if we dedicate the servants to the task. It would be inhospitable to do anything else."

"It is inhospitable to invite them here," Norling said. "We should move back to the palace and be done with this charade."

"Unwise," Thorn said. She leaned forward. "Our enemies may strike again."

"And what use is security, if it makes us look weak?"

"It is better to look weak than to be weak."

We should leave the Fort. This wasn't where the court belonged. It was so dark here, so old. Fear seeped from the walls. But the palace wasn't safe. It wasn't designed to protect anybody. Hundreds of people had died there, and we still didn't know how or why.

I didn't want to die.

"We should stay here," I said. "For now. Where it's safe."

Sten exhaled, a tiny beat of laughter. I stared at him. He had barely spoken in this meeting, but it was clear he didn't approve. Was he laughing because he thought I was a coward, or because he thought it *wasn't* safe?

His expression gave nothing away, and he did not speak.

"A wise decision," Holt said, as Norling said, "Your Majesty—" But Holt plowed ahead. "A decisive break with the old court will do us all good. There is too much grief at the palace, and too many habits that are bad for the kingdom. A new reign, a different reign, will be what matters now."

"A new reign?" My father frowned. "Things are already too new. We need consistency, so that people can feel safe."

"The decision has been made, Titus," Holt said. "Your Majesty, you will want to greet these nobles in proper fashion, of course. I think some sort of gathering the night before the funerals . . . and a speech of some kind. To introduce yourself. I believe most of them do not know you."

"I can't give a speech." Just the word made me feel on the verge of throwing up. I couldn't stand up and speak to a hundred people.

"Don't worry, Your Majesty," Holt said. "We will guide you."

He was watching me closely. He must have noticed my sudden panic, because he nodded once and said, "Perhaps we should adjourn this meeting until tomorrow. We already have much to do, to prepare for the funerals and our guests, and anything else may overwhelm us. And I must admit, Your Majesty, I am an old man. The past few days have been rather draining."

I felt a rush of relief at his kindness. I smiled at him and stood. Everyone around the table stood as well, and bowed. Was this what it was like to have power? To be able to make everyone fall in line with a single movement of your own?

But they bowed because they were expected to, not because they respected me. Who knew what they were thinking behind those blank expressions?

"I will walk my daughter out." My father stepped away from his chair. "Freya?" He offered me his arm.

We walked from the room together. The guards trailed behind us, their footsteps loud on the stone floor.

"Be careful, Freya," my father said in my ear, as we turned down the corridor. "People will turn on you if you fail. You *can't* fail."

"I know that."

"Do you?"

"Yes," I said. "I do."

"Then don't speak so carelessly. You must make yourself allies. You must learn how to be queen. And keep your head down, if you want to keep it attached to your neck."

"Keep my head down?" I pulled my arm away. "I'm the queen. How can I keep my head down?" A queen had to stand out, by definition. I couldn't hide away.

"Agree with your council. Change nothing. Don't make a

fuss. And hope the Forgotten are kind to you, wherever they may be." He paused, reaching for my arm again. "Stay alive, Freya. Make your mother proud, make all of this worthwhile. Stay alive."

SEVEN

THE LIBRARY WAS A DARK, DUSTY PLACE HIGH UP IN the Fort, filled with rotting pages and crumbling spines. It must have been a great collection, once, packed with rare and important books from all over the world, but that had been centuries ago, when kings still lived here. All the valuable books had long since been moved to the palace, and the rest had been abandoned, falling page by page into disrepair. Since then, the library seemed to have been used as a dumping ground for any books the royal family did not want. Most of the newer books were in foreign languages, clearly gifts from the occasional visiting ambassador or king.

But there might be something useful here. I didn't exactly expect to find a book called *How to Be Queen,* but there might be etiquette books, discussions of court rituals, treatises on various approaches to ruling.

My council would try to teach me, as well as they could. But ignorance was weakness now. I needed to go to my lessons with knowledge already, so I could remain calm, so I wouldn't look completely hopeless. I had to win over the council first, and then I could worry about the others in court.

So I needed all the information laid out in a book, a step-by-step guide to ruling and the court, or as close to it as I could find. If I could just find the rules, written plainly and clearly, I'd at least have somewhere to start.

But half the books here proved unreadable, or so delicate that they crumbled when I tried to open them. The rest . . . well, the rest had been stored here for a reason. Records of the court's income and outgoings a hundred years ago. Studies on obscure subjects, so dull that their dedication to the king felt like more of an insult than an honor.

I did find one etiquette guide, intended to help naive young girls when they first arrived at the court, when it had been centered in the Fort. They needed to arm themselves against the "monstrous tricks" of male courtiers, or so the author claimed, and I had to wonder how many of these tricks he had performed himself, to be an expert on the subject. The book seemed unlikely to provide much insight, but it was the best I was going to find.

I tried to drag myself through the pages, but I couldn't concentrate. Etiquette rules were important, I knew that, but it still all seemed so . . . pointless. What did it matter how shallow someone curtsied, when so many people were dead? I needed to know—who had killed everyone, how had they done it, *why*?

Why was the strongest question, nagging at me every time I tried to turn my thoughts away. The killer had been willing to kill hundreds of people, indiscriminately. The only thing that could explain it was fervent, blinding belief—in the justice of their cause, in their need for power, in *something*.

As long as I didn't know, I was in danger, too. If I crossed the person responsible, if I stood in the way of their goals without realizing it . . . I needed to fit in at court, but ignorance now was far more dangerous than a social faux pas.

If this were an experiment, a challenge in my laboratory, I'd start by making lists. Gathering every fact and every possible idea together on paper, letting those words guide me to my next step.

I turned to the back of the etiquette book and grabbed a pen.

Sofia Thorn suspected the Gustavites. I scribbled it down, but the thought didn't fit, whatever my advisers believed. Groups didn't jump from doing nothing to successfully murdering hundreds of people, with no steps in between. There would have been warning signs, whispers, more minor attacks. But no one had heard a word from them. No pamphlets had been distributed, as far as I knew. No one had made any passionate speeches or tried to convince people of the justice of their cause. And no one in the group had claimed the attack. What would be the point of making a statement with violence, if you didn't tell people you'd made it?

I scribbled all these points down on one half of the paper, and then, on the other half, I wrote, *They have motive.* It was hard to imagine that one person would kill hundreds of others in one go. It was too big. But a group, one with political motivations, one that thought they were acting for justice . . . that seemed possible.

Next, there was Madeleine Wolff. If I hadn't left the ball, she would have been queen. That gave her motive, too, or at least suggested that someone might have acted on her behalf.

Holt had said she'd been away from the capital for a few months. She could have traveled to the countryside to keep herself safe, or to remove herself from suspicion. But if she'd organized this from afar, she would have left a trail of evidence behind. It would have been hard to be subtle with messengers traveling back and forth. But it was possible that someone had murdered everyone to put her on the throne, even without her knowledge.

William Fitzroy, the king's son, was my next thought. How had he survived, when everyone else closely related to the king had died? But he wasn't a likely suspect, not really. People always whispered that the king would make Fitzroy his heir, but he hadn't actually done it, not yet. When the king died, Fitzroy

had lost not only his father, but also his chance at the throne—
and why would he murder hundreds of people he knew, when
the throne could come to him through much less bloodthirsty
means?

I hesitated, then added Torsten Wolff. The king's best friend,
and another surprising survivor. I had no evidence against him,
beyond the fact that he unsettled me, but still, that feeling . . . he
might have wanted to give Madeleine the throne, or planned to
supplant her in the chaos, with her so far away. He seemed the
type who would be capable of stealing his cousin's inheritance—
serious, angry, aggressive.

But was he really the kind to murder his supposed best friend
to do it? I didn't know.

And then—I paused, my pen barely brushing the paper.
Then there was my father. He had always been ambitious. How
else did a common merchant end up with a daughter in line to
the throne, acting as adviser to the king? He had the motive. But
his expression, when he saw me in the lab . . . he had genuinely
thought I might be dead. He'd have prepared better if he wanted
to take the throne. He wouldn't have insisted I attend the ball.

Unless that was a plan to save me from suspicion. Unless he'd
only panicked because I had disappeared.

I frowned and added his name. This was research. It didn't
matter how I felt about the evidence. I just needed to record it,
and the truth would emerge in the end.

There were my other surviving advisers, too. Holt. Thorn.

Norling. I didn't really know enough about them to know if they had any motive. What could they possibly have gained, unless they wanted me as a puppet queen? Thorn had missed the banquet, which was slightly suspicious. But it didn't mean much.

I stabbed the nib of my pen into the paper. I couldn't solve this by plucking suspicious names out of the air. It was too imprecise. I needed to know everyone who had attended, everyone who had survived . . . the guests, the servants, everyone. Then I could work down the list and see where the evidence fell.

"Your Majesty?"

I jumped, and the pen snapped in my hand. Torsten Wolff had walked through the doorway.

He couldn't see what I'd been writing. Not my suspicions of him, not my words about his cousin. I slammed the book shut. "Can I help you?"

"Isn't that what I'm supposed to say to you? As queen?"

My heart was pounding, for no good reason at all. I forced myself to take a breath. "Were—were you looking for me?"

"No," he said. "No, as hard as it may be to believe, I was looking for books."

Obviously. Because we were in a library. Now I looked skittish *and* stupid.

Try, Freya, I thought. You suspect him? Try speaking to him. Try distracting him.

"Holt said—he said you were interested in military history."

It was a start.

"Among other things," he said. "And you, Your Majesty? What interests you here?" He moved closer, until he loomed above me. He might have been a scholarly man, but he was built like a wall. He peered at my book. "Etiquette lessons? Surely court has prepared you beyond some old man's ramblings."

What could I say to that? If I agreed, I looked stupid for even touching the book. If I disagreed . . . well, if I disagreed, I just looked stupid.

I snatched the book to my chest. Better to look naive than have him investigate further and find my notes. He was probably the type who thought writing in books merited beheading, accusation or no.

"You will need to do better than this, if you wish to hold on to the throne. The court does not forgive mistakes."

I squeezed the book tighter. "Are you threatening me?" It was amazing how clear things became, when I really was in danger. No lip-chewing over the right thing to say. My stomach was twisted into knots, and my hands shook, but something like strength rose in my chest, driving me to speak.

But he looked surprised by my words. "Threatening you? I would never threaten you, Your Majesty. It was a warning. Or advice, if you prefer." He stared at me, his bushy eyebrows pulled into a frown. His jaw was so square it could have been smashed out of stone. "Why? Is there a reason I should threaten you?"

"I know you don't want me to be queen."

"Of course I don't want you to be queen," he said, his voice low. "My friends are dead. Someone murdered them and made you queen instead. Why would I be happy about that?"

"I'm sorry," I said. And I was. I needed him to understand that. I hadn't wanted this any more than he had.

"Where were you?" he said suddenly. "During the banquet? How did you survive?"

"I was at home. With Naomi."

"Home and safe." He spoke softly, but the words were almost mocking. He turned away. "I will leave to your studies, Your Majesty."

"What about your book?"

"I will look later. I find I've lost my interest for reading."

With a nod at me, I strode back out of the room. Once he was gone, I placed the book on the table, and flicked to the final pages again, adding one more note.

Sten suspected *me*.

EIGHT

QUEEN MARTHA HAD HOSTED MEMBERS OF THE COURT almost every night, rotating ladies into favor and extending invitations to whichever gentlemen she found the most entertaining. I'd only been invited a couple of times. I'd spent the evenings sitting as close to the corner as possible, answering the queen's smiling questions as quickly as I could. Her ladies had echoed my responses, laughing and tossing their hair and thinking how strange I was, and although the queen said I was *wonderful entertainment*, I made whatever excuses I could to avoid going again.

Now it was my turn to host. "I know you don't enjoy these things, Freya," my father said, while a maid fluttered about,

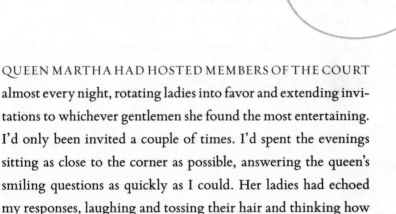

trying to convince my hair to adhere to a giant wire form in the shape of a bow. Some women could have achieved this look with their hair alone, or so the maid had muttered when she thought no one was listening. But I couldn't, and my father had insisted that nothing else would do.

Naomi had already gone to bed with a headache. So I had to get ready without her help. My father had scowled when I told him, but her brother was *dead*. Why should she have to pretend to be happy if she just wanted to hide away?

"You have to act like one of them, to make them accept you. When I married your mother, no one in court wanted me there. I was just a merchant's son. I didn't belong. But your mother just smiled and continued to be her lovely self, and I talked to them, Freya. I dressed like them, I acted like them, I charmed them. And eventually, they forgot. My differences became endearing, and then they simply became normal. But the first step was proving I was the same as them. That has to come first."

The maid hissed through her teeth as another strand of my hair slipped out of her hands. I swallowed the urge to apologize. "But you were just trying to join them. You weren't trying to *lead* them."

"You still have it easier than I did. You are a noble. You are the rightful heir to the throne. If you act the part, you will convince them."

I didn't really believe it, but I nodded. My hair tumbled again, and the maid bit back a noise of frustration.

"Sorry," I murmured. "I'm sorry."

"I want you to walk into that room," my father continued, "and smile at everyone as you enter. Make eye contact, but make sure it's a benevolent sort of smile. One that shows appreciation, but also that *you* are the one giving favor here. Come, try it."

I tried.

"Freya, you look like you're in pain. Look *kind*."

"How?" The word snapped out of me. "How can I make a smile look regal and powerful and benevolent and kind and superior and welcoming and whatever else, all at the same time? It's just a smile!" I'd never thought about my smile before. I couldn't possibly consider all those things and look even vaguely natural in the process.

"You saw Queen Martha smile."

"Queen Martha's smile was mean."

"Then imitate that, Freya. For goodness' sake."

"You said to look kind!"

My father sighed and pressed a hand to his face. I'd never seen him so frustrated. But it wasn't obvious or easy, whatever he thought. He had been a born courtier, and he hadn't even been born to it. My mother's and father's talents seemed to have canceled each other out, leaving me no skill at all.

I closed my eyes. I had to try. Just—just try.

"What about my mother?" I said eventually. "Did she smile like that?"

"She could," my father said. "Yes, she could."

Then I'd think of my mother, and try to smile like her.

My father continued to list rules, and I repeated them in my head, drumming them deep. I had to sit in the center of the room, and remained seated. Encourage people to approach me with smiles. Correct the harp player if the music was not cheery enough. Encourage people to dance, but not dance myself, not tonight, not with my clumsy feet. Suggest a game, something fun—perhaps charades. I couldn't let grief settle into the room.

Could I really be so callous? Plow on like nothing had happened, smooth over absences that no one would really be able to ignore? But my father had survived something like this before. He had convinced the court to accept him. He knew what I should do.

According to tradition, I had to host the court in my own rooms, so servants had cleared a parlor on the top floor of the Fort. The entire remaining court was already there by the time I entered. I paused in the doorway. The old tapestries had been removed and replaced with colorful paintings in gilt frames, making the room look brighter, but taking away its one defense against the cold. Red-velvet chairs had been placed under a huge chandelier, and hundreds of candles and oil lamps flickered around the room, making it almost as bright as day.

The courtiers were gathered in small groups, their clothes looking particularly garish against the drab walls. William Fitzroy leaned against the wall in one corner, not speaking to anybody. He stared into the distance, hands shoved into his pockets, shoulders hunched. Others looked more social. A couple of the queen's old maids-in-waiting stood together by a painting of white horses, whispering together behind their hands. Torsten Wolff was talking to an older gentleman whose name I had forgotten. And Rasmus Holt stood near the middle of the room, his back to the door.

"Her Majesty, Queen Freya!" the guards announced. The room fell silent. Every single person looked at me. Torsten Wolff, William Fitzroy in his corner, the gossiping girls. They bowed and curtsied, almost as one, but no one lowered their eyes.

Rasmus Holt had turned at the announcement. He watched me now, his eyebrows raised. He looked over my hair—still enormous, still in place—my skirt like a muffin, the jewels shimmering on my skin. He frowned in disapproval. I gripped my left elbow with my right hand, fighting the urge to cringe away.

He took a step toward me, revealing the person he had been talking to. It was Madeleine Wolff. My new heir. She was as petite as always, stunningly beautiful, with honey-brown hair and large brown eyes. She oozed confidence and elegance, from the little quirk of her head to the angle she held her thin wrist.

My stomach flipped at the sight of her. She was so effortlessly regal, like the world was moments away from falling at her feet. For a moment, a flash of thought, I *hated* her. She was everything I needed to be, and she didn't have to try. But even as I thought it, I knew I couldn't really despise her. She was enchanting.

I tore my gaze away, searching for the grand chair, the one my father had told me to take. My gaze settled on William Fitzroy again. He stood straighter now, and he was looking at me. My heart thudded. He frowned, like he was debating something, and I quickly looked away. The chair was at far side of the room. I just needed to reach it. But as I began to walk toward it, Holt intercepted me.

"Your Majesty," he said. "May I introduce you to Madeleine Wolff?"

"Your Majesty." She sank into a perfect curtsy. "It is so wonderful to meet you. I am sorry I missed your coronation. I so wished to be here, but my estate is a day-and-a-half's journey away, and by the time I learned of it, it was too late to attend. But I hurried here as soon as I learned the news."

"Thank you." It felt like the wrong thing to say, it didn't really make sense, but I had to say *something*. My heart had started pounding again, like Madeleine was about to attack me. But she wasn't. Of course she wasn't. I needed to stop panicking. I needed to *stop*.

"Young Madeleine just arrived," Holt said. "I told her she should rest, but she wished to see you immediately."

Madeleine did not look like someone who had stumbled from a carriage after a day and a half on the road. She looked flawless.

"Her Majesty mentioned to me that you had never met," Holt added to Madeleine, "but I am sure you will get on wonderfully. Madeleine is an artist, Your Majesty. A very talented one."

"You are too kind," Madeleine said. "I paint, yes. But I would not call myself an artist."

"What do you paint?"

"Landscapes, usually. The kingdom. The things I see from the window. The things I wish I saw." She smiled. "Do you paint, Your Majesty?"

I shook my head. "I'm not very artistic."

"Oh, I'm sure that's not the case. That's the wonderful thing about art, I find. You can always create *something*, and it's certain to have worth if you look at it with the proper eye."

Her words sounded like the usual court babble, but she didn't seem to be mocking me. She rested her fingers on my forearm as she spoke, like we were the best of friends already, and I couldn't resist leaning closer, too.

"Your Majesty." My father strode toward us. "Do you not wish to sit?"

"I am sure the queen will sit when she wishes, Titus," Holt said. There was a note of warning in his voice. "She is getting to know Madeleine Wolff here."

"I should sit," I said quickly. That had been the rule. I needed to look powerful. I needed to make people come to me.

But it felt so unnatural to stumble through the room and

take the largest chair, facing the lingering court. Conversation had picked up again, the remaining people clinging together in twos and threes. People glanced at me, but no one approached. They seemed happy to analyze from a distance. My eyes met William Fitzroy's from across the room. He stared back at me, but I couldn't read his expression.

I shifted on the chair, an itch running down my legs. I couldn't remember how to place them.

Madeleine Wolff followed me and sank into an elegant curtsy. "May I sit, Your Majesty?"

I nodded, and she slipped into the chair beside me. She glanced around the room, taking in the surviving faces. "It is so strange," she said. "To be back. I was close to so many people here, so many who are gone. The queen. Rosaline Hayes—did you know Rosaline? I have never met a sweeter person, or a meaner one. Oh, she was so kind to her friends, but if you crossed her, she would strike you down so cleverly and succinctly that it would take you a week to realize she had mocked you."

Yes, I remembered Rosaline. She had clearly never considered me worthy of whatever kindness she possessed. She usually just raised her eyebrows and laughed whenever I was near.

"Oh, you did not like her?" Madeleine said. "I can tell by your expression. She was difficult to like, I suppose, if she did not want you to like her. But I would prefer to think everyone has something worthwhile in them, if only you take the chance to look."

This was not what I'd expected from Madeleine Wolff, popular court figure and new heir. She seemed so . . . genuine. It didn't fit, that someone at the center of court could be genuine, even kind, that she could actually like *anyone*, no matter how evil or how sweet.

But she could easily have been manipulating me. I couldn't let myself be won over too easily. I needed to change the conversation, flip it back onto her. She was suspicious, a potential suspect in the murders, and I needed to take the opportunity to speak to her, not marvel at how elegant she was.

"It is strange to be back," Madeleine continued, "after being away for so long. And to have everything changed—"

"You were away because you were unwell?" The words came out too fast, too blunt.

"Yes," Madeleine said. If she noticed my rudeness, she was skilled enough to hide it. "For several months. The doctors thought the country air would do me good. And it did, I suppose. I had a lot of time to think, a lot of time to paint. It is a shame you do not enjoy it, Your Majesty. I find it so fulfilling. But it was lonely. Too much rest can be as damaging as not enough, don't you agree? We have to have something to keep us busy."

If she had been ill for months, she probably hadn't left the palace to avoid the poison. And it was hard to believe she would have poisoned all her friends.

Her lips were very pink, like dewy rose petals. She looked

like a queen. And that made her dangerous, even if she were innocent.

"Are you all right to be here?" I said. "If you weren't well enough to attend the king's birthday—"

"I was sorry to miss it. Perhaps I could have gone. But the doctor thought the stress of it would make me unwell again. Obviously he was mistaken—I feel perfectly all right. Perhaps it is the distraction of this grief. Or perhaps I really am getting better. Either way, I am glad to be back. I missed this city, and everyone here." She paused, then shook her head, like she was shaking the words away.

"Were you alone, in the country?"

"My aunt was there. And the servants, of course. My aunt likes the peace of life in the country, but it did not suit me so well. I find I like to be around people, to see them, to get to know them. I must admit, I went against the doctor's orders many times. When I felt well enough, I took many walks."

"I thought doctors liked walks."

"Not when they are to the villages to meet people. A country stroll, with the birds and the trees . . . that is 'restoring,' they say. But going to the village, or even a *town*, meeting with people, going to shops, going to chapels, talking to *commoners*, bringing them gifts and supplies . . . oh, that could never do. My aunt would not have liked it. But of course, my aunt did not know." Her smile was decidedly mischievous now.

"Your aunt? Sten's mother?"

"Oh, no," she said. She glanced over at her cousin, who was now talking to Holt. "No, no my father's youngest sister. She is only ten years older than Sten, you know. No, Sten's parents both died, when he was quite young. He's lived with my family ever since I was born. And then, when my mother and father passed away, my aunt took control of the estate, and he brought me to court, to keep me out of her hair. I suppose the estate is technically mine, but . . . my aunt loves running it, and she is welcome to it. I much prefer being here. And so does Sten, I think."

"Does he? He never looks like he enjoys court that much."

She laughed. "That's just Sten. He's not as serious when you get to know him, I promise."

Of course not. King Jorgen would not have chosen a best friend who lacked a sense of humor.

She leaned closer. "Don't look now, Your Majesty, but William Fitzroy is staring at you."

I couldn't stop myself from glancing over my shoulder. Fitzroy still stood alone in his corner, eyebrows pulled together.

"I said *don't look*," Madeleine said. "He's been watching us talk. I think you might have an admirer."

She wouldn't say that if she'd seen how he looked at me a few days ago. He was probably wishing we were alone so he could tell me exactly what he thought of me again. I sneaked another glance at him. He'd walked away.

"How are you coping?" Madeleine added, in a lower voice.

"With being queen. It must have been quite a shock."

"I—I'm managing."

Madeleine took my hand with both of her own. Her skin was creamy, smooth where mine was callused and scarred from experiments gone wrong. Even her nails were perfect little ovals, colored pink with tiny jewels on each tip. "I want to help you, Freya," she said. "Please, think of me as a friend. If you need *anything* . . ."

"Your Majesty?" A servant floated toward us, holding a tray of pastries. "Would you care for a tart?"

I didn't, really. My stomach was still roiling with nerves. But it would be too awkward to refuse. Unsociable, maybe. "Yes," I said. "All right." I picked a tiny pastry off the silver tray and smiled at the server. She bobbed into a curtsy, keeping the tray perfectly balanced. Madeleine smiled and reached for one as well.

I held the tart in front of my lips, steeling myself to eat it. The fruit smelled sickly sweet, and my stomach turned again. But there was something else there, too, a strange scent . . . slightly bitter, but almondy, too. I couldn't see any almonds in the tart, unless they were baked into the pastry.

Almonds, I thought. I knew something about the smell of almonds, some long-forgotten fact . . .

Cyanide. Cyanide smelled of almonds.

"Don't eat it!" I knocked the tart from Madeleine's hands. "It might be poisoned!"

The servant dropped the tray. It clattered on the floor,

sending tarts flying everywhere. Someone screamed. I stared at the crushed pastry, the smears of raspberry on stone. Poison.

Two guards ran forward and grabbed the server by the arms. Her legs flew out from under her, and she stumbled.

Madeleine clutched my sleeve. She was gasping for breath, eyes huge, skin white. "It's all right," I said. "You didn't eat it. It's all right."

I wiped my hands on my skirts, scraping any remnants away.

Sten crashed across the room and grabbed his cousin by her shoulders. He spoke to her in a low murmur, and she nodded, as another guard grabbed me and started hurrying me out of the room.

My father ran up, too, as the guards practically pushed me into the corridor, so fast I stumbled. The shouts faded behind us, but I could still feel it in the air, the panic radiating through the walls.

My bedroom was eerily quiet. The guards searched the room, pulling back curtains and tugging open wardrobes like an assassin might be curled up in a corner. Naomi peered out of the side room—her new bedroom, once they had finished preparing it. Her eyes were red, and her hair was braided for sleep. "What's going on?"

"Poison," I said. "I think someone tried to poison us." The words hit me then, what they really meant. Someone had tried to kill me. Me, personally, directly. My legs shook. I sank into a chair.

"What?" Naomi ran over. "Are you all right? Is anybody hurt?"

"I don't know. I don't think so. I mean, I'm all right. I don't think anyone is hurt."

"All clear in here, Your Majesty," the guard said. "Is it all right for this girl to remain with you?"

"Yes. Yes, of course. She lives here now."

"Then I'll lock the door, if it please Your Majesty. Until we are certain things are safe."

I nodded. I didn't know what else to do. My father strode over and squeezed my shoulder. "Things will be all right, Freya," he said. "I have to go and help deal with this. I'll return when we know more."

I nodded again. There was little else I could do. And then my father was gone, and the door was locked, leaving me and Naomi alone.

Naomi grabbed my arm. "What happened, Freya?"

I stood, nervous energy filling me again. I needed to move. I told her about the strange smell, about my suspicions, and I paced, my feet thudding against the floor.

"But everyone will be fine," Naomi said, a little too loud, a little too fast, once I was finished. "Nobody ate any of it, did they? Everyone will be fine."

"Madeleine couldn't breathe."

"But she didn't eat it. She was just scared, Freya. She must have been scared."

I nodded. It made sense. But what if she *was* hurt? One bite of cyanide was enough to kill. What if someone had eaten some before they were brought to me? What if Madeleine had taken a bite, and I hadn't noticed? What if more of the court was dying, right now, from poison meant for me?

"The servants brought them straight to me. It was aimed at me."

I'd expected this to happen, but that didn't make it any less terrifying. Someone wanted me dead. Me, specifically me. And I had no idea who it might be.

The killer would have let Madeleine die, too, if I hadn't stopped her from eating the tart. That had to mean Madeleine was innocent, didn't it? That the killer at the banquet did not want her to be queen. Unless the servant was an innocent bystander, unaware of the poison, not knowing that she was only meant to give the tarts to me.

Over an hour passed before my father appeared again, looking pale. "You were right," he said, once the door closed behind him. "The tarts were poisoned."

The words weren't as frightening as I'd expected. The possibility of being poisoned, the question of it, had made my legs shake, but now it was fact, it was concrete, with details and truths to unlock. I could deal with facts. I hurried toward him. "How do you know?"

"The taster. She tried some and was ill immediately."

"The taster?" He couldn't mean what I thought he meant.

"You gave it to a taster? After I told you it was poisoned?"

"We needed to know, Freya. And that was the only way."

My hands clenched, and my heart pounded, faster than when I had discovered the poison. They had forced a woman to eat cyanide, for my benefit, to protect me. "The only way was to make someone eat it, and watch to see if she died?"

"She is not dead, Freya. She may well recover."

"But she *might* have died." She might still die. Cyanide usually acted in seconds, but surely if a dose wasn't immediately fatal, it could still kill more gradually, breaking down the body piece by piece.

Even if the taster didn't die, she was suffering. Suffering for *me*. I raked my hands through my hair, ripping it loose from the pins. Was this what it meant to be queen? To have my life in danger, and throw others in the way instead? Surely a queen was meant to protect her subjects, not hide away and let them die for her sake. I closed my eyes and took a steadying breath. "What about Madeleine? Is she all right?"

"She is unsettled. But she seems well enough." My father sighed. "You were smart there. I am proud of you. If you hadn't noticed that smell . . . any food should have gone through the tasters, but it seems that servant did not bring them from the kitchens. And our guards, it seems, are a disgrace. You saved lives today, Freya. You saved your own life."

But I might have killed a taster instead.

"Was the server—was she from outside the castle?"

"We don't know yet. But we will find out. It would be best if you remain here for the rest of the night. We must check the castle for any more threats."

"What will happen to the server? The one who brought the tarts. She might not have known what they were." She deserved a chance.

"That is unlikely, Freya. But we will investigate all possibilities. In the meantime, don't eat anything anyone brings you unless I'm here to tell you it is safe. Perhaps we can find a taster to try every dish immediately before you eat it. I am not sure."

"I don't want that." To have someone stand beside me, to watch them to see if they died in my place? I couldn't do that.

"Either way," my father said. "We must do something."

He left the room, and I began to pace again, while Naomi stood at the far side of the room, watching me.

"No one died," she said softly. "Even the taster is still alive. That's—that's really lucky. It's good."

It was. I knew it was. But the thought wasn't comforting. Someone had tried to kill me. I had been seconds away. If I'd been hungrier, if I'd been distracted . . . I probably wouldn't have survived. Madeleine wouldn't have survived.

The fact was too terrifying to consider. I scrambled for something else, a problem I could fight. "Why would anyone be a taster?" I said. "After what happened at the banquet? Why would you eat things to see if they're poisoned?"

"People need money," Naomi said. "It must pay a lot, to risk your life for the court."

"We should have another way to test the food. Using people—it's ridiculous, Naomi." I'd always known that the king had tasters, *always*, but I'd never given it more than a second of thought. No one was actually going to try and poison the king. But now—now people were risking their lives to protect *me*, and my skin crawled at the thought of it.

"I don't think there's another way," Naomi said. "They'd use it if there was."

It had to be possible. Anything was possible, if you thought about it in the right way. Had people tried before, or had no one been concerned enough to research it?

I continued to pace. At least it gave me something to do.

"I don't want other people to get poisoned for me. It doesn't even work. It didn't stop whoever killed the king at the ball. And it won't stop anyone now. What if they use a slow poison? We won't find out until that night, or the next day. If we use a taster then, that's just one extra person who dies."

And I would die, too. I shoved the thought away. I had to be practical. Focus on solutions.

"There has to be another way. There has to be. Poison is a foreign element introduced into food, isn't it? So there must be some way it can be detected, a more reliable way than using a person, something that would reveal it straight away. Some powder it would react with, *something* . . ." I turned. "It has to be possible. No one's done it before, but perhaps they didn't care to. Why would they? Only royalty have testers, and they don't care about anyone."

"That's not true," Naomi said. "You're royalty, and *you* care."

"There must be a way. There has to be. People just haven't found it yet."

"And you think you can find it?"

"Why not? Someone has to. And I have the motivation." I had to get started. Right now. I looked around for my book-shelf, but of course it wasn't here. It was at home, with my lab, with everything of use.

"Freya," Naomi said softly. "Are *you* all right?"

I paused. "No," I said softly. "I'm not all right. But I'd rather not think about that."

Naomi nodded and sank onto the arm of a chair. "Do you think these were the same people who attacked the banquet?"

"I don't know. My advisers said the attackers used arsenic then. But this was cyanide. And if the attackers wanted to kill everybody, cyanide would be a stupid way to do it. It acts too quickly. A bite, a breath, and you're dead." I started pacing again. "Cyanide is an idiot's poison, really, if you think about it. Everyone knows it's deadly, and it smells of almonds. Not everyone can smell it, but some people can. And if people had access to all that arsenic, and could put it in a cake at the banquet without anyone knowing, why would they be so unsubtle now?"

"You think someone else is attacking you?"

"I don't know." How many people could want me dead? How many reasons could there be? "It makes sense."

"But *why?*" Naomi said. "Why would they want to kill you? Because they want the crown for themselves?"

"Perhaps." But then I shook my head. "That servant—if she was involved, why would she sacrifice herself like that to put some other noble on the throne? Unless she's innocent, she had to have known she'd get caught. She had to have known. Why would any servant do that to have one person on the throne instead of another?"

"Blackmail, maybe," Naomi said. "Money. You know how court works."

But the pieces didn't fit. It had to be something more, something that carried more weight than gold and threats. The servant had to *believe* I needed to die, believe so deeply that she was willing to die herself to ensure that it happened. Which suggested the Gustavites, as Thorn had said.

And yet the attacks were so different . . . how could they be from the same group, with the same motivation?

I had to learn more. I had to know what they believed, what they wanted, what motivated them. I had to understand them, if

I had any hope of surviving.

I raked my fingers through my hair again, and turned back to Naomi. "But I don't know how court works," I said softly. "That's the problem."

NINE

"HOW CAN YOU NOT HAVE KNOWN ABOUT THE POISON attempt last night? You should have eyes *everywhere*." My father banged his fist against the council table, making it shake. I flinched, but Thorn, master of intelligence, stared him down.

"We do have eyes everywhere," she said. "But mistakes were made."

"Mistakes where the queen is almost killed."

"Yes," Thorn said. "I can only apologize for that, and apologies mean little. But the taster is alive, and no one else was harmed."

"That is not an excuse. Your queen could have died."

"Perhaps you should not be serving on this council, Sofia," Norling said, "if you cannot perform your job correctly."

"I am doing my job," Thorn snapped. "And now we have more evidence to work with. The servant last night had connections with the Gustavites. She told us so."

I leaned forward. "What do you mean, connections?"

"Your Majesty?"

"Is she one of the leaders? A new recruit? What did she say?" The need to understand burned inside me. I had to know *why*. But Thorn only shook her head.

"She was not specific, Your Majesty."

"But she told you she had connections with the Gustavites?"

"Not in so many words. She was raving. In between her pointless protestations of innocence, she talked about the corruption of the court. She said it needed to be purged. To me, that suggests a strong connection with Gustavites. They were responsible for the attack at the banquet."

"It doesn't prove it, though," I said. "It doesn't even prove she's one of them."

"The most obvious answer is usually the right one."

"But do you have *evidence*?"

"The information suggests—"

"But that information failed to notice someone was going to try and poison the court, twice. We don't need rumors. We need proof. I'm just saying we shouldn't jump to conclusions. It isn't safe. The first poisoner used arsenic, didn't they? But this one used cyanide. Why would they change that, when cyanide is so much easier to detect?"

"We will not jump to any conclusions, Your Majesty," Holt said. "But it is possible they were attempting to obscure the connection, or they felt a more direct approach was necessary. Either way, we must prevent this from happening again."

He began to lay out additional security measures, and everyone around the table nodded, and agreed, and planned. Mostly this seemed to involve extra security at the Fort's entrance, a thorough check of all current staff, and the use of additional tasters, from the raw ingredients to the moment before I took a bite.

They didn't spare a word for *why* a group might want to poison us all. And the why was everything, wasn't it? No matter how many checks we had, someone could always figure out how to slip through. We needed to understand them.

"Do we have a copy of their book?" I said, in a pause in the discussion.

Holt frowned at me. "Which book, Your Majesty?"

"Their book. Gustav's book. It would be useful to study it, to understand them better."

"Freya," my father said sharply. "You cannot be seen with that book. And what would it tell you, that you don't already know? They want to kill you."

"But *why?* If we can figure out why they hate us so much—"

"They hate us, Your Majesty, because we have more than

they do," Thorn said. "Nothing more or less than that. The court has money, and it has power, and they want that for themselves. Jealousy can be a powerful motivator."

If they hated how extravagant and wasteful the court was, I could sympathize.

"Your sensitivity does you credit, Your Majesty," Holt said. "But we cannot take a soft approach, not with all that has happened now."

"Is it really *sensitivity* to care about the feelings of mass murderers?" Sten spoke quietly, his expression fierce. It would have been easy to forget he was here, near silent but always listening, if it weren't for the intensity of his gaze on me. "I would ask why Her Majesty sympathizes with them, when they killed almost everyone any of us knew. Is that how we should conduct our diplomacy now?"

"No," I said quickly. He continued to stare at me, and I couldn't fit my thoughts into words. "I only thought—"

"Your Majesty may have a tender heart," he said, "but you should remember why we are all here. It would be dangerous to appear too sympathetic. Do you not agree?"

A shiver of fear ran down my spine. He was still suspicious of me. If I seemed too sympathetic, I'd look like I was involved. And I wasn't sympathetic, not to the idea of killing hundreds of people, not to any of it. But this was a puzzle, and you had to look at it the right way, without letting emotion muddle your thoughts.

But I couldn't do that here.

I sat in silence, picking at the splinters underneath the table, as they returned to their discussion of guards and patrols. How could I get that book without any of them knowing? I couldn't exactly buy it from a bookshop, even if I could leave the Fort. Someone like Thorn might have a copy, one she'd confiscated if not one she'd read, but she didn't seem likely to share.

"We still need to find more tasters," Norling said, "after the loss at the banquet. But to find people we can trust—"

"We should find a way to avoid using tasters at all," I said. "They clearly don't work—"

"They work far better than the alternative," my father said.

"Then we need to find another alternative. Some other way of detecting it, some test. If we get scientists to study—"

"Freya!" My father's shout almost made me jump. He was glaring at me, his face red. "All our resources must go to finding and punishing these murderers, and on protecting you. I suggest you focus on keeping yourself safe, as well."

"I don't want other people at risk because of me."

"But they are. That's what it means to be queen."

I swallowed. A lump wedged itself in my throat. "How many tasters died at the banquet, for nothing?"

"None of them, Your Majesty," Norling said, her voice a little softer than I'd heard it before. "Three tasters died, but not the one who was actually assigned the dish. It seems the tasters were eating anything returned to the kitchens, as well as performing their duties. By the time we realized there was an issue with the cake, several of them had eaten it, and two of them died. But not the one doing his job. So you see. Two poison attempts, two tasters who have survived. Put the worry out of your mind."

"Although of course, the first taster has been arrested," Thorn said. Norling glared at her.

"Arrested?" I said. "Because he didn't die?"

"If hundreds of people die and the taster is not among them, then the taster *must* be considered suspicious. Perhaps he added the poison, perhaps he was warned and knew not to eat too much of it. Either way, we have to investigate."

"He was warned, but he didn't tell his friends not to eat any? You think he'd let the other tasters die for no reason?"

"It's possible. If he warned them, they might have warned *us*."

"Is he here? In the Fort?" I needed to speak with him. Whether he was guilty or innocent, he must know something. He must have seen *something*.

"He is in the dungeons, Your Majesty. In the dark cells. Until we have answers."

I stood. "I wish to speak with him."

"That would be unwise, Your Majesty." Holt's voice slid over the many words that simply meant *no*. "Especially after what happened. You would be unsafe."

"I'll be safer once we know exactly who has been murdering the court."

"And we will know, Your Majesty. But you need not concern yourself with the question."

But I did. Obviously I did. It was my life, my rule. And even then . . . I wanted to know. The mystery nagged at me. I wanted to be doing *something*, using what skills I had. But I wasn't supposed to speak to the suspects, I wasn't supposed to read their texts . . . my advisers were keeping me as far away from the investigation as they could, and the question of *why* thrummed through me. Why were they hiding things from me, why didn't they want me to know?

The tiny beginnings of an answer twisted in my stomach. I couldn't jump to conclusions here. I would gather the facts, and then I would see.

"What have you learned so far?" I said instead. "If you're keeping him in the dungeons, then you must have some intelligence against him?"

"Nothing useful, as of yet," Thorn said. "He claims he saw nothing."

"Then maybe he saw nothing. You don't know he's lying."

"We don't," Thorn said. "The problem is, murderers tend to say they saw nothing, too."

I hurried away as soon as the meeting was over, my guards walking behind me. Every step away from the council room fed my anger, making my hands shake. I'd spoken. Loudly and clearly, over and over, as *queen*, and they still hadn't heard. They'd dismissed me or ignored me every time, even when I *knew* I was right. I'd managed to speak to all of them, interrupted them, argued with them, and it hadn't meant anything. My stomach still shook slightly from the effort, and yet . . . nothing.

They weren't helping me. Not really.

Or they were helping me to become *their* image of a queen. To rule the way they wanted me to rule.

And my father had said to listen to them. I stopped suddenly, pressing my hand against the wall. My guards stopped behind me without comment. I needed to be completely unexceptional, my father had told me. To fit their expectations so snugly that they couldn't possibly think to complain. Perhaps that was right. But I couldn't continue like this. I needed answers, and I needed to act, to just . . . to be myself, and to fight for my own solutions.

My gut told me to march straight to my laboratory and start work there. But my lab was a couple of miles away, far out of reach.

Or *that* lab was out of reach.

I turned to my guards. The gray-bearded man wasn't on duty, but I recognized the younger, dark-haired man, and a blond girl not much older than myself. Both of them wore the dark-blue coat of the guard, still bearing the old king's insignia. I needed one of my own. "I want to set up a laboratory," I said. "Do you know anywhere in the castle I could use?"

The black-haired guard frowned. "I am sure there will be somewhere, Your Majesty."

"It needs a fireplace. And sturdy tables and cupboards. Some sort of ventilation. And it would need to be in a place I wouldn't be disturbed."

"Your Majesty, if I may—" The blond guard hesitated. "I know of a room, but—"

"What? Where is it?"

"Well," the guard said, as though her words might offend me. "This castle used to house the kingdom's most dangerous enemies, when such things were a threat."

"I know."

"Well, Your Majesty, there is a room—it hasn't been used for a hundred years now, and no one will go near it—but the room was used to interrogate prisoners, and it has—well, it has all the things you require."

"You mean a torture chamber?"

"I'm sorry, Your Majesty, I know it is a bold idea. But it has all the things you need, and I thought—"

"Yes," I said. "Yes, it's a good idea." A gory past couldn't hurt, as long as it definitely *was* past. The kingdom had considered torture barbaric for a century at least. And if other people were disturbed by the memory, they'd be less likely to visit and disturb me. "Could you take me?"

The guard led me deep underneath the castle, where the stone dripped, and the only light came from iron braziers that stuck out every few feet. The walls pressed even closer here, and the air felt heavy and old.

"It's here, Your Majesty," the guard said, gesturing toward a wooden door. "But I'm not certain—"

"Is it locked?"

"No, Your Majesty. No need." Her expression suggested that no one in their right mind would ever sneak in. Which made it perfect for me.

"Thank you." I grabbed the handle, and then paused. "I'm sorry. I don't know your name." It hurt to ask it—even that question made me feel like I'd reached out too far. But we'd be spending time together now, and she'd helped me. I had to try.

"I'm Mila Erikkson, Your Majesty," she said, with a bow. "I'm sorry, I should have introduced myself earlier—"

"No, no, I should have asked." I turned to the black-haired guard. "And—and you?"

"Reynold Milson, Your Majesty."

"Thank you. It's—it's good to meet you. Even though we've already met. It's good to—thank you." I bit my lip, as though I could shove the babble back into my mouth. Then I turned and pushed the door. It stuck slightly in the frame, and when it finally shifted, it let loose a cloud of dust. I coughed and waved it away.

The room beyond was large and square. Its uneven floor was spattered with suspicious-looking stains. But it was spacious enough, with a fireplace, a large table in the middle of the room, and many cupboards around the sides. Strange devices hung from some of the walls, and jars cluttered the cupboard tops. I'd need to wear a good pair of gloves when I investigated those, and possibly a mask. Who knew what poisons they might contain?

"This is good." It needed cleaning up, of course, and I'd need to move in my own supplies, but I could work with this. I turned back to Mila. "Find someone to come clean this place tonight, but don't let them touch any of the cupboards or the jars. Just sweep the floor, clear out the cobwebs. I'll need some wood for the fireplace, too. And I need someone to go to my house and fetch my things for me. The books, the vials, the bottles, the flasks. I'll make up a list—or I can go." I glanced at Mila. "No, I can't go. But you can go. Now. Please."

"I'm not supposed to leave you unguarded, Your Majesty."

She could leave, in theory. The guards had always followed the king and queen's commands, including making themselves scarce if need be. But Mila clearly thought any such order would be unwise right now, and she was probably right, after all that had happened. "Then someone else can go," I said. I looked around the room again, already imagining it transformed. It would be perfect. Larger than my old laboratory, and safer for storing my more dangerous ingredients. I could definitely work with this. "Please," I said. "Find out for me?"

"Of course, Your Majesty." Mila bowed and stepped out of the room.

"Would you prefer me to wait inside the room, or outside it, Your Majesty?" Reynold said.

"Outside." The idea of being watched while I explored made me feel far too self-conscious. "Please."

Once he had closed the door, I walked over to the nearest set of jars. They were coated with dust. Anything potent in there might have lost its power years ago. But maybe . . . I wiped a finger along the counter, leaving a line in the dust. Perhaps it would be better if I cleaned this place myself, so no one could disturb anything.

I picked up one of the jars and held it up to the light. Someone had written something on it, once, but it had faded half away. Whatever it contained, it was almost certainly unpleasant. Something that poisoned, something that burned, something that would convince a victim to reveal all their secrets.

I explored the rest of the room carefully, looking through drawers—mostly empty, but a few pairs of tongs remained—and mentally cataloging whatever I could.

I couldn't wait for the messengers to return with my things. I definitely couldn't wait for someone else to clean up the space. I needed it *now*, needed to research, to create something that was *mine* once again.

I grabbed a cloth and began to dust.

TEN

I SPENT HOURS IN MY NEW LABORATORY, SORTING through its secrets. My silk dress was quickly covered in dust and years of untouched grime, and I didn't think I'd ever get the bloodstain off the table, but the space was good, and I'd begun to catalog the strange jars around the room. Many of them contained the remnants of herbs with healing properties—not what I had been expecting. I suppose you couldn't have your prisoner dying of blood poisoning before you had all the information you needed, or at least before you got the chance to kill them yourself. Other jars contained far more expected chemicals—a few poisons, liquids that burned, a powder that, when mixed with water, was good for getting blood off the skin.

Someone knocked on the door. "Your Majesty?" It was Reynold Milson, the black-haired guard. "I am sorry to interrupt, but you intended to see Rasmus Holt at three."

I wiped my hands on my skirt. Holt was supposed to be teaching me more about being queen, or at least more about how *he* thought I should be queen. Traditions, and presentation, how to speak, and how to think.

He might have a chance with the first two, but no amount of speaking lessons were going to help the rest. Even if he gave me a script for every encounter, it would all fall apart the moment someone else spoke.

"What time is it now?" I said.

"Three, Your Majesty."

I looked down at my dust-covered dress. I'd wanted to make an impression on my council, but this wasn't exactly what I'd had in mind. I hurried to the door, where Reynold and Mila waited, one on either side. At least they didn't comment on my appearance.

"I've sent the order for your things, Your Majesty," Mila said. "But it may take a couple of days. For reasons of security."

"Thank you," I said.

They led me out of the dungeons and up to the third floor of the Fort. But someone stepped out of a doorway as we turned the corner, missing collision by inches.

"Oh!" It was Madeleine Wolff. She took a tiny step back,

but even when startled, her mask of courtesy did not slip. She glanced at my grimy gown as she swept into a curtsy. "Your Majesty. Are you all right?"

Of course Madeleine Wolff would be the one to collide with me when I looked like this. I forced myself to smile back at her. "Yes," I said. "Yes, I'm fine. I'm sorry, I—I wasn't looking where I was going."

"No, Your Majesty, it was my fault."

What was I even supposed to say? I was already late, and the awkwardness was a physical presence between us. "I'm sorry, I have to—"

"Wait, wait." Madeleine grabbed my hand. "I wanted to speak to you. To thank you. For saving me yesterday. I would be dead if it wasn't for you."

I didn't deserve her thanks. She had only been in danger because of me. If she hadn't spoken to me, she would never have picked up one of the tarts in the first place. I shook my head, scrambling for words, and she squeezed my hand.

"I'm grateful," she said. "Truly."

"I—I'm just glad you're all right."

Madeleine beamed. "There was one other thing, Your Majesty. I know now might not be the best time, but it's not really a matter I wish to bring up in front of the court."

"What is it?"

"There's an orphanage in the city. I've been supporting it for years, but—well, it's struggling, Your Majesty. I hoped you might be willing to visit it with me. They would love to see you."

"That would be—I'm not sure it's safe."

"Of course, Your Majesty. Things are so uncertain now. But please consider it. Perhaps when things are more settled? I—it would mean a lot to me, to know you might be thinking of them."

"All right," I said. "I'll—when things are safer."

"I know it seems odd," Madeleine said, leaning closer. "Bringing this up now, when you have so much to deal with. But—it's very important to me, Your Majesty. And I hope—I hope things like this will also be important to you."

She curtsied again and stepped aside for me and my guards to pass. I nodded at her, no idea what else to do. She seemed so earnest, but why would she bring that up now, in the corridor, whispered in my ear? The strangeness of it made me shiver. But I had to hurry on. I was already stupidly late.

When I reached Holt's door, I knocked without pausing to catch my breath.

"Come in."

"I'm sorry I'm late," I said, as I swung through the door.

"That's quite all right, Your Majesty," Holt said. "A queen is not capable of being late." He smiled as he rose from his chair. He'd settled into his new office quickly, with papers already covering his desk, and rows of books lining the walls. His smile caught slightly as he took in my appearance. "Your Majesty, is something wrong?"

"No," I said. I batted at my dress, as though that would make the grime vanish, but it only sent a cloud into Holt's otherwise spotless room. "I was just—I was cleaning."

"We have servants for that, Your Majesty." He sounded rather bemused.

"I didn't want to risk them," I said. He wouldn't consider my laboratory very queenly, but he also couldn't forbid me from using it, not with my title behind me. Advise against it, perhaps, but not *forbid*. And my secret was hardly a secret, with servants fetching supplies and me running around covered in hundred-year-old dust. "I was cleaning out a space in the basement"—the word *dungeon* felt too ominous—"to use as a laboratory. For—for my studies."

I cringed slightly, expecting Holt's frown of disapproval, but he simply nodded. "Ah, yes. Your father told me you're quite the scholar. It should come in useful in the days ahead. And you intend to continue your studies here, in the Fort?"

"There's no rule against it."

"No, no," Holt said. "Of course not. An intellectual queen. It is certainly a change, but it will be a welcome one, I think. And you plan to work on the test for poison that you mentioned in our meeting?"

"It's the right thing to do."

"Oh, I agree with you, Your Majesty. If it can be done, it should be done." He smiled, and the look was almost grandfatherly. "Although, there will be other factors to consider. Shall we sit?" I nodded. "Being a taster pays well, Your Majesty. A test would deny people work. They might not thank you for it."

"They might not thank me for their lives?"

"I am not saying it is a bad idea, Your Majesty. It would be a valuable tool. But we do not force anyone to become a taster. They assess the risks themselves, and they consider them worthwhile."

"But they must be desperate if they continue now, after two different attacks." There were choices, and then there were *choices*. People could say "everything is a choice" with as much haughtiness and superiority as they liked, but that didn't mean desperate people wouldn't take a third option if they could. "No one would choose that if they really had another option. We should develop a test, and we should find other jobs for people, so they do not need to risk their lives for me."

"Indeed, Your Majesty. It is a good thought. I just wished to remind you that a good queen should consider all the options, and all the potential consequences. Situations are rarely as simple as they first appear. Consider things complexly, Your Majesty. It always helps."

"Then why didn't you support me in the meeting?" I said, the words bursting out of me without thought. "When the others were speaking against me?"

"As much as I dislike it, they were right, that we do not have the resources to spend at the moment, when so much else is at risk. We have to put your safety first. But if a test were to appear, well . . . it would be a good thing, don't you agree?"

After that, he talked through the etiquette of the court, rules I should have known, rules I'd never imagined before. Which fork to use for every possible dish at a banquet. How to greet different people of rank. The different tiers of nods and curtsies, depending on what one wished to be conveyed. He didn't actually demonstrate the curtsies, but he described them in minute detail, and commented as I practiced, correcting the slightest shift in my posture. When I wasn't bobbing around the room, I took frantic notes, desperate to cram every scrap of detail into my brain.

It had all seemed completely pointless to me before, and a part of me still wanted to laugh at all this meaningless ritual now. But the nobles expected it, and I had to appease them. I had to cling to the things that they knew.

And I had very little time to learn. The funerals would take place in a few days, which meant two incredibly awkward banquets. One the night before, to welcome everyone who had traveled to the city, and one afterward, to commemorate the dead.

And that speech, of course. I didn't want to think about that.

Holt, however, clearly considered it a priority. He handed me a copy of their current draft for my comments. It all seemed fine to me, as diplomatic and bland as I could imagine, and I ran through it once or twice with Holt, tripping over the words. Just reading it in front of Holt was enough to make my heart race. I couldn't possibly recite it in front of the entire new court.

But Holt was surprisingly patient. "I remember my first speeches," he said, with a smile. "I was terrible, Your Majesty. I wrote and memorized them myself, but I still stumbled over the words. You'll do well, Your Majesty. We just need to practice. Develop your confidence."

I couldn't imagine ever being more confident.

"Do not worry, Your Majesty," Holt said. "Etiquette matters, yes, but you do not need to attempt to emulate our departed queen. And you must not emulate our king, the Forgotten protect his soul. So much has changed. Perhaps it is best to embrace that."

I paused. "What do you mean?"

"King Jorgen . . . I do not wish to speak ill of him, of course. And he guided us in his own way. But so much has changed now. Perhaps it is time for something new. Less waste, Your Majesty. Less show. More heart."

But without all the rules and rituals, what did I have left? Just me, hiding beneath twenty layers of skirts. Perhaps Madeleine could act naturally and show her heart, but only because her heart was what everyone wanted to see. Not me.

"My father thinks I should try and—" What had it been? "Try to make things smoother. Make it so people don't feel the difference between my reign and the previous one."

"But of course they'll feel the difference. As painful as it is for all of us to admit, almost everything about the old court is gone. And this . . . this is an opportunity, Your Majesty. A great one. The Forgotten have given us a chance. We must not waste it."

"The Forgotten?" I swallowed. "You think they wanted everyone to die?"

"Not that, Your Majesty. But perhaps it was more than coincidence that you were not in the palace when the poison was served. I can see their hands in that, guiding the situation as they desired, helping us to help ourselves."

As though the Forgotten would have guided the kingdom toward me. But Holt seemed sincere. "Do you really think they can still influence things?"

"They are divine, Your Majesty. They are not constrained by the laws of this world, as we are. Yes, they are gone *physically*, but their influence remains."

"I thought they chose to leave. Why would they keep influencing things here if they wanted to be gone?"

"They left because we failed them. We did not deserve their presence. But they want us to be worthy. We have been climbing toward worthiness for hundreds of years, away from ambition, away from war, from all the brutal darkness of our past. But we were still extravagant, selfish, and wasteful, and they cannot abide that. So perhaps . . . perhaps, Your Majesty, they chose you as a different type of queen. One they could support. One who could make Epria into a land they could return to again."

If the Forgotten were really all-seeing divine beings, they

would have chosen someone better than me. Even Holt had to see that. Did he really believe all he was saying, or was it a comforting lie he was telling himself, to reason away so many deaths? To make my cluelessness seem like a gift and not the result of a senseless tragedy?

If he believed it . . . it probably meant I could trust him. And if he didn't . . .

"I hope you're right," I said. "I hope this all goes somewhere good."

"It will, Your Majesty. As long as you remember that the Forgotten chose *you*. You, not King Jorgen, not his brother, not even the delightful Madeleine Wolff. They value your strengths. And so should you."

My strengths had nothing to do with being queen. But I nodded. He had faith in me, at least. That was more than most people had. It was more than I could honestly say for myself.

"Then . . ." I let out a breath, steeling myself. "I need you to help me. Please. I need a list of everyone at the banquet, everyone who died, everyone who survived. I should know all I can about the remaining court. Shouldn't I?"

He nodded. "Of course, Your Majesty. Your concern does you credit. I will see that it is done."

"And then could you get me a copy of Gustav's book? My strength is with research, and if I can understand—"

He held up a hand. "That, Your Majesty, I cannot do. I certainly do not have a copy, and I do not believe it would help.

These people now calling themselves Gustavites . . . their beliefs are a corruption of a corruption, far detached from the man's original views. They use the memory of his words to serve their own ends, and hope people will not see the flaws in their logic. Here, let me see . . ." He pulled one of his desk drawers open and shuffled through the contents. "Yes." He pulled out a weather-battered pamphlet and handed it to me. I took one glance at it, and my fingers tightened around the paper, bile rising to the back of my throat. It was cheaply printed, the lines thick and blurry, but the imagery was unmistakable. The king lay on the ground, gold piled around him, a spilled goblet rolling from his hand. The queen lay next to him, with a line across her throat that must have been blood. And I stood on top of them, pressing them into the ground, dripping with jewels, sipping from a goblet of my own.

"Kill the Corruption," it said at the top. Below the picture, more words had been hastily printed, calling the court and my rule an affront to the Forgotten, rallying against the wickedness it claimed we spread through the kingdom.

"Where did you get this?"

"They've been scattered around the city. We don't know who actually distributed them. But you see, Freya. Their views aren't based on reason. They aren't based on anything."

"These are all over the city?"

"Some parts of it, yes. We have destroyed any we've found. And we are increasing security, of course, adding more patrols and searching the printing presses. We will stop them."

But sending guards after these people wouldn't stop what they believed. They hated me. Hated all of us. Even if we found their presses, found *them*, their ideas would hold. I tightened my grip on the paper, bending it.

"Don't worry, Your Majesty," Holt said. "We will find them."

We spent another hour going over etiquette and rules, but Holt's enthusiasm waned as he discussed every showy ritual, like he did not really believe in it. Eventually, he called the session complete, and I stood.

"Thank you," I said. "For all your help." He nodded, and I began to walk toward the door.

"Your Majesty, if I may offer you another piece of advice?" He sounded tentative. I paused, turned back. "Be wary of William Fitzroy."

"Fitzroy? I've barely ever spoken to him." The last words we'd exchanged had been outside the banquet hall on the day of my coronation. He was hardly eager to befriend me.

"Perhaps not," Holt said. "But it would be wise to keep it that way. Fitzroy has always been popular, and he is a dangerous element here."

"You think he's dangerous?"

"He is the old king's son. Closer to him in blood than you, regardless of the law. If he decides that he wishes to take the throne, he could be quite a powerful enemy."

I remembered Fitzroy's words that night at the funeral and shivered. *You don't belong here.* But he had seemed to be grieving, even in his aggression. They hadn't been the words of a murderer.

"Thank you," I said softly. "I'll keep that in mind."

ELEVEN

THE SOUND OF NAOMI'S SINGING ECHOED THROUGH
my chambers. Her voice was softer than usual, sadder, but determined. Some people sang when they were happy, but Naomi
sang when she didn't want to think, letting the lyrics block any
words of her own. I peeked through her bedroom doorway to
find her hanging dresses in the wardrobe, hair tucked behind
her ears. There were three open trunks in the middle of the
room—her other possessions must finally have arrived from her
house in the city.

"Hi, Naomi," I said, as I slipped through the door.

She smiled. "Hello, Your Majesty."

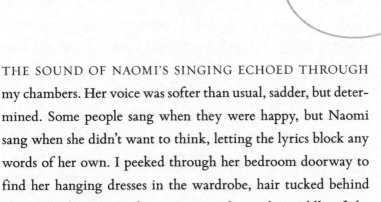

"That had better be a joke," I said, as I walked to the nearest trunk. "Because if you start calling me that seriously, I'm going to have to reconsider our friendship."

"Oh, I'm sorry, Your Majesty. I didn't know I wasn't allowed to address you properly."

"I'm not above killing you, if necessary. I get enough of that from everyone else."

Naomi paused, smile frozen on her face, and I suddenly realized what I'd said. "I mean—I'm sorry. I didn't mean to—"

"It's all right," she said, but her voice was fainter than before. "I know what you meant."

I opened my mouth to reply, but I had no idea what to say. I was saved by a rather demanding meow from the doorway. Dagny strutted in, her tail held high. She spared a second to rub against my legs, before hopping into Naomi's open trunk of dresses.

"Dagny!" I hurried to sweep her up. "She's so rude."

"As long as she's comfy in there," Naomi said.

"She'll get hair everywhere." Having a fluffy cat was only fun until you realized that the fluff didn't actually stay on the cat. Absolutely everything ended up covered in gray hair when Dagny passed by.

"Well, maybe we can start a new court fashion," Naomi said. "A better way to wear fur." She reached to take Dagny from me and held her against her shoulder like a baby.

"What's that you've got there?" she said, nodding toward the speech I still clutched in my hand while she swayed Dagny back and forth.

"A speech." I smoothed it out and held it up, as though I hadn't already read through it about forty-seven times. "Holt gave it to me. For when all the nobles get here."

"So is that where you were today? People were talking. Not to me, but I heard them, while I was eating—they were wondering why you were hiding."

"I wasn't hiding," I said, more forcefully than I intended. "I was studying with Holt for some of the day. And I was setting up my new laboratory in the dungeons."

"New laboratory?" Naomi's whole face brightened. "To work on the poison detector?"

I nodded.

"You should have fetched me! I would have helped."

"I'm sorry. I just got so overexcited with the idea—"

Naomi laughed. "Yes, I know what you're like." Dagny wriggled, so Naomi set her back in the trunk. Dagny leaped away, kicking the dresses for emphasis. Naomi sank onto the ground by the trunk, her skirts poofing up around her. "I heard from my parents today." Her tone made clear that it wasn't good news. A letter from Naomi's parents was rarely ever good news.

I sat down beside her. "Oh? What did they say?"

She reached into another chest and began to pick out books, lining them up on the floor beside her. "They aren't coming."

"What?"

"They won't come to the capital. Not even for the funerals. My father would struggle, and my mother—well, you know what she's like. I think she blames the court for my brother's death. She doesn't want to see it." She let out a long breath, eyes closed, then shook her head. "They've asked for Jacob's body to be sent to them in the country. I'm supposed to travel back, too."

"Will you go?"

She shook her head again. "I should. But—I don't know. I want to stay here. I haven't been back there in years. It'd be too strange now. And Jacob—you know he hated it there. He never got along with them. It'll be so strange . . ." She sucked in a breath through her teeth. "And I want to remember him properly, as he was, not as he'll be during—not as he is now." She straightened the books with shaking hands. "I need to be here. So that's what I'll do. Maybe I'll find something to include in the funerals for him. He would have liked that. More than—than going home."

"He was lucky to have you, you know. As his sister."

"I was lucky to have him." She stroked Dagny, her hand running along her tail. "Will a lot of people be coming for the funerals?"

"Almost everyone, I think." If I knew little about the members of the old court, I knew nothing about the nobles outside the city, the ones who survived by being hundreds of miles away. Some were older family members who preferred to let the younger generation charm the king, some had been disliked by the king, and some . . . some held the court in disdain, or lived far enough away that they ruled their land almost as kings of their own, as long as the real ruler did not think to check on them.

All but the most stubborn or unwell would be traveling to attend the old king's funeral and see their new queen.

I shifted forward to consider the books. "How do you want to organize these? Alphabetically?"

"Let's sort them by genre. Then size. Then—color, perhaps?"

I laughed. "That's not very efficient."

"But it'll look good on the shelves."

I wasn't much help. To me, most of Naomi's books were just novels. To her, they had mountains of nuance, and each tiny subcategory had its own space in her visualized shelving system. But it was fun to guess each book's category as I passed them to her, getting more and more specific and ridiculous with every try.

It made Naomi smile, at least.

We were interrupted by a knock on the door. I opened it to see Reynold Milson holding a sealed envelope. "A message for you, Your Majesty. From Rasmus Holt."

"Thank you."

"Of course, Your Majesty." He bowed, and I had to stop myself from curtsying back.

"What is it?" Naomi asked after the guard bowed again and strode back to his post.

I turned the envelope over. It was sealed with red wax and stamped with an eagle crossed with swords. I still didn't have a seal of my own—something else my advisers were probably worrying about. My father had one, a bolt of cloth representing his old trade and the star of nobility, but it wouldn't suit a queen. I needed to stand for something before I could have a seal of my own. I needed a message to send.

The paper inside was heavy and slightly stiff, and it was covered in writing. Name after name, well over five hundred of them. The list of guests at the banquet. Most had been crossed out. The rest were marked with stars or small Xs.

The king's name was at the top, crossed out, and the queen, and his brother, and his brother's son . . . all gone. My own name was far down the list, with a star beside it—the mark of a survivor, then—while Sofia Thorn's name had an X.

Deaths, survivors, and absentees.

If this was the official guest list, it wouldn't include anyone who showed up uninvited. I flicked to the back page, in case any names had been added and crossed out, but there were no other marks.

"Why has Holt sent that to you?"

"For my investigation," I said. "My advisers think the Gustavites were responsible, but it doesn't quite add up. I thought we could look through the list of guests at the banquet. Maybe there's something suspicious there."

"Makes sense," Naomi said. "I'll grab some paper."

While she walked over to the desk, I scanned the list again. Nothing stood out. They were just names, after all. But we needed to investigate them, find out what they had done that night. Some must have survived because they were lucky, but some may have known what was happening, and some may have been spared for a reason.

I didn't know much about most of the people listed here. But the same few names stood out. Torsten Wolff, the king's best friend, and first in line of the survivors who had been at the ball. William Fitzroy, the king's rejected son. Rasmus Holt, the new head adviser. The conspicuously absent Madeleine Wolff.

Naomi sat down on the floor beside me with a pile of paper and two pens. We split the pages between us, and wrote the name of a survivor at the top of each one. The list seemed much longer, when laid out across the floor. Twenty-four pages total.

Fitzroy had been the highest ranked to survive. Then me, then Sten, then Naomi. The rest were nobles much further down the line of succession, or not in line at all. My advisers, a few young courtiers even more insignificant than me, a great-aunt who always had a disapproving glare.

"Do you think they were definitely a guest? The murderer, I mean," Naomi asked.

"I don't know." It would have given them an easy way into the event, and something of an alibi if they were caught sneaking around. But a servant was probably involved, too, to have access to the kitchens. That meant someone could have ordered the attack and still kept their distance.

I inserted pages for Madeleine, for the Gustavites, for the vague and nebulous "cook" and "kitchen staff" and "tasters," before Naomi and I started to add to each page. Everything we knew about the person. The people close to them who had died. Their relationship with the court. Their behavior since the banquet.

Naomi had a lot more to contribute than I did. She noticed the details—that her great-aunt Katrina doted on Elva's twin children, and could never have wanted to kill them, that Carolina had looked rather green for most of the evening, that this person and that person had been caught up in a fight. My observations were mostly restricted to gossip I'd overheard—not exactly reliable—and what I'd seen since we'd moved to the Fort.

Dagny kept batting the pens away every time we put them down, so Naomi started balling up spare pieces of paper and throwing them for her. So far, two crystal jars and one silk bed-hanging had been damaged by her frantic pursuit of these new makeshift toys, but at least it kept her from troubling us. And watching her tear around the room made Naomi smile.

"We're going to need to talk to everyone," Naomi said quietly, as she watched Dagny chase the fifth paper ball under the wardrobe.

It was pretty much the last thing I wanted to do. We'd not only need to speak to people. We'd need to charm them, challenge them, guide the truth out of them. Judge them on their stories and their excuses.

But I could do this. I could speak to people. I'd spoken to Holt, and to Madeleine. I'd stayed calm, when the city was in chaos. I could cope with this. It was too important for me to shrink away, to hide behind Naomi and hope the answers would appear out of the air. It was just another problem, another question to unpick. I could do it.

"Then where should we start?" I tapped my fingers on the pages. "My advisers blame the Gustavites, but we can't exactly go out and interview them. If we had that book, or more of their propaganda . . . but my advisers are *very* determined for me not to see any of that."

"But they're not determined to keep *me* away," Naomi said. "So that'll be my task tomorrow. I'll see what I can do."

"You're brilliant," I said. "You know that, right?"

She shrugged. "I guess it's been said. Once or twice."

But that left me with interviewing duties. At least people couldn't refuse to meet with me, like they might with Naomi. Even spending time with a suspect might make things clearer.

Sten's name seemed to glare at me from the page, challenging me to question him. But that conversation in the library had unsettled me. He seemed to suspect *me*, genuinely, truly. The murderer wouldn't do that.

I'd speak to someone else first. Ease myself into the investigation. I scanned across the row of names again, and my eyes settled on William Fitzroy. Not technically in the line of succession, but close to the king. He had always been in the center of court. Even if he was innocent, he must have *something* useful to tell. Some secret to uncover.

"All right," I said. "Tomorrow." Tomorrow, we'd begin.

TWELVE

THE ODDS OF FINDING FITZROY ALONE SEEMED pretty slim, so I needed to exert some of that queenlike authority and summon him. I could hardly go into the makeshift throne room for this, so I strode down to my half-furnished laboratory. Perhaps a meeting in an ex–torture chamber would startle some honesty out of him.

If my guards were surprised by my request, they didn't show it. One of them disappeared to deliver the message, and I waited by the far cupboard, trying to figure out what I was going to say.

Ten hand-shaking minutes later, my guard knocked on the

door again. "William Fitzroy, Your Majesty."

I turned. Fitzroy stepped into the room. Gone was his rumpled, grief-racked look. His blond waves were swept back with casual confidence, and his blue eyes were alert again. Like nothing had changed. He looked princely, and for a moment, he stared me down, like he was challenging my place. I stared back at him, forcing myself to meet his gaze, my heart pounding. Then he offered me a shallow bow.

"Your Majesty," he said. "To what do I owe the pleasure?"

William Fitzroy, courtier extraordinaire. Why should I be afraid of him, when he'd never had a serious thought in his life?

He was serious when you saw him in the corridor, a voice in me said. *When he told you you didn't belong.*

I stepped forward. My heels wobbled beneath me. "Fitzroy. I wanted to talk to you."

"I gathered that." He moved farther into the room, letting the door swing closed behind him. "This is an unusual meeting place, Your Majesty. Unless you're planning to torture me?"

"No!" The word shot out of me, and I blushed. "This is my lab," I said, forcing myself to sound confident, in control. "There's not a lot of choice for space in the Fort."

"Ah, so you're planning to *experiment* on me." He strode past me, elbow brushing mine, to peer at the jars lined up on the cupboard tops. "Hemlock? Arsenic? What are you *doing* down here?"

"Those were already here." More words rushing out before

I could stop them. Why was I letting him unsettle me? "From before."

"Strange, that the labels haven't faded at all in a hundred years. And the bottles are so clean. They must have been blessed by the Forgotten, don't you think?"

"I suppose they must." I'd been an idiot to hope he'd be anything other than mocking and rude, considering what I knew of him. His friends always loved to make people like me feel small.

"I'm studying them."

"To see if they're poisonous? Because I'm pretty certain they are."

And this was the problem with William Fitzroy. Or one of them, at least. I was supposed to be interrogating him, yet somehow here he was, guiding the conversation, putting me on the defensive. I wouldn't let him do it this time.

"I'm trying to find a way to test for the presence of arsenic, as a way to replace tasters."

He paused. Whatever he had been expecting, it hadn't been that. "Do you think you can do it?"

I didn't hesitate. "Yes."

He clearly hadn't been expecting that, either. He watched me for a long moment, and I felt a rush of victory. He must have known he'd lost that round, because he shifted his weight, and shifted the conversation. "So, Your Majesty. Why have you summoned me to your torture chamber laboratory? I assume it wasn't for my winning conversation."

"Obviously." He grinned, and I let out a breath. "I just—wanted to talk to you." I ran my hands along the side of the table, letting the movement distract me. "We haven't spoken yet, not since—"

"Not since I shouted at you in the corridor?" He ran his fingers through his hair, rumpling the curls. "That was rude of me."

I stared at him. Had he just admitted to a fault? And a social fault, at that. It had to be some sort of trick, to throw me off balance again. "That wasn't an apology."

"Oh," he said. "Let me try again." He knelt before me, his head bowed, and I scurried backward a step. "Your Majesty, I am grievously sorry for the insult I have caused you. I throw myself upon your mercy."

He was awful. I shouldn't have expected anything else. My fingertips tingled, the first hints of panic, but I clenched my fists. I wouldn't let that control me today. "Don't make fun of me."

He looked up, lips parted slightly. "I was joking."

"You weren't joking." I turned away, counting the length of my breaths. Three beats in. Four beats out. Calm.

He stood again. "I was trying to joke. I didn't mean to upset you."

"You didn't mean to upset me, but you meant to make fun of me." Of course he couldn't respect me. Anyone loved by the old court was bound to be cruel to someone like me. But he had been a courtier, and that usually meant he'd at least be slightly subtle in his mockery. Apparently, I wasn't even worth that.

But the quicker I asked him the necessary questions, the quicker he could leave. "I wanted to talk to you about the night of the murders. I want you to tell me everything you saw."

"And why would you want to know that?"

He couldn't be serious. "Because someone murdered everyone in the old court. I want to find out who."

"And you think it might have been me."

I spun to face him. He still stood casually, but his expression was a little more focused now, a little more intense. "I didn't say that."

"No, but you meant it. I grew up in court, Freya. I know how to read people, and you have the least subtlety of anyone I've ever met."

"What happened to calling me 'Your Majesty'?"

"I think we're on a first-name basis once you start indirectly accusing me of murder."

Something about his expression had changed. He looked less polished now, a rawness bursting through. I felt a stab of guilt. "I didn't accuse you of murder. I just—I need to know what happened."

He stepped closer. "You don't know me, so I'll say this clearly. Almost everyone I knew died at that banquet. My father, my friends. And you think there's a chance that *I* killed them?"

"Anyone could have killed them. And the king was angry with you, at the banquet—"

"My father was angry with me at least half the time. He was angry I existed half the time. That doesn't mean I killed him and everyone I knew."

"I know." And I remembered how he had looked the morning after the banquet, when I bumped into him on the stairs. He looked broken. But a person could still murder and feel bad about it, couldn't they? If they thought it needed to be done? "Why was he angry with you?"

"I don't know. My father was too important to actually tell you why he was angry. You were just supposed to figure it out. It was lucky that he changed his mind easily enough, too."

I'd never really thought about it before. I knew the king had fallen out with Fitzroy on a near-weekly basis, but it had just been a fact of the court, nothing that actually affected people. It was strangely uncomfortable to look at Fitzroy now, to see him as a person, not a figure at court. "So what *did* you see, at the banquet?"

He sighed, then leaned against the countertop. The move seemed like the final drop of his courtly armor. When he spoke again, his voice was a little lower, a little rougher. "I was there, although I didn't eat much. Whatever had upset my father, he wanted to make a point of it, because he wasn't exactly sending the choicest foods to me."

"Your father made you come onto the dais, for the fire-eaters."

"He did. I survived, I sat back down, things went on. Until the end of the feast."

"With the cake?"

"Yes. With the cake. Every part of it was gold, so obviously he wasn't going to waste any on me. He wanted to make a point. So everyone around me got a piece, and I got plain sponge. Just plain. Everyone commented on it, so I made some stupid joke, acted like the plain sponge was the real prize, since no one else had it."

"Were you upset?" There was something about this rawer, quieter Fitzroy that made me shift closer. He was compelling, almost magnetizing—all the things his usual persona tried so hard to be. Succeeded in being, for everyone but me.

"Was I upset? A bit, I guess. But I'm used to it. That's just my life, isn't it? Or it was. And it turned out I was lucky. Gerald was next to me, acting completely normal, and then he started coughing. Acting like he couldn't breathe. I asked him if he was all right, and he turned away and threw up. And before I could even react to that, everyone else around me started reacting, too."

"All at once?"

"No," he said, a little quieter. "Not all at once. That was the most frightening thing. A lot of people fell ill at the same time, but people *kept* getting ill. Everyone was terrified, pushing and shoving to get out of the hall, as though the outside would save them."

I closed my eyes, heart pounding. I could picture every breath of it. I didn't want to, tried to shove the images away, but they burst to life before my eyes, all the faces I'd seen for years, the golden plates clattering on the floor, the terror of it. "I'm sorry."

Fitzroy swallowed. "People didn't know. They felt dizzy, or felt sick, and they thought it was poison, so they panicked . . . but it could have been panic making some of them unwell. We didn't know."

"How did you feel?"

"I was watching everyone I knew suffer and die. How do you think I felt?"

I flinched. "I just—I'm trying to understand."

"So am I," Fitzroy said. "I didn't know what to do. You think, if something terrible happened, you'd do the right thing. Maybe not be the hero, but do *something*. I just stood there. Gaping. Then the guards grabbed me and hauled me out of the palace."

"Why?"

"Why was I such an idiot, or why did the guards grab me?"

"You aren't an idiot." I'd called him that in my head a hundred times, but one brief conversation with him was enough to prove that wasn't true. It had never been true. He was . . . I wasn't sure what he was. But he wasn't an idiot. "I mean, why did the guards—"

"I guess they thought I might be king, with my father dead."

So there had been at least some movement toward crowning Fitzroy that night. Some assumptions. "Did you want to be king?"

"What, then?" He laughed. It was a painful sound. "It was pretty much the last thing on my mind."

I couldn't bear to look at him. I fixed my eyes on the floor, breathing in and out. "I'm sorry," I said. "About your father."

Silence. Then: "At least I survived. That's more than most people can say from that night."

"Yes. I suppose it is." My hands shook and I felt an unexpected urge to comfort Fitzroy. Instead I said, "You're being very honest with me."

"Isn't that what you want?"

"Yes. But—" I didn't know how to explain it. "I didn't really expect you to be. I thought you'd laugh at me."

"You are the queen."

"That didn't stop you from mocking me earlier."

"I didn't mean—" He ran his hand through his hair again. The gesture made him look vulnerable—far softer than the laughing, boisterous Fitzroy I was used to seeing at court. "I was just being ridiculous, Freya. I make jokes. It's how I survive."

"How you *survive*?" That was a bit melodramatic.

"Of course. I was a threat to pretty much everybody there. I still am, I guess. So I had to make people like me."

"You didn't consider just being nice?" I didn't mean to attack him, but the questions poured out of me, demanding to be answered.

"Nice? In this court? Not for me. People would think I was weak and tear me apart. Or think I was being manipulative, and tear me apart."

"So you make fun of them instead?"

He sighed. "I didn't mean to make fun of you. I was just—it's awkward, all right? All of this is awkward. I thought you would laugh. But you didn't. And I'm sorry."

It was a strange feeling, to believe him. "Is that why you were honest with me? Because you felt guilty?"

"I don't—" Another sigh, definitely frustrated now. "I don't know where you got your opinion of me, Freya, but it's not true. I was honest with you because I have nothing to hide. I've seen you, over the past few days. You seem honest. I'm not sure that's such a good thing, from your perspective, but I trust you. I don't know. Something about you makes me want to trust you."

"And you think I should trust you?"

"You probably shouldn't. I am the last king's son, after all." The words should have been another one of his jokes, but his tone didn't change. "Not really one that counts, but I'm sure your advisers will be quick to tell you how much of a threat

I am. Just try not to cut my head off, all right? I rather like it where it is."

Still no change in tone. I shivered. "I'm not cutting off anyone's head."

"I'll take that as a promise." He turned away, stepping toward the middle of the room. The tension between us snapped, leaving the ground unsteady underneath me. "Here's why you can trust me, Freya," he said. "For all my father's spontaneous sulks, he was in the middle of legitimizing me. He wanted to make me his heir. If he hadn't died, I would have been the next king. Even if you think me ruthless enough to kill my father and everyone at court for the sake of my own ambition . . . even then, it couldn't have been me. I would have been king. I would have been accepted here, surrounded by everyone I care about, and now I'm not. I'm not your murderer, Freya. And if you find them, let me know. I'd like to be there to skin them, myself."

He gave me a little smile and a casual tilt of his head, as though that were a joke, too, nothing serious meant at all. But the strain in his shoulders ruined the illusion. He might not actually be willing to murder the person responsible, but he wasn't entirely joking, either.

"I will," I said. "Don't—don't worry about that." I wanted to say something else, something more, but I didn't know what. It felt like something significant should follow, but instead the silence hovered between us, waiting to be broken.

Part of me wanted to continue the conversation, to draw it out, to dwell in the rawness of it. But my hands were still shaking, and my heart was beating too fast. It felt dangerous, all of this. Far too open. "Thank you," I said. "For coming here. For answering my questions."

He nodded. "It was my pleasure. I mean, without the pleasure, but—still." He stared at me for a long moment. "I hope your investigations come to something, Freya. Try and survive until then."

THIRTEEN

I FELT ON EDGE FOR THE REST OF THE DAY. I WAS CON-fident I could cross Fitzroy off my list of suspects, after that conversation, but I was even more confused and uncertain than I had been before I'd summoned him. I tried to organize my possessions as they arrived in the lab, but it was almost as if his piercing blue eyes were still watching me from across the room. I could still feel his *rawness* filling the air.

Shame swirled in my stomach as I worked. I'd always thought Fitzroy was a fool, but I had never paused to think that it might all be an act, that there might be something more sub-stantial underneath. I'd never even really thought of him as a person. First Madeleine Wolff, now William Fitzroy . . . was it the murders that had brought out these sides in people, or had they always been there, lurking underneath the court's gold veneer all along? What did that say about my observation skills, if I'd never noticed?

What did it say about me as a person, if I'd never cared to try?

Naomi slipped into the lab in the afternoon, but she was no closer to getting her hands on a copy of the book. It would be too dangerous to let people know about her search, considering all that had happened, and although Naomi was brave, she wasn't stupid. She'd spoken to as many people as she could without raising suspicion, turning the conversation to the Gustavites, using flattery to convince the older members of court to explain the problems to her, again and again, teasing out each person's beliefs. The survivors of the banquet had been more reticent, she said, but many nobles had begun to arrive for the funerals, and to many of them, the situation was more a source of gossip than one of grief.

"Everyone I spoke to thought the Gustavites were stupid, though," Naomi said, curling her toes around the slats of her stool. "No one seemed to support them. But I suppose they wouldn't want to give that away, would they?"

"I suppose not." After my encounter with Fitzroy, I was wary of dealing with people again. They were too unpredictable. I longed for science—clear, indisputable, easy-to-understand science. "Let's work on the poison test," I said to Naomi, shuffling our piles of notes aside. Perhaps that would give me somewhere solid to stand.

I pulled on thick leather gloves and tied a cloth over my face before passing a second cloth to Naomi and reaching for the jars of arsenic left by the room's original inhabitants. We had both the white powder form, perfect for poisoning enemies, and the pure metal, flaky and gray.

Step one, I decided, would be to burn it. Different metals produced different-color flames when thrown into a fire, and if the arsenic was distinctive enough, we could simply burn some of the food to detect it.

There was no chance that the solution would be that simple. But it was a good place to begin.

I lit a candle and broke off a piece of pure arsenic with my tongs. Naomi stepped back, her face covered too. I held my breath as I pushed the arsenic into the flame.

The fire turned blue, and a garlicky smell filled the room.

"You did it?" Naomi said, shifting closer. She sounded unsure.

"Not yet." I placed the pure arsenic in a bowl and snuffed the flame. "It's the powder that's used to poison people. If that has the same reaction . . ."

It didn't. I couldn't hold the powder in my tongs, so I lit another candle and sprinkled it on top, letting it settle in the slight dip of melted wax. Nothing happened. At least, nothing I could identify. The smoke might have been a little thicker, perhaps, but the powder just sat there, completely uninterested in doing anything useful.

I took notes anyway, making sure I didn't leave out a single detail. That garlic smell felt like the key here. If I could get the powder to release the same gas, then it would be easy to detect.

My pen was too loud as it scratched the paper. I could feel Naomi watching me.

"It'll be all right, you know," she said softly.

"I know. The answer's here somewhere."

"That's not what I meant." She touched my shoulder. "I meant—court. The funerals. All of it. I know you can do it."

I chewed my lip. "I wasn't made for this, Naomi. I was supposed to *leave*. I was supposed to be doing *science*, not—not worrying about court gossip and fashion and the right way to smile. I was supposed to escape all this. I don't fit here."

"Freya—"

"Do you think I'm selfish?"

Naomi stared at me. "Freya, no. Of course not. You—"

"I think I am." I stared at the stains on the table. It seemed so important, suddenly, to say it out loud. Not to get Naomi's reassurance that I was wrong—what would be the point?— but to let myself accept that I was right. I'd found a huge flaw deep within me, one I'd previously thought was a strength . . . what was I supposed to do with that? "Fitzroy—he's not who I thought he would be. And Madeleine, when she bumped into me, she just wanted to talk about charity. About orphans. And

I thought maybe she was just putting on an act, but . . . I think she really is like that. I think she really does care. And I always dismissed her, because she fit in, and I didn't. How can I be the queen of these people, when I think like that? *I* wouldn't even accept me."

"Freya. Listen." Naomi pulled her stool closer, so we were practically sitting on top of each other. She wrapped an arm around my shoulders, and I sank into the strange sideways hug. "I don't think you're selfish. Things were different before. You didn't feel like you fit in here. Neither of us did. You wanted to leave. Of course you didn't want to make friends, or think the people making you miserable were nice. But now things are different, now you're a part of it . . . you're seeing things differently, too. And that's okay, isn't it? It means you *aren't* selfish. You're thinking about them as people. That's all right. That's what you need to do."

"I don't know." I closed my eyes, shifting closer. Her hair tickled my nose. "How am I ever going to understand them?"

"They're just people, Freya. You'll be all right."

But even that thought was terrifying. People were complicated. I'd never be able to please them all.

More visitors poured through the Fort's gates the following day. Since none of these nobles had been at the banquet that night, and many barely knew the victims, they didn't talk in the same somber tones as most of the survivors—they greeted

one another with enthusiasm, their voices swelling in speculation. When I passed them in the corridors, they would fall silent,
bowing and curtsying, before resuming their gossip as soon as I
was out of sight.

I tried to smile as my mother had, to walk as though the
corridors belonged to me. I needed the visitors' approval—as
my father had told me, over and over again. They held far more
power than any ruler would like to admit. They collected the
taxes in their regions. They were the face of law and justice to
whoever lived under their rule. Common people knew them,
respected them, or feared them, as the case may be, and they
had old families, old connections, knowledge of the land and
resources that the crown never saw. I needed their support. How
could someone declare themselves queen in one city, when all
the land around disagreed?

I had no chance to go to my laboratory. Instead I practiced
my speech with my father until I knew it so well that my ghost
would probably recite it in these halls a thousand years from
now. I answered Holt's questions about cutlery and curtsies, and
whenever I had a spare moment, I scribbled down ideas for conversations, phrases I could say, anything to make me feel more
prepared.

Naomi helped me to dress in near silence, pinning my hair
up so it looked like a spiraling black pastry balanced on my scalp.
It looked ridiculous, I thought, as Naomi added another ten pins
to ensure in stayed in place, but it was a familiar style. I just

needed to be familiar. Naomi dusted silver over my eyelids, and tied me into another huge skirt, layered with cascading silk and studded with yet more jewels. It swamped me, making my face and hands look inhumanly small, and I scowled at my reflection, willing it to shift into proportion.

When my father came to collect me, he looked calm and confident, as he always did in court, but he worried the edge of his sleeve with his thumb as he nodded his approval. He was nervous.

We met Holt outside the throne room. He looked over my dress, my hair, my jewels, and he frowned. But he didn't get a chance to speak before my father barreled ahead.

"Do you remember your speech?"

I nodded, feeling too sick to reply.

"The Forgotten are with you, Your Majesty," Holt said. "Even now. Have faith that they knew what they were doing, when they brought you here."

It wasn't comforting, but I nodded again, and Holt steered me toward the door. "Smile, Your Majesty," he said, "and all will be well."

Servants opened the double doors, revealing the throne room beyond. "All bow to Her Majesty Queen Freya, ruler of Epria!" a guard shouted.

People must have worked nonstop to transform this room since the feast after my coronation. Banners hung from the ceiling—still bearing King Jorgen's sigil—and paintings were hung on every inch of the walls, making it look slightly less like a dungeon. The coldness had lingered, though, even with the crowd now waiting inside.

Some of the people were familiar—Fitzroy was there, and Torsten Wolff—but there were many strangers, too. A hundred unfamiliar faces, all staring at me expectantly, eyes burrowing under my skin.

Smile. I just had to smile. I could feel the corners of my lips straining, the muscles in my cheeks twitching. They must all have seen the falseness of it, the fear in my eyes.

I slowly crossed the room, heading for the throne. I wanted to stare straight ahead, to pretend I was walking alone, pretend it wasn't real, but I *couldn't*. I forced myself to look left and right, to meet people's eyes, to smile to them. Challenging myself to notice the details.

This time I didn't trip. That was a blessing, at least.

I stopped in front of the throne, and felt another jolt of fear. The throne had belonged to the king, and had been designed for a king's frame, a king's clothes. My skirt was twice as wide as the seat, and the crinoline was not going to bend. I wouldn't fit. I could possibly sit *over* the throne, my skirts ringing it and hiding it from sight, but that didn't exactly seem like a dignified solution.

But it would be fine. It was fine. I'd just have to stand. Standing would be fine.

I tried to turn gracefully to face the nobles, but the skirt was too large, and I wobbled. A few people in the audience laughed behind their hands, and my face flushed.

But I could do this. I could do this. I just had to say the speech, and everything would be fine.

The words caught in my throat. I knew them, I did, but they wouldn't travel from my brain to my tongue. A hundred people watched me, waiting, judging, expecting me to fail, and the more I snatched for those perfectly memorized phrases, the quicker they danced away. The silence stretched on.

"Welcome," I said eventually. It came out as a rasp. "Welcome," I said again, but that time the word sounded too loud, like I was shouting at them.

Had my tongue always been this large? The room spun at the edges.

I could do this. I *could*. I just had to speak. Just speak.

"I am delighted to welcome you all back to the capital, although it grieves me that we must meet under such tragic circumstances." That was right, wasn't it? The words were stiff, entirely unnatural, but I was speaking them. It was all right. "We have all lost so many friends in this tragedy, and I know we will all feel their absence tonight. But I also know that we are strong, and we can come together in our grief, to honor and remember them, and forge Epria anew." Once I'd started, the words tumbled out, with the ebb and flow that my father had drilled into me, over and over again. The rhythm of them took over, and I lost any sense of what I was saying or where I was. I just spoke, and gestured, letting it happen.

And then the nobles were applauding, and I crashed back into myself, swaying on my feet.

I had done it. I'd reached the end of the speech. It hadn't killed me. I didn't really know what had happened, or what I had said, but my father was smiling at me, and Holt was walking forward, and I'd *done* it.

I felt proud, flush with my success, but I seemed to have rushed through two days' worth of energy to support myself through that two-minute speech, and I needed time to sit now, to recover.

But of course, we weren't finished yet. I had to meet all of the guests, every single one, in a never-ending parade of bows and curtsies.

"This is Sir Leonard, Your Majesty, and his wife, Isabella," Holt said, as the first couple approached. "They have traveled here from the moorlands in the east."

"Oh, we were so heartbroken to hear of what happened at the feast," Lady Isabella said, sinking into a curtsy. "So many good people—it must have been so painful, to be there."

"I was not there," I said. "I didn't see."

"Thank the Forgotten for small mercies, I suppose."

"I remember your mother, Your Majesty," Lady Isabella said. "She was a wonderful woman. She lit up every room she was in. I was much grieved to hear of her death."

"Thank you," I said softly. "So was I."

"Your Majesty," Sir Leonard said, "when the business of the funeral is over, I am hoping we can discuss the issue of taxation over the marshlands. The people there are not rich, as I am sure you know, and these high taxes from King Jorgen are putting an unnecessary burden on—"

"I will be delighted to discuss such matters with you," Holt said smoothly, "or perhaps you could discuss them with the treasurer, Her Majesty's father? After the funeral, of course."

"I can discuss it with you," I said, the blunt words bursting out of nowhere. "If people are struggling, I want to know about it." Holt stared at me, and I faltered. "Although—I'm sure my father will be able to provide more help. But if you wish to discuss . . ." I ran out of words, as suddenly as they'd appeared, but Leonard was looking at me slightly differently now, appraising me.

"Of course," he said. "I will take you up on that."

More people followed, and I tried to greet them as I should. But I felt slightly detached from it all, and nothing seemed quite right. When I stretched my smile wide and tried to be friendly, welcoming, I felt like I was mocking the occasion, too cheery for the funeral of the entire court that came before. When I attempted to be somber, I was too quiet, too cold, an unwelcoming figure with nothing much to say. And when my true thoughts burst through, I felt a rush of relief, just for a moment, before I remembered how *unqueenly* I was being, and shoved the thoughts away.

After what felt like days, we settled down for the evening's first entertainment. A stage had been built at one side of the hall, and the crowd flowed toward it. A few chairs had been placed there, too—mostly for elderly nobles, but one, nearest the stage, for me. And it had no sides, no arms, which meant I might actually fit in it, skirts and all.

I sank onto it, grateful for the support. I couldn't quite catch my breath, and the sounds around me were a little too loud, buzzing in my ears. But this would be time to recover. Then I could face whatever came next.

The performer was a storyteller, with a light box from across the sea. He told a story as the images shifted and changed, about a poor maiden whose younger brother had been caught stealing bread. She had dressed up as him to protect him, and had been sent into the army as punishment in his place. It had happened during Epria's dark days, when all was war and pain, and the Forgotten had left this world to its corruption. But the Forgotten still watched Epria, still exerted power when they wished it, and they favored this girl's bravery and intelligence. They protected her, gave her power, and helped her save the kingdom from ruin.

The Forgotten were represented by many shadows and shapes—the twist of the wind, the silhouette of a dragon's wing, the elegant curl of a swan's neck. I knew the story, like everyone in court, but the performer was an excellent storyteller, and he made even the most familiar parts thrilling, capturing the wonder of this one poor girl with so much bravery inside her.

I'd seen similar performances before, of course, seen the way artists manipulated light to animate shadow. The whirring picture boxes, the many distinct drawings transformed into one image by speed and flickering lights, the way parts could be added or taken away for greater effect. But I'd never seen a show like this. The light seemed to obey the storyteller's will, bringing the story to life.

"Beautiful, isn't it?"

I jumped. I hadn't noticed Madeleine Wolff move beside me. She leaned close, one jewel-covered hand resting on my wrist. "The way they use the light—one has to be aware of it, of course, when one paints, but he seems to be able to control it here. So fascinating."

I nodded. She leaned closer still, her painted fingernails digging into my skin. "I wanted to warn you. Be wary of my cousin."

What? I forced myself to look forward, eyes on the show. "Your cousin?" I murmured. "Why?"

"He is a good man, and he means well, but . . . he is blinded by his grief for the old king. I think he suspects you had a hand in his death. He doesn't have any proof yet, but—he is not your ally, Freya. Be careful with him."

"Why are you telling me this?"

"You saved my life. And you deserve to know. You're far better than he thinks you are." She leaned back, the same sweet smile on her face. "Such talented work," she said. "I must speak to the performer after it is done."

She slipped away, leaving me to stare after her. My heart was pounding. I'd known Sten suspected me—certainly that he didn't *like* me—but it was different hearing someone else saying it, confirming my suspicions. Her behavior was so strange . . . did she know more than she'd said? Was Sten plotting something?

The show ended, and I applauded with the others, before hurrying toward the performer. Madeleine's parting comment could have been a hint that the performer knew something, that I should speak to him myself. But Holt rested a hand on my arm, steering me firmly away. "A good performance, was it not, Your Majesty?"

"Yes," I said. "I wish to thank the performer. To discuss his work."

"Oh, these men never want to reveal their secrets. Come. I think this story has given the court much to reflect on. It's time for the feast."

And he shepherded me away.

We were served peacock on golden plates, but no one seemed willing to eat the birds. People made a show of it, sticking their forks into the meat, even moving them near their mouths, but not swallowing a bite.

I *had* to eat, to reassure people, but I could barely taste it. I had to force every chew. I couldn't stop thinking about what

Madeleine had said during the performance, what *I* had said during the introductions. I *really* shouldn't have told Lady Patricia that I liked her hair. I'd meant it politely, but it had sounded forced, hadn't it? She probably thought I was mocking her. And that stupid smile I gave Sir Viktor—he probably thought I was an empty-headed idiot. And my speech . . . I couldn't really remember much of it, but that was worrying, too. Maybe I'd mixed up the words, and not noticed. Or what if I'd skipped part of it? And it was probably a monotone, and if they all thought I was bored of them . . .

One of the visiting nobles stood. He held his golden goblet in the direction of the high table, smiling slightly. "A toast," he said, his voice ringing through the hall. "To our rightful queen, who protects us from harm." He raised the goblet higher and took a long drink. Everyone in the hall followed suit.

I froze. The words sounded respectful, but something more sinister lurked underneath. A hint that I was *not* the rightful queen. The possibility that someone else might deserve the throne more.

I had to do something. Say something, act somehow, to put him in his place and take control of the situation. But my mind was blank. I couldn't make a mistake now. But what could I possibly do? I couldn't acknowledge the hint of a threat. I'd have to use pretty words and a prettier smile in response, and I didn't have either of those.

Beside me, my father and Holt raised their goblets. I needed to raise mine, too. Or just nod. Something. But my heart thudded faster and faster, and my hands tingled, and I couldn't move, could barely remember how to breathe.

Smash. I jumped. Everyone stared at Fitzroy, who smiled and shrugged at a shattered ewer by his feet. Red wine spread across the stone floor. "My apologies, Your Majesty," he said, his tone not apologetic in the slightest. "My hand slipped. Seems I'll be playing the fool tonight."

I forced myself to nod. He was a different person from the boy I'd spoken to in the dungeons, back into his courtier's skin once again. But my breath was returning now, the world becoming clear.

"Typical Fitzroy," a man near him said, his voice booming across the hall. "Can't bear for the attention to be off him for a moment."

Everyone laughed, and with that, the conversation started again, more lively than before.

I tried to catch Fitzroy's eye, but he did not look at me again.

FOURTEEN

I STARED AT MY BED'S CANOPY THAT NIGHT, DAGNY curled up beside me. My room was almost completely dark, but I imagined I could see the patterns above me, the embroidery of fire-red birds and stalking panthers and glittering stars.

The funerals would take place at dawn. The funerals . . . I rolled onto my side. I'd only ever been to one funeral before, and it wasn't one I wanted to remember.

I'd had to keep telling myself that my mother was dead, repeating it over and over, drilling the words into my head . . . I still hadn't really believed them. Then the funeral came, and my final chance to say good-bye. The crowd had gathered around us, and I remember wondering what *they* were doing there, hating them for stealing this moment, as though any of them could possibly miss her as much as I would. And then it hit me, all at once, that my mother was gone, that she was never, never coming back. I didn't remember much of what happened next, but people told me. I'd screamed, refused to let the priest near the body on the river, fighting and kicking and shrieking.

Tomorrow I'd be the one intruding on people's grief, pretending it was my own. No one I loved was being remembered tomorrow. I hadn't lost anything. And yet I was to stand in front of them all, as though my sadness mattered most.

I couldn't bear it. I swung my legs out of bed and stood. I needed a distraction, something to *do*, and my laboratory waited downstairs. I would head down there, and work on my poison test. Make sure nothing like this ever happened again.

But when I reached the dungeons, the door to my laboratory was ajar. I pushed it slightly, letting it creak on its hinges.

Fitzroy sat inside, reading through my notes. His blond hair was rumpled, and his eyes bleary. He looked up when he heard the door, and nodded at me. Once again, the charismatic courtier I knew was gone, leaving a softer presence behind. I wanted to run up and snatch my notes from his hands, protect my thoughts from his judgment. I wanted to rest my hand on his arm, to soothe some of that rawness away.

"Fitzroy? What are you doing?"

"I couldn't sleep," he said.

"So you came here?" I shut the door. The thud echoed in the room, too loud.

"I don't know. I mean, yes, obviously. I hoped you would be here."

"Me?" I stepped closer, slowly. My heart pounded.

"I know you don't like me," he said. "But—maybe that's what I need right now. I don't know. We were honest with each other, last time. That was—I'm tired of being *courteous*. And I needed something to—I hoped maybe you were working. And that I could help."

He looked so lost. William Fitzroy was in my laboratory, rambling to explain himself, and I should have been angry, I should have, but the feeling wouldn't come. "All right," I said. "You can help. Let me get some beakers."

My next planned test was to try dissolving the arsenic in water. I had no hope it would help—if it had a detectable effect, it wouldn't exactly be a useful poison—but I needed to explore every possibility, leave nothing to chance.

As I prepared two samples of water, Fitzroy continued to leaf through my notes. "These are very thorough."

"Of course they are. Otherwise what's the point?"

Fitzroy just nodded.

I carried the beakers back to the center table and set them down a few feet from Fitzroy. I didn't let myself look at him. He was too distracting, the sheer presence of him, the way his feelings seemed to crackle in the air. I picked up a piece of pure arsenic with tongs and placed it in the water. Nothing happened. I poked it, as though that might encourage it, but it continued to sit, doing not much at all.

The powder was similarly useless. It dissolved in the water, as I expected it would, but nothing else happened to reveal its presence.

I scribbled down more notes as Fitzroy considered the liquid. I glanced at him, just once—twice. The lab felt too full with him here. Too full, and too quiet.

He thought I didn't like him and I couldn't leave that hanging, undisputed. I *hadn't* liked him before, but I'd never spoken to him. And now . . . I didn't know what I thought about him now. Nor did I understand this visceral *something*, a pull whenever he was near.

"I don't *dis*like you." I inspected the arsenic powder as I spoke, like I wasn't even talking to him at all.

"What?" I could feel him staring at me. I didn't look.

"Before. You said I don't like you. But it's not that. I just—" I didn't know. I looked back at my notes, scrabbling for something to say. "We should test its acidity next. If you want to help— there's paper, somewhere in one of those drawers. Pink-purple strips."

I couldn't see his reaction, but I heard his footsteps as he walked over to the drawers and began pulling them open, riffling through my supplies. I could probably have remembered where I'd stored them, if I focused hard enough, but I couldn't think. I could barely make notes.

"I'm sorry," he said, and I jumped. "You probably don't believe me, but—I am sorry."

He was determinedly staring into a drawer, still searching for the paper. I had no idea what he meant. "For what?" I asked.

"For that first night, at your coronation. When I said you didn't belong here. I—I was upset, about my father, about all of this. And you were *there*, standing in his place, not fitting at all, and I just—I wanted to tear you out of there. I wanted to rip everything back to the way it was before. But it wasn't your fault."

I didn't know what to say. "Fitzroy——"

"Everyone calls me that, you know." He pulled open another drawer. "Fitzroy. *King's son*. They invented the name just for me, to make sure everyone knew I was different. Do you even know what my actual name is?"

"William," I said softly. "William Fitzroy." I stared at my notes again. I hadn't thought—"I can call you William if you like. I didn't know——"

"No," he said. "Don't. Everyone calls me Fitzroy. *I* call myself Fitzroy. But—I don't know. I've never had an identity outside my father. And I never really counted."

"You counted."

He made a soft sound of disbelief.

"You counted more than me."

He didn't reply.

Earlier that night . . . he had helped me, when that noble mocked me. Why would he have done that, made himself look the fool in order to save me? Because he had saved me, in his way. I had been too trapped in my panic to react to the challenge, and he had reset the moment, distracted everyone, made things easy again.

I walked to the row of jars against the far wall. There was nothing I needed there, but I had to do something, to move. I shifted the jars about, looking at the labels, not really reading them at all.

"Why did you help me? At the banquet?"

The silence was a physical presence. It loomed behind me, growing, growing, as Fitzroy did not reply.

"I knocked over some wine," he said eventually. "I didn't help you."

"You made yourself into a joke, to stop them laughing at me. I didn't know what to do, and you—" I pressed my lips together. "I appreciated it." The words were heavier than they should have been, too full of meaning. But I *did* appreciate it, more than I could express. "Thank you."

"You should be careful. Don't let people corner you like that."

"I didn't mean to. I wanted to respond. But I couldn't think."

"You could have done anything," he said. "You could have nodded, or smiled. You could have said thank you!"

He made it sound so simple. I suppose it was, to him. "It's not so easy. I know it should be, but . . ." I didn't have an excuse. I'd tried to be confident, to be elegant, to transform into the queen they desired. For hours, I'd tried. I'd just run out of resolve. The pretense had lasted too long.

"You're smart, Freya. I know you can outthink them."

I paused, my hand hovering over a vial of mercury. "You don't believe that."

"How could I not believe that? Have you seen this place, Freya? Have you seen what you're doing?"

"Court is different. It's not—this isn't about being smart. When I'm there . . . all the thoughts fly out of my head. It's like I'm not even fully in the room any more. I can trust my instincts here, but there—I don't know what to do. I *can't* think what to do."

"Then don't think. Go with your instincts, like you said."

But my instincts were *wrong*. They weren't the instincts of a queen, and I had to act as they expected, or they'd never accept me. I chewed on my lip, that admission a truth too hard to say.

"I found the paper," Fitzroy said. "Should we do the test?"

That meant moving closer to him. I felt every footstep as I crossed the room. He held out the papers, and I took them from him, careful that I didn't touch him.

"What are we looking for?" he said.

"If it's acidic, the paper will turn red."

"And that'll help us?"

"It's useful to know."

I dipped the paper in the poison solution. It turned light red. "Acidic?" Fitzroy asked.

I nodded. "It's not enough to prove arsenic is present, but— it's useful. Perhaps the kitchens can use this to test drinks, at least. Make sure nothing is suspicious."

"That would help." He continued to stare at the solution. "So what's next?"

"Acid," I said. "We try and dissolve it in different acids, and see how it reacts. If it has a smell, or a color, or releases a gas . . ."

"Acids." He nodded. "What should I do?"

I glanced at his hands. "Nothing. I don't have any gloves that'll fit you. Acid is dangerous—"

"I'll be careful." He looked down at his hands as well, and then glanced back at me, with a slight look of desperation. "Please, Freya. I need to help."

I shouldn't. I *shouldn't*. But—"Collect some beakers," I said. "And some pipettes. We'll need to use a different one for each solution."

He was too close. He was at least a foot away from me, but he was far too close. I carried my notes over to the far table, where the bottles of acid all waited in a line.

Science was supposed to be calming. It always helped me focus, no matter what was happening around me. But with Fitzroy here, I felt scattered, so aware of him that I couldn't be aware of myself.

We worked in silence for a while, except for the occasional

question about measurements. I labeled each beaker as we went.

"This is good," Fitzroy said, "if you figure it out. Not just for the testers. You could sell it to other kingdoms, or paranoid nobles and merchants. The kingdom can always use more money."

"This kingdom doesn't need any more money. What would we do with it, make a fountain of liquid gold?"

"Freya." He paused until I looked at him. "You really don't know, do you? The court is rich, but where do you think all that money comes from? The treasury is broke. We need money."

In all the years my father had worked for the treasury, he'd never told me that. "Are you sure?"

"I'm *very* sure."

"So we sell some of the court's riches. Some of those jewels, and the gold. We have lots of money, even if it isn't coin."

"You can't do that, either. People won't like it. They'll think you're not fit to be queen. People won't trust you." He watched me, unblinking, and I stared back, heat creeping across my face. "It's a good idea," he added, in a softer voice. "Selling the jewels. But it's not realistic, not now. The poison test . . . that's good. If you can do it."

I looked away. "I'll do it."

"How do you know?"

"Because. There has to be a way. I'm not going to let myself fail now."

"And you feel that way about solving the murders?"

"I have to." We had shifted closer again as we talked. He was less than half a foot away now, and I could have sworn I could feel the creases on his sleeves against my skin. He was so *unsettling*. Nothing about him made sense. I ran my fingers through my hair, shoving the sensation away.

"You have to," he echoed. "Because you cared about my father and the court? Or to protect yourself?"

The words should have stung, a fierce accusation, but from Fitzroy, it sounded like a genuine question. Like the answer itself less important than the act of knowing it.

"Partly to protect myself," I said quietly. "Partly to protect everyone. If there's another attack . . . a lot more people could die. And it's my responsibility, isn't it, to make sure that doesn't happen. Not that it was your father's fault, that everyone died, but now that we're warned—"

"My father was a horrible person."

I stared at him. The statement had come out of nowhere, shattering everything around it, but he continued to measure out the acids, like he hadn't said anything at all.

"What?"

"My father. He was awful. He didn't care about anyone other than himself." He spoke levelly, but anger lingered beneath the words, long-suppressed feeling pressing against the surface. "If you weren't exactly who he wanted you to be, he'd punish you until you changed. And I was never who he wanted me to be."

"Fitzroy . . ." I didn't know what to say. I didn't know him well enough to disagree. "I—I'm sure that's not true."

"Of course it's true." He sounded so matter-of-fact as he said it. "He wanted me to be a real son. A real heir. But I couldn't. So then he wanted me to not exist at all. But I couldn't do that, either. If he'd picked one or the other, it would have helped, but he changed his mind several times a day. Even if I *could* do what he wanted, I'd never get the chance before he switched it again."

"You were a real son."

He laughed. "I told you, Freya. I've always had to work to make people accept me. I've always been a threat. If my father had a real son, I would have been a threat to him. If he didn't, I was a threat to everyone else. If I was too serious, I was a dull disappointment. If I was too frivolous, I didn't deserve the honor of being his son. And I could never give my opinions if they went against his, or refuse to give an opinion if asked. I spent every minute of my life trying to count. I tried so hard, I don't even know who I am any more. And none of it mattered, in the end."

I didn't know how to help him. I wished I did. "What about your mother?" I said instead.

"I don't know. She didn't really have a part in my life. My father wanted her forgotten."

"What happened to her?"

He shrugged. "She's gone. That's all anyone would tell me. I found out a little on my own, but—" He sighed. "Even after all that, I still loved him. I still wanted his approval. And now he's dead, along with everyone else, and I'm still—" He shook his head. "You asked me if I wanted to be king, before. I don't know if I wanted to *rule*. But if I became king, that would be—I would have his approval then, wouldn't I? So yes, I wanted it. It was all I wanted, sometimes. But I wouldn't fight you for it. I wouldn't fight anybody. It just—it meant something, before. It doesn't mean anything now."

"I'm sorry." The impulse was too strong to resist. I reached across the gap and touched his arm. He looked down at my hand, and I looked at it as well, feeling the weight of it.

Then Fitzroy stepped away, reaching for another bottle of acid, and my hand hung in the air where he had been. "So, how about you? Are you ready for tomorrow?"

I closed my eyes. "I'll never be ready for tomorrow." I had to be honest, too, but it was so difficult, my concerns so selfish. "I feel like I'm going to be an intruder, somehow. Everyone will stare at me and hate me for being there, when the people they cared about should have been there instead."

"They won't," Fitzroy said. "Not tomorrow. They'll be too focused on themselves and their own grief to hate you for it."

"But I'll be there. Right at the front, being *queen*, when I shouldn't be." I glanced at him, suddenly afraid. I shouldn't say that I wasn't really queen, not out loud, not to anybody. But Fitzroy just shook his head.

"If people don't know you, they won't even notice you tomorrow. And if they do, they won't have the energy to spare to hate you. No one will really be watching."

"People are always watching."

"Normally. But not tomorrow."

"I always thought—" I paused, pulling my thoughts together. "I assumed it was easy for you. Everyone always seemed to like you."

"I would have thought it was easy for you. No one would really have cared what you did."

"I cared," I said, more forcefully than I intended. "And my father. People who remembered my mother, and how *wonderful* she was. I felt like everyone was watching me, all the time. And I didn't want to be part of it. I wanted to be here, with my science."

"But you forced yourself to try?"

"No, my father forced me." I let out a breath. "I was going to leave, to study. Be a scientist. Make big discoveries, far away from here. I can't do that now."

"You could," he said softly.

"No, I can't. I'm supposed to be queen, and if I don't hold on to this throne—"

"But you could," he said, more forcefully this time. "If you went far away, across the sea, and changed your name, and never mentioned this at all. They'd make Madeleine Wolff queen, and as long as you never challenged them . . . most people would forget about you. And those that didn't probably wouldn't be able to find you. You could leave."

The possibility had never even occurred to me. I could go. Run far away. Follow all my dreams after all. But the thought wasn't as relieving as I'd have expected. It just made me tenser, more anxious, faced with a possibility that I knew, deep down, I could never pursue. That plan had belonged to the Freya of a week ago, and she felt as far away now as if she were a dream. I couldn't leave. I had to make things work here.

"I won't leave," I said.

Silence filled the laboratory again. And then, so softly I almost didn't hear it: "Good."

FIFTEEN

WE WATCHED THE RIVER AS THE SUN ROSE.

The nobles sat in huge stands along the banks, dressed in the soft yellow of sunlight and spring. Their jewels glittered in the dawn.

Everyone else stood farther down the river. The crowd heaved as people pushed forward to reach the water. Many of them held flags or banners, some official with the three stars of King Jorgen, some crafted from old clothes and scraps. A few unscrupulous merchants walked the street near the bank, offering tokens to wave for the king's final journey, alcohol to toast him with, special lucky coins to toss as the bodies passed.

The dead were by the riverbank, too, upstream of the crowds. Hundreds of wooden boats bobbed in the water. Some were plain, but others had carvings on the sides, etched names or drawings that represented the person or their family. The richest victims lay in elaborate boats—given swan necks or mermaid tails or the wings of a hawk—with silks as blankets.

The king and queen lay in a boat together, on a mattress of gemstones. The jewels wouldn't get far. People would be scouring the river as soon as the funeral was over. Even a single stone could feed a family for several years. People would fight over them. They would drown in the river for the hope of finding one.

It was such a waste. All of this was a waste.

I glanced at Fitzroy. We stood on a wooden platform by the water's edge, inches from the royal boat and his father's body, but he wasn't looking at them. He stared resolutely at the trees on the opposite bank, his jaw clenched.

I wanted to reach out for him, as though doing so could fix even a tiny part of this. But the priest from my coronation stood between us, talking on and on, flanked by huge glowing metal torches.

"We can take comfort in this tragedy," he said, "that our beloved king and queen, all those we loved here, have now begun their journey to join the Forgotten. Their travails in this realm have helped to move them closer to their true place in this world, and they await us in the bliss to come."

Dawn was coming, reds and golds spreading across the sky. The priest bowed his head at me, and I stepped forward, a huge wooden torch clutched in my hand. My dress floated around me.

I held the torch above the fire. The flames leaped across, and I flinched at the sudden heat.

All along the riverbank, other people, relatives of victims or important well-wishers, raised their own lit torches. Naomi was somewhere in the mass, I thought, as I glanced over all the flames. I hoped she was all right.

I stepped toward the bodies of the king and queen. They had been doused in pitch, and the smell partly disguised the slight stench of decay that even the best preservation attempts could not stop after a week of death. They both looked peaceful, eyes closed, faces relaxed. Someone must have arranged them, I thought dully, to cover up the horrors of their deaths. The queen looked younger without her hair piled a foot in the air, kinder. The king looked as stately as ever.

I knew they were dead—of course I knew—but my stomach jumped when I thought of setting them alight. They looked so real, like maybe we could wake them, if we just shouted loud enough. If I burned them, they'd never get that chance.

"Your Majesty?" the priest murmured. Everyone was waiting for me. I stretched out my arm, the torch shaking slightly, and touched the flame to the king's feet. The fire caught with a rush, sweeping over the two bodies.

I stepped back, and Fitzroy moved forward, his father's

sword in his hand. He cut the boat free with one quick stroke. The current swept it up at once, carrying it downstream as the flames grew and grew, black smoke billowing. Once the boat reached the middle of the river, people all along the banks lit the other boats, too, cutting them free so they followed the king.

"May they find peace," the priest intoned. "And may we meet again."

"May we meet again," the crowd repeated, but the solemnity of the words was belied by their enthusiasm. As the king's ship passed, they waved their flags and tossed their lucky coins into its wake. Some cheered when the coins landed on the ship itself, as though the feat had won them extra luck for themselves for years to come. As though it was lucky to throw in your lot with someone who had died at his own birthday celebration.

Already, jewels were falling from the ship, sparkling in the water as they fell to the riverbed. How long would it be before someone dove in after them?

The first of the other boats pulled level with me. I stared at those fires, too, at the faces being swallowed by the flames.

Fitzroy still stood beside me, inches away now, staring at the water, seeming to see nothing at all. I wanted to comfort him. To do *something*. But I barely knew him, and even taking his hand felt like an intrusion. So I stared at the water, and so did he, as the boats passed.

Coins splashed into the water. The wood crackled and

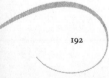

buckled. And the crowd cheered, and wept, and waved the old court away.

My carriage rattled through the streets after the funeral. The horses plodded so slowly that I could have walked faster myself. I sat alone in an open-topped carriage as crowds of people pressed around me. I had assumed—naively, it seemed—that most people would be by the boats, giving me a quiet journey home. But either people had chosen to wait here, or they had left the funerals before me, because the streets were packed now.

I forced myself to take a deep breath. Fitzroy had been wrong here, too. The nobles might have been too consumed by grief to watch me, but many people weren't. The crowds stretched on forever, tens of thousands of them, each with their own voice, their own thoughts, their own reasons to reject me.

People were shouting different things at me, but all the voices mixed together, the words indistinguishable beyond vague cries of "Your Majesty!"

Then something wet splatted against my face. I flinched away, my hand flying up to rub my cheek. Sticky red liquid clung to my fingers and dripped onto the blue silk of my dress, as another tomato splattered against my shoulder. I looked up, my heart firing into overdrive.

"Long live the queen!" a woman said, as she hurled a rotten turnip at the carriage. It struck the door and exploded on impact. The rest of the crowd shifted away from the group as my guards advanced, grabbing the protestors by the arms.

"Long live the queen!" they all shouted again, voices ringing together as they were dragged away. I wiped my cheek with shaking hands. What had I done to earn that? Rotten fruit was a huge step down from an attempted poisoning, but those people must still despise me, to risk themselves in that display.

My carriage plodded on, and I leaned forward slightly, straining to hear the shouts of the crowd. They all still blurred together, but I could make out a few words, being said over and over by different people. *Money* was one. *Curfew.*

I spun around to look at the people I'd just passed. A woman must have realized that the crowd had my attention, because she leaped forward, grasping for my hand. "Your Majesty!" she said. "Your Majesty, please. We couldn't pay the funeral fee, and my husband has been arrested, please, let him go. We can't afford it, truly we can't, but no one will listen—"

Her pleas were cut off as a guard grabbed her and wrenched her away.

"Wait!" I said. "What funeral fee?" But the carriage continued on, the woman almost out of earshot. "Stop," I said to the driver. "Stop, I have to speak to that woman."

"I'm sorry, Your Majesty," the driver said. "It wouldn't be safe."

"That doesn't matter. I need—" But the woman had been swallowed by the crowd again, and the carriage was relentless, plowing its way down the street.

I turned to look ahead again, feeling suddenly sick. I had no idea what the woman had been talking about, but I should have. I was queen, and people were getting arrested in my name, because they couldn't afford to pay for—for all this? And no one had told me?

The words hit me like a punch to the chest. I was queen, and I had no idea what was happening in my kingdom, beyond the Fort's walls. I'd been concerned with the murder, and with the nobles, while my advisers were doing things in my name, making decisions that changed people's lives. No one had told me about a curfew. No one had told me about a funeral fee. I hadn't known to ask, but I should have. It was my responsibility now, but I hadn't recognized it.

Like the jewels in the ships. I'd looked at them, not an hour ago, and thought about how wasteful they were. How people would drown in the river to find them. I'd thought it, and I'd done nothing, even though I was the one person with the power to change it. If people drowned in the river, they should blame me. If we didn't have enough money to fund the kingdom after throwing all those gemstones away, that was my fault.

I hadn't thought. I was spending all my time worrying about murders and nobles, a single threat and a couple of hundred people at most, when hundreds of thousands of people filled the kingdom, their lives relying on whatever I did.

And no, I hadn't made any of these decisions. I hadn't even

known they were being made. But I was *queen*. Ignorance wasn't an excuse.

As soon as my carriage stopped in front of the Fort, I leaped out and marched through the front gates. I had to find my father. I had to speak to him.

I didn't have to search for long. He was waiting for me in the corridor. "Freya!" he said. "What happened?"

"I need to speak to you. Right now."

"About the tomatoes? Freya, what—"

"Right now." I strode over to a side room and yanked open the door. I was almost shaking with anger. I was failing, and my father was letting that happen. He was treasurer, wasn't he? And he hadn't told me. *He hadn't told me.*

"What's the funeral fee?" I said, leaving the door to hang ajar behind us.

My father frowned, like he still couldn't understand what this was about. "It's a fee, Freya. To pay for the funerals."

"I never agreed to a funeral fee."

"We needed to fund the funerals somehow. Freya, why are you asking me about this?"

"A woman grabbed me in the street." My voice was shaking. My whole body was shaking. "She said she couldn't afford to pay the funeral fee, so her husband was arrested."

My father nodded. "We have to be fair to everyone, Freya. Everyone must contribute. There must be consequences if they refuse."

"They're not refusing if they can't afford to pay! Are you actually saying that you're arresting people for being unable to help fund a funeral where we burned silks and threw hundreds of jewels into the river?"

"May I remind you, Freya," my father said, his voice sharp now, "that you are the one who wanted us to involve all of the dead in the funeral? That was not cheap. If all the city's dead were included, all the city must pay for it."

"But it wasn't all the city! These were nobles who died because they ate a cake that was literally *made of gold*. And then we say we can't afford their funerals, so people in the city have to go hungry to pay for it?"

My father rested a hand on my shoulder. He looked annoyed now, as though I were the one being unreasonable. "Freya, calm down. You don't know what you are talking about."

"If I don't, it's because you kept this a secret from me. *I* am the queen. *Me*. You are not to impose any more fees—any more laws—without my explicit agreement. Do you understand?"

"Freya—"

"Do you understand?" My anger was spilling out, washing all shyness away. My father had betrayed me in this. He'd done an awful thing, and claimed it was in my name, and I couldn't let it happen again, not ever.

"I am your father, Freya."

"And I am the queen. Either you agree that all *my* laws will pass by *me*, or I will find a new treasurer."

My father stared at me.

"This woman was taken by the guards. I want her and her husband freed. And the fee will be returned to *every* commoner who paid it."

"Freya—"

"All of them."

My father's eyes glinted with fury. "We will discuss it at the next council meeting, Your Majesty."

"Yes, we will discuss the progress you've made tomorrow. And bring me a copy of Gustav's book then, too. I need it." I wouldn't let my councillors keep me ignorant any longer.

I spun back to the door, and jumped. Madeleine Wolff stood there, hand raised ready to knock. "I'm sorry to interrupt, Your Majesty," she said, "but they're waiting for you in the hall, and I heard you needed to change. I came to help, but if it is a bad time—"

"No," I said. I took a deep breath, forcing the anger down, away. "No, we're finished here. Thank you."

Madeleine followed me up to my rooms in silence. When we reached my bedchamber, she stepped back, looking over my dress. "This will have to go," she said. "But if we dab at your hair, and rearrange it slightly, I think we can get away without washing it. Otherwise you'll be hours before dinner."

She searched through my wardrobe for something else I could wear. The choice couldn't have been particularly inspiring for a girl like her. A few of my old dresses, a few of the queen's dresses that we didn't know what to do with, and the four or five new dresses that had already been completed by the sleep-deprived seamstresses. "I was going to ask you if you wanted blue or yellow, but it seems we won't have that choice." She leaned back, head tilted in thought. "Red," she said finally. "Like sunrise. You'll blend in with all the yellow, but still stand out. And this neckline will look perfect on you if we add a single chain."

She pulled the dress out of the wardrobe and nearly stumbled over Dagny. The cat had appeared out of nowhere, and was now sniffing around her feet. "Oh," Madeleine said. "Hello, beautiful."

"That's Dagny," I said.

"Dagny," she murmured, bending down to stroke her. She was slightly tentative, as though unsure what Dagny would do. Probably a normal reaction for someone not used to cats, but a strange one to see from the ever-poised Madeleine Wolff. Dagny arched her back and twisted her head, demanding more attention, and Madeleine smiled. "Oh, aren't you wonderful!"

"Why are *you* helping me?" I asked. "I mean—is Naomi all right?"

"Naomi is still by the river." Madeleine stood. "Her brother died at the banquet, didn't he? This morning must have been difficult for her. I thought I could help, in her place."

"You noticed she didn't come back?"

"I notice a lot of things. And, I admit, I've been wanting

the chance to talk to you again. Maybe even talk about fashion?" She draped the red dress on the back of a chair and moved to stand behind me. "You have a different kind of beauty from Queen Martha, I think. I'd love to see what we could do with it." She began to unfasten the back of my dress while I frowned. What could I even say to that? It was obviously flattery—"different kind of beauty" was code for "not pretty," I knew—but even so . . .

"Why did you warn me about your cousin? At the banquet last night."

Madeleine walked over to the side table, where a bowl of water still waited from this morning. She dipped a sponge in. "I thought you needed to know. I don't have anything to tell you specifically, but . . . I am wary of him. He's been so angry since the king died. Not entirely like himself. He is looking for enemies in every shadow, and since you are now the queen . . . he has been assessing you. But not accurately, or I don't believe so. I don't think he will do anything foolish, but I thought you should know. So that you can be wary, too."

"So that I can appease him, you mean?" How could I appease someone who suspected me of mass murder?

"No. I think, were he in his usual mind, he would appreciate you. But he is not in his usual mind. Just . . . be patient with him. He is an intelligent ally, once he is willing to listen. I hope he can see you, as I have."

"You think you see the real me?"

She laughed lightly. "I do not know whether I should say this, Your Majesty, but you are incredibly easy to read. You don't try to hide your feelings, not when they count. For someone like Sten, used to everyone lying around him, that might look like a lie, too. Another trick. But it is refreshing, Your Majesty. Or at least I find it so."

She dabbed at my cheek, peering close as she worked. "I heard what you said before," she continued. "About the fee. I think you're very brave."

"Brave?"

"Yes. It can't be easy, to stand up to your father and your advisers and everything that's come before. But you did."

"It's not bravery. It's just the right thing to do."

"Not everyone would see it that way."

I bit my lip as she tilted my chin, dabbing the sponge behind my ear. "So your advisers didn't tell you?" she said. "About the fee?" When I hesitated, she added, "I didn't mean to eavesdrop, Your Majesty, but I couldn't help overhearing."

Then there was no point lying to her. "No. They didn't."

"People will always try to see their will done, when things change like this. They want influence for themselves, I suppose. But you have good instincts, Freya. You can make things right."

"And what about you?" I said. Anger still brewed inside me, making me bold. "What do you want to influence?"

"I want to make things better," she said. "Nothing more or less than that."

★ ★ ★

The feast seemed to go on for hours, despite the fact that nobody ate a bite. People whispered together, their voices a harsh buzz, and I tried to eat, forcing the pheasant down my throat. But I couldn't stop thinking about what I'd seen in the city. What else had I missed, while I sat blindly in this castle, worrying about speeches and jewels? People had been shouting so many things, too many to make the words out . . . what other crimes had been committed in my name, without me knowing at all?

I'd been so wrong. Everything I thought I knew was shattering away. I'd thought all the old courtiers were callous and selfish and shallow, but just a few days had taught me how unfair and judgmental I'd been. And then I'd thought that a ruler's job was to lead the *court*, with barely a thought for the kingdom beyond. Perhaps King Jorgen hadn't thought about the kingdom, either, but that was why he had been a bad king, wasteful and ridiculous and *wrong*. This job was far more than learning how to speak in front of crowds and perfecting my smiles. I held everyone's fates in my hands. And I'd made things worse for them. I'd been so blind.

When the so-called feast ended, we had more entertainment, more forced conversations, before we finally, finally retired for the day. Naomi was asleep when I found her, curled in a ball in bed with her back to the door. I tried to sit in my chair with Dagny, to rest and recover now that the funerals were finally over, but my head was too full of thoughts to sit still. The moment I stopped moving, all the day's discoveries crawled through me, the horror of the funerals, the number of the dead, the pain I'd caused because I hadn't been paying attention. My eyes ached with exhaustion, but I couldn't possibly sleep. Things were so confused now.

So, once again, I headed down to my laboratory, desperate to do something productive.

And once again, Fitzroy was already there. My chest tightened at the sight of him, the way his presence filled the room. "You couldn't sleep?" I asked, as I closed the door behind me.

"No."

"Me either."

He had said good-bye to his father today. He had said good-bye to everything he knew. And then he had come *here*.

He didn't have anywhere else to go.

"All right," I said softly. "Where shall we begin?"

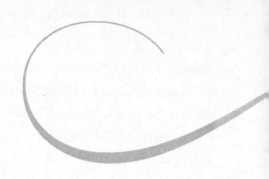

SIXTEEN

THE TESTS DID NOT GO WELL. THE ARSENIC STUB-
bornly refused to dissolve in most acids. It did vanish, with a
little nudging, in spirit of niter, and with no nudging at all in
spirits of salt, but I couldn't smell or see anything to identify it.
It might have had a detectable *taste*, but I wasn't so far gone that
I would willingly put arsenic *and* acid in my mouth, not even
for answers.

Yet despite the lack of progress, despite my exhaustion, the
evening felt like a success. Fitzroy's presence was soothing, even
as it set my nerves on edge, and I found myself trusting him

again, letting all my worries spill into the air between us.

"You didn't know," he told me, as I shared my fears. "But you do now. That's what matters."

And maybe I was just desperate for comfort, but I believed him.

When the council meeting began the following morning, I was ready. Drained from lack of sleep, heart stuttering with nerves, but resolved.

"Every new law must go through me," I said. My voice only slightly shook. "I need to approve every tax, and every big expenditure."

"But Your Majesty," Thorn said. "That will be incredibly time consuming. That's why you have us as advisers."

"I have advisers to advise me," I said. "Not to rule for me. And these secret changes are unacceptable."

"They were not secret, Freya," my father said. "You knew what we were doing. We just did not inform you of the how."

"So now you will. Taxing the people for the court's funerals? Arresting them when they can't pay? And I heard something about a curfew?"

"Necessary, Your Majesty," Norling said, "while we investigate the murders. We need to ensure that people remain in their homes, so they cannot scheme at night."

"Then people will just scheme during the day!"

They were all looking at me like I was a spoiled child,

throwing a tantrum because I didn't want a nap. All except Holt. He watched me with steady eyes, nodding slightly. He did not speak.

"All the *how* will go through me from now on," I said. "And we have to repay the funeral fee. Say it was a mistake."

"Your Majesty—"

"I told you, Freya," my father said. "That will be impossible. We must pay for the funerals somehow, and they were incredibly expensive, as is our investigation of the murder. We do not have the money."

"Then dredge the river," I said. "Hunt down the funeral boats. There were enough jewels there to pay for everything else a hundred times over. If we are poor, we shouldn't be throwing jewels away."

"Your Majesty," Holt said slowly, "I am not sure that is wise. It may be seen as an insult to the court. Those jewels were sent off in honor of the dead. It may be wasteful, but—"

"The dead can't use jewels. We can."

The more I spoke, the more irrational I felt, as they watched me with raised eyebrows and poorly disguised disbelief. But no matter how they spun things, they couldn't charge the city's poor to pay for a funeral where hundreds of gemstones were thrown away. I wouldn't let that be how my rule began.

"Your Majesty," Norling said, leaning forward slightly. "May I make a suggestion? There is distrust in the city for you, as you have seen. And if you do this, there will be distrust in the nobles, as well. It might be best to organize a distraction. An open trial, for those who tried to poison you, and other criminals we have apprehended recently. Show people that justice still rules in this city."

If people thought the laws were unjust, having a trial wouldn't help. But it would give me, and everyone else, a chance to see exactly what was going on. "Yes," I said. "All right."

"Perhaps Her Majesty should make sure she knows what her laws *are*," Sten said softly, "before she rules on them."

I stared at him. "I understand the laws," I said quietly. "I just expect people to tell me when they start manipulating them."

"Then perhaps you understand that we are not used to a tyrant for a ruler. King Jorgen listened to his advisers. And to his friends."

"It's hard to listen to your advisers when they don't tell you anything."

"Yes," he said. He didn't look away. "Yes, I suppose it is."

He suspects me, I thought again. It was the only way to explain that look of careful assessment, the distrust and dislike lurking behind his eyes.

"Pay back the money," I said. "That's my final decision."

My father escorted me after the meeting, his hand tight around my arm. "You are being too rash, Freya," he said, in a low voice, once we were out of sight of the others.

I clenched my fists, digging my nails into my palms. "It isn't rash to treat people fairly."

"This decision will have consequences. Your council are supposed to be here protecting you from that, but if you plan to ignore us—"

"I'm not ignoring you," I said. "You are the ones who've been ignoring me. I just—" I closed my eyes, all the fight rushing out of me. "It's one thing to pretend to be someone else, when it's speeches, and dresses, and balls. It's another when it affects *people*. When people are suffering from decisions that I hate. I can't—I can't do that."

"This will affect *you*, Freya." He stopped and placed his hands on my shoulders, leaning closer, beseeching. "Sometimes, rulers have to do things that they don't like, because it's the best of bad options. Because fewer people will suffer than if you take the other course."

"But you didn't even present me with options," I said, pulling out of his grip. "You just decided for me, and people hate me for it. I would never have agreed to this if I knew. *Never*."

"Freya—"

"How can I trust you now? You were already willing to lie to me. How can I know you're not manipulating me, as well?" I shook my head. "I can't trust you. I have to make my decisions for myself." I stepped back. "Have that book sent to my laboratory. And I'll see you at the trials tomorrow."

"Freya!"

I walked away.

The book, when it arrived, wasn't much of a book at all. I'd been expecting an ancient tome, with hundreds of pages of philosophy and religion. Instead, *Gustav's Treatise* consisted of roughly six leaves of paper, tied at the spine with string. Naomi and I read it together at the laboratory's central table, and I scribbled notes as we went.

The essay inside wasn't what I'd been expecting, either. Gustav had been an exiled radical, a man who despised the nobility and everything we stood for, but his book was hardly a call to mass murder. He claimed that the nobles originally appeared as false heirs to the lost Forgotten, people eager to fill the vacuum they'd left and claim their influence for themselves, but their descendants were now simply misguided, not wicked. The power to convince the Forgotten to return lay in all our hands, through good work and humility. We must purge the corruption from *ourselves*, and be examples to others, for only true atonement in each person's heart would be enough to win favor again.

His ultimate goal, he wrote near the end, was to break down the line between the nobility and the people, as we were all equal under the Forgotten's divine influence. But he recognized that would be a long and difficult path, and a more pious and thoughtful nobility would be the first step—a movement that must come from the nobility themselves.

And this, apparently, was enough to see him exiled and his work banned forever.

I couldn't imagine how this was connected to the attacks. But Holt had said the work had been twisted over time, forced to mean whatever people wanted it to mean. People could have taken the words about pretenders and forgotten the rest. Even so . . .

I leaned back, dropping my pen on the paper. "I don't know," I said. "I can't think."

Naomi stretched beside me. "It's a hundred years old, and illegal to own. It makes sense that it doesn't tell you much about what these people want."

"They call themselves the Gustavites! They should be following what he said, shouldn't they?"

"Or maybe they are," Naomi said softly. "They aren't exactly around to answer questions, are they? Maybe your advisers are wrong about them."

"But what about the woman who tried to poison me?"

"She might not represent the rest of them. She might have nothing to do with them."

And I had thought it was unlikely, when I first heard the accusation. My head pounded. There were so many things to worry about, so many threats. I could barely keep track of all the strands, let alone see how they tangled together. "A break," I said, pressing the heels of hands against my eyes. "Let's have a break."

Naomi stood and stretched again. "You must be tired," she said. "You haven't been getting enough sleep."

"Who needs sleep?"

"Where did you go last night? I came out to look for you, but . . ." She shrugged. "You weren't there."

I looked up again. If she'd wanted to talk to me, on the night of the funerals, and I wasn't there . . . "I'm sorry. I thought you were asleep."

"I woke up. It's all right, I was just wondering. Were you working?"

I nodded. "Not that I made much progress." I drummed my fingers on the table, wondering how much to tell her. But my conversations weren't secrets. There was nothing unmentionable about them. "Fitzroy was there."

"Fitzroy?" She shot me a sideways glance. "Is that why you didn't make much progress?"

"Naomi!" I stared at her, and she grinned.

"Well, you've never mentioned Fitzroy before. Last I heard, you didn't know him at all. And now he's helping you in your lab? How suspicious."

"Suspicious? You think he's manipulating me?"

"Noooo." She drew out the word, the vocal equivalent of an eye roll. "I'm just wondering why you never mentioned that before. Why you're keeping secrets, hmm? *Why* you didn't get any work done, maybe?"

"It's nothing like that. It's—new. We talked, like I said, about the murders, and . . ." How could I possibly describe it? "He wasn't what I expected."

"So you invited him back to your lab?" She still spoke in that teasing, singsong voice, elongating her words, eyes dancing.

"He was just there, when I went to work the night before the funerals. And then last night, too. I think he's lonely."

"Yes, that's why he keeps coming to your lab. He's lonely." She leaned in closer. "I think he likes you."

I could feel myself blushing, but it was ridiculous. Nonsense. "Naomi, you haven't even seen him."

"As though he could possibly resist."

"He could easily resist." But my stomach twisted as I said it. Fitzroy didn't like me, not like that, it was completely nonsensical. We were *working*.

"Wait," Naomi said. "You actually like him. I was just teasing, but you actually like him. I can tell by your face."

"I can't like him. I barely know him."

"But you *like* him." The grin melted off Naomi's face, and she sat back on her stool. "Oh, Freya, be careful," she said, in her normal, steady voice again. "He's the old king's son."

"I know that." I scraped my fingers through my hair. "He's just—not who I thought he was."

"Who did you think he was?"

"Just—nobody. An idiot. You saw how he acted in court."

"And who *is* he?"

The answer was too big, too nebulous, to put into words. "Fitzroy," I said. "Just—Fitzroy."

"Freya—" Her voice rose in warning, but I shook my head.

"We should get back to work. We have a lot of research to do."

"All right," she said slowly. "But if you want to talk—"

"I know." But not then. Her teasing had knocked something loose inside me, like the realization that your finger hurt after someone pointed out it was bleeding. The knowledge buzzed at the edge of my thoughts, but I didn't have time to examine it now, not with so much else going on.

I barely knew Fitzroy. He was an interesting person. That was all.

I had far more important things to worry about than him.

SEVENTEEN

THE TRIALS STARTED EARLY THE FOLLOWING morning.

I'd expected more of a mix of people, from what Norling had said, but only courtiers waited in the throne room, sitting on wooden benches. An aisle passed between them, leading to the throne. My council sat behind a large table, facing the rest of the court, and guards lined the walls.

This time, at least, someone had taken my skirts into consideration. I still wore about ten layers of them, but the wires were missing, making me look like a confection, but a human-sized one, and one that fit in the throne.

Even then, it was lucky I was tall. My long legs only just reached the floor when I sat. I forced myself to sit straight. I couldn't let the throne overwhelm me. I had to look like I was in control.

Once everyone was settled and Norling had talked through the formalities, the guards led the server of the poisoned tarts into the room. She was trembling. Her black hair had matted around her shoulders, and she looked at the ground as she walked, chains rattling between her wrists.

"Felicia Cornwell," Norling said. "You have admitted to attempting to poison your queen. If you name your co-conspirators, Her Majesty may see to have mercy on you."

The woman continued to tremble. "I didn't work with anyone. I acted alone."

"You worked alone?" Norling said. "You found the poison alone, prepared the food alone, broke into the castle alone, got into Her Majesty's rooms alone. Is that what you are claiming?"

"I was already a servant at the palace," she said. "But—yes. I worked alone."

"Tell us who you worked with," Norling said, "or I will be forced to punish you for treason."

The woman stared at the floor, her face ghost white, but she did not flinch. "I worked alone."

But Norling was asking the wrong question, I thought. We could find out who she worked with ourselves, with the right information. If we wanted to understand the attacks, she was the only one who could help us. I leaned forward, steeling myself to speak before the crowd. "Why did you attack me?"

Norling stared at me. "Your Majesty?"

I continued to address the woman. "You must have had a reason for trying to kill me. You knew you'd end up here, whether or not you succeeded. You must have had a reason."

The girl remained silent. I stared at her, willing her to speak. If she would just tell us, if she would just *explain* . . .

"Mistress Cornwell," Norling said. "Her Majesty asked you a question."

"Because of this!" she burst out. "All of this! The court with all its gold, while people outside it starve. You spend more on *sweets* than most people have to live on their whole lives. The Forgotten *want* to return, the deaths were a sign of that, but until we burn out this corruption, they never will!"

"Do all the Gustavites believe that?"

The woman's expression closed off again. She stared at me again, her face red.

"His book—it doesn't mention murder," I said, trying to keep my voice as friendly as possible. I couldn't let it shake. "I read it, to try and understand what you were fighting for. But it was a pretty peaceful book. Do you really think he wants you to do this?"

"Your Majesty—" Norling said, in a warning voice, but the woman seemed angrier now.

"We must burn out this corruption," she said, meeting my

gaze. Words from the book. But incomplete ones.

"We must burn out this corruption in *ourselves*," I corrected. "Change must come from within. He never thought the Forgotten wanted us to become murderers. Has your group read his book, or just heard about it?"

"Most of them are fools," she snapped, so angry now she didn't seem to notice her mistake. "They think we can do this peacefully, and they're wrong. He didn't know what we would be up against. But the rest of us—we know. And so if I'm going to die—" Her voice caught on the word. "If I'm going to die, I want to do it stopping all of you."

"You're not going to die. We don't execute people in Epria."

The silence that followed was too sharp, too loud. "Your Majesty," Norling said, rather carefully. "Epria has not executed a criminal in many decades, it is true, but that does not mean we should not respond to treason. One attack against you would be enough for that. And this woman may have been involved in murdering your predecessor, in slaughtering this entire court."

"I was not!" The woman's whole body shook. "That wasn't me!"

"I find that hard to believe."

"It was an opportunity," she said, "but I wasn't involved in the murders. You must believe me!"

"I believe you," I said. Her surprise and panic seemed clear enough. "And there is no execution in this kingdom."

"Your Majesty," Holt said. "Regardless of anything else,

regardless of her beliefs, this woman attempted to kill you. If not for your quick thinking—your divinely bestowed suspicion—you and several others may have died. We cannot let this go unpunished."

"It won't go unpunished. Where do attempted murderers usually go? Is it Rickstone Castle?" An isolated stone fortress on the moors, a good hundred miles from the capital, and perhaps fifty from the nearest town. It had been built by a rather eccentric noble, desperate for quiet and increasingly convinced that someone might attack him to take that solitude away. He had no relatives, no friends, and so the crown had taken the castle when he died and turned it into a prison. It was, I'd heard, nicer than the dungeons of the Fort. It had never been intended for such grim purposes. "Mistress Cornwell will be sent there, as she has confessed," I said. "No one will be executed."

"Your Majesty!" Norling said, as furious whispers whipped through the crowd. "I am your minister of justice, and it's my responsibility—"

"And I'm *queen*," I said. "We're not executing anybody."

"No executions?" Sten stood. It was the loudest I'd ever heard him speak. His eyes were black and hard, and all his usual steadiness was gone. Fury radiated from him, his hands clenched into fists. "This woman helped kill most of the court. She killed her king, and the queen, and hundreds of others. And you're going to show her mercy?"

"She didn't kill them!" I said. "She denied it, at least, and she happily admitted to attacking *me*. We can't execute her for that."

"Torsten," Holt said, his voice soothing. "You are still griev-ing for your friends, as we all are. But Queen Freya has chosen mercy, until we have indisputable proof of guilt. It would not do for us to lash out in grief and destroy a hundred years of peace."

"The peace was broken when filth like *this* attacked the king." Sten's fists twitched. He shoved his way to the aisle and strode out of the room. The crowd whispered in his wake.

My hands shook, but I would not move. "No executions."

Holt nodded. "As you wish, Your Majesty."

The accused was led from the room, and my advisers had a hurried conference before addressing the guards again. While they talked, a few other nobles followed Sten, whispering as they went.

Next the guards led a man into the room. He looked about my father's age, with a patchy mustache and gray speckled in his hair.

"Henry Goodram," Norling said, reading from a large sheet of paper before her. "Accused of forging diamonds, endangering the stability of the kingdom for his own personal gain, at a time when our kingdom needs its stability the most."

"Begging your pardon," the man said, "but I didn't know what was going to happen at that ball when I did it." A few nobles behind him leaned forward in interest, but some of the others stood up and started drifting out of the room. I guess they had anticipated more discussions of murder, not jewel forgery.

"How could I have known? If I had, I wouldn't have—"

"You expect us to believe that you didn't *intend* to take advantage of the situation?" Norling said. "That you only had innocent intentions?"

"I didn't know they weren't real diamonds," he said quickly, as though he hadn't basically admitted his own guilt ten seconds before. "Someone sold 'em to me, the price was too good to be true, maybe, but I didn't know they were fakes."

"Were they convincing?" I asked. After all the fuss over the poverty of the kingdom and the need to drape ourselves in jewels, realistic fakes might be useful. They must have been good, if they posed such a risk to the economy. Or did they just pose a risk to the nobility's pride?

"See them for yourself," Norling said. She gestured at a man to her left, who walked forward and presented me with a tiny handful of jewels. I held one up to inspect it in the light. It gleamed a thousand colors, shifting as I moved. I wasn't exactly an expert on diamonds, but it looked realistic to me. Someone like Madeleine Wolff would probably spot its inadequacies immediately, but I would never have noticed.

"I didn't know!" the man said. "You must believe me, Your Majesty. I didn't know they weren't real."

"But you did, sir," I said. I shifted in my seat. His rambling desperation made my skin itch, horrified that *I* was the cause, but if he admitted to it himself, I couldn't exactly let him go. "It was the first thing you said. *You didn't know what would happen at the ball when you did it."*

"I meant—I might have suspected they were fakes," he said. "But I'm not an expert, so I went on what I'd been told. I wasn't involved."

I looked back at the diamonds. They sparkled in the light, revealing colors at their hearts. Just like real diamonds. "How were they made?" I asked slowly.

"From glass, Your Majesty," Norling said. "With a lot of lead added to create that gleam. They make a paste, I believe. We're not certain of the exact method."

"They're very convincing," the accused man said quickly. "Anyone would believe they were real."

"Do we have any more proof?"

"Yes, Your Majesty." Norling picked up another sheet of paper and talked through the investigation, those who had spoken against Henry Goodram, how the trail for the source had turned cold with him. Add in his own slip-up here, and the truth seemed obvious.

"I will not go against my advisers' recommendations," I said carefully, hoping they were the right words. "But these are impressive fakes. Tell us how they're made, exactly how, and we'll consider that when we—with the punishment. We'll take it into consideration."

Someone in the crowd laughed. "Is Her Majesty planning to get into the fake diamond market herself?"

"If we can understand how fakes are made, perhaps we can

use that knowledge. It could help us identify them. Or they could be useful in some other way." Like maintaining the extravagant look of the court without it costing endless riches. "Knowledge is a good thing."

"Including criminal knowledge, Your Majesty?" Norling asked.

"It shows intelligence. Ingenuity. We need those things."

"But I didn't make them, Your Majesty. I swear I didn't."

"That's my offer," I said, quieter than I would have liked. "Do with it what you will."

The trials went on for hours. The nobles left the room in dribs and drabs until only a couple remained. Madeleine stayed through the entire thing, her hands settled carefully in her lap, and Fitzroy stayed, too. I tried not to look at him. My conversation with Naomi was still too fresh, and I felt a jolt of uncertainty every time he caught my eye. I had enough to think about, with the parade of cases presented to me.

Norling was the chief of justice, and she was the one responsible for making decisions, but the word of a queen could always overrule her, and I wanted to be certain that everything was fair. I had the power to dole out justice, or to destroy someone's life, and I wanted to do the best that I could. I wanted to do better than my best.

But hours of speaking to people, of being watched and measured, left me feeling scraped raw inside, too tired to think. The moment the trials ended, I hurried away with my guards, avoiding Fitzroy's gaze again.

I'd been fascinated by the fake diamonds, the way the light shifted and changed color inside them. I'd always heard that those colors were part of diamonds' hearts, but if a mixture of glass and lead could have the same effect, perhaps there was more to it. I'd asked that they be sent to my laboratory, and they were waiting on the center table when I returned. I picked one up and watched the colors again. Was it something to do with the light?

I lit a candle and held the jewel up to the flame. Again, the colors shifted inside. I'd left a piece of paper on the table, and the colors danced there as well, forming a rainbow.

I looked across at my supplies on the other side of the room, and then stopped. Something was wrong. I'd organized my metals in order of reactivity, to make my experiments easier, with the uncertain and untested ones in alphabetical order at the end. Now they were out of place. Mostly the same, but a few jumbled or reversed.

Someone had been in here.

It could have been Fitzroy. Naomi knew to keep things organized in the lab, but Fitzroy might not have known the system. Yet the hairs on my arm stood on end. I knew, *knew*, something was wrong.

I hurried over and inspected the jars. Nothing was missing, as far as I could tell. But someone had been looking for something—

I seized the jar of arsenic. It looked the same, though. That was good. No one had taken any.

Why hadn't I been locking the door? I'd trusted that no one would really care to interrupt me here, but I should have realized the risk the moment Fitzroy first appeared. These chemicals should be locked away.

The door creaked. I spun around, but it was just Naomi, peering into the gloom.

"Freya? Are you all right?"

"I'm fine. Are you all right?"

She nodded. Then she glanced at the jars scattered across the countertop. "What are you doing? You'd glare at me if I made a mess like that."

"So you haven't been here today? Reorganizing these?"

"No. I wouldn't touch them, you know that. Maybe Fitzroy was here?"

"Yes," I said. "Maybe." But I didn't quite believe it.

Naomi sat on the stool and pulled my notes toward her. "I think we need to get started on talking to more people," she said. "Now that the Gustavites and Fitzroy are off our list. Fitzroy is off our list, isn't he?"

I nodded.

"Sten acted so strangely at the trials. I know he lost his friends, but—he's acting oddly. One of us should really speak to him."

"And you think he'll tell me anything, after that?"

Naomi shrugged. "He might. If you're direct with him. Or I could try and speak with him."

"Somehow," I said, "I doubt most people will be as willing to spill their secrets as Fitzroy was."

"He spilled all his secrets, did he?" Naomi said, giving me a slight sideways grin.

"Shush, you." I joined her by the notes. "I suppose you're right, though. My advisers haven't found any more evidence or linked it to anyone. It feels like it *has* to be someone here. Sten must have seen something."

"Can we find out who ordered the cake?" Naomi asked. "I know sometimes people would pay for particular dishes. As a gift to the king. If we knew who it was—"

"It was my father." We both jumped. Fitzroy stood in the doorway. "Your guards let me pass," he said, in answer to my unspoken question. "Since they see me so often here, anyway."

"So much for security." I stared at him. He hadn't heard what we'd said before, Naomi's jokes, had he? "What was your father?"

"He was the one who arranged that cake. Do you think anyone else could afford it? That's why it was such an insult when I didn't get any. It was for people he liked only. Or at least people he didn't despise."

"He did always like spectacle," Naomi said.

"But he usually preferred to live to appreciate it." I bit my lip. "If there were any official records, my advisers would have gone through them already." Assuming they could be trusted.

"They won't have everything," Fitzroy said. "My father always locked his study, and that's where he kept everything not *entirely* official. Personal letters, notes he was working on, things like that."

"And I suppose you know where to find the key?"

He smiled. "Of course. It was my father's secret study. I'm an expert at breaking in."

"Who knew you had a history of crime?"

"Freya, there's so much you don't know about me."

Naomi grinned at me, and I quickly looked away. "So we should go," I said, all businesslike. "See what we can find there."

"Your guards aren't going to let you just wander back to the palace alone," Fitzroy said. "I'll go. No one cares if I leave the Fort. I'll collect everything I can find and bring it back to the lab."

It made sense. I didn't *like* it—staying here, waiting for someone else to bring information to me—but it made sense. "Good idea. Bring it back here, and we'll figure out what to do."

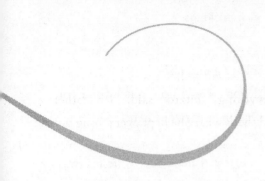

EIGHTEEN

I COULDN'T BREATHE. SOMETHING WAS PRESSING against my mouth, cutting off the air.

I jerked awake. A small shape loomed over me in the dark.

I tried to scream, but the sound was swallowed by the figure's hand, the cold rings pressing against my lips. The figure leaned closer, honey-brown hair catching the moonlight.

It was Madeleine Wolff.

"Shh." She glanced at the doorway. "You have to leave. Quickly. I'm going to move my hand now, but you can't make a sound." She took her hand away, and I scrambled out of bed, feet landing hard on the floor.

"Madeleine," I hissed. "What's going on?"

"You're being attacked. I don't know how much time you have, but you have to hide. Or run. Get out of here."

I froze. "Who's attacking?"

"My cousin. And his supporters. I managed to lie my way past your guards by pretending I was involved, but they're in on it, too, and they won't wait long. You have to move *now*."

I stared at her, fighting to understand. My mind was still fuzzy with sleep, and—Sten was attacking me? "Why did you come to warn me?" I said. "Why didn't you fetch more guards?"

"Because I don't know where they are, and I don't know which ones you can trust. Freya, that doesn't matter. We have to *leave*."

"We have to warn Naomi."

Madeleine scrambled after me. "They don't want to hurt Naomi. They want to hurt *you*. They're going to kill you." She grabbed my arm, her perfect painted nails digging into my skin. "Do you think you can fight them, Freya? You have to hide. Now."

It didn't make sense. Sten was trying to kill me? *Sten* had been the murderer? I pulled my arm out of Madeleine's grip and ran into Naomi's room. Naomi was still asleep, dark hair falling across her face.

"Naomi," I hissed. I shook her, making her hair shake. "Naomi, wake up."

Her arm flew out, knocking me away. She blinked. "Freya?" She scrambled up, shoving her hair away from her face. "What's wrong?"

"Madeleine says Sten is attacking. We have to leave." Back in my room, Madeleine clattered through the drawers of my dresser. She pulled out a long, delicate gold chain, with a ruby cut like a star. It was one of the jewels I'd worn at my coronation.

"Madeleine, what are you doing?"

"Let's hope you don't need this. But just in case—"

The front door rattled and slammed, and Madeleine jumped. "I wedged a chair against the door," she said. "But it's not going to hold them for long."

"There must be another way out of these rooms," Naomi said. "They're supposed to be safe for the king, aren't they?"

"If there are other ways out, I don't know them."

"There are storage rooms in the back," Naomi said. She hurried for the door. "Covered up. There must be something."

I nodded. Naomi led us out of the bedroom into the corridor, as the guards rammed on the door again.

Naomi grabbed my hand at that, squeezing painfully tight. She tugged me around the corner and into a room at the end of the corridor, before shutting the door quietly behind us.

The room was dark except for one sliver of moonlight, creeping in through the arrow-slit window. I could just make out the shapes of several large pieces of furniture, but Naomi seemed to know where she was going. She pulled me toward what appeared to be a wall in the dark, then reached out and opened a space where the door must have been.

"Wait!" I said. "Dagny! They'll hurt Dagny." I pulled my hand out of Naomi's grasp and turned back.

"Freya, wait—" But I'd already thrown open the door, and ran back into the corridor. I couldn't let them hurt Dagny. She relied on me to take care of her, and if they touched her . . .

I pulled open the door to my bedroom. Please let her be somewhere obvious, I thought. Please don't let her have wandered off.

But Dagny wasn't there. Not that I could see. I pulled back the blankets and peered at the top of the wardrobes, but there was no sign of her.

A door creaked. Someone was walking through the corridor.

I ducked and looked under the bed, but I couldn't see anything. Why was it so *dark*? "Dagny?" I hissed. "Dagny, where *are* you?"

A meow came from behind me. I spun around. Dagny leaped out of a slightly open drawer, her tail fluffed, eyes glowing. "Dagny!" I ran forward and scooped her up, pressing her fur against my nose. Dagny meowed again, and she whacked me on the chin with her paw.

"Queen Freya." I spun around. The black-haired guard, Reynold Milson, stood in the doorway. "Why don't you put the cat down, and come along with me now?"

I tightened my grip on Dagny. The only other way out of the room was into Naomi's bedroom, and that had no other door, no other means of escape. Which meant I had to speak, not run. "What do you want?"

He stepped closer, still blocking the doorway. "Come on, now. Let's not make it any harder than it needs to be."

I took a slight step back. If I could lure him closer, make him step fully into the room, I might be able to dart around him and escape into the corridor. But he would have allies, wouldn't he? Other people helping him. Should I pretend to surrender? Pretend to trust him, make him relax?

No. Madeleine had barricaded the door. He knew I was afraid of him.

"I take no pleasure in this," he said. "But justice must be done. You understand that, don't you?"

I shifted Dagny's weight, trying to free one of my hands. There was a heavy candlestick on the table on the side—if I could just reach it, if I could use it as a weapon . . .

Milson stepped closer again, and something glinted between us. A sword.

I couldn't fight a sword with a candlestick. But I wasn't going to go quietly, either. I took a small step to the side, trying to make out the shape in the corner of my eye without looking away from him.

More men would come. More people to drag me away. I couldn't fight them all. But that didn't mean I wasn't going to try. I snatched up the candlestick, feeling its weight, holding it between us.

"That isn't going to help you."

A loud crash shook the room, and he staggered forward.

Madeleine stood in the corridor, a candlestick raised above the guard's head, ready to strike again. I ran. The guard struck out with his sword, but his aim was slightly off, dazed by the attack, and I swung my own makeshift weapon wildly. It hit the blade with a shriek of metal on metal. The force of the blow knocked it from my hand, but I didn't pause to care. I twisted past him, and Madeleine grabbed my arm, hauling me away.

More shouting from down the corridor. If the guards had had any hope of being subtle, that crash would have destroyed it. More attackers would follow now.

Madeleine dragged me back into the room we had entered before. The lock clicked behind us.

"It won't hold them for long," Naomi said. She was pushing a huge shape forward, her voice straining with the effort. Madeleine darted forward to help. The furniture—some shelves, I thought—scraped against the floor. The door thudded as someone tried to open it from the other side. And then the shelves were wedged there, and we were running again, through the next door, and the next. We stopped in a room full of strange shapes—a storage room, maybe—slamming the door closed behind us. I clutched Dagny tight as Naomi and Madeleine maneuvered a cabinet in front of it.

"Is there a way out from here?" I asked.

"We don't know," Naomi said. "But it's safer than being out there."

"There has to be some sort of passage," Madeleine said. "We have to look."

But the darkness was everywhere. I bashed my leg on another piece of furniture as I pushed farther into the room and felt the walls for any kind of door, anything useful for hiding.

"You went back for the cat?" Madeleine said in disbelief. "You risked your life for the cat."

"Of course I did. She's my cat."

I hit my hip against the corner of a table, and fought the urge to swear. We couldn't hide in here. The attackers had seen us come in, they'd find us. How long would it take for the rest of my guards to realize something was amiss? Until morning? Or did they already know? Were they *all* against me?

I hoisted Dagny into the crook of my elbow so I could hold her with one hand, and began to search the room. Dagny meowed in my ear, her claws kneading my upper chest.

My fingers brushed behind worn tapestries, but I only found more stone. I found a wardrobe, but it was slightly away from the wall, with no secret passageways behind its doors. If there was another way out of this tower, it wasn't in this room. And the longer we spent searching, the less chance we had to form another plan, to hide, to do *something* . . .

"We have to go out of the front door," I said. "That's the only way out."

"But they're out there," Naomi hissed. "They want to kill you."

"And I won't hide in here until they break in. You heard Madeleine. No one's coming for us." I began to pace. "They won't expect us to burst out and run toward them—"

"Because it's suicide!"

"It'll give us an advantage."

"Against swords?"

"We have to do *something.*"

"Can you make something?" Naomi said. "A—a weapon, or a bomb, or something?"

"Not without my equipment. Not in the dark."

I glanced around the room again. The window was tiny. None of us would fit through it, even if we weren't high in the air. Even during daylight hours, the room would be dingy, too dark to properly see. "There have to be lanterns in here somewhere," I said. "And a way to light them. We have to find them."

We scrabbled against the walls again, hands sweeping over the tables, looking for any strange shapes that might provide light.

A metallic thud, and a hissed cursed from Naomi. "Here. But I knocked it over, I think the oil is pouring out."

"Then pick it up," Madeleine hissed back. "And light it."

"I can't see—"

I scrambled over, trying to balance Dagny with one hand as she began to squirm. The lantern was the usual oil sort, like thousands of others in the city. I reached under the base, brushing over the sandpaperlike material that coated it until I found the small compartment of matches. One scrape against the base, and the match was lit. Even that small amount of light seemed too bright in the darkness.

The glass door on the side was already open, so I tossed the match inside and slammed it closed against the rush of fire. It singed my fingers, and I flinched, but the lamp was lit, there was light in the room.

I passed it to Naomi so I could clutch Dagny closer to my chest. She was fond of hugs, for a cat, but not fond enough to put up with being held through all this noise and chaos. "Shh," I murmured, stroking her back. She nipped my wrist in protest.

Naomi raised the lamp higher. Now I could see her fearful face, Madeleine's stubborn calm—and another door, half concealed behind some crates.

"There!" I scrambled toward it. Naomi and Madeleine heaved the crates aside and pulled on the door handle. It resisted once, twice, sticking in the frame, but one final pull and it flew open, slamming into us.

The swinging light illuminated the space beyond the door at intervals. It was a narrow stone staircase, twisting down out of sight. Cobwebs stretched between the walls, and the worn steps were coated with dust. They looked like the slightest weight would make them crumble away.

"Go!" I said, jerking my head toward the space. Dagny squirmed again, hitting me in the chest with her tail, but I wasn't going to let go now. "Quickly."

They didn't argue. Madeleine ran ahead, and Naomi gestured for me to go between them before pulling the door closed.

The floor was like ice against my bare feet, and the autumn chill settled through my nightgown, making me shiver. Cobwebs tangled on my arms as we ran down and down, praying the staircase was safe, praying more men were not waiting wherever it let out, our elbows bashing against the jagged stone walls. The passage was clearly one of the oldest parts of the Fort, not renovated even after a thousand years.

Ahead, Madeleine gasped. Naomi raised the light higher.

Water filled the narrow corridor below. It did not look too deep, but that could be deceptive, especially in the dark. Who knew how many steps it covered before it reached the floor?

"It must have come in from the moat," I said. "Are we that far down?"

Madeleine stepped tentatively forward, holding her skirts high. She was wearing heels, I suddenly noticed. "There should have been a boat here," she said. "It would have been tied there, look." She gestured at a metal ring on the wall. Assumedly it had been there to stop the king from getting his feet wet if he ever had to flee his chambers. But there was no boat now. I peered into the darkness, as though it might be floating just out of reach, but no. Nothing.

"We'll have to swim," I said. Swim, with an oil lamp and a cat, in our nightgowns and Madeleine's heels. But we had to do it.

"Or not." Naomi followed the steps down, her white nightdress floating around her as the water rose to her knees, and then her waist, and then the bottom of her chest, and then . . . stopped. "We can walk. Come on."

I wasn't going to argue. I hoisted Dagny a little higher, but if the water reached Naomi's chest, it would only come up to my waist. We'd be safe, as long as it wasn't too full of disease. The water must have been down here a long time.

"It used to be deeper," I said, nodding at the walls. There were lines about a foot above our heads, a difference in the color of the stone. "It must have drained somehow." The water pushed against my waist, weighing me down, making every step a struggle. My white nightgown had puffed up around me. At least it was a fashionable size now, I thought distantly, and snorted despite myself.

Something skittered against the wall, and Dagny pricked up her ears. I didn't pause to see what it was.

We passed the ruins of a boat once the stairs were no longer in sight. At least, I assumed it had once been a boat. Only rotten scraps remained.

A few minutes beyond that, stairs rose ahead of us again,

eroded by the now-drained water. I stopped to listen. No voices, no signs of chaos ahead.

"Have we left the Fort?" I asked, as we picked our way onto the steps. The cold air hit me again, and I shivered. My skirt stuck to my skin, outlining my legs. Madeleine's silks were stained by the water, but they were less see-through, at least. And she still wore those heels, apparently without concern.

"I don't think so," she said, looking ahead. "I don't think we've gone far enough."

I looked back over the water. The tunnel had vanished into darkness again. No sign of pursuit.

"We could wait here," Naomi said, peering into the darkness as well. "It's probably safe."

"No," I said. "I want to see what's happening." I wouldn't wait here for them to find me. I strode up the steps, pressing my bare feet decisively into the stone.

The steps ended in a metal gate. It was locked, with a large padlock rusted shut across the handle, but the whole gate had warped with age. I shoved it with my shoulder, and it lurched, leaving a small gap. Another shove, and it bent sideways, leaving a space large enough to squeeze through. Naomi went first, her nightdress catching and tearing, and then she reached out to take Dagny before I climbed after her.

We emerged in the dungeons, tucked in one of the alcoves designed for guards. Everything was silent. "My lab," I said. "This way." We'd be able to find things to defend ourselves with there, chemicals and heavy instruments and things that made the eyes burn. But when we turned the corner, someone was already standing in the entrance to the lab. Madeleine raised her candlestick again. The figure turned at the sound of our approach.

It was Fitzroy.

"Freya!" he hissed. "You're all right. Where have you *been*?" It almost sounded like a reproach.

"I've been *running*," I said. "The guards turned on me, some of them attacked us in our rooms—"

"I know," he said. "I was looking for you! And then I saw your lab—"

"What do you mean?" He hesitated. I pushed past him.

It was chaos. Vials and jars had been smashed, their liquids and powders spreading across the counters. One patch of wood bubbled as what must have been acid ate away at it. My journals had been torn apart, pages now littering the floor. My weighing system was smashed, the metal dish above the fire ripped down and dented. My beautiful lab, all my work . . .

"Why? Why would they do this?"

"They're hunting for you," Fitzroy said. "To bring you to Sten. I guess when they didn't find you here—"

"How did *you* know?" That was suspicious, too. "How did you know to look for me?"

"They asked me to join them. They thought I'd be on their side, considering who my father was."

"And you didn't tell anyone?" Naomi said. "You didn't tell the guards?"

"I found out ten minutes ago," he snapped. "And all the guards I've met are part of it. I hoped I'd be able to find you and warn you. I told them I'd join them, and ran up to your rooms, but the guards were already inside, destroying things. I thought you were *dead*, Freya, or captured, until I realized they couldn't find you. So I thought you might be here. I came to warn you."

"They let you go?" I said. "After you said you'd join them?"

"I'm a familiar face at court, Freya. And they're saying you murdered my father, so you could take the throne for yourself. Of course they trust me."

"My father!" If they were after me, they must be willing to hurt him, too. I twisted out of the laboratory. "What happened to my father?"

"I don't know," Fitzroy said. I began to run down the corridor again, but Fitzroy grabbed my arm.

"If the wrong people see you, Freya, they'll kill you."

"And what happens when people find *him*?"

"Nothing as bad as if they find you. You're the queen, Freya."

"Apparently not," I said. "Not a welcome one."

"So stay out of their way." Fitzroy looked around. "We have to get you out of here. We don't know who we can trust. You have to leave."

"Leave?" I laughed. The sound echoed off the walls, a little desperate, a little hysterical. "Leave and go where? They'll hunt me down and kill me. The Fort is supposed to be the safest place in the kingdom!" If I left, I would no longer be queen, and I'd have no protection at all. I'd be even easier to kill.

I couldn't run. I'd just be murdered in the hills, or on the streets. I squeezed Dagny so close she meowed in protest again. "We have to defend the Fort. It's my only chance."

"Where are the other guards?" Naomi said. "They can't *all* have turned against us!"

"I assume they've been attacked, too," Fitzroy said. "That, or they've joined Sten. Many won't even be here—most don't live here."

So I was unlikely to get help from them. But I had to try. "Fitzroy, you go and find them. See if you can get any to help us. If they've all turned against us, pretend to be on their side until you can escape. They respect you."

He nodded. "What are you going to do?"

What *was* I going to do? I let out a long breath. I had to be calm. Logical. "I'm going to the throne room," I said. "If they want to kill the queen, they can do it while I'm sitting on the throne. See if they're brave enough then."

"Make them remember your power," Madeleine said softly. "Sten will hesitate at that."

"Hesitation is all we need, if we can bring the guards." And I refused to die cowering in a corner of the dungeons, in the vain hope they wouldn't find me.

Fitzroy shook his head. "It's risky."

Madeleine let out a little huff of air. "Yes," she said. "Of course it's risky. Come on." Her heels clicked on the stone floor as she strode away.

I nodded to Fitzroy. "Stay safe."

He squeezed my shoulder, fear seeping through into his expression. "You too, Your Majesty."

I hurried away.

No guards watched the corridors now. We passed no one at all, and saw no signs of struggle—how could there be, when there was nothing in the corridors to knock over, nothing to displace at all? It looked like the contents of the castle had already been swept away.

We turned a corner. Two guards hurried toward us. On the left, Mila, the young blond girl who'd shown me my laboratory. On the right, a gawky brunette who often guarded the halls, but had never guarded *me*, as far as I could remember. I hesitated, but Madeleine did not pause. She kept walking, head held high, staring them down.

"We are heading to the throne room," she said. "If you will excuse us."

"Your Majesty," Mila said. "We were looking for you. I'm so glad you're safe."

"She is not safe yet," Madeleine said. "Please let us through." And they did. They stepped aside, and our group strode past, moving closer to the throne room with every step.

"We want to protect you, Your Majesty," the brunette said. "We were on patrol, when one of the other guards told us . . . we wanted to find you. Please, how can we help?"

"Wait at the door," Madeleine said. "Do not let anyone in without permission."

The brunette nodded. "What's your name?" I asked her.

"Carina, Your Majesty. Carina Carlsen."

Carina Carlsen. I tucked that knowledge away. I hoped I could trust her.

The throne room had been attacked, too. The banners, the paintings . . . all of it had been torn down, shredded. The gold plates had been knocked off the table, the crystal shattered on the floor. But Madeleine stepped straight over it, and I followed. The throne loomed at the far end of the room, and I would certainly fit in it now, in my soaked, bedraggled nightgown. I doubt I'd ever looked less like a queen. But I would be more like a queen sitting on the throne than gawping beside it, so I sat.

"Straighten your back," Madeleine said. She ran her fingers through my hair, working out the knots. Then she pulled some pins out of her own hair and stuck them between her teeth, twisting mine into something that must have resembled a style. I couldn't see what she was doing, but it didn't seem like the extravagant, heavy styles of the court. Just the feel of it made me sit straighter, feel more regal somehow.

I could hear people speaking outside the throne room—or

maybe above it. The Fort carried sound in strange ways. But Madeleine did not seem concerned. She continued to arrange me, her hands steady.

As a final touch, Madeleine pulled out the necklace she'd rescued from my rooms. She draped it around my neck, leaving the ruby to gleam against the white of my nightgown.

My heart pounded in my throat. I wasn't ready for this.

Then I heard footsteps outside the door.

"Stop!" one of my guards said. "In the name of the queen."

I had to invite them in. I had to stall them, but if I looked like I was in control, like I didn't really care about their threat . . . I had to be in control.

"Let them in," I said, as loudly as I dared. The words seemed to bounce around the destroyed room.

"Your Majesty—" one of the guards began. I cut her off.

"Come in, whoever you are."

Torsten Wolff strode through the door. A sword gleamed in his hand. It was clean, though—he hadn't hurt anyone yet.

"Cousin!" Madeleine said, stepping forward slightly. Her voice was all sweetness and light. "How good to see you."

More men entered behind Sten. None of them were bothering to conceal their faces, I realized. They didn't care who knew about their involvement. Perhaps they didn't expect any witnesses to survive.

I kept my own expression as impassive as I could. All I had to do was look like a queen.

"Lady Freya," Sten said. "Hiding on your stolen throne."

"Not hiding, cousin," Madeleine said, her voice still so calm, so *lovely*. "This is a queen's place, is it not? On her throne?"

"It is," he said. "A queen's place. But she is not a queen."

"Clearly, you are mistaken."

"How can you stand there beside her, Madeleine?" he hissed. "She murdered our friends."

I clutched the arms of the throne. "I didn't murder them!"

"Did you think no one would notice? I've been to your laboratory, Freya. It's full of poisons. Notes on their effects. You're experimenting in an old torture chamber, and you didn't think anyone would suspect you?"

"I'm trying to solve the murders." Calm, I thought. Stay calm. I couldn't manage the same light tone as Madeleine, but I could at least seem somewhat collected. "Why would I keep arsenic with me if I'd used it to kill the whole court? You can't think I'm that foolish."

"It would be foolish," Sten said. "But I am not convinced that you are not a fool. I suspected you from the beginning. You attended the banquet, and then left with your friend before the poison struck. But I didn't *know* until yesterday, when you decided to pardon your accomplices."

"I didn't pardon them." *Calm.* I took a deep breath. "I didn't want them to be executed. That doesn't mean I support them."

"And yet you have no respect for the dead. You stole tributes from the river. You admitted to reading a book that says we should all be killed. And you do your strange little experiments, with *poison*. You can't be queen."

"So you're planning to kill me?" I was proud of how steady I sounded. I tilted up my chin, just a little, so I was looking down at him even more. Imperious.

"I want you to come quietly," he said. "Admit your crimes, and face justice."

"I didn't do it, Sten. It wasn't me."

He glowered at me, his hatred so strong that I almost flinched. "Get up," he said. His eyes lingered on the necklace that Madeleine had given me. "Take off those jewels and come along quietly. I don't want to have to kill you, no matter what you've done."

If I moved an inch, if I gave any sign of breaking, he would murder me and leave my blood to soak into the stones. I could see it in his eyes. And he might murder me either way, but Madeleine . . . Madeleine believed. Madeleine did not look afraid.

"It is my throne," I said quietly. "I will not move for you."

Sten stepped forward, sword held before him. Dagny hissed at him. He glanced at the necklace again. "Do you think you can rule?" he said. "Do you think you can hide in this fortress and really be queen? No one will support you. Half of them have already joined me. You'll *rot* in here."

"And if she does," Madeleine said, her voice still all politeness, "she will rot as queen."

Shouts and running feet. Someone called "Your Majesty!"

and then Fitzroy's voice, "Freya!"

He'd found the guards. It was enough to make me sit straighter, to meet Sten's gaze.

"My guards are coming," I said. "If you plan to kill me, you'd better be quick."

He glanced down at the necklace again. Then he reached forward with his free hand, snatching for my arm. Dagny spat and struck with her claws, leaving streaks of gleaming red blood on his wrist. Sten flinched, and in his moment of hesitation, guards crashed through the doors.

"Stop!" one of them shouted. "In the name of the queen."

Sten spun around, sword raised. Another group of guards surged into the room, some wearing their usual jackets, some in loose shirts and breeches, a few holding swords, others wielding only fierce expressions.

"Step away from the queen."

"This girl," Sten spat, "is a murderer. She must be brought to justice."

"Stand down, Sten." That was Fitzroy. My heart pounded. He didn't have a weapon, but he stepped forward, as the new guards moved around the walls, surrounding Sten's men. Several stepped in front of me, blocking me partially from view. But they didn't have any weapons. I could taste blood at the back of my throat, that metallic tang of fear.

No one moved to attack. For a long moment, everyone stared at one another.

Then one of my guards grabbed for Sten's arm. Sten swung his sword. Not enough to actually collide with the guard, but enough to make him flinch back. Enough to break the tension in the room, to make his men pull out their swords, too, to turn the standoff into a fight.

I couldn't follow what happened next. Two of the guards stood so close to me that they were practically on my toes, and there were too many voices, too many men wearing the same shirts and coats on either side. I could smell blood on the air, hear the shouts, the clangs of metal, the thuds of flesh on bone.

But my men outnumbered his now, and they were on the outside, pressing the enemy in. We *had* to win.

Sten must have reached the same conclusion. "All right, *Queen* Freya," he said, and his voice seemed to cast a spell over the room, freezing the fighting men in place. "I'll leave you to your throne." He spat onto the floor. Behind him, a few of his men were bleeding, and a few of mine, but no one was dead, not yet. "But you'll wish you surrendered. I promise you that."

NINETEEN

STEN MARCHED AWAY. HIS MEN SURGED FORWARD again, protecting him, clearing the way. One of my guards tried to block the door, but Sten shoved her aside, and then he was gone.

I clutched the pendant around my neck, and I stared at the door, listening to the fading footsteps. Fitzroy and my guards chased after him. I held my breath, waiting for more shouts, the sound of another fight.

A man yelled, and I leaped to my feet, forcing Dagny to bound to the floor. Madeleine grabbed my shoulder, holding me back. "Wait here," she said. "They're leaving."

"But the guards—" *Fitzroy*.

"If he wanted to kill your guards, he would have done this in a very different way. He thinks he's being noble, Freya. He thinks he's *right*. He won't want to kill anyone he doesn't have to."

"And when my guards attack him?"

"He'll defend himself," she said. "But then he'll *leave*."

"Until when?"

"Until he thinks he's stronger. But it gives you time."

My guards had captured a couple of Sten's men, but most of them had escaped. I'd barely stopped anybody.

I stepped away, twisting the necklace in my hand. I pressed my feet firmly against the stone. The cold helped me to focus. No time to panic now.

More shouting down the hall. I jumped, my grip tightening on the necklace.

"What is that?" Naomi said, nodding at the chain. "Sten kept looking at it."

"The Star of Valanthe," Madeleine said.

I stared down at the jewel with dawning realization. Valanthe had been one of the Forgotten, or so legend claimed, known for her justice and kindness. She had been the last to leave Epria, the most reluctant to abandon the kingdom, and had left a jewel to remind us mortals of her desire to return. Or so the legends said. "I wanted him to think twice about the possibility of crossing the Forgotten," said Madeleine. "To remember that *you* are the anointed queen."

"Does that matter, if he thinks I'm a murderer?"

"Probably not in the end. But it made him reluctant enough to do anything in that moment, didn't it?"

Dagny rubbed against Madeleine's ankles, and Madeleine bent down to stroke her.

More footsteps echoed from outside the door. I stood ramrod straight, my stomach twisted. Please let them be my men. Please let Fitzroy be all right.

Fitzroy was the first through the door. Relief rushed through me. He looked fine. He looked perfect. I ran forward and threw my arms around him. He let out a little *oof* of surprise, and then his arms settled around my back, my chin tucked on his shoulder.

"Are you all right?" he asked quietly. His breath tickled my neck. The sensation ran all down my spine.

"Yes," I said. "Yes, I'm fine. Are you—"

"Yes. Yes, I'm fine." I stepped back, suddenly aware of how close we had been. Too close. Stupidly close. He scraped his hand through his hair, making it even messier than before, and nodded at me. Such an awkward nod. I didn't know Fitzroy was even capable of being awkward.

"Was anyone else hurt?" I said quickly. "Did Sten and his men leave?"

"They escaped, Your Majesty," a guard to our right said. "We sent men after them, but they evaded our soldiers."

"So no one else is hurt?"

"No one, Your Majesty."

It felt too good to be true. Surely we hadn't survived this so easily.

"Thank you," I said to Fitzroy. "For fetching the guards."

"They were already looking for you. I just pointed them in the right direction."

One of the guards stepped forward. "When we realized the Fort was under attack, Your Majesty, we wanted to help."

"You wanted to help *me*?"

"It's our duty, Your Majesty. And you're no murderer. Some of us appreciate what you've done, pardon my saying so."

"What I've done?" I'd barely done anything.

"Returning that money, Your Majesty. Things are tight these days . . . and then refusing to kill that servant. Some would say you're too soft, but the rest of us—well, we appreciate it, Your Majesty. Things have been hard for everyone recently."

The words seemed to reach me through water, slightly fuzzy and hard to make out. I'd actually done something right. "Thank you." I didn't know what else to say.

"Stop!" A guard by the door shouted into the corridor. I turned. Rasmus Holt was in the doorway. He was paler than I'd ever seen him, and his beard twitched with nervous energy.

"Your Majesty," he said. "You're all right. When I heard what Sten intended, I thought—but you are truly protected by the Forgotten."

I hurried toward him. He looked unharmed, too, if shaken. "Have you seen my father?"

"Your father . . ." Holt winced. "He was with me, at the time."

My stomach dropped. If he was reluctant to tell me, if it was that bad . . . "And? What happened?"

"They locked us in. To ensure we did not interfere. Your father was—he was concerned for you. And then Torsten Wolff appeared and said they were leaving. I assumed you were dead, but then . . ." He shook his head.

"And my *father*?"

"He went with them."

No. I stepped back, shaking my head. It didn't make sense. "How could he have gone with them?"

"Sten took him. As leverage against you."

"And you didn't try to stop him?"

"Me, stop Torsten Wolff? I am an old man, Your Majesty. I am an adviser, not a soldier. And someone needed to remain here to help you, if you survived."

I'd argued with him. Last time I'd seen my father, I'd shouted at him. Anger rose inside me, sharp and irrational. "So you should have gone in his place. You should have protected him."

"They would not have thought me as valuable a hostage,

Your Majesty. They only left me because they did not consider me worthwhile. And you need advice, now more than ever."

He was right. It wasn't his fault. But my father . . . "What will they do to him? What will happen?"

"I am certain he will be safe, Your Majesty. He would want you to focus on your *own* safety now."

"How can he be safe? Sten just tried to kill me."

"There is nothing you can do, Your Majesty!" Holt's voice rose for the first time, the whites of his eyes gleaming. "Half of the court is gone, and several of the guards. No doubt Sten has gone to his own lands in the south, where he will have all the men he needs to support him. You cannot fight him."

"I *have* to fight him." I clenched my fists by my sides. "Call the council. Or what's left of it. We need to plan."

He bowed. "Of course, Your Majesty."

The remaining council, it turned out, was Holt and Norling. I suppose it made sense that Thorn had betrayed us. Surely the spymaster would have heard of Sten's plan if she hadn't been involved.

The council room had been left untouched, as cold and somber as always. The table seemed even more awkwardly large now, but I sat at the head of it anyway, pushing my fear away. I was too exhausted for preamble. "How long will it be before he attacks again?"

"It is hard to predict, Your Majesty," Holt said. "He will

gather support elsewhere in the kingdom first, to prove his right to the throne, and then I do not doubt he will return."

"He has already started a campaign of words against us," Norling said, "claiming Her Majesty was the one who poisoned the court. If people believe him, he may not even have to fight us himself."

"At least we know who was responsible for all those attacks against us," Holt said. "Sten has shown his hand now. He wants the throne for himself."

"No," I said. "That's not right. The second poisoner . . . it seemed like she wanted to get rid of the throne entirely. Why would Sten be involved in that?"

"He could have allied himself with them, even if he did not share their beliefs. And it does seem likely now that he was involved in the attack on the banquet."

"Perhaps," I said. But I did not think it was him. He had seemed so *convinced* when he accused me of murder. So furious. He could have simply been a good actor, but . . . I didn't think so. "We don't have any evidence yet. Do you think he'll gain a lot of support?"

"Unfortunately, Your Majesty, I have to say that I do. Some have already left with him, and he will be even more popular outside the city. People know him, and they trust him. They do not know you."

"But he attacked me in my sleep. He took my father. People can't support him."

"Not everyone, Your Majesty," Norling said. "But those will be seen as actions of justice, if people believe you are guilty. You should not have shown mercy to your attackers, or insulted the memories of the dead by taking jewels from the river. People here are not inclined to support you."

The *nobles* here weren't inclined to support me. My guards had seemed reasonably happy. But all my efforts to appease the court clearly hadn't been enough, and a ruler without nobles behind her . . . I shook my head. "If his argument is that I killed the king, we have to focus on finding out what actually happened. If I can *prove* it wasn't me, he'll lose support." And maybe, *maybe*, if I found proof, Sten would stop his attack, as well. Perhaps that was irrational, or it was naive, but . . . he'd always seemed sincere in his grief. He wanted to find his friends' true killer. If I could prove I hadn't been involved, he wouldn't attack me again. "I need the poisoned cake brought to my lab. I need to study it."

Norling frowned. "Your Majesty, I'm not certain—"

"But I am."

Holt shook his head. "We cannot fight him that way now. We have to secure the city, gather support for you. Come up with a counterstrategy."

"And we will. But I need that cake."

I stared at him until he nodded.

"He'll return to his own lands first," Norling said, into the quiet that followed, "to gather more strength. But I don't doubt that will only be the beginning. The balance of power in the kingdom has been shattered by recent events. If I were a betting woman, I would say he would start in the south, and then sweep around the kingdom, building his support one region at a time."

"If he does that, it will be difficult for us to stop him from winning their support. We have no one to send as envoys to the other regions," Holt said. "Not if we wish Her Majesty to have any protection left. No, Her Majesty must focus on *here*. We will have to win this with words."

"And actions, too. Some people don't like me, but some— they don't know me. If I can show them I'm worth supporting—" Continue to do what I thought was right. Hope it was the right thing to do.

"The nobles may be hard to convince," Holt said, "and you cannot run after those who have left. But perhaps you are right. The people of this city have seen very little of you, and those extremists have been whispering in their ears. If you can prove you're not as corrupt as King Jorgen and his court—" He nodded. "Going into the city will be the first step. Perhaps some charity work. There are already rumors that the Forgotten were responsible for all the deaths at the banquet. If you can show them that you are worthy of the Forgotten's favor, as we all know you are—that may work for us. People will fight for the Forgotten's chosen queen."

I twisted the ruby pendant again. The idea of the Forgotten had worked for me once, hadn't it? The sight of Valanthe's pendant had made Sten hesitate, long enough for my guards to arrive. Could the same idea inspire people to protect me, as well? If they did, they'd be risking their lives for a lie. But terror had gripped me, deep in my stomach. I did not want to die.

It wouldn't come to that. I'd find a way to avoid fighting him. And this way, I could help people. Even if it was through a lie. "Madeleine supports an orphanage," I said slowly. "I'll go there. Make sure people see it. That might help, mightn't it?"

"Yes, Your Majesty," Holt said. "An excellent idea."

"And I want you to distribute copies of *Gustav's Treatise*. Place them everywhere. Make it so anyone can read it."

"Your Majesty?"

"It's become legendary since it's been banned, and it's being used against me. But the actual text might *support* me. At least, it doesn't support trying to kill me. I think we should try it."

"If you're sure, Your Majesty—"

"I am." I wasn't, but it was worth trying, at least.

"As you wish, Your Majesty," Holt said. "But then, we have another issue we must take into account. If you are to present yourself as one favored by the Forgotten, then we must look to the court, and the company you keep."

"The company I keep?"

"People have noticed, Your Majesty, how you and William Fitzroy have been growing closer. I understand that he is a— pleasant young man, but it is not good for you to be seen with him, in such circumstances. As I mentioned before—"

"You said he might be a threat, I know. But he protected me, when Sten attacked. He could easily have turned against me."

"That is not the only issue," Holt said. "Fitzroy's existence is symbolic of the past court's corruption. If you wish to separate yourself from that, you must separate yourself from him."

Anger flared inside me. "He isn't a symbol. He's a person. And I can't kick him out of the court because of that."

"Not kick him out, Your Majesty. But maybe—do not associate with him. For all our sakes."

"There is one more possibility we must consider," Norling said, her voice cutting over the silence left by Holt's suggestion. She seemed determined to move the conversation on. "Sten is out of our reach for now, but his cousin, Madeleine, remains here. She may prove a useful bargaining piece."

I frowned. "What do you mean?"

"He has your father, Your Majesty. No doubt he means to use that against you. But we have his cousin. I suggest we arrest her, and—"

"No." I didn't need to hear the rest.

"Your Majesty. If it might help us—"

"No," I said again. "Madeleine has done nothing wrong. She saved my life tonight."

"This is war, Your Majesty," Holt said softly. "Sometimes we must act in ways that—"

"*No.* Madeleine is to be left alone. Sten knows she's still with us. That will have to be enough."

I returned to my rooms, limbs aching, as the sun rose. Mila and Carina stood watch, promising to keep me safe despite their exhaustion. I locked the door of my quarters anyway, and shoved a small table in front of it. Just to be safe.

My rooms were half ruined. Chairs knocked over, tapestries torn down, the dresses in the wardrobe shredded by swords. Naomi had clearly tried to start the cleanup, but she was now asleep in a chair, a circle of neatness around her. Dagny, curled up on Naomi's lap, pricked her ears when I entered the room, but she didn't move.

I began slowly, carefully, putting things back into place. My brain was too full of the night's events to sleep.

"Your Majesty? Freya?" I spun around. Madeleine Wolff stood in the doorway to my bedroom, hands clutched carefully in front of her.

"Madeleine. What are you doing here?"

"I hoped I might be able to help you."

"I locked the door. I barricaded it—"

"I've been waiting for you to return. I didn't want to wake Naomi, so I was exploring a little. I hope I didn't startle you." She took a step forward. "Are you all right?"

"Am I all right?" I scraped the hair away from my face.

"No. No, I'm not all right." My father was gone, and I'd been attacked, and the danger of the situation felt all the clearer now, the metaphorical dagger hanging by a thread over my heart. "Why are you here?"

"Because I think you are a good person. I don't want to see you hurt. And I think—I think you might need my help." She stepped closer. She hadn't changed out of her water-stained dress, but somehow, she managed to make the damage look deliberate. "I can help you, if you'll let me. You need to win people over, make allies, more than ever. And I'm told I have a talent for that."

"Why would you want to help me? Your cousin—"

"My cousin is wrong. And you . . ." She paused, her pink lips slightly apart. "You saved your cat."

That was the last thing I expected her to say. "What?"

"When you were running for your life. You came back to fetch your cat. I knew you didn't deserve what Sten had planned. I knew you were going to be a good queen, and that I should warn you. But when I saw that . . . you're a good person, Freya. I want to help you. I know you'll be a good queen, if given the chance."

She was supporting me because of *Dagny*? I turned away, raking my fingers through my hair. "You think I'm a better person than Sten?"

"Does it matter? Sten was part of the old court, yes, and he would probably be a good ruler. But it's not his throne."

Madeleine had saved my life. But for her to turn her back on her cousin, on everything she had known . . . I didn't know if I could trust her. It didn't quite make sense. "You liked the old court. Didn't you?"

"Yes," she said softly. "And no. I liked the people. I liked the laughter of it, the glamour. Always being around people, different people, learning their ins and outs . . . yes, I liked that. But it could be a cold place, too. Callous. Too wrapped up in its own extravagance to notice anyone or anything outside it. It was hard. But my friends were there. My life was there. I missed it whenever my doctors sent me to the countryside. They clearly knew little about me, if they thought peace and silence would make me feel better. But I suppose they did save my life, in the end."

"What was wrong with you?" It was too blunt a question, but perhaps if Madeleine answered that, I'd know whether or not I could trust her.

"Melancholy. Nothing more or less than that. I have suffered it often. Not because I do not like the court, but because . . . well, I do not know why. It is just one of those things." She brushed her hair over her shoulder and smiled slightly. "This time was particularly bad, though. It was so strong it was like a physical illness. I had never had stomachaches like that. But the doctors said it was melancholy, *just* melancholy, and that time away would heal it. 'A fragile disposition,' they called me." She laughed. "As though one needs to be fragile to be sad."

"What were you sad about?"

"That is not the question to ask. I did not feel sad over anything particular. I just felt sad. Have you not had the sensation? You are lucky if not." She sank onto the floor, her skirts swelling around her. Dagny stretched and leaped from Naomi's lap, before strutting over and butting Madeleine's hand for attention. "You should arrange more entertainments," she said. "I know it may seem crass, considering the circumstances, but if people do not see you as queen . . ."

"Yes," I said. "Yes, I understand. But I can't be what they want to see."

"And have they told you that?"

"They've always judged me, even before all of this."

"Are you so sure? Few of the people who survived the banquet were close to the king. And have you ever given them reason to like you? Spoken to them? It might be that they are nicer than you think. Be yourself, Freya. It's the only way you can succeed now." She stroked Dagny under her chin. "I would love to help you. If you'll accept me. And I'd love to stay here. With my cousin gone, and all my friends . . . please, Freya. Will you accept me?"

I chewed my lip. "Yes," I said. After the warmth of her words, it was all I could say. "Yes, please help."

TWENTY

"TELL ME, YOUR MAJESTY, WHERE WERE YOU ON THE evening of the banquet?"

"I, um—I went home."

Fitzroy shook his head. I was perched on the side of the center table of my laboratory, to emulate my throne, while Fitzroy paced, bombarding me with questions. Dagny was grooming her paws beside me, while Naomi stood next to the cabinets, preparing different metal wires for the next round of tests. "If you wanted to sound suspicious, congratulations. Otherwise, no."

I had listened to Holt's advice. I'd even considered it, for a moment. Just long enough to confirm that I thought Fitzroy was a person, a *good* person, and that I could never throw him aside because of something he couldn't control. I wanted to survive, but I wasn't willing to sacrifice that.

"But it's the truth," I said to him now. "I did go home. I left with Naomi."

She shook her head, not pausing in her work. "I can't save you from this one, Freya. It did sound suspicious."

"It's not what you're saying," Fitzroy said. "It's the way you're saying it. Like you think your words might be cause for someone to murder you."

"My words *might* cause someone to murder me."

Fitzroy raised his eyebrows at me, trying to look stern.

"Well, how *should* I answer it, then?" I frowned down at the paper where I'd written all the sample questions and answers we'd practiced so far. Fitzroy's introduction to Not Getting Ousted was supposed to prevent me from making the same mistakes I'd made the last time someone challenged me, but so far all it had done was reinforce how ill-prepared I was. "If I tell them I ran home to do experiments in my lab, I'll only discredit myself more. Sten accused me *because* of my lab."

"So you can't hide it," Naomi said. "You might as well be honest. I think it makes you sound interesting. And intelligent."

"It makes me sound like not a queen."

"It's not the answer they would expect," Fitzroy said. "But maybe that's good. You're not exactly an accomplished liar. And the court likes a bit of novelty. Maybe it would intrigue them."

"My experiments are not a bit of novelty! They're important research, and—"

"I know, Freya," Fitzroy said. "Do you think I'd be here if I didn't know? But does it matter if people think that? If it's based on the truth and it makes them like you, then you should use it." He cleared his throat and stood up straighter, shifting back into the role of interrogator again. "So, Your Majesty. What were you doing on the evening of the banquet? I didn't see you there."

"I went home," I said. "I, uh—I wanted to do an experiment."

"No."

"You are not helping."

"All right," he said. He stopped in front of me. "Just tell me. Stop worrying about every word, and tell *me*."

"But I can't stop worrying about every word. Isn't that what this is for? Because my words are useless?"

"You're smart, Freya. You're convincing, when you forget to worry. When you're talking about your experiments, or your theories. Just let yourself speak like that."

I took a deep breath. Fitzroy never let me feel completely at ease, but at least I could trust him to be honest. His emotions were always so clear around me that I didn't have to worry about what he might think but not say. I should just address my words to him. "I was inspired at the ball," I said slowly. "I thought that hairpins might be the key to an experiment I've been working on, about—about creating portable, long-lasting heat without flame. To help keep hands warm in the winter. I hurried home to try it, along with Naomi. I was there when I heard the news."

"It still doesn't sound very diplomatic," Fitzroy said. "But it's much better than before."

I tugged my fingers through my hair, pulling it half loose from its braid. At least I was making progress. I could do this.

"Did the experiment work?" Fitzroy asked.

"Will that help my defense?"

"I don't know. I was just wondering. Did it work?"

"No," I said softly. "No, it didn't work." I shook my head and stood, stretching out my shoulders. The pile of papers at the far side of the room caught my eye. Fitzroy had gone to the palace this morning and brought back as many letters as he could carry. The disorganization made my teeth clench. But there was no good way to sort them before reading them all, and I didn't want to lose time. So the pages were just piled there, to be read in whatever random order Fitzroy had gathered them in.

I'd spent two hours on them already, with Fitzroy and Naomi. We'd found nothing. Fitzroy planned to return to the palace for more papers that night, but I didn't have time to go through the rest now. I needed to practice, and to prepare. I would be visiting people around the city that afternoon, and trying to convince them I was not as horrible as Sten and the extremists claimed.

There was no realistic way it could go well. But if I dwelled on that, I'd never get out the door. I had practiced my words and my smiles. I could do this.

I walked across the room now, practicing my "regal but welcoming" gait. Dagny leaped from the table to follow, which didn't really make walking any easier. Fitzroy watched me, but he did not comment, while Naomi worked in the corner, double checking the weights of all her samples.

"Your Majesty?" The brunette guard, Carina, poked her head through the door. "Madeleine Wolff is here to see you."

"All right," I said. "Let her in."

"Freya," Madeleine said, as she stepped in. "I was told I'd find you here. We need to start getting ready for your outing." For the first time I could remember, Madeleine was the one who appeared out of place. Her skirt was huge, the silk ruffles skimming the dusty, bloodstained floor. She smiled as she looked around the room, but her posture wasn't entirely composed. "The old torture chamber is a strange choice."

"It was the best place for what I needed to do."

"Not torturing people, I hope. That would be terrible etiquette for a queen."

"It would be traditional," Fitzroy said.

"Then I'm glad our queen is not a traditionalist." Madeleine moved farther into the room, looking over the bottles and vials, the books, Naomi still sorting out the wires. "Naomi," she said. "What are you doing?"

"We're going to try placing different metals in arsenic

solution," Naomi said. "Freya thinks it might be a way to detect it—"

"I can't be certain," I said. "But I think it's possible. And we have to try something."

Madeleine nodded. "You—you're working on finding the murderer?"

"Among other things."

"I suppose my cousin is your main suspect now."

"I don't know," I said. "He's suspicious, but—" It didn't *fit*. It didn't feel like he was responsible. That was terrible reasoning, I knew, but it just didn't fit. "He doesn't have the motive. For him to kill all his friends . . ." I shook my head. "I have to find out who it was. I have to find proof."

"So people will fight for you?"

"I'm hoping we won't have to fight at all."

Madeleine sat on the spare stool at the end of the table, her skirts cascading around her. "You think finding the truth will stop him from attacking you?"

"It won't," Fitzroy said. "Sten's committed to this now."

"My cousin—he's always been a very logical person, ever since we were children. And he believes in justice, more than anything else. But I think he's blinded himself to that now, or to the truth, at least. He's convinced himself you are responsible, because it would be so straightforward if you were, and he so desperately wants an answer to this murder. He wants something he can do, to fight against it. Now he's on this path . . . it will be hard to change his mind."

"But you said yourself, he's not a murderer," Naomi said. "If Freya could prove she was innocent, or find who was responsible, and bring the evidence to him . . . if he really wants justice, he'd have to stop fighting her. Wouldn't he?"

Madeleine sighed. "I wouldn't place all your hopes on it," she said. "He might well assume you're trying to trick him, and finding evidence will be hard. It would be best if—"

"If we fight him?" I said. "That can't be the best thing to do." I raked my fingers through my hair. "It's worth a try, to convince him."

It was worth more than that, though. I couldn't imagine that I would fail, not when success was so important. I could picture it already. I'd go to him, with Madeleine—he trusted Madeleine, so she would be a good person to use. She'd tell him the truth, offer him a pardon. He'd refuse to accept it at first, but when he saw the evidence, when Madeleine implored him to see reason, he would surrender. We'd catch the murderer, and everything would return to normal.

I had to be right.

Madeleine had been happy to take over Naomi's styling duties, and Naomi had been more than happy to let her. Madeleine had brought hundreds of pots of makeup and hair ornaments with her when she moved into my chambers, and she laid them out on the table now, considering them before starting her masterpiece.

She styled me without reference to anyone, dressing me in an elegant dress without too many layers, and leaving the makeup light and bright. It wasn't the fashion of the old court, but the look in the mirror suited me. I looked regal.

Madeleine separated out sections of my hair, sweeping it back one way, and then another. "The king was sick," she said softly. "Did you know that?"

I shook my head.

"I don't think many people did. He was unwell, for the past six or seven months at least. Not life-threatening, I don't believe, but it scared him. He didn't want anyone to know."

"But you knew?"

"With my own illness . . . it was very different, of course, but I think he thought I might understand. It was strange, to hear him speak of it. He seemed so vulnerable. I was not accustomed to seeing him as a vulnerable man."

"You were friends with him?"

"Not especially, before that. I'd never thought he cared for much outside himself and his own comfort, and that makes for a poor friend. And I did not always approve of his politics. The nobility have so much here, and everyone else is left to scrape for themselves, but he never made any effort to change things."

"What would you want him to have changed?"

"People dying because they don't have access to simple medicines. People kicked out of their homes because they cannot afford the rent. Farmers who go hungry because they can't afford their own food. It is time somebody noticed. My cousin notices. But he is not helping things, with this attack."

"I wouldn't have thought you'd be interested in politics."

"One can be interested in both fashion and politics, don't you think? They so often go hand in hand. Appearances, saying the right words, making people like you . . ."

"I wish politics wasn't like that."

"Me too. But we have to do it, if we want to help."

I stared at our reflections in the mirror. Madeleine ran her fingers through my hair, and prickles chased over my scalp. "I think my mother felt the same way. About court."

Madeleine smiled. "What was she like?"

"Perfect. She always saw the good in everything . . . she told me people are waiting for you to let them in, if you'll just give them a chance." A lesson I'd decided several years ago only applied to people like my mother.

"I heard she was a legend of the court. The king's relative, running off and marrying a merchant. And somehow convincing them all to accept it, without any consequences at all."

"She could have convinced anybody of anything." She'd even convinced me of my own worth, once. That I should embrace my own strengths, and others would love me for them, regardless of how I doubted myself. It had been a beautiful lie to a nine-year-old, but no one had been around to perpetuate it since.

"I don't remember much about my mother," Madeleine said.

"She died when I was four. But I remember, she always smelled of turpentine, from the paints she used. I don't remember her painting, but we still have her work in our manor, and so it is like *she* is there, too, or her perspective is, the way she saw the world."

"Is that why you started painting?"

"I don't know." She considered my reflection for a moment, and then reached for a fine paintbrush on the table. She popped it in her mouth, almost absentmindedly, smoothing the bristles, before dipping it into a pot of red lip color. "I didn't start until a couple of years ago, when I was home after my first bout of illness. I was terrible at it. But there was something soothing about it . . . it's somehow freeing but methodical, you know. I felt like I had a connection with my mother as I worked. And luckily I have something of her in me, because I learned quickly enough. And now I am the one who sometimes smells of turpentine."

"My mother smelled of lavender," I said. But as I spoke the words, I wondered if they were true. I knew my mother loved lavender, she'd had a little water spray . . . but did I actually remember the scent of lavender, or was it just the idea that I clung to?

Madeleine swept the red paint over my lips, and then stepped back. "There. All done. What do you think?"

She must have spun some kind of magic. My hair looked extravagant and sophisticated, without overwhelming me or making me look like the uncertain girl I really was. The way the sides swept back created the illusion of cheekbones, and the spirals at the back of my head created volume without seeming overdone. A small curtain of black hair fell down from the bun, as straight as always, but the straightness looked purposeful now, refined rather than limp.

As a finishing touch, Madeleine draped the Star of Valanthe around my neck. It was the only jewel I wore.

"It looks wonderful," I said. "Really, thank you."

"I told you. You need to look like a queen. No one said you needed to look like the last queen."

I nodded. The pins didn't shift as I'd have expected. I felt confident, secure. I stood up and pulled Madeleine into a hug. Madeleine flushed, her smile growing. "I'm glad you like it. My art is useful, is it not? Now, let's go and show those people what sort of queen you can be."

TWENTY-ONE

RAIN HAD DRIZZLED ALL MORNING, LEAVING PUDDLES on the roads and a light mist in the air. My carriage moved slowly through the streets. The two gray horses had looked pure and regal when I'd stepped out of the Fort, but they were probably covered in mud now.

The rest of the city seemed to have decided to stay inside, out of the rain. I peered around the curtains, but I couldn't see any passersby. The sky was a gray canvas above us.

"Where is everybody? Did they not want to come out to see me?" The words sounded arrogant, but that had been the point, hadn't it? I couldn't convince people to like me if they couldn't see me.

"We didn't announce that you were heading here today," Norling said. "It wouldn't be safe. We'll go to the orphanage, but we'll do it quietly."

"We can't do it quietly." Without an audience, the whole exercise was useless. I wasn't putting my life at risk and my nerves to the test if it wouldn't help me. I *had* to make people like me. "Stop the carriage."

"Your Majesty?"

"Stop the carriage. I want to walk."

"But, Your Majesty—"

"I need to be seen." My father had pushed for aloofness, but he wasn't here anymore. I only had Holt, and Norling, and my own wits, and I couldn't be aloof now. Acting like the old king, when half the people seemed to have hated him, when people wanted to get rid of the nobility altogether . . . what good would that do? I needed to prove that I wasn't like them, that I wasn't snobby and corrupt. That perhaps I was a person the Forgotten could approve of after all.

And for that, I would need to walk.

I stepped out the moment the carriage stopped, and Madeleine and Naomi slipped out behind me. Once I got past the narrow vantage point of the carriage window, I saw that there *were* people farther down the street—a few shoppers, striding along with baskets over their arms, a gang of teenagers on the corner, merchants and traders and other distracted figures hurrying about their business.

Holt and Norling climbed out of the carriage, too. Holt smiled slightly, but Norling was looking about in frustration. "All right," she said. "All right. Guards, lead the way. We will be proceeding on foot."

"Make way!" one of the guards shouted, as he marched ahead. "Make way for Queen Freya!"

That got people to look. I forced my spine straight, rotating my shoulders back, trying to remember everything my father had taught me about being queen.

Except that *wasn't* what I was doing now. Good posture might help, but otherwise, those displays hadn't benefited me yet. Holt and Madeleine had told me to be different, to be myself, and . . . well, that had to be easier than these shows of royalty. I smiled at the group of shoppers, a little weakly perhaps, but still a smile. One of them curtsied.

Another of them stared me down. She didn't shout anything, gave no other sign of aggression, but I could see it in her eyes. She'd heard I was a murderer, and she was assessing what she saw.

One of the merchants tipped his hat. "Good afternoon, Your Majesty. What brings you out into the city?" It was bold, greeting the queen like that. Would King Jorgen have accepted it? Would he have laughed and replied, or had the man arrested for rudeness?

It didn't matter. All that mattered was what *I* wanted to do. "Good afternoon," I said. My voice shook slightly, but it wasn't too bad. "We're traveling to the Stonegate Orphanage, on the northern side of the city."

Another man laughed. "And you care about things like that, now you've been accused of being a murderer?"

A guard strode toward him, but I held out my hand. "I always cared. I just realized I should be doing more to show it."

The man frowned at me, and I took the opportunity to walk on again. The shoppers bobbed into curtsies as I passed.

"Your Majesty," Norling hissed, as we walked on. "That was not appropriate."

I knew. But lying or ignoring people wouldn't help me. Maybe this would.

We passed more people as we walked farther into the city, and other carts clattered past us. I could feel myself shrinking inward, trying to increase the space between me and the crowds, but I kept my back straight, and counted the length of my breaths. I tried to focus on the details as we walked—the moody gray of the sky, the splash of water under my feet, the way the streetlights were reflected in the shop windows. Be present, I told myself. Don't panic.

As we turned toward the poorer neighborhoods on the north side of the city, a woman stumbled toward us. She must have been in her fifties, with a gaunt face and an eager expression. My guards moved to intercept her.

"Your Majesty," she said. "Please. Let me have your blessing."

"My blessing?" I stepped around the guards and moved closer. "What do you mean?"

"My business is in trouble, Your Majesty. Too many debts. I don't want your charity, Your Majesty, but I hoped—perhaps if you could bless me, in the name of the Forgotten, I mean . . . that might help."

It was the strangest request I'd ever heard. "I can't do that," I said. "I can't bless you."

"But you're the Forgotten's chosen, Your Majesty. Please."

I stared at her. I couldn't lie to her. A few comforting words wouldn't help her at all. But she looked so hopeful. I leaned forward and rested a hand on the woman's shoulder. "I—I bless you," I said. "In the name of the Forgotten. May all your debts be solved, and your business flourish." I paused. "What is your business? And your name?"

"Mary, Your Majesty. Mary Howard. I make buttons."

If my father had been here, he would have known how to advise her. But I was on my own with this now. "Come to the Fort tomorrow. We'll see what we can do."

"I don't want charity, Your Majesty."

"It won't be charity. But I want to help. In the name of the Forgotten."

That last part felt a bit much, but the woman beamed at me and curtsied again.

I couldn't settle as I walked on. People asking for my blessing was less frightening than people asking for my head, but I was no chosen one, no savior. This had to be Holt's work, convincing people that the Forgotten had selected me somehow, but for people to believe that . . .

A few more people asked me to bless them, but most watched in silence, perhaps stretching to a tip of the hat or a curtsy. I could feel them assessing me, this unexpected queen walking through their streets.

The sky darkened as we left the main streets behind and headed into the more dangerous alleys beyond. I'd never stepped foot in this part of the city before. The buildings were crammed close together, bending slightly over the street, as though threatening anyone who dared walk beneath. The streets smelled, too, of waste and rot and too many bodies crammed together. Madeleine strode ahead, nodding for me to follow her. She led us deeper into the maze of streets, until she stopped before a rickety door. Young voices shouted from inside.

I forced myself to take a steadying breath as Madeleine knocked on the door.

The woman who finally answered was in her sixties, with cropped gray hair and wrinkles around her eyes. She looked completely exhausted, but she beamed when she saw Madeleine.

"Lady Madeleine!" she said. "You're back. I'm so glad. I worried, when I heard what happened at the palace—"

"I wasn't there, Susan," Madeleine said. "I was all right. But I've brought you a visitor." She gestured at me. "May I introduce you to Her Majesty, Queen Freya? I've told her all about your work here, and she wanted to come and visit."

"Oh!" Susan stared at me for a long moment, her mouth open. Then she seemed to realize what she was doing, and sank into a curtsy. "It is an honor to have you here, Your Majesty. I'm afraid the place is a bit of a mess. The children, you know. They can be quite a handful."

I wasn't sure what to say in response to that, so I just nodded.

"Please. Come in, come in." She tried to beckon Madeleine forward while also curtsying respectfully to me. She didn't entirely succeed.

The inside of the building did not match Susan's warm demeanor. The stone walls were damp and bare, with mold growing near the ceiling. A few cracks ran up from the floor, and the few pieces of furniture had more repairs than actual material. The sounds of children playing and screaming echoed from somewhere above us.

Susan must have seen my surprised expression. "I know, Your Majesty, it's not suitable at all. But it's the best we can do, really, with the money we have."

"Can—can I help?"

"That's very kind, Your Majesty. We always appreciate donations, of anything. Food and clothes and toys as well as money. But, well." She pressed her lips together. "If you don't mind my saying so, Your Majesty, we need a lot more. You're helping us just by being here, making people take notice, but—the children need more than donations. They need more than this place."

That was fairly clear. I'd always felt so *sorry* for myself, the awkward girl who never fit in, but I'd had a home, and my father, and enough money that I'd never even thought about it. I'd been such an idiot. "What happened to them?"

"Many things. They all lost their parents, one way or another. I used to just take in orphans, but when people heard about my work, they started leaving babies on the doorstep. There's nowhere else for them to go, you know. The older ones are on the street otherwise, while the younger ones just starve."

A little girl appeared in the doorway to the left. She had wisp-blond hair that hung to her waist, and freckles all over her face. She scowled at me. "Who are you?" The question came out as a challenge.

I moved closer to her. Her front tooth was missing. "I'm Freya," I said. "I'm a friend of Madeleine's. What's your name?"

"Lucy." She continued to scowl at me. "Have you come to play with us?"

I nodded, and Lucy reached out to grab my hand. "We don't play in this room," she said firmly. "It's not allowed."

"All right."

Lucy looked me up and down again. "Are you a princess?"

"No," I said softly. "Not a princess."

"I'm so sorry, Your Majesty," Susan said, hurrying forward. "Lucy, this is Queen Freya. She's the woman in charge of the entire kingdom."

Lucy did not look impressed. She stuck up her chin. "I'm going to be a princess," she said, almost daring me to disagree. "When I'm grown up."

"Lucy, I've told you," Susan said, her voice harsher now. "Only very special people are queens and princesses. They're not like you and me. I'm sorry," she added again, seeming to address everyone in the room.

But I didn't want her to be sorry. I knelt in front of Lucy. Small children usually made me uncomfortable—you never quite knew what they were going to do—but Lucy would clearly not accept uncertainty or dismissal. "I wasn't a princess," I said. "I was never one of those special people, and I became queen."

Lucy nodded, like she suspected it all along. "We can only play in the playroom," she said, as she let go of my hand. "You should come." And she strode away.

"I mean no disrespect, Your Majesty," Susan said, "but I do wish you hadn't told her that. It's no good to give them false hope. What these children need is food, a home, a chance for work when they're older, maybe. Hope won't keep them alive."

After leaving our gift purses at the orphanage, our group began to walk back to the carriage. The driver had followed us most of the way through the streets, but the carriage couldn't fit down the narrow alleys in this part of the city.

I was happy to walk again. It helped me think.

Playing with Lucy and the others had been surprisingly fun. She had a boldness that reminded me a little of myself when I was little, but was seemingly unconcerned with people's reactions. It was impossible to be reticent around her.

She had been intelligent, too. Intelligent and brave. She'd achieve great things, if given the chance.

I moved to walk beside Holt. "I want to call a council meeting when we get back," I said.

He nodded. "Are you planning to make a bigger donation?"

"I'm planning to get them what they need." Surely I could find some way to fund a *real* place for the children to live.

Holt nodded again. "I'll see that it's done."

TWENTY-TWO

"WE COULD DO SO MUCH," I SAID TO FITZROY, FOR AT least the fourth time that night. "Just think about it. We have so many empty manors in the city after the attack. We could easily give one to them. We could even make it a day school, as well, for children who can't afford tutors. Everyone would have a chance to learn." I was practically bouncing on the spot from excitement, but Fitzroy didn't look convinced.

"I don't think people will be happy if you take away their houses," he said, leaning against the central table of the lab. "They still belong to *somebody*. And how will you pay for it all?"

"The court is full of gold," I said. "We could easily sell some of it."

"And what about when that runs out? How will you get more?"

"That's far in the future," I said, even though I knew he was right. But the gold was wasted in the palace, and we had time to come up with more solutions. "We could ask people to pay to stay at court. We could trade more abroad. We could do lots of things."

"Maybe sell this poison detector?"

"Maybe. If we ever figure it out."

I turned back to my notes. Nothing had really reacted with the arsenic solution so far. The closest thing to a breakthrough had come from mixing the powder with spirit of niter—it had dissolved, reluctantly, and when I distilled the result, it left glassy crystals behind, almost like salt. It probably wouldn't work as a test, but *something* was happening there. What if I added something else to make the reaction more obvious? Something to catalyze it?

I'd try metals first. "Could you prepare me some more baths of spirit of niter?" I said to Fitzroy, as I climbed off the stool.

"Got another plan?"

"Something like one."

I crossed the room and considered the jars of metals.

I began to weigh out some copper. Beside me, Fitzroy pulled on his gloves, ready to measure the acid.

"I guess you never thought you'd be doing anything like this," I said softly.

"What, playing with acid in the old torture room? That's how I've always spent my evenings."

I smiled. Then Naomi's teasing words came back to me. It wasn't possible that Fitzroy liked me, not in the way she had joked. It wasn't possible for me to like him, not considering all that had happened, not when I hardly even knew him. He was— he was a presence that I was always aware of, my skin prickled when he accidentally brushed against me, my heart was beating a little faster as I thought of him, yes. And yes, scientifically, when I gathered that evidence together, perhaps an impartial observer would hear those facts and reach that conclusion. Possibly. But they'd be wrong.

However, a lot of things weren't entirely logical right now. Like why Fitzroy was still here, when he'd known Sten so much longer, when he had no evidence that I hadn't been involved.

"Why did you stay here?"

He was quiet for a long moment. "What do you mean?"

"When Sten left. You've known him for years, and you don't hate him. You've barely known me a couple of weeks, and I'm not—" I removed the copper from the scales. "I'm not likely to win this. Anyone with good sense would have left. So why did you stay?"

"Lots of reasons," he said. "I think Sten's wrong. You didn't kill my father, and you definitely don't deserve to die. I think you'll be a good queen. And travel is so annoying. All that dust, and never having anywhere to sleep? Why would I choose that?"

I laughed, but the tension remained in my chest.

"Plus," he added, his voice slightly lower. I could sense him arranging the vials beside me, still working, constantly moving. "I like you."

I turned my head to look at him. He was studying the jars. "You like me?"

"Of course. What's not to like?"

"I—" He was speaking so casually. What did he mean? Was he saying he liked me as in "We're friends, of course I wouldn't betray you"? Or as in "You're not an awful person, and I'm happy for you to be queen"? Or . . . or did he mean he liked me, as in he *liked* me? As in had feelings for me?

I should ask him.

I was definitely not going to ask him.

"Are you ready?" I said, with more confidence than I felt. "We'll start with the copper."

Fitzroy raised his eyebrows at that, but then he nodded.

The first two attempts yielded nothing of use. The copper was uninterested in reacting, the iron similarly bored. Then I tossed in some zinc.

The reaction was almost immediate. The zinc fizzed, releasing a gas that smelled strongly of garlic.

"Get back," Fitzroy said. "It could be poisonous."

But I just stared at the gas. A reaction. I'd finally gotten a reaction, a visible, testable reaction. Had I done it?

I had to be sure. "Quick. Fetch me some food."

"Food?"

"So I can poison it! I need to lace something with arsenic, and then test it, to make sure it works." I waved my right hand at him, already reaching for more of the powder with my left. "Fetch some, quickly, quickly!"

Fitzroy nodded and strode out of the lab, and I laughed. Spirit of niter and zinc! I'd known the answer was lurking here somewhere. I'd known I could do it.

I grabbed another bowl and filled it with more acid, ready for Fitzroy's return.

When he finally came back, he carried a piece of bread with jam spread on top. It had a bite taken out of it—he must have stolen someone's supper. I sprinkled arsenic powder into the jam, stirring it with a knife until it vanished, and then took a glob of it and added it to the acid. I threw in another piece of zinc and waited.

Another cloud of garlicky gas burst out.

"I did it," I said, as Fitzroy pulled me away from the still-streaming gas. "I did it!" I wanted to jump up and down. I wanted to spin on the spot. I wanted to squeal. And why not? I did all three at once, the world spinning around me, already slightly dizzy from how wide I was grinning. And Fitzroy was there, grinning too, looking at me like . . . like I was someone who'd just figured out how to jump up to the moon, like I'd figured out how to fly, like I could solve all the world's mysteries if I put my mind to it. So I threw my arms around him, pulling him close, still laughing and squealing. He pressed his hands against my back, holding me steady, and another thrill ran over my skin, the sense of him so close.

I giggled and twisted back to look at the central table again.

"Now we have to test the cake," I said. "Just to be sure."

The poisoned sponge was growing mold in a cupboard. I hoped the addition wouldn't affect the test.

It didn't. That test worked, too. Fizzing zinc, garlic gas. I jumped on the spot. I'd solved it. A test for arsenic. A way to save lives. A way to find the murderer, if I used it right.

I hugged Fitzroy again. I could do this. I was almost there.

I went to Holt's office first thing the following morning, carrying spirit of niter and zinc. When I told him I'd found a way to test for arsenic, he stared at me.

"Are you sure?"

I nodded. "Watch." And I demonstrated the test, talking him through the theory, as far as I understood it.

"Spirit of niter is dangerous, of course, so we'll have to be careful how it's used. But the materials are common enough, so the test shouldn't be too expensive. And if we train the current tasters to use the acid safely, we could pay them for that. I mean, we'll still need tasters for a while, because this is just one poison, but—it's a start, isn't it? Even having a reliable test will discourage people from trying it."

"Yes," Holt said. "Yes, it will." If he wasn't so dignified, I might have described his expression as a grin. "This is most impressive, Your Majesty. Most impressive. We are lucky to have you, truly we are."

"It was simply science."

"But you made the effort to do it. The Forgotten chose well in you, Your Majesty. Once we get through all this, you will be magnificent."

"I—thank you." I picked at the skin around my fingernail. He'd meant to praise me, but his words were unsettling, somehow. They reminded me of that woman I'd encountered in the streets. Mary. "About what happened yesterday—that woman who asked for my blessing. I don't understand why she thought that would help."

Holt templed his fingertips together. "I've told you, Your Majesty, that I believe you were chosen by the Forgotten. It is no surprise that others have reached the same conclusion. Or that they would think you have divine powers of your own. The past weeks have been unusual for the kingdom, to say the least. It is not surprising that people are looking for their own explanations."

"But I don't have any powers. I couldn't say I didn't then, but—I don't have any powers like that."

It felt so dishonest, to let people imagine that my touch, my words, could do that good. That I was somehow innately blessed.

"These things can work in strange ways, Your Majesty. I think anyone expecting to wake up with a pile of money at the foot of their bed because of the kindness of the Forgotten will be very disappointed. But they find their ways to help us, when they wish to. They have their agents in this kingdom, their believers, their chosen. Putting a mind like yours on the throne . . . that could still be their blessing."

"But—how can people think the Forgotten care about us, and also think that they wanted the entire old court to die?"

Holt considered me in silence for a long moment. "The old court was choking this kingdom, Your Majesty. You have to weed the garden before you can plant flowers, must you not?"

I stared at him. "People aren't weeds."

"You are right, of course, Your Majesty. I only meant—we cannot always understand why the divine act as they do. But we must have faith that it will all work out for the best in the end."

But cold had settled inside me, too deep for his apology to dislodge. The Forgotten had agents in this world, he said. What if he believed he was one of them?

TWENTY-THREE

THE NEXT MORNING, MY ADVISERS BROUGHT MORE bad news. Sten had attacked the convoy to Rickstone Castle, and captured all of the prisoners. And then he had taken control of the prison himself.

He'd left the guards unharmed—they, he claimed, had done nothing wrong—and one had returned to the capital to warn us. The rest had defected to Sten.

"He's gathering support in the south, as we expected," Holt said, his fingers trailing over a map on the table. "Most of the minor nobles are siding with him—hoping for the favor of a new king, no doubt—and providing men for his cause. The

Darkwoods in the east have also been contacted by him. We can hope they won't get involved, after so many deaths, but if they believe you were the killer . . ." Holt shook his head. "We have received letters from other nobles around the kingdom, telling us how loyal they are, but how difficult it is to support us. Asking for lower taxes, more land, special favors. We cannot grant them all."

"Subtlety is a lost art," Norling said, wrinkling her nose.

"Indeed," Holt said. "Well, we could try to bribe these nobles to support us, but to be frank, Sten, with his vast fortunes, can offer them more."

"A low price to pay, if Her Majesty survives."

I sucked my bottom lip under my teeth. I didn't know what to do. I had wanted all decisions to travel through me, but my advisers had been right. I really didn't know what I was talking about. I didn't know what would be best. "We can review laws," I said slowly. "And of course we'll change anything that's unjust. And if land is not being used, perhaps we can find new owners for it, once all this is done. But maybe—we could suggest our disbelief that they'd only support the queen for monetary gain. It seems unworthy of the greatest nobles of Epria."

The words sounded utterly ridiculous. But Holt was nodding. "Perhaps invoke the Forgotten there, too. Why would they demand land in order to support their chosen queen?"

I didn't like the idea of more lies, building a legend around me. But these wouldn't hurt anyone. We needed to do it.

"We believe Sten is staying in Newsam Manor, here," Holt said, pointing to a spot on the map about seventy miles south of the capital, "but he will not remain there for long. No doubt he has gone there because the Manor has the greatest collection of old weapons and armor that we know of, beyond his own."

"You cannot support an army with a mishmash of old relics," Norling said.

"Yet he lacks the time or the skill to forge new ones. It'll help his cause that *we* don't have weapons or armor, either. The ones we do have are more ceremonial than sharp. Even without supplies or training, he will be better prepared than we are."

"More people have been leaving the city," Norling said. "Mostly nobles, but some merchants, too. We've lost the Renshaws, and Nicholas Anderson. More will follow them."

"Do you think they're joining him?" I asked.

"It's unclear. They could just be trying to avoid the entire situation. I suppose we cannot blame them. And people are angry, Freya, with your actions."

"With what, exactly?"

"*Gustav's Treatise*, Your Majesty. It hardly paints the nobility in a good light. To see you *distributing* it . . ." She shook her head. "They think you don't respect them, and the old ways. But I do have one piece of good news. I have information on Sofia Thorn. She is not helping Sten, it seems, or providing him information. She has returned to her own lands in the west with her husband."

"Then why did she leave, if she's not against me?"

"Her husband truly is sick," Norling said. "I assume she wanted to retreat from the capital before anything else occurred, like so many of our potential allies. No one wishes to be caught in the middle of this. They will all return, I am certain, once things are settled. The cowards probably expect a pardon."

"And my father? What have they done with him?"

"He is at Newsam Manor, too," Holt said. "Unharmed, we believe."

"Has Sten made any threats against him?"

"No, Your Majesty," Norling said. "He claims he is keeping your father for trial, after you have been captured. To see if he was involved in the murders, too."

"But he wasn't. Of course he wasn't."

Except—I couldn't know that. Not for certain. All I knew was that *I* hadn't been involved. Would my father have been that desperate to increase our influence? I didn't think so, but it was possible. Anything was possible.

"Do you have any more evidence about who *was* involved in the murders?"

"Not yet, Your Majesty," Norling said. "We lost a powerful resource in Thorn, and I admit, we have been distracted with more immediate matters of security."

"But, Your Majesty, it grieves me to inform you that there have been more rumors about you," Holt said. "Notably, about you and William Fitzroy."

"Me and Fitzroy?"

"Nobles had of course noticed that you have grown closer, since the murders. Many are speculating that you intend to marry him, perhaps that the two of you schemed together to put yourselves on the throne. Nonsense, of course, but it is sordid enough for people to enjoy spreading it."

"If they've noticed we weren't friends before, how could we have plotted together?"

"They say you were concealing your relationship, to protect yourselves. Absolute nonsense. But still, I must warn you again—be wary of Fitzroy. Both because any contact with him threatens your position, and because we do not know that he was not involved."

"We've also lost a lot more of our guards," Norling said, into the quiet that followed Holt's statement. "They seem to think they'll die if they remain. I recommend making it clear that leaving is not an option."

"No," I said softly. "No, I can't threaten them into staying, if they think they're going to die."

"Then we must increase our remaining guards' patrols immediately," Holt said. "Increase the work hours of those who remain. And we will have to recruit more people from the city."

"Untrained! Untested!" Norling said. "Who knows if we can trust them? What sort of men will want to become guards at such a time, with Torsten Wolff bearing down on us?"

"We don't have a choice," Holt snapped. "We must get it

done." He sighed, pressing his hands on the table. "It will be all right. We are seeing more true believers by the day. People want to support their queen."

"True believers?" I sat straighter, apprehension prickling through me.

"Your campaign is working. People are talking about your goodness, your new scientific discovery. Some are calling it a sign that the Forgotten want to keep you safe."

"It's science," I said. "Not divine intervention."

"But if people use it to support you . . . do not mistake me, Your Majesty. You still face a lot of opposition in the city, and a lot of mistrust. We are trying to stop people from speaking against you and your court, although it is difficult to do so when we have so few men at our disposal. But you have supporters, too. We can use this to our advantage."

But *what* advantage, I wondered, as I walked down to my lab after the meeting. What was Holt's goal? I couldn't forget his words about clearing out the weeds. If the murderer was on my side, as Sten suspected, if he had killed them for *me* . . .

I had to find more evidence.

I tested every part of the cake I could separate, but the results weren't particularly revealing. The arsenic was in the sponge. It was in the icing. The flakes of actual gold were safe to eat, but the rest of the cake was deadly.

"It could just be in the sponge," Naomi said, peering over

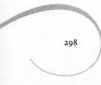

my shoulder at my notes. "It might have left traces on the icing, after so long."

"Possibly." Then I shook my head. "Then there'd be traces of it on the gold flakes, too. Unless the gold is interfering with the results? But why would it? It's unreactive." I tapped my pen on the table. *Think.* "We need the recipe. It'd be pointless slipping the poison into both the cake *and* the icing, too much risk. So it must have been hidden in one of the ingredients. What ingredients are in both cake and icing?"

"Sugar," Madeleine said. "Sugar and water."

"It could have been hidden in the sugar, maybe," I said. The arsenic powder would probably mix well with sugar granules, if no one looked too closely. But then the recipe would have gone wrong. It wouldn't have been sweet enough, unless the cook knew to compensate.

But if someone had diluted the arsenic in water, what could we possibly do next? The killer couldn't have added it to the palace water system—everyone would have died, far sooner, and not only at the banquet. So someone with access to the kitchens must have added it that night. Which once again narrowed the list of suspects down to pretty much anybody.

"If it was in the water . . ." Madeleine closed her eyes. "What if it was an accident? The king was unwell. So what if someone was poisoning him gradually? Not enough for anyone to notice, but slowly. Over time, it might look normal to anyone in the kitchens. Someone doing their job, putting something in the king's water. I wouldn't be surprised if he had his own special supply."

"If he did," Fitzroy said, "I never heard of it."

"But you think someone could have been poisoning him?" I said. "A different someone from the attacker at the banquet?"

"Or the *same* attacker. Accidentally. Maybe someone put the poison in the wrong place, or they used too much, or something else went wrong. And a single target became the entire court."

"Maybe," I said. Then: "No. That doesn't make sense. You couldn't kill an entire court with a dose meant for one person." I ran my fingers through my hair, thinking. "But the water supply—that might be helpful. Could he have asked for special water for the banquet?"

"Special water?" Madeleine repeated. "As in, water imported from some fabulous mountain spring, rumored to grant its visitors eternal life? That sort of water?"

"Yes. Something like that. If that was the case, the water could have been poisoned long before it entered the castle, and kept locked away until the cake was made."

Naomi turned to Fitzroy. "Did you hear your father mention anything like that?"

He shook his head. "If he planned that, he didn't mention it to me. It might be in his letters, but—my father liked to brag. If it was special, he would have told somebody. And he would have used it in other dishes, wouldn't he?"

But all this speculation was pointless, when we could simply perform a test. "We have to get to the palace kitchens. It's the only way we can know. We'll test the ingredients there."

Fitzroy nodded. "I'll go tonight."

"*We'll* go tonight," I said. "You can't carry everything back here, and you might miss something important."

"Is that safe?" Naomi asked.

"It'll have to be."

The first challenge was getting out of the Fort. My guard was somewhat depleted now, but it wasn't gone, and people continued to watch both the front gate and the bridge. As queen, I could probably have ordered my way through, but I couldn't let my guards tail me through the streets. I couldn't draw attention to the investigation.

In the end, dropping my guards was fairly straightforward, if unpleasant. We all retired for the night, and then left the rooms through the hidden passage we'd found before. Fitzroy distracted the guard placed on the other end, and we emerged slightly damp, but otherwise unscathed.

Leaving the Fort itself was harder, but Fitzroy's solution was sheer brazenness. With no makeup, wearing plain dresses and coats, our hair in simple braids, Madeleine, Naomi, and I blended into the background. No one would expect the queen to sneak out of her own castle, and so nobody looked too closely when I did. Fitzroy was more noticeable, so he didn't even try to hide his identity. He strode confidently to the front gate and asked the guard to open it for him and his friends.

"Getting out of harm's way, are you, Fitzroy?" the guard said. "Can't say I blame you."

"Not tonight, Mills. Just wanting to get out of these dreary walls for a while."

"Can't blame you for that either," the guard said. "Wish I could join you. Hang on, then." And, as simple as that, the front gate opened, the drawbridge lowered, and we escaped into the city.

For the first time I'd ever seen, the palace windows were dark, the sweeping lawns untended and slightly unruly. It looked almost peaceful through the wrought iron fence, undisturbed, the river reflecting the stars.

The gates had been left unguarded, fastened with a heavy padlock. Fitzroy pulled a key out of his pocket and opened it. I didn't ask where he'd gotten it. "I think we'll be lucky," he said. "All the death should have kept away the looters."

"The looters?"

He raised his eyebrows at me. "The castle is practically lined with gold," he said. "Of course people are going to take what they can. But the murders probably put them off the idea for a while."

It wasn't very reassuring. Surely gold was gold, no matter what superstitions people wove around it. A little unpleasantness wouldn't stop any otherwise willing thieves.

But as we followed the narrow path down the lawn, we saw no one. The scraps of floating lanterns lay in the grass, and banners flapped sadly between the trees, half ruined by the wind and rain.

"No one's been here," I said. "No one's cleaned up at all." My voice sounded too loud, shattering the silence.

"Your advisers wanted it left untouched."

"For the investigation?"

Fitzroy nodded.

We approached the rear of the palace and the double doors that led into the ballroom. Even now, weeks after the event, one of the doors stood slightly open, inviting us in. It was as though the entire palace had been frozen in time, stuck in the moment its court fell.

The door creaked as we pushed it open and stepped inside.

The feasting tables were still in place, but many of the chairs had been knocked backward, the golden plates abandoned on the floor. Doves still cooed in the rafters. Instruments lay abandoned in the corner. And there, there at that table, that was where I had sat, where I would have died if I hadn't walked away.

Madeleine's eyes glistened with tears. "So this is it. This is where they all died."

"This is it," Fitzroy said. He walked the length of the hall, past the scattered chairs and jewels spilled across the floor.

I turned on the spot, still staring. It was unsettling, to see the hall so empty, so quiet. Disturbed in the middle of a feast and left to gather dust. Someone had clearly made a quick attempt to clean up—removed the bodies, removed the mess—but otherwise, the feast might have simply paused. As though everyone had wandered away and forgotten to return.

"We need to head to the kitchens," I said. "Do you know the way?"

Madeleine nodded. She led us out through another door, into a corridor lit solely by moonlight. The gilt walls glimmered.

Footsteps echoed from farther down the corridor. I clutched Fitzroy's sleeve and jerked my head in the direction of the sound. Looters. What would they do if they saw us? Would they recognize me as queen? Or would they see us as rival treasure hunters, standing in their way?

The passage was cluttered with statues and human-size vases. I ducked behind one of the vases and Fitzroy pressed behind me, pushing me even closer against its cold surface, his heart thudding against my back.

Madeleine and Naomi darted behind a statue of two lovers entwined.

The footsteps moved closer. Fitzroy's breath brushed my ear.

The person came around the corner.

It was Holt.

I gasped, and Fitzroy pressed a hand over my mouth to stop the sound. Holt was striding down the corridor, looking for all the world like he belonged. His cloak flapped behind him.

What was he doing?

I waited until he turned the corner again, and then I slipped out from behind the vase and crept after him. Fitzroy snatched for my hand, but I pulled away. I had to see what Holt was up to. What was he doing here?

Around another corner, and another. Fitzroy grabbed my arm, pulling me to his side. "Stop," he hissed in my ear. "I know where he's going."

I raised my eyebrows at him. *Where?*

"The shrine to the Forgotten is this way. It's the only thing down here."

"There's a shrine in the palace?"

"Of course. Even if my father didn't care in the slightest about the Forgotten, he wouldn't miss a chance to show off his gold."

I nodded and stepped forward again, but he pulled me back. "Wait. We can look once he's gone."

"What good will that be?"

"We can see what he's done, without him seeing us."

I wanted to argue further, but he did have a point. If Holt saw us, we'd have no chance of uncovering whatever secrets he was hiding. And he'd know we'd been here, investigating. I couldn't let him know that, not until we could rule him out as a suspect.

So I waited. Tucked in an alcove by a statue, twisting the

ends of my hair around my fingers, my friends beside me. None of us spoke.

Why was Holt here? Surely, if he had an innocent reason, he wouldn't have come in the dark, alone. But what could he possibly be doing?

The minutes crawled by. Then more footsteps, and Holt hurried past again.

I peered around the statue. Holt was carrying a sack in his arms, like its contents were precious beyond words.

Once he was out of sight, I stepped into the corridor and paused for Fitzroy to lead the way. But when we got there, the shrine was empty. A little moonlight fell through the narrow windows, but no gold glinted, no statues loomed, no relics decorated the walls. There were a few wooden pews, and a wooden altar at the front, but otherwise, nothing.

Or not quite nothing. Flowers had been left on the altar. I stepped closer. They were fresh, the petals still bright and blooming.

"Well, the looters have been here," Fitzroy said.

"There was more?"

"Much more. There was gold plate, and tapestries . . . jewels embedded in the walls. It's all gone."

"Holt," I said. "Do you think he stole them?" He'd been carrying something precious. But he wouldn't steal from the Forgotten.

"Maybe," Madeleine said. "If he convinced himself it wasn't

stealing. He thinks the old court was too extravagant, doesn't he? Maybe he considered the gold an affront to the Forgotten."

"How convenient," Fitzroy said.

I picked one of the flowers off the altar. The petals were smooth under my fingertips. This was what Holt considered a suitable offering. Fresh, delicate, pure. I was tempted to put the flower in my bag, as evidence, but I paused. It was a genuine offering, and although I didn't believe in the Forgotten myself, I didn't want to disrupt that. I laid it carefully on top and turned back to the others.

"Let's go down to the kitchens," I said. "Before somebody else comes along."

TWENTY-FOUR

THE KITCHENS WERE NEAR THE BANQUET HALL, DOWN
a twisting staircase that, although unadorned, matched the opu-
lence of the rest of the palace. It was certainly nicer than any
part of the Fort, lined with neat white stone and sweeping metal
banisters.

The kitchen itself was two huge redbrick rooms. Ovens
covered one wall, and there was a large table in the middle of
the room, still covered with chopping boards and knives and
abandoned pans. More pans hung from hooks on the walls, and
hundreds of empty plates were piled up on the side.

Where we looked depended on when the cake had been

made. There were no traces of the cake or its ingredients on the center table, so I strode into the second room and started searching through the cupboards instead.

"Empty sugar sacks over here," Fitzroy said.

"Put them on the center table. Madeleine, Naomi, look for anything that might have contained water."

"Especially if it has any fancy labeling on it," Naomi said.

"Yes." And I would look around for other clues—the cake recipe, perhaps, or remnants of the gold decorations.

I found nothing. The sugar tested negative for arsenic, and we couldn't find any signs that water had been imported for the cake. I scraped my hands through my hair. There had to be *something*.

"What else goes into cake and icing?" I said. "What have we missed?"

"What about coloring?" Naomi said slowly. "The cake was golden yellow, right? What if the poison was hidden in there?"

Madeleine gripped the table. All the color rushed from her face. "No," she said, in a strangled squeak. "Oh no."

"Madeleine?" I ran over and grabbed her shoulder. She looked like she was about to be sick. "What's wrong?"

"The color," she said. "What if it was in the color?"

"What do you mean?"

She let out a shaky breath. "There's a color, a beautiful vivid green, that has arsenic as one of its ingredients. It's fine, you don't eat it, but artists—when artists use it, they get lines on their fingernails. Black and white ridges, from the poison." She scraped at her own painted thumbnail, until a bare patch peeked through. She held it out to me. White lines ran across the nail. "See? That's just from painting with it. I don't know what color was used in the cake, but what if it had arsenic as an ingredient, too? If nobody knew that . . . what if it was an accident? What if nobody meant it at all?"

Naomi frowned. "Why would you put poison in your paints?"

"Because artists will do anything to create the exact color they want. As long as they don't eat the paints, it's not going to kill them. But if someone didn't know, if they got a new color, an exciting rare color that also contained arsenic, and they baked it into the cakes . . . the cakes would have been full of it. Every piece. Every single bite of it. It's just dye. Just color. If you saw it, and you didn't know . . . oh no no no." She sank onto a kitchen stool. "What if they died for nothing? Nothing at all?"

"We don't know that," I said. "We don't even know if there was poison in the dye. And if there was, someone could have used it on purpose. We don't know. We have to find it, first."

We searched through jars, looking for even a hint of the dye. The rich smell of spices tickled my nose, but we didn't find anything even vaguely gold or yellow.

Four large jars like those that held spices had been left on the side of the counter. I hurried over and pulled off the lids. Nothing but darkness inside. I moved the lamp closer. The first jar was scraped clean. The second was the same. But in the third . . . in the third, a little yellow powder clung to the sides and to the base.

"Here. I found it." It was difficult to tell in the dim light, but it looked the same as the cake. And how much yellow-gold powder could there be in a kitchen?

I used a spatula to scrap a few clumps of yellow powder out of the jar and deposit them in the zinc and niter bowl.

The dye dissolved. The zinc fizzed. Garlic smoke exploded out of the bowl.

My friends flinched back, but I stayed close, staring at the bubbling metal, the powder dissolving into nothing. Here it was. Here was the answer. I'd expected to feel more excited. More accomplished. Now I just stared at the mixture, horrifying certainty settling into my stomach. This was how the murderer had done it. This was what had killed them.

"All right," I said. "All right. We found the source of the poison. So now we need to find the source of the dye."

Madeleine let out a shaky breath.

"It wasn't necessarily an accident," I said. It couldn't be. If it had been an accident, I had no defense against Sten. No one would believe me, not even if I had all the evidence in the world. "It's a possibility, but—we have to keep investigating. We have to assume someone planned this."

I picked up the jar. It was heavy and awkward to hold, but I wasn't going to risk scraping out more powder now. I needed to take the rest back to the lab.

"Well, then. What are you lot doing down here?"

I jumped. Two men stood in the doorway, each holding a large sack. I could see gold candlesticks and decorative cups peeking through the top of each. I tightened my grip on the jar and stepped back. My hip banged against the counter. If they realized I was queen . . .

But they wouldn't. Why would the queen be here, in the kitchens, dressed as simply as this? They'd think we were other looters, at worst.

"After the spices as well, are you?"

Madeleine stepped forward, smiling prettily, all trace of paleness and panic gone. "Oh, sirs," she said. "Are you here to help with the cleanup? We've been struggling here. The queen's council told us that more men would be following along soon enough. We've been trying our best, but, well, we're not near strong enough to move everything by ourselves." She watched them expectantly, that pleasant, hopeful smile still on her face.

The man stared at her. "That's right," he said. "We're just here to help out."

"Excellent. Oh, but you seem to have run out of sacks. I think there are some piled in that closet. Let us check for you."

She began to walk toward the door, but the man stepped forward. "Hang on," he said. He reached for my jar. "Let me take this. It looks cumbersome."

"No," I said, fighting not to stutter. "I'm all right."

"What's in there? Spices?"

"Rubbish," I said. "Things I swept up." I didn't sound particularly convincing.

"I'll take it. Dispose of it for you."

Logic said I should give him the jar. If he opened it, he'd find nothing worthwhile inside and discard it. It was the safest course of action, the most sensible thing to do. I knew that. I knew it, even as I flinched away from him, my arms tightening around the jar. I knew it even as I knew my actions had been suspicious, that he'd never believe it was worthless now.

The man snatched for the jar. I dodged back, but I didn't move quickly enough. His fingers scraped against the ridges around the rim, and his nails found purchase. He tugged as I pulled away, throwing me off balance. The heavy jar teetered, and I tried to tighten my grip, but the man snatched again, and it fell. The pottery smashed on the floor.

I dove after it. "You idiot." I shoved the shards aside. One rough edge scraped my finger, drawing blood. There had to be some dye left, something stuck to the pot . . . but I could barely see in the darkness, and the floor was dusty, unswept since the night of the banquet. I couldn't see anything.

"Freya!" Naomi grabbed my arm and hauled me backward. Madeleine ran for the wooden door, wrenching it open to reveal another dark corridor beyond. Naomi yanked me along, too, half dragging me across the room and into the corridor, as Fitzroy ran behind us. One of the men shouted, but Madeleine did not stop. Honey-brown hair streamed out behind her as she led us up the stairs, through doors, up and around and out into the palace gardens again.

My sides burned. I could barely breathe. But I kept running, gripping Naomi's hand, the taste of grass choking in the back of my throat, until we were out on the city streets again.

"I don't think they followed us," Naomi said, when we stopped for breath. "Just didn't want us to interfere."

I leaned against a wall, gasping. "We lost it," I said. "We lost the dye. We lost the proof."

"But we still know," Madeleine said. "We know what caused it."

"No. You don't understand." Without the dye, I couldn't prove it. Why would anyone believe me without proof? "I have to prove it wasn't me. How can I do that now?" It's lost in the dust.

"The dye didn't prove that," Naomi said softly. "It was just a start. And you still know it's poisonous. You'll find something else."

I nodded, my breath rushing out through my teeth. She was right. There was no point in panicking now. We still knew the dye was responsible. We had *something*. "We need to go through the letters again," I said. "If we can find where he ordered it from, or who might have suggested it to him . . . that's what we have to do."

The letters were less than helpful.

It was easy to tell which notes had been taken by a scribe,

and which had been written by the king himself. The scribes' handwriting was always elaborate but clear, their pens flowing across the pages. The king's writing was nigh illegible, a mixture of jagged scratches and ostentatious loops. But as I tried to decipher the words on page after page, reading his comments on proposed laws and taxation decisions and pleas from his advisers to find a new wife who might give him legitimate heirs, I had to admit that he, too, was not exactly as I thought. Yes, his court was wasteful, dramatic to the point of ridiculousness, but he'd responded with care to every issue presented to him. And there were so many issues—as many as I had faced and more, a deluge of needs and questions and problems to be faced.

But then I'd pull another page from the pile and see his demands for more and more—more jewels for the queen, more clothes, new paintings to fill the supposedly "empty" parts of the palace. A better cook, additional guards, more and more things, while he waved away concerns about finances with a casual flick of his pen.

Then, after what felt like a hundred useless pages: "I found something."

Fitzroy looked up from his own pile of papers. "What was that?"

"Here." I scanned the page again to be sure. "Listen to this. 'We're continuing the search for King's Yellow, as Your Majesty requested. The people here call it orpiment, and they tell us that it can cure all manner of impossible ailments. One must suspect they are merely trying to raise the price, but we will continue to negotiate.'" I looked up. "King's Yellow. That would fit."

"But it sounds like he's talking about a medicine, not a color," Naomi said. "Who would confuse arsenic with medicine?"

"It *is* a medicine," I said. I'd heard it before, the details lurking deep in my brain. "I think—I'm not sure." I flicked through the pile of letters, as though the answer would be hiding there. "I've heard of it being used. In very small amounts, when someone is very sick." To purge the sickness out of them.

"Madeleine," Fitzroy said. "Have you ever heard of a color called King's Yellow before?"

She shook her head. "Never. The dye didn't look familiar to me—I've never seen that exact shade before."

"But if my father discovered something new, of course he'd name it after himself."

"There's more," I said, flicking back to the letter again. "'We are told the mineral forms in the hot springs in the mountains, which explains the extreme expense, and why, as Your Majesty believed, it is only available in Rejka. We send another sample to Your Majesty with this letter. If the quality is satisfactory and the price good, we will acquire more.' The king's written something else at the bottom." I peered at the scribbled handwriting. "'Spare no expense.'" The letter was dated a few months ago. "Madeleine. You said the king was unwell, didn't you? He had some stomach complaint. So, what if someone gave him this dye as a potential *cure* for his illness?"

"The golden wine," Fitzroy said slowly. I looked at him in confusion. "My father's wine looked gold. I noticed it a couple of months ago. I assumed it was just his goblets changing the color, but what if he dyed it instead? If he was taking King's Yellow as a medicine, he could have mixed it with the wine. It would have suited his arrogance."

"And then he was so impressed by the medicine that he decided to make a show of it in the banquet?"

Madeleine shook her head. "If he found a magical cure for his illness, he wouldn't share it like that. He'd hoard it all for himself."

"Perhaps he wanted to show it off," I said. "If it's a rare and expensive medicine, what better way to show how rich and powerful he is than to throw all of that away at a banquet? On his birthday? Like a—like a declaration that he's well again, and he can do whatever he likes."

"I don't know, Freya," Fitzroy said. "If it was rare enough to shout about, why didn't he shout about it?"

True. But there had to be *something* in here. We had a name—King's Yellow—and a source. We knew it was rare and expensive. But they were scientific answers, not explanations. Who had introduced the king to it in the first place, if even Madeleine had never heard of this dye? Had it been an accident, or had someone prompted him to do it? And was the poison in the dye he'd ordered, or had someone changed them along the way?

I placed the paper to one side and continued to read.

TWENTY-FIVE

I WATCHED HOLT CLOSELY AT THE COUNCIL MEETING the next morning. He looked tired, but he didn't look guilty, and he didn't seem to know that I'd been in the palace, too. I wanted to ask him what he'd been doing there, accuse him of some connection to the murders, but I swallowed the words, down down down, until I nearly choked on their bitterness.

I didn't *know* that he was involved. Not yet. And if he was involved, and I revealed what I knew too early . . . I could lose the chance to prove it.

"We are running out of time," Norling said. "Sten has swept east, and is marching back to the capital. The Darkwoods have joined him, as have the Solbergs, with all of their own resources at his disposal. The kingdom is against you, Your Majesty, and Sten will not hold back when he arrives."

"How many men does he have?" I was almost afraid to hear the answer.

"Ten thousand."

"And how many men do *we* have?"

"Trained guards and soldiers?" Norling said. "Perhaps thirty. I would estimate around twenty thousand people remain in the city, but most will not fight for you. You have gained some supporters, Your Majesty, but most people want to survive, and if staying quiet and allowing Sten into the walls is the best way to do that, that is what they will do. I suggest that you run now. Before it becomes impossible to leave."

"No," Holt said. "She cannot run. If she leaves, she will forfeit the crown."

"At least this way, she will live."

"She'll live," Holt said. "But for how long? Sten will hunt her down, and without the crown to protect her, how will she hide from him? Where could she go? She couldn't possibly hope to evade him forever. And then what will happen to the kingdom? It will be stuck with a blasphemous usurper rather than their rightful queen. We cannot allow it. We must stay and fight."

"Fight?" Norling laughed. "Fight how? This isn't going to be a civil war, Rasmus. This will be a massacre."

Her words rang in the silence. I'd known, of course, that my chances against Sten were slim. But to hear my closest adviser insisting that I was going to die . . . my first instinct was to run to the library, pull out books on military strategy, history books about battles where impossibly small forces defeated their larger enemies, but what would be the point? I couldn't become a better strategist than Sten or my advisers in a few days. I could only win through invention. It had taken me years of study to be able to think inventively in the lab. And now I had to pretend I could learn how to think inventively in battle by the end of the week.

"Norling," I said quietly. "You've always advised me to appear strong before. To return to the palace, to punish people, to fight. But now you want me to run. Isn't that weak, too?"

"Perhaps, Your Majesty. I have always advised you because I want your reign to be strong. But now—I am concerned for your safety now, Your Majesty. I am concerned for *you*. Do not continue with this folly and put your life at risk."

"The Forgotten support our queen," Holt said in a low voice. "They will protect her. We will find a way."

"The Forgotten are not *here*, Rasmus!" Norling snapped. "They have never been here. They will never be here. This is not some story of divine justice. There will be no magical intervention. This is a tragedy. We must leave."

"I won't leave," I said, my voice shaking slightly. I couldn't, not when people were relying on me, not when my father was at risk. I pressed my hands against the desk. "If I leave, I'll just look even more guilty. I have to find a way."

"Your Majesty—"

"No. I can't leave."

"A wise choice," Holt said.

"A foolish one," Norling said.

Holt ignored her. "We must focus on fortifying the city," he said. "Rationing must be put in place, in case of a siege. I will send men to protect our water supply—"

He talked through the strategy, and I tried to focus, but everything he said was defensive. We would strengthen the walls, add to the guards, protect the food. As though we just needed the resolve to hold strong until Sten gave in.

So if my plan didn't work, if I couldn't convince him to stop his attack . . . what would we do then?

All I had on my side was science, and the bubbling rumors that I was *chosen* by the Forgotten. They didn't exactly mesh together, and most people couldn't *really* believe in my supposedly divine ascension. The Gustavites had planned an entire campaign around the idea that I was rotten, just like the court, that the Forgotten despised me. And maybe their feelings had come from an honest place, once, a desperate need for change, but they had still tried to murder me, still encouraged others to turn against me. They'd been quiet since Sten's attack, since I'd distributed those pamphlets, but they were still an unknown quantity, potentially dangerous.

But I wasn't who they thought I was. I cared, I did, and I wanted to make changes. I wanted to help people. Even if I wasn't really chosen by the Forgotten, surely our aims might fit together. If Sten took the capital, it would be back to the way the court was before, undoing all of the Forgotten's supposed interventions.

"Do you have anything to add, Your Majesty?" Holt said.

It was an insane idea. To convince the Gustavites to be on my side, to somehow twist around their entire agenda. If I could gently alter their ideology . . . but it would take subtlety, and time, and the nobles would be furious. It wasn't exactly the perfect solution.

"I'll go to the Minster this afternoon," I said instead. "To pay my respects." Make another show of my connection to the Forgotten, and let people think of it what they would. It seemed that faith would stop people from abandoning me, even if it wouldn't do much more.

But could I really use people's beliefs against them like that? If Holt had been involved in the murders, if he had been manipulating me all along, a puppet queen for his twisted agenda . . .

Could I manipulate them, too, to save myself?

Yes, I thought, and I hated myself slightly for the knowledge. I would manipulate them if it meant staying alive.

Norling was the first to leave after the council meeting concluded, marching off to arrange the Minster visit, while Holt reflected on his notes. I paused, too, standing behind my chair. I could ask him about his trip to the palace, or at least about things related to it, find some way to uncover the truth.

But if it *had* been suspicious, and I revealed what I knew too soon . . . it was too risky.

I had begun to walk toward the door when Holt spoke.

"Your Majesty? I hoped I could speak to you. In private."

I glanced at Norling's now-empty seat, and my heart started pounding. What could he want to say to me, that he couldn't say in front of her? "All right," I said carefully. "What is it?"

"You know that I am here to support you, Your Majesty. My goal—my *only* goal—is to help you survive."

"I know." And I did. Despite all my suspicion, I'd never doubted that he genuinely supported me. His belief was fervent, unsettling in its force. I was frightened by what he might have done in order to create this new court, what he might *still* be willing to do, but I knew he wouldn't directly hurt me.

Which made his statement all the more unsettling.

"So you know that I am speaking to your best interests when I say that William Fitzroy is a danger to you, in more ways that you realize."

"I know," I said again. "You've told me."

"But obviously I have not made the details clear enough, because you have ignored my advice. I told you that people are talking about you, saying you plotted to take the throne together. There are some filthy lies in there, Your Majesty, things that I do not wish to repeat, but Sten is more than happy to endorse them, and they are doing real damage to you. They are eroding our message of the Forgotten's chosen queen."

"I appreciate your concern," I said, "but if people are already talking, I can't change that now. It'll only look more suspicious if I push him away, like they stumbled onto the truth."

"That is not all, Your Majesty. I know you wish to see the good in people, and I respect you for that, but I have been conducting my own research into the murders, and into Fitzroy's behavior. Something has not been right."

"Why can't Norling hear about this?"

"She disagrees with me, Your Majesty. As she does about many things. She did not consider the avenues worth pursuing. But I believe she is wrong."

"And you've—found evidence?"

He'd been assembling a case against Fitzroy. Not openly, not with Norling, but in secret, alone. Because Fitzroy was a problem, and he needed to be dealt with. Because he damaged Holt's idea of the perfect chosen queen. An official investigation would find nothing on him, but if Holt was determined enough, and manipulated the evidence enough . . .

"I found a mention, in the diary of King Jorgen's chief adviser. He commented that the king planned to disinherit Fitzroy."

"Fitzroy was never *in*herited to begin with."

"But he always had that hope. We all knew that, Your Majesty. It seems very possible to me that Fitzroy was tired of being out of favor, and decided to act to change that."

"By murdering everybody?"

"He murdered many people, Your Majesty. Everyone who might have known anything about his so-called legitimacy. He wished to unsettle things, so that he could step into the throne instead."

Holt looked terrifyingly sincere. That would be odd if he were the murderer himself. But I didn't trust the sanity of anyone willing to kill so many people. If Holt could convince himself that he was an agent of the Forgotten, murdering for the greater good, surely he could convince himself that Fitzroy deserved to be punished, as well. Surely he could perform this one final task.

"Fitzroy didn't make any move for the throne," I said carefully. "He didn't want it."

"When he realized that someone in the city had survived, I believe he changed his strategy. He decided to win you over. Whether for a later betrayal or to gain the crown through marriage, I do not know."

"Stop." The word burst out of me. "That's enough. I trust Fitzroy. Which is more than I can say for you right now."

I almost asked him about his presence in the palace. The words were on the tip of my tongue, ready to be thrown at him, but then I saw his expression, and I paused. He looked resolved. As though the last piece of a terrible truth had fallen into place, and now he only had to react to it.

"I am sorry that you feel that way, Your Majesty," he said. "But the problem must be dealt with, regardless of your feelings. If you will excuse me."

He bowed, rather stiffly, and strode out of the room.

The problem must be dealt with. The words rang in my ears. Dealt with, like Holt may have dealt with the rest of the court. Like a weed, needing to be ripped away in order for his precious new queen to flourish.

I found Fitzroy in the lab, going through more of his father's papers. He glanced up as the door creaked open.

"Fitzroy." I closed the door behind me, sealing the rest of the castle away. "You have to go."

"Go?" He frowned. "Freya, what's wrong?"

"Holt—he thinks you're a threat."

He shook his head, turning back to the notes. "People always think I'm a threat. I've survived so far."

I had to make him understand. I hurried forward, grabbing his shoulder. "He says you have to be *dealt* with. He's going to kill you, Fitzroy."

He didn't even look up. "He's not going to kill me."

How could he be so calm? "You have to leave. Find some-where safe to go." I turned away decisively, as though he would move just because I willed it so. "Once this is all over, you'll be able to come back, whatever happens."

"Leave?" That got his attention. "I'm not going to leave."

"Yes, you are. It's common sense, Fitzroy! He's planning to kill you. You shouldn't stay here." I grabbed his arm, ready to haul him off the stool, but he didn't budge.

"Holt is not going to hurt me, Freya." His voice was low and calm, as though *I* was the one who didn't understand things here. "He's a bit strange, but he's not a murderer."

"You don't know that. Somebody here is. And he wants to get rid of you, either way."

"So I won't give him the pleasure."

"I'm your queen." I stuck up my chin. "You're supposed to do as I say."

"But I won't."

I could have shoved him. I almost did, to jolt some sense back into his idiot brain. "I could order you," I said. "I could kick you out of the Fort. My advisers would be more than happy if I did."

"You could. But you won't." He turned back to the notes again. I tugged on his arm, pulling him back around.

"Fitzroy—this isn't an empty threat. I don't want you to get hurt."

"Good," Fitzroy said. "Then let's concentrate on figuring this out who the murderer is." When I didn't move, he sighed. "You need me here, Freya. You can't expect me to leave, just because Holt is acting oddly."

"Fitzroy," I said again, softer this time. "Don't—I don't want you to get hurt because of me. All right?"

"And you think I want you to be hurt because of me?"

"I might be," I said quickly. Anything to convince him. "I might be, if you stay."

"Because I'm going to betray you and take the crown for myself?"

Why couldn't he take this *seriously*? "Because people are suspicious of our friendship. People are gossiping—"

"People always gossip. They'll be happy to have something to talk about other than impending death, and even happier to move on to a better subject when one appears."

"But you've heard them. They're saying we schemed together to kill your father. They think we're murderers, plotting to get us both on the throne."

"I know," he said, his voice slightly quieter. "But most of them won't believe it. Not if you give them a better story." I opened my mouth to argue again, desperation surging through me, but he shook his head. "Freya. I won't leave now. No matter what you say."

"But that makes no sense! You have to protect yourself. Why would you stay if it could kill you?"

He looked at me, steady, unblinking.

"Okay, I know *I've* stayed. But I have to stay. I'm the queen, Fitzroy!"

He frowned. "And I'm what? No one?"

"*No.* But you're someone who can leave. You can go, and

come back later, and survive this whole mess. Why wouldn't you do that?"

"Freya."

The words were rushing out of me now, getting faster and faster. "We don't need you. We can stop Sten without you. And we'll be able to solve this more quickly if we don't have to worry about your death. It's better if you leave. You have to go."

"You really haven't been paying attention, have you? You really think I'm going to leave?"

"Why wouldn't you?"

"You know why, Freya."

My heart was still pounding, and now the air in the lab felt too thin. I'd never been good at reading people, at understanding them, and I didn't want—I couldn't let my imagination get carried away. "What do you mean?"

He kissed me.

It couldn't have lasted more than a second. Just his lips pressed against mine, soft and warm. My stomach flipped, but before I could react, before I could *think*, he was moving back, hands resting on my shoulders.

"What are you doing?" I whispered.

He laughed softly. "You know what I'm doing."

"But—"

He glanced at my lips again. I couldn't breathe.

But then he turned away, stepping back to the table. "We

have to find out where my father learned about that pigment."

My skin prickled. I still—I needed him to leave, to be safe, but . . .

I couldn't force him to leave. I didn't want him to go, even though I did, even though it was the only sensible thing to do. "All right," I said eventually. "Let's—let's keep looking."

But it was hard to fight the urge to grab him and kiss him again.

TWENTY-SIX

I SET OUT FOR THE MINSTER THAT AFTERNOON. IT WAS
supposed to be a show of piety, a desperate attempt to help my
cause. But as I walked through the city, I could not stop thinking about Fitzroy.

He had kissed me. William Fitzroy had kissed me.

And I wanted to kiss him again.

What was wrong with me? My life was in danger, and I'd
been told, again and again, that Fitzroy made the situation
worse. Fitzroy's life was in danger just by being here. I shouldn't
even have been speaking to him, and even if I *did* speak to him,
even if I did have feelings for him . . . now wasn't the time. I had

a throne to keep, a city to protect.

I did not have time to think about this.

So I very decidedly did *not* think about Fitzroy. I didn't think about him when I walked down Main Street, my feet splashing in the puddles. I didn't think of him when a gentleman bowed and asked how my day had been. I didn't remember the warmth of his lips, or the way his eyes lit up when he was amused, or the thrill of him being so close. I *definitely* did not think about what would happen when I saw him again.

But I couldn't help wondering *why* he had done it. I knew why he'd *implied* he'd done it, but that didn't mean much. Words could be misconstrued. It could have been the adrenaline of our life-or-death situation. He could have just been trying to distract me, so I wouldn't force him to leave. Had he been using my feelings against me?

Not that I had feelings for him. But the feelings he assumed I had—I definitely did not have, because now was definitely not the time for any sort of ill-directed attachments.

And he'd kissed me, but he hadn't *kissed* me kissed me. Surely, people normally kissed you kissed you, when you seemed happy to be kissed? Surely he shouldn't just sort-of kiss me and then go straight back to research, not when he had never kissed me before.

It was supposed to be more. Did it count if it wasn't *more*?

Then again, it was probably a good thing it hadn't been more. I could barely think as it was.

The Minster loomed ahead of me, its tower swept up in the fog. The bells tolled as I approached, marking the hour. People crowded its courtyard, calling out my name as I passed. I smiled at them, nodded my head, but walked through the front doors without further incident.

The inside of the Minster was almost empty. The priest stood by the altar, and he bowed at me as I entered, but he did not speak.

I walked down the aisle, my heart pounding. So much had changed since the last time I had walked here. Since those people had watched me, waiting, their expectation and grief filling the air.

I stopped before the altar and stared up at its carved faces. I couldn't have identified even half of them. I knew the most common names of the Forgotten, like anybody, but that didn't mean I could match them to whatever idealized images people created. But, as I considered them all, I decided that the tall woman had to be Valanthe. She had a kind face and determination in her eyes. Like someone who would never be cruel, but would never give up.

She'd saved me, in a way, when Sten had attacked. Not directly, not with any divine intervention, but the idea of her . . . her necklace had made him hesitate. And now the idea of the Forgotten was helping me again, making people support me, making them fall to their knees and ask for my blessing.

I didn't believe in them. Perhaps beings had lived in Epria

a long time ago and been smarter and wiser than people were now, but they weren't immortal, they weren't watching out for us, they weren't influencing us and preparing to return. I had to use my own wits to survive.

But I sent a silent wish to them, anyway. Just in case.

"So," Madeleine said, as she pinned my hair in place that evening. "What happened?'

"What do you mean?"

She tapped lightly on the back of my neck. "You've been in a daze all afternoon. You keep smiling to yourself. I know that smile. Tell me."

"There's nothing to tell." I picked at the skin around my fingernail. I'd been *not thinking* about Fitzroy all afternoon. I hadn't seen him. Maybe because he was avoiding me. Maybe because he'd listened to me. Maybe because . . . I really didn't know.

Madeleine shook her head, but she didn't argue.

"Do you think—" I stopped.

"Occasionally. Should I be thinking about something in particular?"

"I was just wondering. Fitzroy. He—you knew him, before all this happened. Didn't you?"

Madeleine twisted more strands into place. "I did."

"Do you think—I never spoke to him, before. Do you think he could ever like me, really? If all these things hadn't happened?"

She was quiet for a moment, considering. "If all these things hadn't happened, perhaps not. You'd never spoken to each other, and I don't know if that would have changed. But if you're asking me if I think he could truly like you now . . . yes, I think so. He has always worked hard to make people like him, but he seems genuine to me." She plucked more pins off the dresser, smiling. "So. Tell me. Did you kiss him, or did he kiss you?"

"What?"

"I'm guessing you kissed him, if you're asking me whether he could like you."

"Who's kissing somebody?" Naomi swung into the room, half her hair pinned up, half of it still loose. "What are you saying? Freya kissed somebody? Was it Fitzroy?"

Madeleine smiled. "Freya was just going to tell us."

My face burned. "I didn't kiss him. Why would I? I can't think about that right now. There's so much going on. I . . ." I couldn't finish that sentence.

"Ah," Madeleine said. "So he kissed *you*."

"How—?"

"I told you, Freya. You have that expression."

"Fitzroy kissed you?" Naomi practically bounced over to us. "That's fantastic! It's fantastic, right? Because you like him. Did you tell him you liked him?"

I stared at the remaining pins on the dresser. "It wasn't like that."

"Then what was it like? I need details."

Madeleine leaned closer, adjusting my curls. "Was it a good kiss?"

"I don't know," I said honestly. "Yes. I think so."

"You only think so?"

"I've never had a kiss before. I have nothing to compare it to."

Naomi sank into a chair beside us. "Did your stomach flip? Did he put his hands in your hair?"

"He didn't put his hands anywhere."

"Not *anywhere*?"

"It was quick." I should have more to say, shouldn't I? Did that mean it *hadn't* been good? "My stomach did—flip, though."

"I knew it," Naomi said. "I knew you liked him."

"Perhaps you'll have to kiss him again, if you're not sure," Madeleine said. "Gather more evidence. In the name of science."

"Madeleine!" I pushed her away, and she swayed, giggling.

"But you want to, don't you? I can see it in your face."

That thought was terrifying, too. Almost as terrifying as the thought of *not* kissing him again. "Maybe."

"Only maybe?" Naomi said.

"No. I mean, yes. Yes, I want to kiss him again. But it's not the right time!" My voice rose, the words rushing out of me. "There are too many other things going on for me to worry about this. And people have already said that Fitzroy and I are plotting together. I'm not going to be foolish about this."

"I don't think it makes you foolish to think about it,"

Madeleine said. "And clearly you have been thinking about it, whether you want to or not. There's nothing wrong with that."

"But . . ." I sighed. It didn't make sense. "I don't know. He kissed me. And he said he liked me, before, and he said he wanted to stay, but—I don't know whether it *means* anything."

"You don't know if it means anything for him to kiss you and say he likes you and refuse to leave when an army is marching on us as we speak?"

"I know he's my friend," I said quickly. "But I don't know—I don't know whether it was just a kiss. If that makes sense. Some people—I'm sure some people will kiss anyone, when they feel like it, and not have it really mean anything. And some people will only kiss people if they really like them. I don't know which Fitzroy is."

"I don't know if you can say anyone is only one type or the other," Madeleine said carefully. "I think it depends on both people, and the circumstances. From what I've seen, he cares about you, Freya. But I'm not the person you should be asking."

"I can't ask *him*."

"Of course you can," she said with a grin. "You're queen. You can do anything you like."

Norling accosted me in the corridor outside the meeting room that night. "Your Majesty. May I have a moment?"

I nodded. She stood near the wall, almost in the shadows, and she beckoned me closer. "I need to tell you, Your Majesty, that we have found some of the Gustavites. We know where a few of them are staying, and the location of one of their meetings, tomorrow. What would you like us to do?"

We should arrest them, I knew. They'd tried to kill me, they could still have been the ones who killed the king. And yet—and yet. That idea came to me again, that perhaps I could talk to them, perhaps, if they knew me, they might be willing to support me.

It was a crazy, dangerous idea. And yet.

"Don't do anything," I said. "Not now."

"This opportunity won't last long, Your Majesty."

"I just need to think about it." And figure out whether my idea was complete lunacy, or only mostly insane.

Norling frowned, but she didn't argue. "Of course, Your Majesty."

I stepped toward the door again. The entire remaining court would be waiting inside, whatever that meant these days. Five people? Four? I still had to win them over, still had to seem like a good queen, despite all the things I'd done to upset them, despite everything.

And Fitzroy would be in there too. *Fitzroy.* My stomach jumped. The only thing scarier than seeing him again tonight would be *not* seeing him again, knowing he was hiding from me.

I let out a long breath and stepped through the door.

There was no fanfare this time, no startling announcement

of my importance. But everyone looked up as I entered, sinking into bows and curtsies. The group was bigger than I'd expected. Twenty people, perhaps—Holt, Naomi, Madeleine, and Fitzroy, but also others I'd barely ever spoken to, people with no personal motivation to be here.

And none of the women were wearing the old fashions of the court. None of them. Their skirts were smaller, slighter, with less layers. Their hair was half loose, half pinned, no strange shapes and huge wire forms in sight. Even their jewels were kept to a minimum, as though they had all decided, as one, that such things were rather gaudy after all.

This was Madeleine's doing.

It was *my* doing.

Madeleine's, because yes, she had changed the way I dressed, altering the styles so that they didn't swallow me, so that any natural hints of regality in me shone through. But mine, because they were emulating me. They wanted to look like I did.

That meant acceptance, didn't it? That I was the leader, not the outsider, that these people, at least, were happy to see changes in the court. They were embracing me, symbolically at least, showing their support.

I felt stronger, just looking at them. The people who stayed. I'd spent my whole life terrified of failing to be who people wanted me to be, unable to speak in case the words were wrong, in case people laughed . . . but people had laughed at all my pretenses, all my ostentatious attempts to be queen. This group, this small group, was still here, still showing their support. And it might be fake, it might be politics, all part of the game, but not to all of them. Madeleine believed in me, and so did Fitzroy, and if they could, why couldn't others? How many had just been playing the game of the court before, loathing it but continuing because everyone else acted that way? How many had avoided the capital to avoid it all?

I was done pretending. The court had been shattered, and we couldn't rebuild it, not without a million cracks showing through. I had to be honest. I couldn't trust my advisers, and the murderer might have been on my side, so what else *could* I do, in the face of all that, except stop playing any sort of game and just *be*? Be queen as *I* wanted to be queen, in the court and out. Be myself, be Queen Freya, be whatever sort of person that turned out to be.

I stepped forward to the front of the room. "Hi," I said. An awkward start. "I just wanted to say something before—while things are quiet." Don't cringe, I told myself. Don't think. Just keep going. "I know things are incredibly uncertain right now. Uncertain, and frightening. And I'm going to do everything I can to keep everyone safe, but it's still scary, not knowing what will happen. For you all to remain here—I really appreciate it. Not in terms of lands and bribes and favors, but in real, genu- ine—" I stumbled for the words. How could I finish that? "I appreciate it," I said again. "And also—I know some people have been upset with the things I've done since I became queen. Torsten Wolff, certainly. That I haven't been harsher on our enemies, that I've been too concerned with the people and not put all of you first." I could feel everyone watching me. I could feel Fitzroy watching me. "But I think that—everyone in Epria deserves a chance. I was just nobody, twenty-third in line, and now I'm queen, and I think . . . we can be so much *greater*, so much better, if we help everybody. If we care about *everybody*. We don't need to throw jewels in rivers and cover ourselves in gold to show our worth and our strength. We can do it in other ways, by making the kingdom greater, by treating people well, by—we can be better than we are now, I know we can. We have so much, and we enjoy so much, and we can still enjoy it, still live our lives, but if we don't use that power to make things better, who even are we? And perhaps Sten disagrees, but . . . that's what *I* believe. I hope you all believe it, too."

I held my breath, standing, waiting, as the world crashed back into me. The knowledge of who I was, where I was, what I'd done. I might have made a mistake. I could have ruined everything.

Everyone was silent, waiting for me speak again, or else just unsure what to do. "Anyway," I said, to fill the quiet. "I think we need . . . we should relax. Have some music?"

Madeleine smiled, sweeping back into her perfect courtly

role once again. "How about charades, Your Majesty? We haven't played that in ages. Perhaps you could adjudicate?"

"Yes," I said. "Yes, that sounds perfect."

Nobody ran from the room. No one muttered angrily when I stepped out of earshot. We played, and we talked, and I felt *right*. Still slightly drained from all the interaction, still slightly unsure of what people might do next, but something had clicked, some knowledge that I could *actually do this*, I could be queen the way I wanted, and the consequences would be whatever the consequences would be.

"It was a good speech, Your Majesty," Holt said, later that evening. "A little spontaneous, perhaps, but good."

"Thank you." I said, even as I cringed away from his praise. The speech had been messy, I knew that, but I felt liberated by it. I'd laid everything out, and I'd survived.

And so I knew what I needed to do. "Norling mentioned that you found the Gustavites. I want you to contact them and ask them to meet with me. Tomorrow."

"You want to invite them to the Fort?"

"No, I'll meet them wherever they're planning to meet. Make it clear that we know everything about them, but that this *isn't* a threat. I need to talk to them about their ideas."

"Your Majesty! They tried to murder you."

"One of them did. But she said the others didn't help her.

That most of them didn't agree. And I need to find out what they think. It's important."

"It's dangerous, Your Majesty."

I looked him in the eye, hands shaking slightly. This man who might have killed everyone, for *me*, the man who might want to kill Fitzroy, too. "What isn't?" I said.

TWENTY-SEVEN

I COULDN'T SETTLE TO SLEEP THAT NIGHT. THE DAY'S events still pulsed through me, and, now that I was safe in the dark, I finally allowed myself to dwell on that kiss.

Fitzroy hadn't really spoken to me all evening. Shouldn't he have at least given me a significant glance? Something? Things shouldn't continue as normal, unless the kiss didn't mean anything at all.

And all right, yes, I wasn't *entirely* hopeless. I could weigh the evidence, gather the facts, and see where they might point in any other scenario. His refusing to leave, his telling me he liked me, that kiss. The pointed looks during our conversation, the fact that he opened up to me, even when we had just met, despite almost never opening up to anybody . . . a bystander might look down the list and decide the answer was obvious.

But that missed the clear argument to the contrary. This was happening to *me*. I could imagine people occasionally deciding to be my friend. They'd listen to my ideas, yes. But they couldn't like me *beyond* that.

I was queen, but I was still me. People like me might get one small, brief kiss of friendship. And we might confuse that for something more. But we didn't . . . it didn't make sense.

With a grunt of annoyance, I climbed out of bed, waking up Dagny from her spot by my feet, and grabbed some paper. Written down, the evidence for and against seemed ridiculously unbalanced. "Because it's me" did not look like a reason at all, once it was detached from my brain. But still . . . it *felt* like reason enough.

"Freya? What are you doing?" Naomi peered around her bedroom door, rubbing her eyes. "I saw your light. Did you have a breakthrough?"

I clutched the paper. "No, it's all right. I was just thinking. Go back to sleep."

"You're making a pro and con list about Fitzroy, aren't you?"

"It's not that." She raised her eyebrows expectantly, and I sighed. "It's a 'what does Fitzroy think about me' list."

"Just go talk to him, Freya. He's the only one who could tell you."

I could, technically, but . . . "I don't know where he'll be."

"He's waiting down in the lab for you. Where else would he be?"

"You don't know that."

"Oh, I do."

At least if I asked him, I would know. I could stop this obsessing. The thought terrified me, the risk of humiliation too great, but I'd faced the court, hadn't I? I could do this. "I guess I could—gather evidence. To reach a proper conclusion."

Naomi laughed. "Well, go on, then. Be sure to tell me how it goes."

Naomi was right, of course. I wasn't sure whether that was relieving or annoying. Fitzroy was in the laboratory, more papers spread in front of him. He looked up when I walked into the room, and his smile was a little more tentative than usual. Maybe slightly awkward. Because of how I was acting? Because he regretted the kiss?

I had to speak before doubt got in the way. "What did you mean," I said, "when you said you liked me?"

His smile shrank another fraction. He looked decidedly unsure now as he stood. "Was it not clear?"

"Well, I assume it means you like me. But *how* do you like me? It's an imprecise word, really, don't you think? I mean, do you like me like I'm your friend, or do you like me like you—like me in a different way."

He was walking slowly toward me. I resisted the urge to take a step backward. "You said 'like' a lot there. It was confusing."

"You understood what I meant."

"I did." He moved closer still. An arm's length away. "Do you tend to kiss your friends like that, Freya?"

"No." The word came out quieter than I'd like. "But some people do. And it was just a tiny kiss, and—"

I knew this time, a moment before it happened. Fitzroy moved closer, and I shifted forward to meet him.

My second kiss. I was kissing Fitzroy. Fitzroy's hand was curled around the back of my neck. Fitzroy's fingers were tangled in my hair. Fitzroy was . . . Fitzroy.

How could I possibly have ever thought I didn't like him? That the way my stomach swooped, and my heart raced, and my thoughts calmed, was an inconsequential thing?

I was aware of every breath, of the blood racing through my veins, of the spot where Fitzroy's nose bumped against mine. The slight difference in height, the tiniest shift of Fitzroy's hand. I cataloged every detail, savoring them, saving them.

He pulled back, paused a couple of inches from my face. "Does that answer your question?"

I shook my head, just an inch, left and right. "No." My voice came out breathy, like someone else was speaking. I had to *know*. "There are many potential interpretations for that."

"Such as?" His eyebrows rose in a challenge.

"You just wanted to stop me talking. Or maybe you want to practice kissing. Or you just want to kiss the queen, but you can't admit it, so you keep kissing me so you don't have to lie to me. Or you're just . . . very friendly . . . with your friends."

"Then how's this?" The question sounded grandiose, something Fitzroy the courtier would say, but then he paused. "I like you not just as a friend. And I don't usually go around kissing my friends like that."

"Not usually?"

"Not as a rule. I like you because you're *you*, Freya. In all your stubborn strangeness. And because you make me feel like me. I told you the first time I talked to you, that's not—I'm never sure who I really am. And it's different when I'm with you."

"Well," I said, with a slight smile. "I think I like you, too."

"You think?"

"I think."

He laughed softly. "But do you like me as a friend, or as a lab assistant, or perhaps as the old king's son who now won't leave, or—"

"I like you as Fitzroy," I said, with a decisive nod.

"Well," he said. "I guess I'll take that."

And he kissed me again.

The Gustavites did not agree to meet me. Holt didn't even ask them. "They would run, Your Majesty, before the request was complete," he said the next day, in a soothing voice. "They'd think it was a trap, or else lay a trap for you."

And so we were surprising them. I wasn't sure that was *safer*, considering how they might react, but I wasn't going to shake in my resolve now.

I cared more about fashion that morning than I ever had before. I tried on five different crowns and tiaras, not wanting to look too extravagant, not wanting to hide the fact that I was queen. Eventually, I settled for a simple diadem, the Star of Valanthe hanging around my neck.

Fog had settled low over the city, cloaking the alleyways, making the world feel close. Nothing seemed to exist beyond my carriage, my guards, and our small stretch of road as we proceeded through the quiet.

I was going to be sick. It was all I could think about. I was always nervous before speaking, often forgot how to breathe, but now I truly, genuinely felt like the contents of my stomach were about to spill all over the carriage floor. What was I *doing*?

The right thing, I told myself. The thing I needed to do.

It wasn't much comfort, as acid bubbled in my throat. My fingers tingled with the beginnings of panic, but I counted my breath, willing it away.

The carriage stopped outside a nondescript manor house on a normal-looking street. I stepped out, ordering myself not to vomit. It wasn't that it was dangerous, although that should really have been my concern. It was that I didn't know what to expect. I had no idea what I was walking into, and yet I needed to speak to them. I *knew* these people hated me, and I still needed to try and change their minds. It wasn't exactly a task I was well suited for.

But I was here. I could do this.

A couple of guards went ahead, to announce my arrival. I'd instructed them to be as nonthreatening as possible, but I still cringed as they knocked on the door. If this ended in violence . . .

It didn't. They were too sensible for that, at least. Better to pretend it was a normal gathering, to deny and deny until the lie sounded like truth. The man who answered the door remained calm, not betraying even a flash of concern when he saw the guards. When my men told him that I wished to speak to them, with no mention of who we believed they were, he bowed without hesitation, his lips forming words of joyful surprise. Inside, people must have been scrambling to hide anything suspect, but the man was the picture of calm.

He bowed again as I approached.

"It is good to meet you," I said.

"And you, Your Majesty."

He was a good actor. He would have done well in court.

He led me and two of my guards through the entrance hall and into a busy sitting room. A mishmash of people had gathered there, from boys younger than me to a woman with ghost-white hair and more wrinkles than skin. Some were dressed in rough cotton and wool, some finer clothes, a couple dressed like the lower edges of nobility—people from all parts of the city, all parts of life, perhaps thirty of them in all. The group was bigger than my court.

They weren't all as good at acting as the man who opened the door. Fear vibrated through the room, and while some looked at me with wide, uncertain eyes, others looked almost aggressive, their expressions daring me to challenge them. They would be the ones to watch.

No one moved to acknowledge my arrival. They all seemed too startled, or else too angry. I guessed it would never have crossed their minds that the queen might stroll into their meeting this afternoon and give them a not-quite-natural little smile. If the king had walked into my home a month ago, I'd have fallen over my own feet in shock, and I had seen him frequently, even if it was usually from afar.

No one spoke. They didn't seem to know what to do. "Thank you," I said eventually. I didn't vomit on them—the first success of the meeting. "Thank you for agreeing to see me."

More stares. Then the elderly woman near the door seemed to remember herself. "Your Majesty." She stood, slowly, and began to curtsy. Her face contorted from the effort, like she was in pain.

"No, no," I said quickly, darting forward and putting my hand on her arm. "Don't worry about that. We aren't in court."

"No," a man said. "No, that we're not." He was one of the

aggressive ones, with a voice sharp as wire.

The elderly woman stared at my hand. "Thank you, Your Majesty," she said eventually.

She didn't want me to touch her, I realized. I quickly let go.

"Was there something you wished to say to us, Your Majesty?" the aggressive man said. "It must be important, for you to have come personally."

"I like to say things for myself. And hear them for myself. I think it's easier to get the truth that way." I was still standing in the doorway. I considered walking forward, finding somewhere to sit. But perhaps it was better to stand. To not get too friendly. "I wanted to hear what you had to say. You're—I know you care about Epria, I know that. And things are changing now, as I'm sure you've seen. I wanted to know what you think. About the kingdom. I've read the original pamphlet, of course, but—" I ran out of momentum. It hadn't exactly been the eloquent plea I'd been hoping for.

Again, everyone was silent. The wary still looked wary, the angry still looked angry, and more people looked confused. "What pamphlet, Your Majesty?" the aggressive man said. Like I was trying to trick him into admitting treason.

"*Gustav's Treatise.*"

"Never heard of it," the man grunted.

"Really? It's been all over the city."

A round-faced girl near the window spoke up. "Why did

you allow it again? I thought it was forbidden."

I considered her. "I don't think knowledge can be a bad thing. And banning something doesn't make it disappear. It just lets people twist it. People a hundred years ago might not have liked it, but I thought it had good ideas, too. The court *is* wasteful. I don't agree with radicalism, or with murder. But perhaps if people read his actual words, they might rethink that. It seemed important."

"So you think people misunderstand him?" the aggressive man sneered.

"I think he's not as controversial as some people might believe. And I wanted people to know that—I understand."

"Forgive my rudeness, Your Majesty," said the man who opened the door, "but I don't see why you are telling us this."

This definitely wasn't what I had imagined. I'd hoped for *some* reaction. But it would be all right. It was all right. No violence, no danger. I could say my piece, and maybe it would linger here. Have an effect in time.

"I just wanted everyone to know that—anyone involved in attempted murder, or in hurting *anybody*, will be punished, of course. But others . . . I want new ideas in my kingdom. I want things to be better than they've been before. If people want that . . . you're welcome here. As long as it's peaceful. And I guess that's all I came to say. And if you have anything to say to me . . . come to the Fort. I do want to hear."

Still no reaction. I nodded at them, once, and turned to leave.

"Why?" someone said from the room behind me.

Why? It was a good question. I looked back at them. "Because," I said. "There's no point in fighting for the throne if you're not going to make a difference."

TWENTY-EIGHT

STEN CONTINUED HIS MARCH. WE HAD THREE DAYS now, just three, before he would arrive at the city gates.

We could be mistaken about his plans, I told myself. He could stop for a few days, head elsewhere to gather more support. But our spies said he was returning, and that was unlikely to change.

I had nothing. I knew it, my advisers knew it. I could win the support of the people and talk endlessly about the Forgotten, but I couldn't fight Sten and win, and I'd done little to stop his attack. I didn't know who the murderer was. It was possibly Holt, *probably* Holt, but I needed to be able to prove it, and to prove my innocence, too.

I couldn't sleep now. I needed to use every moment to prepare.

I tiptoed out of my rooms, careful not to wake Naomi or Madeleine. The front door of my chambers was ajar, and two night guards were speaking, their low voices buzzing through the gap.

"But Sten's a good man," one was saying. "I know he's not the heir, not by the way we've always done it, but he's a good man, and a good leader, too. Shouldn't that count for something?"

"It counts for everything," the other guard said, "when his opponent is a little girl with no knowledge of war. What can she do against him?"

"Then why are you still here?"

"Safest path, isn't it?" the second guard said. "And I got nothing against our new queen. She's a nice girl, at least. If she holds out against him, then good for her. I'll be happy to support her. And if she doesn't, then Sten'll be happy enough for us to join him when she fails. He's always been a reasonable man."

"True enough," the first guard said. "True enough, that."

I paused by the gap in the door. Their words made my stomach clench, but they weren't being treasonous, just honest. I couldn't blame them for wanting to live.

I crept back to my bedroom door and closed it a little more loudly. The guards stopped talking at once. By the time I reached the door again, they were standing to attention, as though the conversation had never occurred.

"Can we help you, Your Majesty?" the guard on the left said.

"No, that's all right. I'm just restless." I stepped into the corridor. "I'm going to walk down to my laboratory, I think."

"Then we should go with you, Your Majesty."

They should. But after that conversation, I really wanted to be alone. I didn't want to be protected by people who knew they could not protect me, not now. "No," I said. "I'll be safe inside the Fort. Wait for me here." And, with the authority of a queen behind me, neither of them could protest.

The corridors were eerily quiet. Sconces sent orange light flickering across the stone walls, and the high ceilings vanished into shadow. Sounds echoed and distorted in the stillness of the night, so faraway whispers seemed close. I saw no one.

My lab was empty, too, devoid of Fitzroy for once. Maybe he was actually sleeping, like a normal human being at three o'clock in the morning.

I itched to conduct more experiments, to have focus like I'd had working on the arsenic test, but I had no idea what to do. I had nothing left to test, no leads that science could pursue. So instead, I began to work through the letters again, hunting for anything, *anything*, that might help. A hint at the king's illness. A mention of Holt.

Nothing. All I gained was more of the dead king's words in my brain, this sense of him as a person, with thoughts and fears and priorities and *humanity*, rather than just the ridiculous caricature I had known.

I didn't want to think of him as a person. It made all of it too real.

Eventually, the itch of working alone became unbearable. Maybe Fitzroy was awake upstairs. Maybe he'd be willing to help.

I passed no one as I climbed the stairs. I knocked on the door to his chambers, but nobody answered. I knocked again, louder.

No response.

"Fitzroy?" Maybe he was asleep. I pushed the door open slightly. "Fitzroy?"

The lamps inside were lit, casting a warm glow across the room. I stepped inside, leaving the door slightly ajar.

The lights were on in the bedroom as well, but Fitzroy was nowhere to be seen.

That was odd. If he wasn't in the laboratory, and he wasn't asleep . . . Maybe we'd missed each other in the corridors.

He couldn't have gone far, though, if the lamps were any indication. He would be back soon.

I wandered over to the bookshelves on the far side of the room. Even though Fitzroy had only been here a few weeks, he'd moved several books here—a couple of novels, a history book, a copy of *The Scientific Method*. I picked that one up, smiling. He'd actually listened to my recommendation.

A few sheets of paper fluttered from between two books on the shelf. One fell to the floor, and I bent to pick it up.

I recognized that near-illegible scrawl. It was a letter from his father.

It was private, I told myself. I shouldn't read it, not without his permission, but the back of my neck prickled as I stared down at it. A single word caught my eye: *heir.*

I couldn't help myself. I read through it at breakneck speed, as though my rudeness didn't count if I did it quickly enough. But the words didn't make sense, *couldn't* make sense, so I read it again, slower, waiting for the meaning to change.

The words stubbornly remained, so I read it a third time. And a fourth.

It was a draft of a decree. A decree to ensure that Fitzroy could never, *never* inherit the throne.

My hands shook. I grabbed the other pages from the shelf. The king had requested an adviser's opinion on the decree. His sickness made him contemplative, he said, and more concerned about the succession than ever. He must be certain the crown was in good hands. And that could never be Fitzroy. If he did not have any other children, his brother must be heir.

A third letter discussed plans to send Fitzroy away. Each suggestion had been analyzed based on how valuable it made Fitzroy look—a survey on his father's behalf, for example, or a diplomatic mission would make him look too important. Perhaps banishment would be better. The king had resisted the idea—Fitzroy was still his son, after all—but had agreed that alternatives were difficult to find.

"Freya? What are you doing?"

I jumped. Fitzroy stood in the doorway, hair mussed by sleep. I tightened my grip on the papers.

"What is this?"

All the color drained from his face. "Freya," he said carefully. "I know what that looks like, but listen to me—"

"You know what it looks like?" I laughed. I didn't know why. The sound was too low, too sharp. "Tell me you didn't put this here. Tell me this is Holt, trying to turn me against you."

He didn't reply.

"You hid this from me." Holt had been right. The certainty of it turned my stomach. "You knew your father wasn't planning to make you his heir. He was going to exile you! And you hid it from me."

"I did. But please, Freya, listen."

He took a step toward me. My heart was pounding in my ears, humiliation burning in my stomach. "What can you possibly have to say?"

"I didn't know that's what my father was planning. You have to believe me. I only found out when I read these notes in the lab, I promise."

"So why did you hide it?"

"I panicked. I thought—I didn't know what would happen if anyone else found out. Your advisers already distrust me—"

"Are you surprised, with this?"

"I didn't want *you* to distrust me, too. I thought, if you read that—I don't know what I thought, Freya, but you have to believe me. I panicked. But I wasn't involved."

"You lied to me. *And* you harmed my investigation." The first was worse, it scalded me, stealing my breath, but I had to mention the science, I had to remember what was *important*. Not me and him. It had never been me and him. "You had the motive, Fitzroy. You had it, and you hid it from me. What else am I supposed to believe?"

"I told you. I lost everything that night."

"You would have lost everything if that night hadn't happened. It says it right here, Fitzroy! So don't tell me you had nothing to gain from his death." I was shaking now, a mix of anger and fear, the weight of the words thrumming through me. Fitzroy stared at me, his face pale. "Is *this* why you kissed me? Why you said you liked me? To distract me?"

"*No,* Freya." He stumbled forward, hands out, and then paused when I flinched, jolting like he was caught on a string. "I do like you. I think you're one of the best people I've ever met. Please—"

"Stop lying!"

"I'm not lying! Freya, listen to me." His hands were shaking slightly, but he stepped closer again. "You know what court is like. If I was trying to distract you and make you like me, do you think I'd have done it like that? That I'd have shouted at you, distrusted you, been so slow to do anything nice? To tell you I liked you?"

"You're clever. I'm sure you could figure out the optimal strategy."

He flinched. "Please, Freya. Just listen to me. Let me explain."

"No." If he had lied before, he could be lying now, and how would I know? I was useless at reading people, so naive. He'd proved that. If I ignored this evidence, because I wanted to . . . how would I ever survive? I'd been the perfect victim for manipulation. Self-doubting, isolated, overwhelmed. All Fitzroy had to do was help me, pretend to like me, and I'd miss every sign of betrayal.

"If you want me to listen to you, if you want me to trust you, then stay here. I'm fetching my guards. If you try and run, I'll know you're guilty. If you weren't involved, as you say, then everything will be fine."

"And you believe that, do you?"

I forced myself to look him in the eye. My hands still shook. "I have to."

Fitzroy did not run. I fetched guards to watch his door, with strict instructions that no one was allowed to enter or leave without my permission. A lump had settled in my throat, and it swelled with every word, pressing against my windpipe.

I couldn't let myself get upset. I had to focus. Sten was still marching on the capital, the identity of the murderer was still unclear, and if Fitzroy was responsible . . . would Sten believe I hadn't been involved, too? I'd look suspicious, as his friend. Just as Holt had warned me.

I would have to hand Fitzroy over to Sten, or at least ensure that his version of justice was done. And if he was guilty . . . if Fitzroy had killed *everyone* . . .

I half ran back to my chambers, the world blurring around me. Once I was safely behind the locked door, I collapsed on my bed and let myself cry, the sobs almost choking me. Dagny mewed in distress, her head butting against my forearm. I ignored her.

A gentle hand rested on my shoulder. "Freya?" It was Madeleine. I turned my head to the left, my vision blurred by tears. Madeleine looked beautiful, as she always did. Her hair was pulled into two braids, and although her eyes were vague with sleep, she looked at me with concern. "What's wrong?"

"Everything," I choked out. "Everything." I pushed myself into a sitting position. Madeleine sank onto the mattress beside me, and Dagny hopped up, kneading my legs, still meowing sadly. I reached down to stroke her behind the ears.

"What has happened?"

"Madeleine—" I closed my eyes, the words stuck in my throat. "It was Fitzroy. I think it was Fitzroy. He lied to me. His father was going to exile him, and—and I don't know what to think, but I had to lock him up, I had to, and I don't know what I'm doing—"

"Shhh." Madeleine wrapped an arm around me, running her fingers through my hair. "Shh, it'll be all right, Freya."

"But it *won't*. I trusted him, and now . . ."

"Do you absolutely know that it was him?" she said softly. "It seems so unlike him."

"I don't know for sure. But he's been lying. He hid the evidence from us. He took letters from my lab and hid them."

"What's going on?" Naomi had appeared in the doorway, blinking sleep from her eyes. "Freya, are you all right?"

I shook my head. Naomi didn't ask any more questions. She walked over and sank onto the mattress beside us, a gentle hand on my shoulder.

"You'll figure it out," Madeleine said. "And even if he's guilty . . . I've known him for so long, Freya. He's one of the few people left from—from before. He must have thought he had good reasons. Maybe it's better to show mercy."

"Good reasons? How can there be a good reason to kill that many people? And with Sten attacking, if I'm going to convince him to stop, I have to—I won't be able to be merciful. Sten wouldn't ever let me. I just—he can't have done it. I can't believe he would have done."

"No," Madeleine said. "No, no one would want to believe that of anyone they knew."

"What am I going to do? I'm going to have to explain why he's gone, and then people will be out for his blood. But I couldn't let him stay free, I couldn't."

"You'll figure it out," Naomi said. "I know you will."

"I just—I've made so many mistakes, and now I'm locking

away my friends, and I can't—"

"Freya." Madeleine shifted on the mattress so we were facing each other. "You are a good queen. Trust me. I know royalty. I've known the court my whole life. And you are a good queen. You will do well. You are doing well. Just believe that you can do it. Believe in your strengths."

"But *how*?"

"You've survived this far, haven't you?"

I snuggled back against her shoulder. "I don't know what I'd do without you two."

"You'd be fantastic," Madeleine said. "Just maybe a bit less fabulous."

I laughed.

TWENTY-NINE

"YOU ARRESTED FITZROY?"

Holt leaned forward over the table, his expression a mixture of satisfaction and disbelief.

"Yes," I said, fighting to keep my voice steady. "It needed to be done."

"I am sorry it had to come to this," Holt said. "But he was too much of a threat."

"No," I said. "This has nothing to do with what you said before. But I found evidence that—I know he's been lying to me. And his father—he wanted to send him away. Fitzroy has the motive, he's acted suspiciously. I had to."

"A wise choice," Holt said. "I had suspected him, as I tried to warn you—"

"Yes," I snapped, all my exhaustion, the hours of crying, bursting out of me. He could act as wise and superior as he liked, but I still couldn't be sure he wasn't involved, somehow. He'd still been suspicious. How dare he act like his good judgment had predicted this? "I know what you suspected. You've been against Fitzroy from the beginning, for no reason. You were determined to think he was guilty, or to *deal* with him if he wasn't. Why? Because his mother wasn't the queen?"

"I only thought—Your Majesty, I wanted what was best for you. I only wished to protect you."

"And did you find any evidence against him? Anything, beyond the fact that his father wanted to send him away?"

"Not as such, Your Majesty, but it was suspicious, and—"

"Suspicious? If we're condemning people for acting suspiciously, why don't you tell me why you were in the palace a few nights ago? What did you take from the chapel?"

Silence. Holt stared at me. "Your Majesty?"

"I saw you. I was there, investigating the murders, and I saw you carrying treasure away. Sneaking into the place where everyone died is suspicious, don't you think? Do you think I should arrest and execute *you* for that, without any actual evidence?"

"Rasmus?" Norling said. "What is this?"

"I was in the palace, Your Majesty," Holt said slowly. "But

I was helping you. That shrine was an insult to the Forgotten, and we need gold if we're to have even a chance of fighting Sten. They would want it to be used to support you."

I could believe it. I wanted to hate him, wanted all the blame for the murders to fall on him, but that, at least, I believed to be true. "Perhaps," I said. "I am simply saying—" I pressed my fingers into my eyes. The strain of the night was too much. I didn't want to think that Holt had been right after all. He had still been prejudiced, misguided. He *had*. "We should not act too harshly before we know the whole truth. I appreciate that you want to protect me. Especially—considering the circumstances. But your job is to advise me. Whether I take your advice or not is up to me." I sighed. "We're not going to do anything, for now. We won't tell anyone. Not until we have more evidence, one way or the other."

"Freya. If you think he's responsible—"

"Think is not good enough. Not for this. Not even with Sten bearing down on us. We have to know."

"You won't be able to keep this a secret," Norling said. "People will gossip."

"Then they'll gossip. If we say nothing, they won't know anything for sure."

"And they'll imagine all sorts of things in place of the truth."

"Then they'll imagine." I stood, scraping the hair away from my eyes. I felt like I hadn't slept properly in days, the tiredness weighing down my limbs. "I need to gather more evidence. I have to know."

"Your Majesty," Holt said. "Sten is three days away from the capital at most. We must work on our defensive strategy. We will man the walls the best we can, but we still lack any forces to meet him in the field. We must prepare—"

"We are preparing. We have been preparing. But this is important, too." More important, almost. I couldn't imagine how I might defeat Sten, what I could possibly do to stop him, if he would not surrender. But I could get to the bottom of this murder. I could solve this, achieve *something*, before Sten arrived to destroy it all.

I wasn't going to be sad, I decided, as I searched through the papers again that afternoon, thinking and thinking about what evidence I might have missed. The facts were the facts, and there was no point crying over them, not when Fitzroy had probably been lying to me all along. I couldn't—I *wasn't* going to get distracted. Not when there were far more important things going on. But I couldn't ignore the issue, not when he now seemed the most likely culprit. I had to find more evidence, one way or the other, and that meant thinking about it reasonably, with detachment.

I wasn't proving very good at it. No matter how often I insisted that I had cried myself out with Madeleine and Naomi last night, I kept remembering his expression when I confronted him, the drop in my stomach when I first read the notes, know-ing, *knowing*, that he'd lied to me, he'd hidden things from me, that even if he was innocent, he hadn't respected me.

There wasn't enough evidence here. I could have his rooms searched, but he would have destroyed anything truly condemn-ing. There'd be nothing in the Fort that could help.

I'd have to go back to the palace again. If I could get into the king's offices myself, if Fitzroy had missed something . . . I bit my lip. That was what I would have to do.

"Your Majesty?" One of the guards peered through the door. "A woman has come to speak with you. From the city."

"From the city?" I had thought that nothing had come of my visit to the Gustavites. I certainly didn't expect anyone to take up my offer of visiting the Fort. But if this woman was one of them . . .

The woman waited for me in a guards' room near the Fort's front gate. Four guards watched her, with another outside the door. At least someone had found her a chair. She stood shakily as I entered, and I realized she was the elderly woman from the meeting, the one whose arm I had touched. She bowed slightly now.

"Your Majesty," she said. "You—you said we could come and speak with you."

"Yes," I said slowly. "I wasn't sure if anyone would."

"You made the effort to visit us. I thought perhaps you

might wish to hear the reaction there. Some people would be furious if they knew I'd come, of course, but these young things can be foolish sometimes. They want things to change, and if you agree, then that can only be a good thing, I say."

"Thank you," I said. "I'm sorry, I don't know your name."

"Bakewell, Your Majesty. Mary Bakewell. I wanted to tell you . . . some people believe you, Your Majesty. In the group. They want to listen to you, and they want to believe that—well, that the Forgotten support you, Your Majesty. But some . . . they want to believe, too, but they want more proof."

More *proof*? "I don't think it's possible to prove something like that."

"I don't, either, Your Majesty, but there we are. That's how they feel. And then there are the extreme ones, of course, the ones who aren't happy if they aren't shouting. I can promise, none of us were involved in what happened to the court. We've never been like that. A couple of them now, they think violence is the right path, they tried to attack you, once . . . but most of them just want change. They just need a little encouragement to believe."

"Encouragement," I said. Short of getting the Forgotten themselves to descend from the sky and give me their endorsement, I couldn't think what more encouragement I could give. But it was something. They weren't all against me. They *wanted* to believe. If only I could convince them.

★ ★ ★

This time, I went to the palace alone. It was dangerous—no guards, no friends, no one to protect me beyond my own wits— but I couldn't trust *anyone* now. I had to see the evidence without giving anyone the chance to interfere.

Nobody tried to stop me. The guards at the Fort's entrance looked uncomfortable with my orders, but they opened the gates anyway. What else could they do, when the queen told them she needed to go into the city?

The halls of the palace were silent this time. Occasionally I heard the rustling of rats, settling into the unoccupied space, but no human footsteps, no other signs of life. The figures in the portraits stared at me, and every step sounded too loud on the marble floor. A large painting of Fitzroy's father watched me as I climbed the stairs, one hand on his hip, the other brandishing a sword he had never used in his lifetime.

Fitzroy had cooperated enough to tell me where his father's study was, at least, and it seemed he had told the truth. It was inside the king's private quarters on the third floor of the palace, and he had left the door unlocked.

I paused on the threshold. I'd never been in the king's quarters before, not even the semiprivate ones, and although he was dead, although I was now queen, it still felt dangerous, forbidden. I didn't belong there.

But I couldn't let that silliness stop me now. I forced myself to step into the corridor.

It wasn't what I had expected. The king had been ostentatious, wasteful, but he hadn't filled these rooms with the usual gold paneling and endless staring statues. A couple of paintings hung on the walls, but otherwise, the place was almost plain.

The king's study was also more sensible than I had expected. A huge oak desk filled most of the room, and several shelves leaned against the walls. No paintings here. I hurried around it, lighting the sconces on the walls until the room flickered with light.

It was mostly empty, thanks to Fitzroy. But he couldn't carry an entire room's worth of papers, even if he wanted to. There had to be *something* here.

And the king, it seemed, had been incredibly messy. Papers had been shoved on top of books on the bookshelf. They'd been piled on the windowsill behind the curtains. They teetered in the corner and under the desk. A quick glance through the stacks on the floor suggested they were almost a year old—probably not relevant, which would explain why Fitzroy hadn't brought them. But I couldn't leave anything to chance. Evidence could be hidden anywhere.

I sat in the king's red-velvet chair, cushioned by its luxury. If only the king had cared as much for organization as he did for comfort and gold.

I looked at the chaos on the desk again. I had no time left, and this would take hours to sort through. But I needed to play to my strengths. I would work out a system, and I would get through everything, bit by bit, until I had the whole picture in mind.

The hours flew past, Sten's army getting closer and closer to the capital, and I found nothing. Nothing about Fitzroy, nothing about the banquet, nothing hinting at the murders. A few letters from nobles, a few drafts of notes to send back to them, pleas from his advisers to consider this or that. A note from Holt, warning the king of the expense of his birthday celebrations, but no sign of how the king had responded.

One letter of note came from Rasmus Holt. In it, he begged the king to consider using some of the gold decorating the chapel to support victims of a flood in the west, but the king had merely scribbled *Find other resources* at the bottom. I ran my finger along Holt's signature. Yesterday, I would have added this to the pile of reasons why Holt must have been involved, why he resented the king and tried to create a new regime. Now, I wasn't sure. It explained his appearance in the palace, confirmed that he supported charity and religious simplicity. It wasn't necessarily a motive for murder.

Once I'd worked through the piles under the desk, I crawled underneath, searching for any dropped pages. When that revealed nothing of worth, I emerged and pulled books out from the shelves and moved the curtains aside, checking for any hidden pages.

Behind one of the curtains was a wastepaper basket. It was full.

Most of the pages here were unfinished letters, full of crossed-out words and apparent frustration. I skimmed through them, but found nothing useful.

After several hours, the king's desk was completely tidy, his notes sorted by topic and author, and I'd found nothing more than a few coins lost in the mess. I slumped back in the chair, tiredness weighing my eyelids down. If I found nothing . . . if there was nothing to find . . .

I couldn't stay in this room any longer. I needed to stretch my legs, to see what else this part of the palace had to offer. There had to be secrets and intrigue behind some of the doors.

I stepped out of the office and stopped. A large landscape hung on the wall opposite the door. It had been obscured before, by the darkness, by my distraction, but it caught my attention now. Rolling hills, tinted orange and yellow by the setting sun. The sky was a rainbow of color, the sunset gliding across the clouds. Near the top, where red blended into blue, there was a streak of yellow that almost looked like gold.

The same yellow that had been used in the cake. The same yellow as the powdered dye when it colored my fingertips. I scrambled closer, until my nose was inches from the canvas. It was here. I searched the painting for a signature, for any sign of its origin, but there was nothing, so I wrenched it from the wall and pried it out of its swirling golden frame.

A note had been tucked inside. It said:

I see these hills from the window of our country manor, and the richness of the sunset makes me long for your company and your court. I hope I can return soon and find you as well as when I left.

It was signed by Madeleine Wolff.

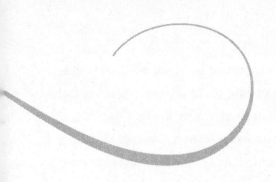

THIRTY

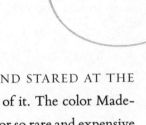

I TURNED THE PAINTING OVER AND STARED AT THE sky. It was King's Yellow, I was certain of it. The color Madeleine claimed she had never seen. The color so rare and expensive that the king had to send thousands of miles away to get it.

Someone had told him about the color. Someone had exposed him to the idea. And Madeleine was close to him, the only painter that I knew of. She'd used the color, and she'd lied about seeing it, and—

I pressed the heels of my hands against my eyes. I had to think. I'd already accused someone I cared about. Was I now going to accuse another, over a painting? The evidence was scant, to say the least, and everyone had lied, with their lives potentially at risk. Lied about religion. Lied about what they had lost. Lied about a small dab of paint in a landscape.

I had to think. *Think*. Fitzroy had reason to silence his father, but to kill everybody, and not make a move for the throne himself? To help me in my investigations—and he had helped, he had brought me closer to the truth—and defend me against Sten? I'd seen him in the Fort, the morning after the banquet, and again after I was crowned. He'd been distraught. He had looked like he could not make sense of what was happening, like he didn't quite believe the pain was real.

I wasn't good at reading people, but Fitzroy . . . Fitzroy had been so *raw*. He was a good performer, when he wanted to be, but I'd seen him without that mask now, and I felt certain I'd seen his true feelings then. His face in that moment, the agony there . . .

Madeleine had been sad, too. Madeleine had grieved. But always in that sophisticated, wonderful Madeleine way, so perfect, with none of the messiness that Fitzroy and Naomi had displayed. And she had been out of the capital when the attack occurred, safe and free from suspicion. If I hadn't left the palace, she would have inherited the throne. And when the poison was a food dye, intended to be in the meal, included on the king's orders . . . who would ever suspect her of murder, even as a painter who had used the color before?

She'd said she was away from the capital because of an illness, one that seemed to have no clear cause. "Melancholy," the doctor called it, but Madeleine said she'd never had such a stomachache from melancholy before. Stomachache, a sign of mild arsenic poisoning. Arsenic like in the paints she used.

And Madeleine licked her paintbrushes. I'd seen her do it, smoothing the bristles on my makeup brushes. If there had been traces of King's Yellow there, it could have given her that stomachache, and if she'd realized the source . . .

Had that given her the idea?

I did not want to believe it. But it was possible. It was beyond possible.

When I got back to the Fort, I did not order guards. I did not make a scene. I walked into Madeleine's rooms to find her sitting in an armchair, a book propped open on her lap. Our eyes met, and Madeleine's lips parted, her face paling slightly. And I knew. There was such a resigned look on Madeleine's face. She stood, her skirts flowing around her like water, never looking away.

"It was you." I was surprised by how calm I felt, how clear. Now it was fact, now I *knew*, it didn't seem worth screaming about. "You killed them."

"I didn't put the poison in the cake," she said, in the same soft tone I'd heard from her before, whenever she discussed the deaths. "But I introduced him to that dye, yes."

"Why?" There was so much I needed to say, but that question pushed away everything else. *Why.*

"It needed to be done."

"You needed to kill all your friends?"

"I did not know he would do it," Madeleine said. "I did not force him to act as he did. I knew he would like it, for the extravagance, but I did not know—I did not *know* he would fill a dish with it at the banquet."

"*Why?* Why would you do this?"

Madeleine tilted her chin upward, meeting my gaze without flinching. "You know I loved the court, when I first came here. It was so lively. Every day had a new distraction. I felt like I belonged, like it made up for everything I'd lost. And then, a couple of years ago, I was sick for the first time. I spent several months back in the country, painting, walking, meeting new people and learning how to breathe. And when I returned . . . I *saw* it, Freya. I saw it for what it really was. The vanity of it, the waste. The day I returned, we had a huge party in the garden of the palace. The theme was gold. Gold flakes in the food, gold flakes in the water, gold on the dresses and in people's hair. It was a celebration of the peace and goodness of the court, the peace we'd had for *so long*. And I stood in the middle of it, seeing how ugly it was. Seeing how no one had really cared for my absence. No one cared about me, no one cared about anyone. They just wanted to have fun, and to be more fantastic than anyone else. The next day, I went to the king. I'd seen people struggling, and I wanted to help. But when I asked him for money, he laughed at me. He said I was too much like my cousin, and the crown did not have the funds to waste. The countryside dealt with its own affairs. He had the money to let his whole court literally eat gold, but not to make sure others were fed. And from then on, I saw it, Freya. I saw what Gustav was talking about, as I know you have. We needed change. We needed it. And it wasn't going to happen by itself."

"Because the Forgotten must return?"

"The Forgotten aren't real, Freya. We're deluding ourselves to think they are. The people who lived here before were just people, with skill and knowledge we don't have. And we'll never have them, because we think we must wait for the Forgotten to give them to us. We use that myth as an excuse. Things were broken, Freya. And someone needed to fix them."

I stared at her. "That was your reason?" There must have been more. That couldn't be it.

"Would it be better, if I had something more dramatic to offer? Some personal grievance, some cry for revenge? Ambition for myself, perhaps? Surely it would be worse, to hurt people for such selfish reasons. I wanted to help. I wanted to create a better kingdom. And I believe I have."

"Don't pretend you intended me to be queen. That you didn't think it would be you."

"I never intended that. I assumed he would hoard it for himself, poison himself slowly, until he told me he was getting more for the banquet. And even then—so many people could have survived before me. It was never about becoming queen."

"But you didn't stop him. You knew hundreds of people could die, and you didn't stop him."

"It had to happen. Epria *needed* it." She looked away, eyes settling on a half-finished canvas on the other side of the room. "It is medicine, you know. That's what the merchant told me, when I bought a tiny pot of my own. It cost a fortune, but I'd never seen a color like it, and I needed it for my collection. He leered at me and told me it was a cure for the pox—and for sweating sickness, too, for many things. Of course, I just wanted the color." She glanced back at me, smiling softly. "And then I fell ill. I saw the lines on my fingernails and I knew it must contain arsenic—I don't paint with it normally because it ruins your hands, and this yellow was the only new color I had, so it had to be the source."

"So you sent some to the king?"

"I sent all I had left, along with the painting I had just completed. And I told him the truth. It was a color, but also a rare and miraculous medicine that people in Rejka thought brought good health and good fortune. I wished for him to have it, as a gold color fit for a king."

"And he put it in his wine."

"I assume so. It gave him stomach pains, of course, as it poisoned him slowly. But he didn't connect those with the dye. Why would he? He thought he was ill, and no one thought to investigate something that the king himself added to his food."

"You said he had been sick for months and months. Long before you last left the castle."

"I lied," she said, and for the first time, I heard a slight hint of remorse. "I am sorry. You were so intent on solving the murder. I couldn't let you find out he had only been sick since I left the capital. I wanted you to think someone had been poisoning him for months, before and after I left."

And *that* was the detail she seemed to regret. Not all the deaths, but a couple of small lies, to interfere with my investigation.

I'd trusted her too much. I hadn't checked her story. Fitzroy had agreed that his father was hiding an illness, and I'd just assumed that all the details she'd added were true, too.

"Of course," she continued, "his arrogance wouldn't stop there. He needed more and more. I didn't have any more to give him, so he sent men to hunt some down. He named it after himself, even though it already had a name, and he wanted to own all of it. I was concerned that someone would warn his advisers that it contained arsenic, but either no one knew, or no one cared. They just knew it was a dye that cured certain illnesses, as long as people did not take too much. And of course, his extravagance meant he could not keep it to himself. He needed to make a big show, to bestow that good health and good fortune on everyone he favored. He had to throw that rare dye away at a banquet, just to show how *rich* and kingly he was. But I knew he would only give it to people he liked, which meant that those he didn't like, those less extravagant than himself . . . they would survive. It would be far more effective at creating a new court than I had ever imagined. I would not stop that."

"Even if your own cousin might die, too?"

"I trusted in him. I knew he wouldn't eat it. The king was angry with him, and Sten was angry with the king, with his wastefulness . . . he wouldn't eat the gold cake, out of principle. And he didn't."

"But everyone else—you just left them to die?"

"Not everyone. I thought perhaps Fitzroy might rule. I wanted to make sure he survived, so I told his father that a rumor had reached me, that Fitzroy was bragging that he'd be king. I didn't say it quite like that, of course . . . I congratulated the king on his decision, said I'd heard it from Fitzroy himself. I knew it would enrage him, just in time for the banquet, and he'd deny him any golden cake, to put him in his place. He'd be safe."

"So you're the reason Fitzroy was going to be exiled?"

Madeleine shook her head. "I didn't know about that. But you must understand, the king was always changing his opinion about Fitzroy. Even if he wished to make him his heir on the day he received my letter, he would have been furious to think that Fitzroy was *assuming* it would happen. And even if he was furious with Fitzroy because of my letter, he would have forgiven him, soon enough. If he had not poisoned them all. That was how the king behaved."

"And the king just happened to have made a more permanent decision, this time?"

"I do not know. He might have been posturing, ready to

change his mind again. But his sickness had made him reflective. And considering what we know about Holt's beliefs . . . he may have been influenced to finally dismiss his son for good."

"And everyone else . . . you killed them. All your friends."

"The king's greed killed them. Not mine."

Her expression wasn't guilty. It didn't show any remorse. It was . . . honest. She met the truth with the same poise with which she met everything else.

"If I arrest you," I said, "people will think it's because of your cousin. They won't believe you were responsible. And when Sten arrives, I'm sure he'll be happy to free you." He'd never believe me if I said Madeleine was responsible. He wouldn't stop the attack now.

"Oh, no," Madeleine said. "Not at all. If he finds out I was responsible, he'll punish me for it, like he wants to punish you. But he will fight his way into the city before he believes you. I do not believe it will help your cause."

Because Madeleine was so beautiful, so loved, so *good*. She was everything I wasn't, or so I'd believed. How could *she* have killed them?

"You were supposed to be my friend."

"I am your friend," Madeleine said. "Whatever else I have done, I am your friend. I did this from kindness, Freya. I did this because it needed to happen, for everybody's sakes. I am not proud of it. I take no joy in it. I've cried over those deaths, and every tear was real. But it needed to be done."

And that was where we could not agree. No matter the flaws of the previous king, no matter who had ordered the poison, no matter how much she had mourned the deaths, Madeleine had plotted to kill, and kill she had. She had killed Naomi's brother. She had killed *everyone*.

"Did you intend to kill me?" I said.

"I did not think of you. I did not know you."

"And did you try to kill me after? After the poison failed?"

"No! No, of course I didn't. This was never about me taking the crown. I meant every word I ever said to you, Freya. I think you are a good queen. The sort of queen we need."

"Then it is lucky Naomi and I left the banquet."

"Yes. It is lucky you did."

I continued to stare at her. I couldn't understand the soft expression on her face, her *calm*. "You let me arrest Fitzroy. You would have let me kill him."

"You would not have killed him. You would have found a reason to forgive him. You have a good heart, Freya. You would have known to trust him, in the end."

"And what about you? What about my heart's decision to trust you?"

"Perhaps your heart is wise in that, as well. I did what was best."

I shook my head. I could almost see Madeleine's perspective, how she had twisted things around, but *so many people* had died. Innocent people, trying to live in the world they'd been given.

Madeleine had punished them all, indiscriminately, just to say she had not done so directly, to say the king's extravagance was the cause.

"Do you believe me?" Madeleine said softly. "Or should I prepare to go down to the dungeons?"

"No," I said. "No, to both of those things. If you really are my friend, you'll stay in your rooms, and you'll help me to stop your cousin. Once we've survived that, then . . . then I'll decide what to do."

"I meant what I said before," Madeleine said. "You will be a great queen. A better one than I had hoped for."

"If I stop your cousin first."

Madeleine stepped back. "You have to use your strengths against him. Unsettle him. I don't know what he believes, but he is too superstitious to be entirely convinced he doesn't believe. If you can somehow convince him the Forgotten are angry with him . . . that might be the only way."

I nodded. It was good advice, no matter the source. "I'll have someone guard the door."

Madeleine sank into a curtsy, her skirts flowing around her, and I forced myself to turn away.

I wanted to run to Fitzroy's rooms, but my legs wouldn't listen. The shock of Madeleine's betrayal had hollowed me out, and I could hardly feel my feet touching the floor. I floated like a ghost through the castle, barely disturbing the air with my presence.

Down the stairs, along the corridor, past the guards, to Fitz-roy's rooms. I hadn't planned what I would say to him, had no time to sort through my feelings, so when the door swung open, I simply stumbled forward, my throat tight.

He sat in an armchair, writing. His shoulders were tense, but otherwise he looked fine, he looked like *Fitzroy*.

"Why did you lie to me?" I said. My voice cracked. "Why did you hide the letters from me, when you knew . . . ?"

He must have noticed the shift in tone, the way my question had moved from accusation to confusion, because he frowned, and when he replied, his voice was softer too. "I panicked," he said. "I didn't know my father planned that, not until I saw those letters, when I was reading in the lab by myself, waiting for you. I thought, if you read them, you'd suspect me. It *did* seem to suggest I might have done it. So I hid them. I didn't want you to not trust me."

"So you did something untrustworthy?"

"I knew they weren't useful for the investigation. They were personal. So I hid them. But I shouldn't have. I'm sorry."

"I—I understand why you did it." That didn't mean I forgave him, but I could see his reasons. It didn't make him a bad person, but—that didn't mean I had to forgive him. "I found the murderer." I had to force the words out. I'd wanted to be able to say them for weeks, but now they were just . . . hollow. All of it was hollow. "It was Madeleine."

"Madeleine?"

"She told me." And I explained all that had happened since his arrest. He began pacing as soon as I mentioned the painting, and did not stop even when the story was done.

"Madeleine," he said. "That—how? How could it have been Madeleine?"

"I just told you—"

He laughed humorlessly. "It was a figure of speech, Freya. But—*Madeleine* killed them. Madeleine. I've known Madeleine for years. She's—how could *Madeleine* have done it?"

"She thought she had good reasons."

"I'm sure Sten thinks he has good reasons to kill you. I'm sure everyone thinks they're doing the right thing. Doesn't mean that they are."

I felt that I should say more, apologize more, dig in more, but—I just couldn't. Fitzroy's betrayal was still raw, hidden underneath the devastation of Madeleine. I'd cried all night. I'd been so reluctant to trust him, and then I had, and even if his feelings were honest, *he* wasn't. I couldn't offer him anything more. I couldn't possibly articulate any of what I felt.

I scraped the tangled black hair away from my face. Madeleine wouldn't be able to style it for me now. "Sten's two days away," I said. "And I still don't—please, come to my lab. I have to figure this out."

He watched me for a long moment, and for once, I couldn't read his expression. Then he nodded.

I still needed to fetch Naomi, to tell her everything that had happened. She hadn't been as close to Madeleine as I had become, but she'd still be heartbroken. Madeleine had killed her brother.

We met her on the stairs to my quarters. She hurtled down them, her face had been drained by fear, and stopped short when she saw us.

"Freya!" she said. "I just woke up, and Madeleine's under guard. No one would tell me what was happening. Has Holt arrested her? What's going on?"

"I'm sorry, Naomi," I said. The words felt too heavy to speak. "Madeleine confessed to me. She killed them."

Naomi opened her mouth to argue, then stopped. She swayed on the spot, still poised to disagree, all the fight falling out of her. "She told you that?"

"She did. I'm sorry, Naomi."

She glanced at Fitzroy then back at me. "How can you be certain?" she said. "How can you know? She could be lying, or she could be confused, covering for her cousin—"

"I know, Naomi. This time, I know." And I told her what Madeleine had confessed.

"So Madeleine killed Jacob."

I nodded, and she repeated the words louder. "She killed everyone, and then she joined us. Then she pretend to *help* us?" Furious tears burned in her eyes. She strode back up the stairs. I ran forward to grab her arm and hold her back.

"Naomi, don't," I said. "We can deal with her later, and we will, but we can't right now."

"Freya—"

"Please, Naomi. Punishing her won't help anything yet. We have to deal with Sten first. We have to. And I need your help."

"You don't need my help."

"Yes," I said. "I do. Please. You're my best friend. We'll deal with Madeleine later. But first—we have to figure out how to stay alive. I need your help. Please."

Naomi looked at me for a long moment, tears still blurring her eyes. "All right," her tone resolved, fierce. "Let's take down this bastard together."

THIRTY-ONE

"STEN'S MEN ARE COMING FROM THE EAST," FITZROY said. He had spread a large map across the lab's central table, and he was negotiating it like a seasoned battle strategist.

I leaned closer. "Traditionally, he'd either wait for us to send our armies out to fight him, or put us in a siege." Fitzroy gave me a questioning look, and I added, "That's what I read, anyway."

"If we had an army, yes," he said. "But we don't. We barely have any men. I'd be surprised if he even expected a fight."

"What, he thinks I'll just open the gates and let him kill me?"

"No," Fitzroy said. "I assume he'll stop outside the capital and demand we surrender. He'll make a show of being willing to negotiate. And if we don't step down, if we don't meet all of his demands, he'll storm the city the next day. He won't expect much resistance, but he's still a tactician."

"That's good," Naomi said. "He doesn't think you'll be able to outsmart him. So he'll sit outside the walls all night, expecting you to surrender. That gives us time. Maybe we can attack him there. Subtly."

"But how?" I said. "I don't want to kill him or his men. If we poisoned them . . ." I did not need to say what thoughts mass poison invoked, considering the events of the past few weeks. "Be smart," I muttered. "Play to your strengths." My strengths were science, experiments, puzzling out the truth. Not much use now. But they were all I had.

Play to your strengths, Freya. *Think.*

I looked around the room, at the different bottles and jars, the attempts at poison detection, the cut glass, the notebooks full of failures and successes.

"What am I supposed to do? Do scientific experiments at them until they think I'm worthy of being queen?"

Naomi stared at me. She began to smile. "It's not the experiments that matter," she said slowly. "It's how people interpret them."

I frowned, the beginnings of hope crackling inside me. "What do you mean?"

"You can't fight Sten with force," Naomi said. "So you have

to make his supporters decide they'd rather support you, instead. As, say, the chosen of the Forgotten."

"Make them see heresy," Fitzroy said.

People wanted proof. That's what the Gustavite woman had said. They wanted to believe, *needed* to believe, but they required that final push. They had to *see* it.

I looked around the laboratory again. The experiments, the explosions, the way I had manipulated light . . . science was my strength, in part because so few people understood it. Because no one expected me to be capable of it.

Play to their expectations. Use their assumptions against them.

I picked up one of the crystals, letting it fracture the lamplight. "I've got it," I said. "I know what we have to do."

Holt was unconvinced. "Your Majesty," he said, a little tentative, considering our last interaction. "This is a dangerous plan. If it displeases the Forgotten—"

"You've told me before that you think they chose me. If that's the case, surely they won't mind me using that to keep my throne. They can't disapprove of me using my brain to help, not when they chose me because of it."

Even as I said it, I felt a slight shiver of fear. *If* the Forgotten existed, *if* they were displeased . . .

It still couldn't be worse than what Sten had planned for me.

I turned to Norling. "Do you think we can get everything in

place before Sten attacks?"

"Certainly," she said. "But Your Majesty, many other things could go wrong. If they see through it—"

"If they see through it, I'll be just as dead as I'll be if we don't try. If that happens, you can surrender to him. Say you were misguided. He'll probably spare you. Short of that . . . it's the best plan we have."

"But Your Majesty." Holt paused, choosing his next words carefully. "This plan is rather—theatrical. You will have to speak well. And you . . ."

"And I've never spoken well in my life?"

"You have improved, Your Majesty!" he said quickly. "Your passion is undeniable. But I do not know if it will be enough."

It was true. Despite all the convoluted details of the plan, that was the part that made me the most nervous. But it was also key to the whole thing. I needed to play my part.

When I'd dealt with people before, honesty had made things click. This plan relied on reaching out to others, on making them believe. And I could do that just as easily with truth, with being myself. "I can do it," I said. "I have to do it."

My life depended on it.

Holt gave me a long look. Then he nodded. "I'll make the preparations."

Sten made camp within sight of the city walls, as Fitzroy had predicted, and sent envoys with his demands for my surrender.

And so once it was dark, I set out with my guards around me. I was dressed simply, for a queen, in a pale-blue silk dress and no jewels, save for the tiara brushing my hair back from my face and that star around my neck. Simplicity—another thing I'd learned from Madeleine. I needed to look like my own kind of queen tonight.

"Who goes there?" one of Sten's guards shouted, as we approached his camp. Mila stepped forward, holding her torch higher. "Representatives of Queen Freya. We wish to speak to Torsten Wolff."

"He hoped you would be willing to see reason," the guard said. "Drop any weapons here."

My guards made a show of placing their swords in a pile, and a couple of Sten's men stepped forward to check for any concealed blades. They paused when they saw me in the middle of the group, my hair flowing loose around my shoulders.

"Your Majesty," the guard said. I waited for a mocking remark, something about being desperate enough to travel to speak on my own behalf, but it did not come. Good. They might not believe in me, but these people had some modicum of respect left for the crown. I dwelled on the thought, turning it into a whisper of a smile.

"Sir," I said, with a respectful tilt of my head. Another of Madeleine's tricks. "May we proceed? It is a chilly night."

I was actually quite warm, blanketed by adrenaline, but delicacy was the best excuse. The guard bowed and led the way into the camp, without checking for the dagger I had tied to my calf. I didn't expect Sten to attack me or my men during a parlay—they had more honor than *that*, at least—but I wouldn't trust my life on it.

The camp was a strange jumble of sights and sounds. Men sat by campfires outside hastily erected tents, and there was a sense of adventure in the air. Yet nothing felt consistent. I passed one man fletching arrows, his hands unsteady, next to a collection of bows—longbows, short bows, bows that had been hastily carved and bows that surely could no longer hold a string from age. Swords of all different designs, armor that ranged from steel plate to leather coats—everything had been thrown together, the war camp of a kingdom that had forgotten how to make war.

The guard led us into the center of the camp, and I stood tall as I walked, glad for once of my height. My guards spread out slightly, as they had agreed, to ensure everyone in the camp saw me among them. And see me they did. Whispers followed us as we walked. I forced myself to keep my chin high, to step firmly, to wear the slight smile of confidence. My heart pounded, but I didn't feel panicked, not this time. The world was sharper, but I could use that to my advantage. I just needed to focus.

Sten stepped out of a large tent as we approached. Good. The more eyes on us, the better.

"Freya," he said, as we approached. "You've come to surrender?"

"Torsten Wolff." Say the person's name first, make them feel *known*. Madeleine had always said it helped people to like you, but perhaps it might be unsettling, too. "I've come to negotiate."

"I don't negotiate with murderers."

"Then it's a good thing I'm not a murderer. And neither, I think, are you. Stop this, Sten, before more people die."

"If they die, it'll be because of you." Sten stepped forward. The light of the campfire flickered on his face, emphasizing the gauntness of his cheekbones. "You are outnumbered. And you still want to fight?"

"I don't *want* to fight. You're the one attacking the city." The words were rehearsed, uninspired, but that was fine. As long as he acted as we'd predicted, I'd be fine. "Where is my father?"

"Safe. And well. But not here. He'll be dealt with justly."

"If you are just, then you will take your men away and surrender now. I have done nothing to hurt you."

"*Nothing?* You have torn this kingdom apart. You killed my friends."

"I didn't kill anyone." But Sten's expression did not change. He was convinced that I was the murderer, that he was doing the right thing. He truly wanted justice for his friend. It would destroy him, I thought, to know his cousin had been the one who poisoned them. For him to be so convinced, and so wrong . . . but I couldn't change his mind with words now. I had to stick to the part I'd written for myself.

"Aren't you afraid, Sten?" I stepped closer to him, fear and anticipation thrumming through me. "The Forgotten protected me, put me on the throne. Aren't you afraid they'll punish you for trying to fight me?"

Sten stared back at me, nothing but hatred in his eyes. "You were not built for threats, Freya."

"Yet you claim I'm built for murder." Don't flinch, I told myself. Don't blink, don't hesitate, don't react at all. I simply had to wait. "You are a fool, Torsten Wolff." I let the words hang in the air, fighting the urge to fill the quiet, waiting for my men to take the signal.

Sten's soldiers gasped. It had begun. I couldn't let myself turn my head, couldn't break the image of defiance I was creating, but I was dying to look. I could only picture what was happening around me, the magic of it. The shadowy images moving across the tents, the way they shuddered and scampered and grew. Ghosts, or the angry forms of the Forgotten, flitting around the camp like creatures from their nightmares.

"The Forgotten will not like you attacking their queen, Sten," I said. The words echoed through the camp.

One of the images danced across the tent behind him, clear in my field of vision, and I fought the urge to grin. It was perfect. So perfect. A few men hidden about the camp, some small magic lanterns, a few words from me on how to make the images seem to grow or move. They were just shapes on card, just pictures, concealed images dancing in the firelight, but by using the tents as lit screens, by making the figures move and loom, I'd created something new. No one seeing them could know they were a trick, not for certain, not in the dark fear of an army camp on the night before battle. It would be enough to put them on edge, and that was all I needed, for now.

"There's no need for bloodshed," I said, my voice ringing through the camp. "Anyone who stands down will be welcome in my kingdom. But the Forgotten are here, and they do not have pity for traitors and blasphemers." I stared straight into Sten's eyes, my face like steel, and saw a flicker of uncertainty there.

Then the flicker was gone, and he spat at my feet. The whole camp seemed to recoil. "Get out."

"It's your choice, Torsten Wolff. I hope you choose well." I walked away, leaving my guards to follow. Every eye in the camp watched me leave. I did not stop until I was beyond the edge of the camp, until I was past the city walls, up the hill, and into the Fort. It was only when I was in the dungeons that I let out a shaky breath and slumped against a wall, my nerves shuddering through me. My hands, so steady when confronting Sten, would not stop shaking.

It went well, I told myself. It went well. But I kept reliving it in my head, going over every word, trying to recall Sten's expressions, the gasps from the crowd. Had they believed me? Or had they been mocking me, a whole crowd seeing through my disguise?

It didn't matter. It couldn't matter. I had to carry on

regardless, to fight the only way I knew.

Naomi and Fitzroy were already in my laboratory, preparing for the second part of the plan. "Did it work?" Naomi asked, when I walked through the door.

"I don't know." I couldn't think about it anymore. I had to move. I braided my hair as I walked toward my leather gloves. "There's a lot more to do. Time to get to work."

THIRTY-TWO

DAWN APPROACHED, AND I WAS READY. MY SPIES HAD harried the camp all night, sending phantoms crawling across tent walls and creating strange, haunting noises, preventing anyone from sleeping.

The Forgotten were not amused.

I worked through the night in the laboratory, too focused to feel even slightly tired. I had too much to prepare, too many theories to test and test again. Now I caught a glimpse of my reflection as I pulled off my leather gloves. I had soot on my nose, and my hair was a tangle of frizz around my face. I should have been afraid, should have been *terrified*, but all I felt was calm. Calm, and focused. It was finally time to do something, to act, to *fight*. I stroked Dagny, taking strength from her presence.

"You have to catch sunrise," Fitzroy said. "It'll be most dramatic that way."

"I know," I said. "Believe me, I know. I just have to get ready." I glanced down at my ruined dress, and then across at Naomi. She could help me, it was true, but if I wanted to look *perfect* . . .

I should have locked her up in the dungeon. I should never want to speak to her again. But Madeleine was the best at presentation, and I needed to make a statement.

And then . . . a part of me still cared about her. That part wanted to see her, wanted to work with her, to prove she wasn't as awful as I now knew she was. As though redemption were possible after mass murder.

So I knocked on Madeleine's door. Madeleine answered it, as elegant as always. I felt a tug in my stomach at the sight of her, honey-brown hair cascading down her back, eyes bright, standing straight and tall. Her smile was a little smaller than usual, a little sadder, but otherwise Madeleine still looked like Madeleine. Just one glance made me want to pause in the moment, forget what I knew.

"Freya? Are you all right?"

I stepped around her into the room. It smelled of oil paint and turpentine. The stone wall at the far side was covered in color, a manor on a hill, sheep in the fields, a sunset, ocean waves crashing against a cliff. Madeleine must have been painting non-stop since I locked her in here. Her paintbrush flying over her makeshift canvas, the uncertainty of her future making her desperate to create. But she was completely composed now, not a drop of paint on her.

"I need you to help me," I said. "I need you to make me a queen."

"You are already a queen."

I shook my head. "Make me magnificent. Make it so when the sun rises behind me, I look like a goddess. Can you do that?"

Madeleine smiled her slight smile again. "Yes. I can do that."

Her fingers brushed against me as she pulled a dress over my head, as she placed my hair just so, as she draped the Star of Valanthe around my neck and dabbed powder on my eyelids to capture the light. And I felt so *safe,* knowing Madeleine would make things right, Madeleine always knew what to do . . . but then Madeleine stepped back, her hands fanning out as if to say, "There"; and I remembered all she had done. All she had put in motion. I stepped away from her, just slightly, and looked at my reflection.

It was perfect. Of course it was perfect. My stomach twisted as I stared at myself, the image of a queen, complete with flowers in my hair and a tiara glinting in the lamplight. Madeleine's work. Madeleine's creation. And I hated her, I did, for all the pain she had caused. But I loved her, too. I couldn't crush that feeling so easily, couldn't deny how important she'd been to me the past few weeks. How Madeleine had brought me here, and how she would help me to live.

"Thank you," I said softly. "It's perfect." I left the room without another word.

The sky was beginning to lighten, but the sun had yet to appear. Everything around us was still. The people who remained in the capital were hunkering down, hiding in their homes and hoping for the best. There were no soldiers in the streets, no guards. They were all on the walls, ready to begin.

My carriage jolted to a stop in front of the city gates, and I stepped out. I paused in front of the steps onto the walls and took a deep breath. I did not have to speak this time, but I had to look the part. Calm. Confident.

I climbed the stairs, my heels clinking on the stone. Rasmus Holt waited in the guard tower at the top. "Your Majesty," he said. "Everything is ready."

"Good." I glanced over my shoulder at the ever-lightening sky and thanked the city builders of long ago. The main gate, the point where Sten's men must attack, faced west, meaning any soldiers attacking in the morning must march toward the rising sun. The builders had intended for it to put glare in the soldiers' eyes. But the sun would serve a different purpose for me now.

"The Forgotten will be with you," Holt said.

I nodded my thanks and stepped onto the walls, alone. Men

were scattered along the ramparts, too few to man it effectively.

Sten's army approached from the west. A mass of soldiers, some on horseback, some on foot, making a slow advance, as though their mere presence might terrify me into surrender. They were a mess of armor and weapons, old tournament helmets and chain mail and leather boots, a thrown-together army of the kingdom's past.

I reached the middle of the wall, and I turned to face the fields beyond. Crystals and cut-glass prisms had been arranged around me, hanging from the gate towers on either side.

I could only hope they would work the way I'd imagined.

Sten's men were approaching, the sun was rising. My own men were gathered in front of the gates, a paltry force, but necessary for the show. Sten did not know about the spies in his ranks, did not know what we'd hidden in the grass in the dark. He didn't know what I was capable of.

I stepped onto the side of the wall itself, so I towered over the fields, so everyone would look up and see me first. I was exposing myself to arrows, I risked falling, risked death, but I refused to look anything other than fierce and serene as I stared down at the approaching army, and the sun burst over the horizon behind me.

An explosion of orange and red framed my silhouette. The rays of the dawn caught in the crystals and prisms, breaking into more shafts of light, more colors, so it bounced and swelled and glared, forming a living halo around me. It stung my eyes, but

I refused to blink. I would not look away. I stared down the approaching army, and the Forgotten lit me up for all to see.

Some of Sten's men faltered, and I let myself smile. My spies had done their work. They were unsettled, ready to believe.

There was another flash of light. Thunder rumbled overhead. I glanced up, but there were no rainclouds, and no rain fell. As I watched, another sheet of lightning leaped across the sky.

I felt a rush of excitement. Rainless sheet lightning. Possible, of course, but rare. I sent a silent prayer to anyone who might be listening, nature or the Forgotten or the flukes of science, for the intervention in my favor. Some of my enemies might see through the prisms and the framing of the dawn light, but rainless lightning in the sky . . . that was harder to dismiss. Even my stomach leaped as thunder rolled again, thinking that maybe the Forgotten were here after all, maybe they *had* chosen me.

It was irrational. I knew that. But it seemed so perfect, and it would help my performance to have at least a flicker of belief.

Sten's army was close now. He was on horseback at the head of the group, looking as determined as ever, while a group of men beside him hauled a fallen tree as a battering ram. But his troops did not seem so passionate now, not when faced with me, surrounded by light, not when rainless lightning continued to flash across the sky.

"Freya!" Sten shouted. "There is still a chance for you to surrender."

I bit back my response. Silence was best. More intimidating.

And if Sten's men took a few more steps . . .

Warning arrows flew at the walls, but none of them struck their targets. Archery had been nothing more than a sport for too long for the army to aim true. I didn't flinch. The men continued to march, but they moved slower now, with more caution. Their conviction seemed to waver. My tricks were working.

They moved closer still, and their boots collided with the spots in the long grass where metal and powder had been concealed, pressing them together, triggering a reaction. For a long breath, nothing happened, as the men strode ahead. Maybe my design hadn't worked, maybe it wouldn't work . . .

Then the men yelled in shock as purple smoke exploded from the grass.

It had been Naomi's idea, based on the one failed experiment that had started it all. Aluminum and iodine, combined to create colored smoke that looked like magic. It had taken a little ingenuity to time it right, though. The dew on the grass would act as the water needed in the reaction, but they could not be allowed to mix too early. So my spies had placed fragile, dangerously thin pieces of glass between the aluminum and the iodine. When the soldiers stepped on them, the glass would shatter, the chemicals would mix, and I would get the spectacle I needed.

And if any soldiers stumbled when the glass gave way, well . . . that might help, too.

Some of the horses reared, and the soldiers yelled, too, stopping where they stood. Another moment, and the concoctions burst into flames, sparks flying into the air along with the smoke.

Then the final part of my plan fell into place, and phantoms danced on the smoke clouds again. They were less defined now that sunlight surrounded them, but they haunted the soldiers still, lurching shadows, vengeful gods returned.

My own archers sent a barrage of arrows onto the field. Another sheet of lightning flashed across the sky.

"Surrender!" I yelled. "And the Forgotten will have mercy."

I couldn't see if my words had any effect. The soldiers might not even have heard me. The air was too full of smoke and fire now, the sound of soldiers yelling and coughing. Those who attempted to run through the chaos would find their eyes streaming, their chests tightening. They could not charge while they struggled to breathe.

I searched the field for Sten, but he had vanished in the smoke and fire.

Still I stood, listening to the shouts. Men emerged from the chaos, moving *away* from the city, running, dropping their weapons on the ground as they went. The first few were men on my side, hidden among the ramshackle army to inspire cowardice in others, but more followed, and more, scrambling to escape that immortal wrath.

One man on horseback whirled around, galloping after the fleeing men. And once that noble had broken ranks, all of his men broke with him, the already disorganized army scrambling over themselves to get away.

"Your Majesty." Holt stood in the gate tower, just out of sight. I did not turn to look at him. "You should come back now. Where it's safe."

"No. I have to stay here." I had to watch my fears play out. Many of the men who'd emerged from the smoke now fell to their knees, staring up at me, a mix of terror and awe in their eyes.

Then the rain came. A downpour, bursting out of nowhere. The raindrops hit a few uncatalyzed spots of iodine and aluminum, creating more bursts of purple smoke and flame. If anyone believed the rain was for Sten, that smoke would disabuse them of those hopes.

As the smoke cleared, I saw Sten, standing at the edge of the chaos, refusing to surrender but unable to proceed as the Forgotten came down around him. Someone was standing in front of him, shouting at him, gesturing with a sword—

Fitzroy. He'd been out in the field? I hadn't told him he could join the battle. My stomach twisted in fear, but he was unharmed, shouting at Sten. Telling him to surrender.

I stepped off the side of the wall. "I wish to go down there," I said to Holt.

"Your Majesty—"

I nodded at him and descended the stairs. The city gates swung open, guards standing alert on either side as I stepped onto the field of ash and fear.

"Your Majesty," the men on their knees murmured, the words forming a chant that flowed through the air. And then, as if the word had more meaning, as though it meant more respect, "*Freya. Freya.*"

I stepped through them, my head held high, to where Sten stood, weaponless now, glowering at me.

"I did not kill your friends, Sten. I did not want them dead. I know you didn't, either. But I am queen now, and I will protect my kingdom from *anyone* who attacks it. And the Forgotten will protect me as I do."

And with no weapons, no army, no one left to support him, Torsten Wolff could hardly disagree.

THIRTY-THREE

"I SWEAR ALLEGIANCE TO QUEEN FREYA, THE ONE TRUE queen of Epria."

I sat in my throne, crown on my head, as a soldier knelt before me, head bowed. I nodded at him, hands folded in my lap to hide my nerves. "Thank you," I said, and I put all my happiness, all my genuine relief, into the words. "You may rise." The soldier stood, head still bowed, and stepped aside to allow the next man before the throne.

True to my word, every man who had surrendered during the battle had been pardoned. Even those captured fighting were pardoned and recruited into my army, if they agreed to swear loyalty to me. And so I had sat on my throne all day, hearing oath after oath, dwelling in the relief that I was *alive*, I had survived. No one else needed to die now.

But there was still the problem of Sten. He was in the dungeons now, and I had to decide how to deal with him. The assumption, of course, was that I'd have him executed to ensure he never posed a threat again. To show the cost of rebelling against the queen. But I meant what I had said, about wishing to avoid more bloodshed. I didn't want anyone else to die. Not even those who'd been trying to kill me. But I couldn't let him go, couldn't exile him. He could easily try to gather forces and attack again.

So was I to leave him in the dungeons for the rest of his life? Somehow, that didn't feel like justice, either.

At least he'd be easier to deal with than any lingering threat in the city. My show had convinced most people—what else could have caused all that smoke and light?—but I couldn't have convinced everyone. There would always be doubters, and if they chose to put that doubt into action . . .

I shook my head. I was safer than I had been. I had followers of my own now, and love and respect, besides. If anyone plotted to kill me, they wouldn't find much support.

And then there was Madeleine. Beautiful, charming Madeleine, who had helped me in the end. If I told anyone else what she had done, they'd scream for her execution. Madeleine would deserve it. But I couldn't bear to see that happen. I couldn't see what good that would bring.

No more bloodshed. No matter what.

When the last soldier had sworn his allegiance, the old throne room emptied out, leaving me and my advisers alone. I stood, my legs aching after too many hours on the throne, and stretched. "That went well."

"Yes, Your Majesty," Holt said, striding to my side. "But there is still work to be done."

I walked into the middle of the room, taking in the somber stone, the desperate attempts to make it appear anything other than a prison. It wasn't enough. This place was too cruel. "I want the court to move back to the palace."

"Your Majesty?"

"This place isn't fit for living anymore, and we're not going to hide here in fear."

"But Your Majesty, the implications of that—"

"It will mean we carry on." I looked back at the golden throne, *my* throne. "The kingdom needs money. It needs *more*. So we'll sell a lot of the gold in the palace, the statues, tear down the ridiculousness of it all. Create a new home for us. Have the palace banquet hall turned into a memorial for those who died. But we cannot stay here."

Holt nodded. "It is a good thought, Your Majesty."

"Then we'll do it. And Sten can remain here, for now. Where he can't cause any trouble."

Holt pursed his lips. "Your Majesty, I really do advise—"

"No more death, Holt. Not even for that."

He looked at me for a long moment, then bowed. "That may be wise, Your Majesty. Or it may be folly. But I would like to see it as wisdom."

I continued toward the door. "Your Majesty," Holt said. "I must apologize, for my attitude regarding William Fitzroy. I must admit that I may have been—biased, in that regard."

It was probably all the admission of fault I could expect. Quite a big capitulation, from a man who had been so convinced before. "I can't trust you," I said, "if you will not trust me." He and I did not always see eye to eye, and sometimes his motivations were puzzling to me, to say the least. But he did genuinely, passionately support me as queen. And he understood things that I could not, things about the Forgotten, things I needed to know. "But I am grateful, to have you as my ally." I slowed my walk. While we were being honest . . . "May I ask you a question?"

"You may ask me anything, Your Majesty. You are queen, after all."

"Why didn't you side with Sten?" He stared at me, and I smiled. "He was the safer option. The known quantity. And he was a reformer, too. Why did you choose to support me, when I looked like the losing side?"

"Because I thought it was the right side, Your Majesty.

Maybe the Forgotten put you here, and maybe they didn't, but you're intelligent. You're thoughtful. And it's your throne by right. I thought it was best, for the kingdom."

"Then thank you. I hope I live up to your expectations."

"You have already exceeded them." But his attention was distracted by movement at the entrance to the throne room.

My father stepped through the doorway, looking as he always had. Not much thinner, not much more worn, except by travel. He smiled as our eyes met, lowering his head slightly in respect. "Apologies for my lateness, Your Majesty. Do you have time for one more pledge?"

I ran to him, my heels clinking on the floor, and threw my arms around him. My momentum nearly knocked us over, and my father laughed. "Steady, Freya. Try to have *some* queenly decorum." His words were warm, vibrant. I hugged him tighter. He patted the back of my head. "It's good to see you, too, Freya."

I stepped back slightly to look at him again. "You're all right? You look like you're all right. I was worried that—"

"I do have *some* ability to charm people," he said. "It worked on your mother and her court, after all." He shook his head. "Sten thought what he was doing was just. Not kind, maybe, but just. I think he genuinely believed you were responsible. And he had no proof I was involved."

"Still," I said. If anyone had been captured by my side, if my advisers had had their way, they would not have remained unscathed. My advisers thought they were being just, too, but their view of justice had become slightly twisted. "I'm glad you're all right."

"You too, Freya." He cupped my chin with his hand. "Your mother would be so proud of you. She was always proud of you, but if she could see what you've become . . ." He swallowed. "*I'm* proud of you, Freya. I know we haven't always understood each other, but—I am proud of you." He cleared his throat, looking suddenly uncomfortable, and stepped back. "Well," he said. "I suppose we had better start rebuilding your council. There is still a lot of work to be done."

"Yes. Of course." I smiled at him, and he smiled back. "I'll leave you and Holt to catch up."

With the duties of the day done, I wandered down to my laboratory. I would have to pack everything away again, all the notes, all the instruments . . . I'd proven the value of a scientist queen, and I wasn't going to put that aside now. My experiments had saved my life, more than once.

Fitzroy was waiting inside. Of course he was. My heart jumped when I saw him, but I had no idea how to feel about him now. Everything had been so focused on survival, but now we had survived, and he was still here, still Fitzroy, still my friend, still someone who had lied to me. What could I possibly do with all that?

He looked up as I closed the door. "Freya. I was hoping you'd come here."

"I'm bound to show up eventually." I walked farther into

the room, taking in the instruments on the walls, the strange stains on the floor. "We're moving back to the palace. We just decided."

"Putting things back to normal?"

"Not quite. But something like that." I ran my hand along the rough wood of the center table. "I'll miss this place." I'd made so many discoveries in this dark, depressing space, truths about science, truths about myself. It would be strange to let it crumble into history again.

"You could come back," Fitzroy said. "To the lab, at least."

I shook my head. It was a makeshift lab for a makeshift queen. Things would be different now.

I caught Fitzroy staring at me, and quickly looked away, pretending to shuffle through my notes. But there was no reason for me to look at them now. No distraction for us, no way to work through the awkwardness. I felt like I had to say *something*, but I didn't know what. I couldn't be honest when I didn't even know the truth of my feelings, myself.

"I'm sorry," I said eventually, almost too soft to hear.

"Because you locked me up?" He didn't sound accusatory, just—like he was checking.

"Because I had to." It was all the truth I had to offer.

Fitzroy nodded. "I'm sorry, too. I didn't—you have to understand. I thought I was protecting myself, but—I was wrong. I should have trusted you."

"You should have," I said. "I trusted you." It was too late to change it now. He opened his mouth, like he was going to say something else, and I could feel the weight of it in the air, the way things would shift . . . and then he turned away, shaking his head. "You know there'll be consequences," he said. "For claiming the Forgotten chose you. People are going to expect a lot."

"It can't be worse than execution." I forced myself to smile. "And how do you know I'm *not* their chosen one? You saw that lightning."

He didn't seize the joke. He stared at me, his expression still serious. "You don't believe that."

"No. But others will." I looked back at him, William Fitzroy, not a prince but son of a king. Far kinder and far cleverer than I had ever imagined. My friend. My—*something*. But he had lied to me. I understood why, but . . . he hadn't trusted me.

And I'd imprisoned him.

It was a poor basis for any kind of relationship. Not insurmountable, but it would linger. I didn't know where things would go from here, but . . . it wouldn't be easy.

I wanted to say something, something bold, but the words wouldn't come. I stood a foot away from him, wanting to move closer, wanting to touch him, wanting to *act*, willing him to act. But I had no reference for this, no theory to work from, so I stood, waiting, hoping, until Fitzroy spoke.

"What are you going to do about Madeleine?"

And the moment was gone.

I looked about the room again, at the stool where Madeleine

had sat. "Leave Madeleine to me."

I knew, in my heart, what I needed to do.

It was the dead of night when I returned to Madeleine's rooms and opened the door. And there was Madeleine, as elegant as ever, her legs tucked beneath her as she slept in an armchair. I paused for a moment, watching her, letting myself remember all the good of our friendship. Then I crept forward, and Madeleine opened her eyes.

"Freya," she said. "Have you come to deal with me now?"

I tossed a bag at her. "Take this. It's money, food, a map. Take this, and leave."

Madeleine stood. "Freya?"

"I don't care where you go. But you have to leave this kingdom. You have to go, and never come back."

"Freya—"

"If I ever see you again, if you are ever heard of in this kingdom again, I will have to kill you. You know that I will." She stared at me, refusing to look away. "I don't want to have to kill you, Madeleine. I really don't. But I will, if I have to. So go, and do not come back."

Madeleine nodded. She clutched the bag to her chest. "Thank you. Your kindness—"

"Don't." My voice shook. "Please just—just leave."

Madeleine nodded. She sank into a curtsy. Perfectly composed, even now. "You are a good queen, Freya," she said. "A good queen, and a good friend. Don't forget that."

She stepped forward until she was level with me, and then she paused. For a heartbeat, our eyes met. Madeleine nodded a final time, and hurried out of sight.

I sighed into the empty room, my eyes settling on the sweeping mural that Madeleine had left behind. The kingdom, as she saw it. The thing she wanted to protect, and the thing she had nearly destroyed.

I stared at the sweeping red paint until my eyes blurred, and then I walked away.

The sun filtered through the palace's high windows, lighting the ruined corridors. They had been ransacked, looted, fragments of urns dusting the floor . . . but there was potential, too. There was hope.

I walked slowly, savoring the brightness of the morning, until I reached the council room. Mila and Carina walked behind me, promoted to chiefs of my guard now, wearing their new uniforms embroidered with my crest—a bolt of lightning on a violet field.

The door to the council room was ajar, and I stepped inside. The chamber had already been stripped of its most extravagant decorations, leaving a map of the kingdom on the far wall, a single large table, and several shelves of books on history, agriculture, language, and religion. Fitzroy smiled at me as I entered, and I smiled back, before glancing around at my council, *mine,* with my father, with Holt, with Naomi, with Norling, with several seats left empty for the people who could fill them, for people whose advice I could trust, whose different perspectives would help me know what to do.

I might not truly be the chosen queen. I should never have stood here, with the crown on my head. But I was here now, I had held my place, and I was going to rule well, or as well as I could. I was going to make sure all the bloodshed led to something good after all.

I slipped into the chair at the head of the room.

"All right," I said. "Let's begin."

ACKNOWLEDGMENTS

Long May She Reign wouldn't exist without the support of many amazing people.

First, my wonderful agent, Kristin Nelson, who makes everything possible. Her wisdom, hard work, and sense of humor keep me going when things get overwhelming, and I would never have even started this story without her enthusiasm and support.

My editor, Catherine Wallace, was the person who made this story click. Her suggestions made all the difference, and I couldn't have done this without her insight and advice. Massive thanks are also due to the whole HarperTeen team, for all the amazing behind-the-scenes work they do.

Rachel Thompson answered endless questions for me in my struggle to make the science in this book as realistic as possible. She opened her super-scientist brain for the picking, found resources for me, and generally guided me through the key scientific thoughts that tied this story together. All remaining mistakes are entirely my own. Rachel also provided incredibly helpful feedback on early versions of this book, for which I'm really grateful.

Phoebe Cattle also gave me a lot of science help, and never once freaked out when I sent her weird messages like, "So, if you poisoned someone with arsenic . . ." and "So, when you dissect a body . . ." The gruesome details she provided on the latter question didn't end up making it into the book, but I still learned a lot from her, not least that I am definitely not cut out to be a biomedical scientist.

When I was halfway through the second draft, Alex Zaleski was the reason I kept going. She read that messy half-a-first-draft with her pompoms at the ready, and has provided endlessly helpful feedback on the many versions of the book since. Thanks so much to her for all her cheerleading, support and advice, and for always believing in me.

Thanks to everyone in Black Scabbard for constantly inspiring me with our adventures; to James Cattle, Pascal Gilbraith, Matt Goodyear, Kim Jackson, and Oz Shepherdson; plus, of course, Rachel and Phoebe, for all the drama, laughs, and goblin cookery courses, and for letting me take inspiration from their characters for the gods of Freya's world.

I'm lucky enough to have amazing friends on both sides of the Atlantic, and huge thanks are also due to Shelina Kurwa, Meg Lee, and Anna Liu, for always being there for me despite the distance.

And finally, endless thank-yous to my mum and dad, Gaynor and Brian Thomas, who always support me, and are the reasons for everything I do.

DON'T MISS THESE BOOKS BY RHIANNON THOMAS

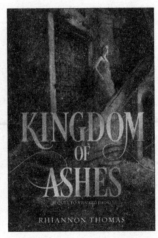